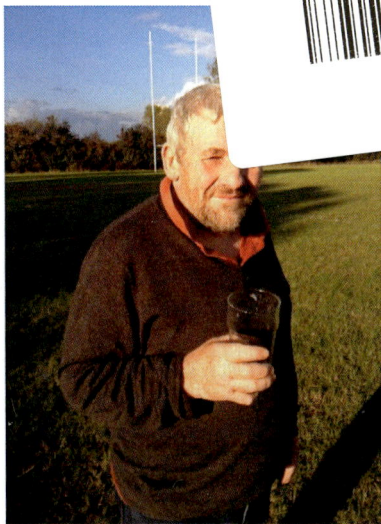

Geoff Martin was born in Epsom, Surrey, but lived for most of his childhood in Ruislip, Middlesex. A "failed" pupil of a good school, he took up catering becoming a chef in the West End of London, moving on to retail management in Norwich and from there to running a small stud farm with his wife, Lou, where they bred both show and racehorses. Retiring from the equine world and latterly with little to do, Martin has taken up writing as a pastime.

To Jack Lots of Love

Geoff xxx

Conquest

The First Horseman

Geoff Martin

Conquest
The First Horseman

Vanguard Press

VANGUARD PAPERBACK

© Copyright 2016
Geoff Martin

The right of Geoff Martin to be identified as author of
this work has been asserted by him in accordance with the
Copyright, Designs and Patents Act 1988.

A CIP catalogue record for this title is
available from the British Library.

ISBN 978 178465 039 1

*Vanguard Press is an imprint of
Pegasus Elliot Mackenzie Publishers Ltd.*
www.pegasuspublishers.com

First Published in 2016

**Vanguard Press
Sheraton House Castle Park
Cambridge England**

Printed & bound in Great Britain

Thank you to Scott, Gabby and Alan for
their help with my computer skills.

CONQUEST

The First Horseman

Into this uncertain world comes a crowned horseman riding a white horse, and his name is conquest. A world where friend and foe can look exactly alike and enemies can walk freely amid their potential victims, where life has little meaning and death can lurk around every corner, where fear, ignorance and intolerance are enemies to all men, whether they are Christian, Muslim, Jewish or any other religion. Nobody is safe from the fickle hand poised to strike them down for their belief, the smallest point of doctrine can render a life forfeit, as the religious zealots eagerly blow into the glowing coals of discord, whipping up an inferno of hatred, causing unrest where brother seeks to kill brother and neighbour plots the downfall of neighbour.

The church has wealth, their wealth is power, power breeds corruption, corruption breeds poverty and despair, which breeds dissatisfaction and the dissatisfied seek solace from the wealthy church, and thus the circle begins. In this world there are none as wealthy as those who spiritually advise the masses, those who control the ignorant, using threats and promises to bend them to their will to do their bidding, hiding behind the sanctity of religion to advance their claims, creating turmoil out of peace, and discord out of harmony.

As the political temperature rises, the paranoia increases eventually xenophobia is the norm. Accusations and counter accusations start to fly, becoming more and more venomous, next threat and counter threat, finally action, possibly as little as a thrown stone can spiral uncontrollably into full-blown warfare. Sometimes fate throws an unlikely hero into the mix, helping restore the balance, deflecting the threat of all out conflict, saving property and lives, keeping sanity a reality, such a man is Peter Cahill, a reluctant hero and a quiet man.

INTRODUCTION

Nobody sees Peter Cahill, he is just not there, and when he walks down the street nobody sees him. It's not magic, nor is it science, it's just him, his appearance, his way of walking, his whole demeanour, most of all his empty soul, the spirit crushed by unhappiness, despair and hopelessness, a sad tortured essence, forged in the fires of war, hatred and last of all lost love. A contrast to the old Peter, once a rich banker with a house, two cars, a beautiful wife and a fantastic life, all was taken away by the fickle hand of fate. Now a shadow of his former self, sad and broken Peter was tempted by what seemed to be the only option to escape the cruelty of the world, he chose to join the underclass of the lost and homeless, among the vagrants, he accepted his lot and then promptly disappeared into social oblivion.

Neither tall nor short, thin with dark hair and a sallow complexion, his intelligent blue eyes now had a slight twitch, like a knowing wink, half hidden by a heavily furrowed brow sitting above high cheekbones and a square jawline, a three-week beard hid his full-lipped stern mouth which rarely smiled exposing his even white teeth, his heavy face was finished with a slightly flattened nose, making him almost, but not quite handsome. Etched now with deep lines of sorrow and deprivation, his once upright frame now had a slight stoop, his gaze cast permanently

11

downward, so as not to look at the world, the world that let him down so badly.

His attire consisted mainly of a grubby old coat draped over his broad shoulders which seemed to weigh him down a little, a woolly hat crammed down tightly over his unwashed hair, faded cheap jeans, baggy patched and frayed, just about revealing the serviceable but old brown brogues, unpolished and scuffed, once expensive, the only remnant of his affluent past. Little did he speak, but occasionally he would surprise those about him, his utterances being those of a very well educated man, his voice marred slightly by almost inaudible sighs, which punctuated his speech especially at times of reflection.

Unlike the rest of the invisible multitude of fallen men Peter never took to the drink, probably due to his upbringing, he was always sober and in total control of his faculties. His unique gift, to be able to listen and hear the quietest of conversations, linked to his ability to lip-read, opened up to him a hidden world of intrigue and deception invisible to most.

He lived where ever he could, scratching about trying to eke out enough to survive, eating whenever the possibility arose, keeping warm to the best of his ability, sometimes in doorways, often in derelict buildings, even on occasions under cardboard boxes, never comfortable, rarely completely dry, the damp conditions playing havoc with an old injury to his knees, but free of the woes of normal life. Generally he avoided the company of his peers, as they tended to find him odd, frightened by his sobriety and perplexed by his whole demeanour. They accepted him, yes, but they knew he was just not the same, almost outcast among outcasts, but he needed them, as they needed him, together survival was more possible than alone.

CHAPTER 1

1982

Peter James Cahill was born on the 12th of April 1982 in the lodgings attached to the British Consulate just north of Riyad, Saudi Arabia.

His father James Cahill an ex-military man, tall, upright, erect and well groomed in his early thirties, never having wanted children, was surprised by the birth of his unwanted offspring. A highly regarded important member of the British trade delegation to oil rich Saudi, his power was great and was used by him, when necessary, to get everything he needed. To the outside world he was strict and uncaring but much admired as being very good at everything he did; to those he loved he was sympathetic and kind. Now he was in a sterner mood than normal, upset by the human fly in his ointment. Peter's mother, Susan was twenty-six years old, dark skinned and petite, pretty with very dark hair, liquid brown pools for eyes that were heavily lidded and appealing; a full-lipped shapely mouth gave a perfect balance to her face, her looks made her always popular with men. She also rued Peter's birth, looking upon it as a curse, likely to ruin her ability to enjoy the high life, which was her only love, apart from her many flirtatious affairs that her husband knew about and chose to turn a blind eye to.

Before the birth the arguments had been many, Susan blamed James, James blamed Susan, each of them bemoaning the expected loss of their freedoms. Susan had enjoyed jet-setting with the rich and famous including sheiks and princes, all of them loved her, her beauty mesmerised men, who would hang on every word, obediently doing her bidding like faithful puppies. Sue, as she was generally known, took to fretting over the possible loss of her perfect figure, worried about her breasts getting overlarge and then sagging, concerned that her undeniable sex appeal would diminish then disappear completely with impending motherhood.

As the birth grew nearer the mood she had always suffered from, grew worse, becoming violent especially towards James whose presence became rarer and rarer. He was not like Sue, he enjoyed work, often burying himself in paperwork, not only just to avoid the rantings of his frustrated wife, but to him it was also an obligation. All night he would pore over graphs and oil yield projections or something similar, he was dedicated to his job and was very good at it. Regularly he would be summoned away to meetings or site visits for days, sometimes weeks at a time. James didn't like the high life, in fact he attended functions only on sufferance, preferring to be elsewhere, involved in work, rather than, "wasting time on pleasantries." He had worked in Saudi for over five years and made many acquaintances, he preferred to remain aloof from, but in time even some of them became his friends; those, that is who could put up with his apparent abrupt mannerisms and stern nature.

The marriage to Susan was virtually a sham. Originally she was beguiled by his wealth and power, and he by her undeniable beauty, not realising how shallow her nature was, and how feeble she was her mind. They only continued together for outward appearances and their sex life was almost nonexistent, in fact the pregnancy was only due to the aftermath of a drink-fuelled evening when they both forgot how much they had grown to hate each other, and ended up in bed together participating in a drunken romp, that resulted in their devastating news.

Sue had always been careful and thought nothing of her missed periods, assuming that it was the result of a virulent foreign bug that she had been suffering from. Forgetting everything about the wild drunken night with her equally forgetful husband, after missing for a third time and noticing a few subtle changes in her body, the stark realisation set in followed by utter dismay. After trawling through her memory banks the full horror hit her. First disbelief then utter terror, followed by floods of tears. She had nobody to talk to, no female friends to confide in, she desperately wanted the problem to be kept secret, so the only option left to her was to speak to her errant husband. With trepidation, and after due consideration she telephoned James, who managed to interpret the hysterical sobs and garbled message, quickly realising the gravity of it all, as was his wont he took control by organising urgent professional help.

Using his elevated status he bypassed normal channels and got things moving rapidly. James hastily organised some medical help, and the next day Sue was visited by a French doctor called Xavier Dubois, a small dark man with apparently uncontrollable jet-black curly hair, a round swarthy face with dark beady restless eyes that perpetually scanned to and fro, until they rested on Sue, allowing his gaze to loiter approvingly for a second or two before moving on.

"You are Mrs Cahill yes?" She nodded nervously.

"You have a little event expected soon yes? I will have a little look if that is OK. It will be fine." He was smoking a Camel cigarette and smelled of raw garlic, her dark mood was momentarily broken as she inwardly smiled at the ridiculous comic-book Frenchman. Yet she was snapped back to reality, by being asked, in very broken English to, "Streep off and put this on then lay on the bed." Again a little inward smile as she duly obeyed, having stripped her lower half and put on a faded green, overlarge gown with frayed tapes that were too frail to tie, which left her half naked and feeling exposed. Sue then lay on the bed and nervously opened her legs. Never before in her whole life had she felt so vulnerable as she awaited the approaching smiling doctor as he put on a long rubber glove, snapping it loudly against his arm. She shivered violently as the examination proceeded and the forthcoming event confirmed. "Fourteen to sixteen weeks, could be more, I am not the gynaecologist," was his only comment as he removed his well oiled gloved fingers from her, "you may get dressed now."

He then promptly demanded twenty American dollars as he snatched off the glove, which he tossed basketball-style into a waste bin that was about twelve feet away, wiping his other hand carelessly on his crumpled white coat and then, lighting another cigarette, he exclaimed shrugging his shoulders, "C'est la vie!" Then in English he consoled, her noticing her tears were not tears of joy. "Sorry, I can do nothing, too late, a little accident I think."

Nodding affirmatively she handed over the money, and then without ceremony he left, along with Sue's hopes for the future, and for the rest of her life either the smell of raw garlic or Camel cigarettes filled her with dread.

On receipt of what was to him earth-shattering news James acted very quickly, reassuring his distraught wife, explaining his plan. Secrecy was of the upmost importance, as the British government would almost certainly recall him if they knew about the pregnancy, there being such political uncertainty in the area.

Attached to the diplomatic lodgings which were supposed to be their home, was a staff flat, and James had arranged for a nanny to live there masquerading as their housekeeper. He explained to Sue that she was a well educated Arab woman, whose father had worked in the Shah of Persia's entourage and he and his wife had been killed in the unrest leading to the coup which ousted the Shah. She was twenty-three years old, had lived and worked in London and spoke very good English, she would be very grateful for the job, as her husband had died in an accident leaving her vulnerable with a baby son, no income and soon nowhere to live. Sue was to hide her expanding midriff and act normally; that is, they were to appear to the outside world as a proper loving couple. She was to completely forego her dalliances and to keep a low profile, he on the other hand would spend more time working at home, and support her needs the best he could, James was not asking Sue, he was telling her. He explained that Xavier knew all about the need for secrecy, and was completely trustworthy. Sue couldn't help but smile as she thought back to her meeting with the comical doctor, and then shuddering at the image she tried to forget him. James laid down a few more house rules, and then

17

waited for her agreement, which after consideration she did, thanking him with a genuine smile, for a fleeting moment it was noticeable that once they had been in love.

Several weeks passed without incident. Sue's waist thickened a little and her breasts grew larger and harder, which she countered by merely wearing tighter clothing. Her newfound life with James was going according to plan, none of their famously violent arguments had occurred, just some relatively normal occasional bickering and the forced peace was holding firm. However everything changed in October, the day when the hired help arrived.

It was very early one morning when Jasmine first appeared. She was shrouded in a full-length black niqab, with only her eyes visible, she was bustled into the lodgings by an immaculately dressed, black chauffer with a broad toothy smile. James looked nervous as he ushered in the woman's belongings, including a tightly wrapped bundle that was a very young child. All her gear was hurriedly taken up a narrow staircase that smelled of new paint; at the top there was a green door, imaginatively labelled STAFF FLAT. This had its own brass letterbox and knocker, both shone to gleaming perfection; James opened it with a large old-fashioned key, and it creaked slightly as it revealed a spacious hallway. James bowed mockingly as he signalled Jasmine to enter. Meanwhile behind them, the chauffeur was struggling upstairs with a huge amount of luggage, which teetered precariously as he rounded the top of the stairs onto the landing, almost losing half of the load, which he cleverly re-balanced with a smart sidestep. James thanked him calling him, Michael and pointing out that two trips would have been easier, winking knowingly, Michael turned and left chuckling to himself, pulling the green door behind him, making it creak back into place and close with a gentle click.

The couple looked at each other in silence, "Has he gone?" Jasmine asked as the downstairs front door was heard closing noisily. James cocked his head to listen, hearing a car drive away he whispered a confident, "Yes!" Jasmine spoke with a polished English accent, that of someone who had been well educated in England. Feeling assured that the coast was clear she pointed to the bundle that was the baby, "Our little Ibrahim," she announced, then pulled down the wrap which covered the screwed-up face of the sleeping infant. James looked at the child for a second or two, feigned a slight interest, and then he asked if Jasmine wanted to be shown around the flat.

"Can I take this off first?" she asked, indicating to the bulky all-covering garment, that some Arab women were obliged to wear in public. Again James nodded yes without speaking. And then at speed the great black shroud was removed, revealing a stunningly lovely young woman, rather like a beautiful butterfly emerging from a chrysalis; underneath she wore a silky tight-fitting trouser suit in pale blue silk, which showed that her figure had not been marred by the recent childbirth. Her raven-black hair fell in soft waves onto her shoulders, as she turned and smiled at James showing her full face, flawless and perfect with skin the colour of milky coffee, bold brown tearful eyes, a narrow straight nose that was perfectly positioned above her luscious mouth, her freshly licked lips glistening as she looked a wan apologetic smile towards James, sniffing at an annoying wayward tear which trickled down her nose, she then rushed to embrace him.

Seeing them together, it became obvious that James and Jasmine were secret lovers and he desperately needed to make sure the story he told his wife tallied with Jasmine's while he still had the chance.

"I told Sue that you had been married, and your husband had been killed in an accident, she thinks you are destitute, and you need this job to survive!"

"I do!" she replied starting to cry tears of gratitude. Whispering thanks and kissing his neck, he shushed to silence her and jerked his head over his right shoulder in the direction of the other bedrooms.

"She's still sleeping, she'll be there for at least another hour or so." He put his finger to his mouth in a quietening gesture, took hold of her hand and started the tour, he led her straight to the bedroom. "C'mon Jazzie it's been ages," James said dragging her to the bed, his manner now that of her lover and not that of her employer.

"The baby! your wife?" Jasmine asked.

"We'll be quiet," he whispered closely in her ear.

"Do you still love me?" She begged him, coyly staring lovingly into his eyes.

"Yes of course," he replied as he started to gently unbutton her top then pulled down a silky loose undergarment to expose her breasts, which he cupped in both hands.

"Don't squeeze," Jasmine said imploringly. He looked amazed.

"Milk!" she answered, "And very tender," Jasmine added with a grin.

"Oh well!" was his reply, as he changed tactics and undid the zip on her trousers, allowing them to fall to the floor; as he gently lowered her onto the bed. Indicated to James that she was trussed by the pulled-down top; he laughed at her struggles to free both arms at once, which she managed only by tearing the material. James removed her panties and at the same time as she was undoing his trousers.

"Curse these button flies!" she said through gritted teeth and wrestled clumsily with unyielding material, "have you never heard of zips, James?" Eventually she succeeded revealing his erect penis, then stroking it like an old friend and addressing it in an overly posh voice, "Hello my dear old chap, how are you, keeping well I hope?" She giggled childishly, then dropped her head down and started kissing, looking cheekily up into James's eyes as she did, he raised her body up to his, still looking intently at each other.

"No fucking, too soon for me after the baby," she said apologetically, lowering her head back down and starting to suck, flicking her tongue up and down and moving her head in cadence to his gentle groans. Wriggling uncontrollably, she unexpectedly started to come with the pure joy of it all, they were both being drowned in the oblivion of sexual bliss, suddenly to be snatched back to reality by a loud hammering on the door.

"Christ Almighty!" James said, his voice lowered to almost nothing, jumping up he mouthed to Jasmine, "Get in the bathroom quickly."

"Where is it?" Jazzy mouthed back, running around stark naked in a state of panic. James nodded feverishly towards yellow door, still trying to quickly adjust his crumpled attire, and stuffing his disappointed semi-erect penis back into his boxers. Immediately the yellow door closed it opened again and Jazzie's head appeared, gazing in the direction of the pile of clothes and then to her niqab. Another more urgent banging on the door ratcheting up the tension, he threw the garments at her, smoothing himself down, he opened it to find Sue standing there in her night clothes with a face of thunder.

"You're up early," he coolly observed, "I've been moving furniture."

"Is that why your face is so red?" she retorted sharply.

"Where is she then?"

At that moment Jasmine appeared covered from head to foot in her voluminous niqab, which completely covered her nakedness underneath, gliding effortlessly up to Sue, Jasmine made a very slight curtsey, and introduced herself and her son, pointing to the bundle that contained the infant. "Thank you Mrs Cahill for this opportunity."

Sue glared at James's groin, held the look for a moment, and then turned silently on her heels and disappeared downstairs, her audible mumblings fading as she went.

"I think we got away with that, don't you?" questioned James.

"You are joking; she's not as daft as you think. She knows, I know she does, I need this job, I can't leave here, they will kill me!"

"Don't worry!" James replied, "They can't get to you here, you're safe, and she needs me, and you as well, for that matter, she'll toe the line! I will just lie convincingly to her."

"You are a very bad Christian James," she noted, once again fighting to remove the cumbersome shroud that was deliberately designed to hide females from public gaze. Once rid of it and re-clad back in her trouser suit, she returned to feeling more relaxed and self-assured.

"And you, my dear, are a perfect example of a dutiful little Muslim girl, aren't you?" retorted James, laughing at her good-heartedly.

"You know what I think of that," Jasmine replied sulkily. In fact her early days in London and her English education had completely westernised her and she enjoyed the freedoms it offered, having first-hand experience of how the fundamentalists in her home country, that was once Persia and now is called Iran, treated women as second-class citizens. Realising how oppressive they were she opted to adopt the ways of her British friends and it broke her heart when she had to leave London and return home on the death of her parents.

The double grief almost destroyed her, obliged to leave her job, her apartment and friends, having to go back to the turmoil that was Persia, where she was reluctantly taken in to the home of a rich uncle, in Tabriz, who was much less moderate than Jasmine's mother and father, forced to wear a niqab, beaten regularly because of her nonconformist ways, ridiculed and spat at by her aunt and cousins, treated as a slave, and then promised in marriage to an older man, Shredding her whole life into tatters, to be trapped in an, embittered extreme world, twisted by hate and jealousy.

Jasmine endured her lot stoically and paid false lip service to her uncle's demands, apparently accepting all that she was expected to. Scrubbing, cleaning and cooking from dawn to dusk, watched over by her idle family, who treated her like a dog, only being fed occasional scraps when absolutely necessary. Inside Jasmine was rebelling more and more, fuelling feelings that were not natural to her. Every day she hoped that she could get away from the evil of her situation, wishing death and destruction on her hated new family. After months of abuse, and immediately before her arranged marriage, she eventually managed to escape. She crept out of the hovel where she was forced to live, and under the cover of darkness, posing as a refugee, she joined the exodus of people trying to avoid the radical reforms of the Ayatollah Khomeini, gradually ending up far away safely in Iraq.

Jasmine had left all her woes back in Tabriz along with the vengeful fuming uncle and a livid fiancée, along with nearly all of her belongings. Her hasty exit had only allowed her the time to gather a little bag of precious relics, which she kept with her always, as keepsakes, to remind her of happier days and better times. Jasmine's newly found freedom gave her hope; once again she was able to seek happiness, and resume a normal life, and she very quickly found work as an interpreter for an oil drilling company in Rafha, on the border of Saudi Arabia.

A lone unattached woman in an extremist Islamic state under sharia law was an extremely dangerous place for Jasmine to be, a place where it is unacceptable for women to travel without permission, and to be raped was usually considered the female's fault, and death sentences were often handed out to the perpetrators of relatively minor crimes. The clerical courts had complete say over anyone who had the misfortune to appear before them, and if found guilty were liable to suffer the many cruel punishments meted out including amputations, stonings and beheadings, which were common place and often considered a public entertainment.

Jasmine begged her new employers to be lodged in the safety of the secured quarters reserved for the European staff. The firm accepted this condition willingly, mainly because her language skills were beyond excellent. It was here she met and fell in love with James, who fell in love with her in return; it was in these quarters they started their steamy affair which led them to tragedy and, almost, to their deaths.

The next time James showed Jasmine around the newly painted flat, he showed her properly; it was clean and well furnished with the once expensive cast outs from the embassy, a lot of them dating back years, but all were newly polished or upholstered. They chatted as they went on the tour, musing on Sue's reaction the forthcoming birth, and other bits of mundane gossip Most of all they discussed how the secret of Jazzie's whereabouts must be kept strictly hidden from the outside world. James reminding Jasmine several times about the need for utter silence, especially when visitors called, giving Jasmine a list of safe contacts in case of emergencies: her top priority was not to alert anyone as to where she was living. James apologised to her earnestly, "I'm so sorry to have to hide you away, but if my people find out about you they'll make me give you up, and then that lunatic uncle will have you killed. One day I will get you out I promise!"

"I know they will do anything to get me, they call it an honour killing. An honour killing! I ask you where's the honour in killing me?" Jasmine replied sobbing bitterly. "I hate my uncle!"

"I will have him killed if you want," James said casually, but meaning it. She nodded no back to him, her cheeks wet with fresh tears. Clasping her head with both hands he kissed her passionately on the mouth, standing so close she could feel the desire coursing through the whole length of his body. Then wrestling with his needs he simply pecked her on her lips, "I've got to go and face the music." He lingered waiting for his erection to subside, wagging his finger at his groin as if to tell it off. He turned to walk away, took two strides, looked back, blew a kiss then departed, leaving Jazzy standing alone, surrounded by unpacked luggage and a waking hungry baby.

Sue was furious, using swear words that James didn't know she knew he denied everything, calling her "paranoid," and accused her of tilting at windmills, telling Sue that she was deluded, probably due to her hormones being out of balance. James advised Sue to call and see Xavier. She replied calling him, in a mocking French accent, "That filthy leetle, garlic-crunching, French pervert fucker," a taunting James pointed out sarcastically, "You mean your doctor?"

"Yes! That Camel-smoking French cunt."

"Mind your language please I'm sensitive," he smirked.

She shrieked, "Want to hear some more, arsehole?" James replied laughing at her, "No thank you, quite enough for one day, ta!" Sue sat down knowing that she could never win. Still mumbling obscenities, she peevishly snatched up an outdated magazine, and pretended to read, ignoring all James's attempts to engage in civil conversation. In the ensuing silence, James pondered on how different he was when he was with Jazzy, as opposed to his time with Sue like Jekyll and Hyde he thought, grumpy and stern on one hand, fun-loving and light-hearted on the other.

During the days leading up to the birth, the rows became worse and more violent, often missiles were hurled at James, who kept his cool at all times, countering the savage attacks with quiet, verbal ripostes, ignoring the tirades of foul language, which grew more and more abusive and included an increasingly higher percentage of expletives. Jasmine kept a low profile, making herself busy house working, sewing and caring for the ever-growing child, always remaining silent, even going as far as watching the television, with the sound turned as low as possible.

Xavier made regular house calls, all at the bidding of James, as Sue wasn't interested the least bit in her well-being during the pregnancy. the fact was that she always felt slightly nauseous when the smelly little French doctor came near her, especially when latex gloves were involved, which they invariably were, Sue suspected that Xavier enjoyed it, as often his well oiled mobile fingers would linger a touch too long.

Apparently, all was going according to plan, the baby was growing normally, despite the skin-tight restrictive clothing that Sue always wore, and the fact that she was on a diet eating as little as possible, always worrying about her swelling waistline and fretting over the size of her blossoming bust. On one such visit Xavier brought a large bag of fearsome ancient surgical instruments with him, "For the birth!" He announced as he threw them down on a nearby table making them rattle noisily.

"A little feel, now that I am here I think?" he suggested. "I hear that you do not like the garlic, and the cigarettes yes," Xavier said, puffing on a huge glowing cigar. Sue wondered what else he'd been told, not everything she hoped, as she duly removed her clothing, her flesh popping gratefully out of the undersized garments. Sue put on the same gown as before, now strangely minus any of the ties to fasten it with, leaving it undone and revealing her complete nakedness. Xavier's lecherous eyes lingered on her body as she lay on the nearby bed as, again, he donned the well-oiled glove, and again she suffered his explorations. This time he breathed faster and heavier and she knew he was enjoying it.

"What was that you called me, a little French fucker? And what else did you say I am, the pervert, yes, that's it the pervert…" he thrust his fingers a little harder as he questioned her, "I forgive you," he said as he removed them, "you like the cigar yes?" He was laughing at her, "Everything is fine. You know James is my friend, yes." He snatched off the dripping glove with his clean hand, turning it inside out as he did so, looking around for somewhere to cast it, he remarked, "Not too far to go now, six or seven weeks I think." Xavier left still clutching the glove, leaving Sue inwardly cursing James for telling tales, but half smiling at the cigar joke, still wondering whether all the internal examinations were necessary, she re-dressed managing to scoop all back together, squeezing herself into the unyielding garments giggling as she did.

Sue felt strangely happy, considering she had just been sexually assaulted by her doctor, was expecting an unwanted baby, isolated, alone, unloved by her husband who had a live-in lover and, last but not least, getting fat. She put her lightness of spirit down to the fact that her hormones were probably out of balance, or maybe just, at last, acceptance of the irreversible situation. Sue thought a lot about her husband's lover; she had only really met her the once, and then Jasmine was completely covered by her niqab, not since her arrival had there been any sign of Jasmine, no sounds, no baby noises, nothing. Her curiosity was taking a hold, the more she thought, and the more she wondered about the guest, what was she really like? Where was she from? She only knew what James had told her, and that was the bare minimum, he was away as usual and she was in the grip of a bout of loneliness. Perhaps it was the reason she wasn't too upset by Xavier's unacceptable behaviour?

A few steps away Jasmine also felt isolated and lonely, just having meaningless conversations with the unresponsive Ibrahim. She was in the middle of one such when there came a gentle tapping on the door; thinking it was James, she rushed to the door, hastily opening it, concerned and surprised to see a smiling Sue standing there. Her intention was obvious, she wanted to talk, so politely Jasmine opened the door wider and asked her in. Hesitantly Sue did so and, on being offered a seat, she took it and sat nervously, perched on the edge of a luxurious Georgian wing chair.

"Tea or coffee Mrs Cahill?" asked Jasmine.

"Tea please? And call me Sue."

"I'll put the kettle on," she replied, disappearing into the kitchen, wondering what it was all about.

Sue was stunned by Jasmine, who was dressed in a lilac silk tracksuit with her glossy raven hair tumbling in waves to her waist, completely without any make-up but still amazingly beautiful, her obviously fantastic figure not quite hidden by the clinging casual attire. Feeling dumpy, pregnant Sue suffered a real pang of jealousy as Jasmine returned gliding gracefully, sporting a tray laden with a very English-looking spread, tea and water pots, cups, saucers, a sugar bowl, milk jug and a plate of digestive biscuits. She put it all down on a nearby table, and then pulled up a chair. Sitting opposite Sue she politely asked, "Shall I be mother Mrs Cahill? Sorry, I mean Sue."

"Please dear, I like mine medium."

The small talk continued for some time, between sips of tea, Sue asking about pregnancy, giving birth and post-natal care. Jasmine was reassuring, giving advice, telling Sue that mixed feelings were quite normal. Sue told of her misgivings and about not wanting children. They became at ease with other, relaxing and laughing, when suddenly, completely out of the blue Sue asked, "Is James the father?" indicating with her head towards the still-sleeping child. Jazzy gulped audibly, and although it did not show, she started to feel her face reddening, and as the answer started to stammer out, Sue blurted, "No that's unfair!" But having read the reaction, Sue knew the truth.

The easy-paced meeting all of a sudden became strained; the tangible tension and the embarrassed talk broken suddenly by the demanding cry of a hungry baby. Jasmine whispered an inward prayer, then rushed to Ibrahim, cradled him and, undoing her top, she offered up an ample breast, which he started to suck greedily; looking an apology to Sue, she continued to feed the infant. Sue left uttering a quiet thanks to her host, gently closing the door behind her, all the time rueing the outburst which called an acrimonious halt to the meeting. She felt even more alone now, having alienated her neighbour and also feeling a consuming jealousy, remembering Jasmine's beauty and her probable liaisons

30

with James. She wondered whether inside she was harbouring hidden feelings for him, or perhaps it was just the fact that on paper he was still hers? She dismissed it all as fantasy.

James returned from his trip late one evening in February, he was tired from a long journey and hungry, frustrated by the failure of his latest talks, he was not in the best of moods. As he entered the front door he was greeted by his pregnant wife, who instantly asked him if he wanted something to eat; taken by surprise he indicated that he did and feeling somewhat bemused by this unusual event he enquired to see if Sue was all right. Michael was with him, staggering behind his boss with a mound of files in one hand and in the other he juggled with a pair of bulging suit cases, which appeared to be fighting each other. Again James advised him not to overload himself, the same smiling indifference was the result, as he carelessly unburdened himself, dumping his load in a nearby corner. Amazingly Sue then turned to Michael and inquired if he was hungry, who was equally surprised, thinking that was a first time for everything.

"Yes please," was his instant response. She disappeared out of the hallway leaving both James and Michael staring at each other in dumb amazement. Having made themselves comfortable in the sitting room, they started to chat about their arduous trek, when Sue entered with a pre-prepared trolley laden with food and drink. "I've been waiting for you," she said sitting down with them both, then handing out sandwiches and pouring drink.

Sue was for a change wearing a loose maternity dress, making her look somewhat rotund and dumpy, but still radiantly attractive in her pregnant state. James was almost speechless, wondering what had caused this sudden change in her demeanour. He did not know about her guilty feelings following the meeting with Jasmine, and her inner need to build a bridge with him, in order to secure her future. She realised without her husband's power, she might slip into anonymity back in Blighty. He had enjoyed the sudden change in Sue, and had slept well that night. In the morning a breakfast was prepared in readiness for him, placed carefully on a tray along with several newspapers; they sat together and chatted for a while about nothing in particular. Sue told him about Xavier's misbehaviour, telling James the whole episode, asking how long ago they met. He informed her of the details, of how they had met, and how Xavier kept bumping into him Riyad, reminding Sue that he was probably the only safe doctor to tend her, bearing in mind the need for secrecy. She mentioned nothing of her visit to see Jasmine, thinking that it might cause a new round of bitterness. Their meal over he went to his office having, "phone calls to make"; after being away James really wanted to see Jasmine, but not necessarily for the purpose of conversation.

The day passed slowly for James, his tired mind not on his work, his aching loins yearning for relief, his brain confused by Sue's unpredictable behaviour. He was also worrying about political climate change, the subject of his recent trip, all these niggles playing relentlessly with his thoughts and were becoming overlarge and all-consuming. He drifted into a fitful sleep, still sitting at his desk, his head slumped forward on his folded arms dreaming of the events of the past few months, yet suddenly awakened by a thumping on his locked office door, strangely, as sometimes happens in the waking stages of slumber when fact and fantasy intermingle, he was himself hammering on Jasmine's door.. Sitting up suddenly, and not knowing where he was, he called out to a secretary who had left his employ several years before. Then rubbing his eyes and realising that he was in his office, he stretched and asked who was there.

"Me!" a timid voice answered whispering, "it's Jasmine!"

Hurriedly he got up and unlocked the office, still rubbing his sleepy eyes. Ushering her in, he then saw it was dark outside he rushed over to the curtains, almost pulling them off the rail as he snatched them together to prevent anyone passing from seeing into his secret room.

Until that moment he was unaware that night had fallen. Yawning a giant yawn he wearily asked Jasmine what the time was.

"Half past midnight," she replied, and then she announced sounding worried, "your wife is behaving in a funny way."

"You're telling me!" James answered, pulling a funny face as he leaned forward to kiss Jasmine. Turning away to avoid his puckered lips, Jasmine needed to say more.

"Not yet! Just listen for a moment." Duly obeying, James listened as Jasmine told him everything about the oddly insincere meeting with Sue, when she deliberately let slip the suspicions she harboured about James being the father of Ibrahim, Jasmine also saying how surprised she was at the strangely unbalanced nature of Sue.

With other, more pressing urgent matters on his mind, James agreed that Jasmine was right to tell him everything, adding that he too thought Sue was becoming odder by the day. Putting the minor annoyance to the back of his mind, James rather impatiently suggested that it might be best if Jasmine went quietly upstairs and waited for him there. "I will join you later, after I've checked her, just in case she's still awake!" Sue didn't even stir when he entered the bedroom. An empty bottle and a half-filled glass of wine explaining why she lay totally unconscious, sprawled face down, snoring loudly and dribbling on the crumpled eiderdown.

Creeping through the house as silently as she could, Jasmine went up to her rooms and positioned herself provocatively on the couch to wait expectantly for James to arrive. After ten or so minutes, a gentle tapping heralded James, who without bothering to hang around for an answer, scurried furtively into the room looking somewhat agog with eager anticipation of resuming the hot and steamy affair which started the moment they first met.

"It's all right, she's fast asleep, she's had a wine or two."

"She shouldn't drink in her state," Jasmine said, sounding concerned.

"She always has a drink before bedtime," he replied, smiling happily, as he loosened his clothes at the prospect of making love with his beautiful soul mate.

Closed the door firmly behind him, James evocatively approached Jasmine, anxious to once again to rekindle the missed passion he felt for the love of his life. Standing up, Jasmine craned her neck to meet his gaze with hers, and then saying nothing, she kissed him hard and full on his mouth. In response, James did the same, and standing toe to toe, they shared sizzling kiss after kiss; he deftly undid her top and let it float to the floor, exposing both her breasts for him to gently caress, a pleading look from Jasmine begging him to take extra care in their tender state.

Wanting to make up for lost time, Jasmine took control of proceedings by grabbing James' hand and dragging him to the bedroom. Used to a submissive role, James went willingly, but found walking difficult due to his already erect penis. His peculiar gait making them both laugh, as she pushed him onto a chair to watch her slip off her garments and reveal her full nakedness.

Temptingly, Jasmine started to masturbate herself in front of him. Slipping her hand between her open legs, she began to slowly caress herself, while James feverishly undressed himself, all the time keeping an eager eye on the temptress he knew would go to any lengths to satisfy him as she had done so many times before. Ripping and tearing at the obstinate clothing, James eventually succeeded to remove his attire; throwing himself naked on to the bed, he lay at full-stretch to watch his private show.

Jasmine was getting more and more excited as her hand strokes became quicker, until with a long stifled groan of pleasure, she collapsed next to her lover gasping for air. Having regained enough of her breath to continue, she cleverly swung a leg over James to straddle his abdomen and kneel in an upright position above his waist; she stroking herself once again, this time at very close range, showing him all as she shuffled closer and closer, until she was near enough to push her vagina down onto James's face, wriggling and writhing on his tongue until she came again, making his sweating face even wetter. Spinning round without losing sexual contact, Jasmine plunged her open mouth onto his cock, taking him to untold depths of sublime pleasure. Stopping suddenly, Jasmine rolled on to her back, opening her legs wide like a gymnast she bid him to enter. Doing exactly what he was told to do, James fucked her slowly at first, his strokes getting faster and deeper, all the time whispering her name between gulps of breath, until with a long guttural sigh of delight, he withdraw, coming all over her breasts. Massaging the sperm around her rock-hard nipples Jasmine begged for more, so bending forwards, James kissed her passionately full on the mouth and started to finger her soaked clitoris, making a voracious Jasmine whimper her satisfaction a third, then fourth time, before finally admitting, at least for the time being, that she had had enough.

Both exhausted, they laid face up panting, trying to regain their breath. He turned to her and whispered, "Wow! I needed that, you greedy little bitch."

"So did I, you male whore," she said playfully slapping him.

"I have got to go now Jazzy," he said, his breathing now almost back to normal."

"Please don't go, pleeeze," she begged hanging on to him.

"I'd love to stay, but I must go, I really must!" he explained gathering up his crumpled clothes, "I love you, Jazzy," he added.

"I love you too James, lots!" She shot him a tender parting look, blowing endless kisses as he left, naked and clutching the bundle, waving goodbye over his shoulder.

Things were as normal as they could be, James was away most of the time, and Sue pottered around downstairs, making herself busy with nothing in particular. Jasmine silently contented herself happily being a mother, always looking forwards to James's next visit. It was April fool's Day when they next saw James, he came home unexpectedly in the afternoon looking worried, as usual he was accompanied by Michael, who looked equally concerned. Sue greeted them with her newly found welcoming manner, only to be virtually ignored by James, "I must see Jasmine now," he said pushing carelessly past Sue.

"Are you that fucking desperate?" she asked as he raced upstairs. Going straight into Jasmine's flat without knocking, James called for her.

Eventually Jasmine appeared out of the kitchen, "I was cooking," she explained, instantly seeing his obvious concern she asked, "What is it James, what's wrong?" Sitting her down, pulled up a chair for himself to explain the reason for his worry.

Looking Jasmine straight in the eye, James leaned close, gripping her hand to tell her about some urgent news he had received concerning Jasmine's uncle. He'd taken up his grievance against her with the elders of his mosque, supported by his friend Jasmine's ex-intended. "They've accused you of adultery," James blurted out.

"I never married him, how can that be?" Jasmine asked confused at how it could have happened.

"They lied and bribed," he replied, then carried on hesitantly, "they've found you guilty." Jasmine gasped her dismay and fear, fully understanding how the strictly religious Islamic courts had dealt with many other innocent females in the past.

"The sentence?"

"Don't worry about that, you're safe here."

"The sentence?" she repeated, knowing the answer and staring at James. Looking intensely back into Jasmine's eyes, squeezed her hand supportively.

"They've sentenced you to death! But they won't get you while I'm alive." Jasmine started to cry; she sobbed once or twice, and then suddenly stood up, shook herself, then having regained her composure, she calmly announced, "Yes! They've got to get me first, haven't they?" With that she spun round and went back into the kitchen, where her cooking had starting to smell somewhat overdone.

Sue had been standing at the open door all the time and heard everything. Looking at James, she simply said she was sorry and then departed moodily downstairs leaving him standing alone and bewildered. James stayed upstairs in the flat, in case Jasmine needed him, sitting quietly he just listened to the busy kitchen noises, when suddenly the crash of a dropped plate broke the spell, hastily James went into the kitchen innocently asking, "Is everything OK?"

"Of course it is," she replied sharply, "why shouldn't it be, nothing wrong here, nothing for me to worry about is there?" Jasmine was visibly shaking, not with fear, but with pure temper, "I should have let you have them killed, when I had the chance." James tried to put a comforting arm around her. "It can still be done, Michael will do it!" She brushed his arm away and shrugged, "It's too late. It won't change anything now; I'm still condemned, aren't I?"

They stayed upstairs together for some time discussing the situation, James sounding reassuring and confident told Jazzy how careful she must be, how nobody could know her whereabouts, no phone calls, no letters, and no communications at all, and now how the need for silence was even more paramount. "I will protect you." he said meaning it. "I must go now," he said apologetically, "I've lots of arrangements to make." As he turned to leave she asked, "How did you find out about it?"

"I have spies," he answered; kissing her goodbye as he departed, leaving Jasmine feeling happier and more relaxed, knowing that James would move mountains for her.

For the next few days Michael stayed faithfully on guard at the window of the downstairs apartment, only ever half asleep, always alert and always hungry, pleased to be in one place for a change. Normally he would be driving James about, covering thousands of boring miles, going all over the place, concentrating for long days along the dusty, never-ending half-made roads. Now he was doing what he was trained for, being a bodyguard.

After about a week James arrived back, with a new driver, an Irishman he referred to as Pat. He was of medium height and weedy with long wiry bright ginger hair tied back into a pony tail, piercing bright blue eyes, closely set, separated by a long crooked nose, over thin pale lips. Most noticeable of his features were his bushy eyebrows that moved endlessly, having their own language like a type of semaphore, unlike his mouth that barely moved as he spoke. Pat obviously knew Michael well as they shook hands warmly on meeting, Pat calling him Mickey and asking how he was. Greetings over, the men departed to the office, locking the door behind them. They then got down to business.

The issues to be discussed were laid down by James, the three esses as he called it: security, safety and secrecy. At length each subject was explored in detail, different hypothetical scenarios were suggested, measures and counter measures considered. James's background as an army officer was being put to good use, Michael and Pat were equally at home with the planning, suggesting ideas and methods. James informing them that he believed a private contract had been put out on Jasmine by her uncle, who euphemistically had referred to Jasmine's planned death as an honour killing; in reality her family were still furious about her escape, and purely wanted bloody revenge. "Be aware," he said as he unlocked the office door, to allow the men to leave and then he shut it, firmly behind them with a loud click.

Having eaten a hastily prepared meal, James and both men sat down with Jasmine, who was cradling the quiet infant close to her breast while she listened as James carefully explained the detailed plan to them, repeating parts of it until it was fully understood, each person repeating aloud their roles, "in case of an incident!" as James had put it. Jasmine felt guilty about involving them with her troubles and decided to stand up in front of the gathered assembly to apologise for bringing her personal woes down on their heads. She offered to save them from any of her problems by running away and losing herself somewhere far off. James was insistent, telling her that to run away was not the solution, promising her that he could and would deal with her uncle. The meeting over, Michael stood up to say goodbye, saying that he had a mission to go on; he looked to James for permission to leave, who nodded affirmatively back to him. Giving a little secret thumbs up to James; he wished good luck to all and then left, "back soon," his departing comment. Also deciding it was time to go, James announced he and Pat had plenty of things to do, so the company all went their different ways, leaving Jasmine sitting alone, quietly wondering what the next day might bring.

Early the next morning Jasmine was laying in bed, gazing through the barred open window, enjoying the sounds and smells of the stirring city, listening to the clamour of preparation for the new day; Ibrahim was waking in his nearby cot. Her first thoughts were all about the safety of both her and the child, all night she been fretting, snatching moments of erratic sleep dispersed among the bouts of worry. The baby's demanding cries were audibly growing louder, forcing her to do something to quieten him, for both their sakes changing him to make him dry and comfortable before returning to the still warm bed to feed him, snuggling together, both mother and noisily feeding child laid happy and peacefully cuddled up. Jasmine, briefly forgetting her troubles, fell asleep with the baby still clutched to her breast, his lips still moving instinctively and making gentle contented little sucking noises.

Suddenly out of the blue, the peace was ripped apart. A piercing scream rent the silence, causing Jasmine to sit bolt upright in bed, waking the startled baby and making him cry. At first Jasmine thought the Mullahs were calling the faithful to prayer, and then after her head had cleared a little, she remembered the situation and wondered if they were being attacked. Another long drawn-out cry of pain filled the air, this time Jasmine recognised it as Sue's voice. Jumping out of bed, she hurriedly placed the still crying infant in his cot, and then raced, tripping and stumbling, still half asleep, towards the source of the noise. Bumping into a panicky looking James on the landing, "What's happened?" she asked, trying to make herself decent, covering a wayward escaped naked breast, "the baby! It's started," James replied panting. "She's been up groaning all night, I thought she had wind."

"Let me have a look," Jasmine said, heading towards Sue's bedroom.

"No she's not in there, she's in the sitting room," he said, grabbing and then dragging the still tripping half-naked Jasmine in his wake.

The vision that greeted her when she entered was not what she expected. Sue was not lying in bed as Jasmine thought Sue might be, instead Sue was sitting, totally nude, with her head between her knees, on a beautiful large sage green velvet settee. Looking up, Sue explained that everything was painful, adding with a grievance that even her clothes hurt her, and she was only comfortable sitting as she was. James announced that he was going to call Xavier.

"NO DON'T!" was the instant yelled response, "I hate him," she shouted, "and I fucking hate you," she added, looking evilly at James, her sweaty, grey face contorted with hatred. Realising there was no time to be wasted, Jasmine took control of the situation, instructing James to find a bowl, soap, clean towels and to put plenty of water on to boil. Turning to Sue Jasmine instructed her how to breath properly, telling her how to save her energy.

"No pushing until I tell you!" she insisted.

Sue obeyed, offering groaned thanks.

"We really need Xavier here, you know," Jasmine said, advising Sue to forget her objections. Another contraction was starting; Sue started uncontrollably grunting with effort. "Remember pant through the pain and don't push," again Sue obeyed, the intensity was building, then as it began to reach its peak, and through a muffled scream Sue started pleading, "Call the doctor, call Xavier, and hurry up!"

Hearing the plea James dutifully scooted off, presumably to make the call.

Several more contractions occurred in the next half-hour or so, getting more and more frequent, each time the insistent Jasmine urging Sue not to push, all the time holding and sympathetically squeezing her hand. The pains were almost continuous when Jasmine peered firstly at Sue's nether regions, and then looked closely into Sue's eyes, telling her that the time was right to start pushing.

"PUSH NOW!"

James was standing in the doorway looking green, unable to help himself from straining and pushing sympathetically, his face distorting with each effort. Jasmine commanded Sue once again, this time raising her voice to encourage her flagging patient:

"P-U-U-U-SH!"

And then even louder: "AGAIN, COME ON!"

Sue was arching her back, sweating, and screaming at each effort, Jasmine was urging and cajoling, saying, "Keep going, you can do it! One more BIG effort… NOW!" her voice trembling with her personal strain.

"The head is out!" Jasmine squeaked excitedly, and then regaining her composure, advising Sue with a reassuring squeeze of her hand, "a quick breather, then one more BIG push." Sue gulped in three giant lungful's of air, and with a giant groan her unwanted baby boy was born.

The couch was ruined, bloodstained, soaked in sweat and torn. Jasmine busied herself with the final acts of childbirth. After dealing professionally with the cord and the placenta, she cleaned the infant, carefully dabbing him with warm water-soaked cotton wool. Totally exhausted and spent, Sue lay back spread-eagled naked on the soaking damaged sofa, her grey face told the whole tale of the strenuous effort of giving birth.

First carefully wrapping the newborn in a soft and fluffy clean white towel, Jasmine offered the baby to Sue. "Not now!" she screamed venomously, pushing the infant from her as she snatched her gaze off the bundle. Surprised and tired, Jasmine looked at the similarly exhausted James, who was standing, propped listlessly in the doorway, her questioning glance answered with a bemused shrug. Without being asked, Jasmine took the spurned infant over to a nearby chair, and sitting holding him close to her breast she started softly humming, making a bond that would never be broken.

Suddenly, in a whirlwind of garlic, cigarette fumes and curly black hair, the tardy Xavier arrived, having been let in by the ever-vigilant Pat, who had been watching over Ibrahim and on guard all the while. The Frenchman looked at Sue, who wearily lifted her gaze towards him, and then resumed her previous position. Using his best broken French accent Xavier mocked Sue, "You like me now, yes?" Perplexed by no response, raising his voice Xavier changed tack, "How close together are the pains?" James gestured over to Jasmine and the baby, who was still humming and rocking the infant contentedly. "Oh!" he said pondering, "The afterbirth?" he asked, arching his eyebrows. Jasmine replied by inclining her weary head in the direction of a washing-up bowl covered with a bloodstained cloth. "It's all there!" and then pausing she stared inquisitively at Xavier, furrowing her forehead, as if trying to drag something from the back of her mind, "I think we've met somewhere before, haven't we?" Xavier shuffled his feet

44

awkwardly for a split second and then, having collected his thoughts, he answered suavely, "I think not! How could I forget such a beautiful face?" With that, James and a puzzled-looking Jasmine retired from the room, so that Sue and the baby could be checked by the embarrassed doctor in private.

James was curious. "How did you know how to do all that?" Her reply sounded tired, "I wanted to be a nurse so I studied, and don't forget I had Ibrahim."

"Where do you think you know Xavier from?" he queried.

"Somewhere from not that long ago, I'm too tired to think! Ow could I forget such a creepy face?" she replied mimicking the doctor, smiled a weak smile, held on to James's supporting arm and went with him downstairs to sit down and recover from her effort.

Pat had made a welcome pot of tea, which he offered to Jasmine and James, who gratefully accepted the steaming beverage, closely followed by Xavier, who on seeing the tea, promptly asked for a cup of coffee, grimacing and twitching his eyebrows, amid a torrent of muttered curses, Pat duly obliged and shuffled off on his errand. Jasmine's questioning gaze never left the Frenchman as they all sat down together, making the doctor feel uncomfortable and fidgety. However Xavier tried to sound unflustered by Jasmine's attention, by announcing that all was fine with the baby, but Sue was in a dreadful mood.

"She is asleep now," he said nervously lighting up a cigarette, "she does not want the baby near her yet," he stated, vigorously puffing and creating a welcome smokescreen to hide in.

"I'll get him," Jasmine volunteered, "he needs to bond, to feel loved!" She then rushed off to fetch the rejected infant and cater for his immediate needs.

CHAPTER 2

1982

Most of April passed uneventfully. A grumpy Sue had shown no interest in her baby, and she wasn't even concerned in the naming of the infant. All that interested her was the regaining of her figure and the future of her social life. Whereas Jasmine felt completely at home with both boys, treating them as odd-sized twins, suckling them in shifts, making sure the greedy Ibrahim didn't take all her milk, often feeding the newborn first, to ensure he got his share. James made regular visits, trying to show an interest in the children, bringing presents and supplies on each occasion, overtly staying the night with Jasmine, apparently caring nothing for Sue's feelings. In fact it seemed that the miserable Sue now sanctioned their relationship, and appeared happier without him in her immediate vicinity. James wanted to call his legitimate new heir Peter James, in honour of his late father. Sue was unmoved, her only comment was that she didn't give a fuck what the brat was called, as long as he was out of her fucking sight. Jasmine on the other hand got really excited when she heard, repeatedly calling the baby by his new name, whispering, "Hello my little Peter James," and, "who's a lucky little Peter, then?"

Sue was getting restless, wanting to be allowed to go out like she used to be able to do, pleading and begging with James to let her go. He still needed her to be his wife, for appearance's sake, as the stuffed shirts that were his masters would frown on any marital disharmony. Sue still needed James's name, as it opened many otherwise closed doors to her, thus the arrangement held firm, with James calling the shots, and Sue reluctantly obeying. James was always vulnerable to Sue's relentless nagging appeals, so on sufferance he assented to let her go out, promising to have a word in the right ear to arrange an outing for her. Having got her own way, and restored the truce made for a happier Sue, who became generally more pleasant to those around her.

The regained peace was relief to all, especially Pat, whose constant presence in the lodgings annoyed Sue, and being the nearest to hand, he bore the brunt of her vile malice. Pat ignored all attempts to rile him, only his mobile eyebrows gave away his true feelings. Appreciating the change in Sue and saying a little inward prayer of thanks, Pat went about his business much the lighter, pleased to be free from the verbal abuse he had been forced to swallow of late.

Michael returned at the end of April. James and Pat had been waiting nervously for his arrival, peering furtively out of the upstairs window on and off for upward of three hours, pacing restlessly in between times. On several occasions a concerned Pat whispered to James secretly, from behind his hand, trying to hide their obvious worry from Jasmine, who despite their efforts was well aware of their concern about his late arrival.

Michael arrived at about half past two in the afternoon, four hours late, and was driving a different car than the one he left in. A big black Mercedes covered in yellow desert dust drew up outside the front door. Michael got out, limping slightly. Knowing how anxious James would be, he looked up at the window, gave a quick thumbs up and a forced smile. Painfully he limped into the hallway through the front door, which had been speedily opened by Pat, who looked glad to see his almost intact old friend. James came galloping down the stairs three at a time, and skidded to a halt in front of the pained Michael.

"What's happened?" he asked urgently, "Jasmine's relations wouldn't listen to reason, I tried to explain to them, but they were still hell bent on getting her." "Were?" repeated James "were!" Michael said nodding affirmatively, "I shot them! They tried to shoot me first," he proffered a bloody trouser leg as a testament to his story. "We will have to get rid of that tank," James said meaning the strange car."

Pat butted in, "I'll take it into the desert and torch it," without being asked he got up to leave, disappearing quickly on his mission.

While all this was going on Jasmine was halfway down the stairs bringing a late lunch for them all. When she heard the mention of a shooting, she stopped and cocking her head she listened instinctively before continuing the descent. Having placed down on the table a tray full of sandwiches, mugs and a pot of coffee, she enquired, "Who has been shot? Apart from Michael," her voice politely matter of fact. Michael looked at James, who looked back at Michael, they both grimaced at each other and then James blurted out, "I'm sorry Jazzy, it's your uncle and his friend, your ex-intended."

"How are they?" she asked pouring out mugs of coffee.

"Both dead, I'm afraid!" interrupted Michael apologetically, "the old one tried to sneak up on me, he just winged my leg. They weren't in the mood for listening, that's for sure." Michael pulled up his bloody trouser leg and to prove he was telling the truth and showed the wound to Jasmine.

"I'd better have a look at that, make certain it's clean," she remarked, seemingly unperturbed by the news she went off to get some first aid supplies.

Michael continued his story, "The others shot the car up as I got away. I got rid of it in Iraq, burnt it and buried the plates, nothing to identify, its clean."

"What others?" James inquired.

"The nephews, I guess, I left them alive and kicking, they're lousy shots." Jazzy came back with suitable supplies in a box with red cross on it, and a bowl brimming with hot water smelling of disinfectant, kneeling at Michael's feet she carefully rolled up the stained tatty trouser leg, cutting a small length of seam to save him from unnecessary pain. As Jasmine was tending the vicious tear in Michael's calf muscle, the two men continued discussing the episode.

"Is it all over then?" James asked.

"No!" Was the immediate answer, "they've paid a couple of thugs, and they're on their way here, somebody's talked, they know where we are."

Jasmine looked up from her task, her frightened expression said more than any words could. Michael reassured her, saying,

"Don't worry, they haven't got a chance, I'll get them if Pat doesn't first, BANG! BANG! All over." Feeling slightly better she carried on dressing the wound. Michael barely showed any sign of pain, even though Jasmine knew that it must have really been hurting him severely.

"How did you get that car?" James asked.

"What the Merc?"

"Yes, the car you drove here, the giant black Merc remember?" James insisted Michael replied sounding shy,

"I borrowed it from some rich raghead, he had several, he won't even miss it. Anyway it's history by now."

The wound to Michael's leg was serious and when Jasmine had finished dressing it, she motioned Michael to try it. He duly obeyed, wagging the bandaged limb like a trained dancer practising a complicated step. Satisfied with her nursing skill, she bent down again, this time to repair the damage to his trouser leg, to make it less obvious.

Later that evening Pat returned with another car. He refused point blank to explain its origin, but he assured James that it was genuine, calling it "a favour called in", adding that the Mercedes "was lost forever."

Jasmine noticed that more animated Pat became, the busier his eyebrows worked, and as James related the whole story of Michael's mission to Pat, his expressive brows changed to suit each emotion. She stared at him both fascinated and amazed, in the corner of his eye he caught sight of her fixed gaze, and realising the object of her attention he laughed, his blue eyes twinkled mischievously

"They frighten little children you know, they can't make them out." Pat wiggled them wildly at her.

She giggled saying, "Nor can I!" Still enthralled by Pat's amusing mannerisms Jasmine sat watching him. All of a sudden realising she'd forgotten something, she exclaimed apologetically, "Sorry Pat, I forgot you haven't eaten, you must be starving?"

"I'm starving miss," he replied softly in his Irish brogue, still laughing and tickled by Pat's obscure sense of humour, Jazzy left to prepare him some well appreciated food.

Sue hadn't involved herself seriously in anything of any importance since the birth. She didn't even bother to thank Jasmine for her help, she merely whiled away her time playing patience, reading glossy magazines and watching inane television programmes about nothing in particular. Only when James told her that she was getting fat did Sue promise to become more active. He asked her to go and see the little boy, using the fact that they had been invited to an Arab horse-racing meeting in Dubai as an inducement, and the prospect of the races really perked her up. Sue begged him for a new outfit for the occasion, but, no matter what bribery James used, she still refused to see the young Peter. Knowing that nothing would move her to take responsibility for her son, James reluctantly told her that he would accept the invitation on both their behalves, and she could go out to buy herself some new clothes, giving her a strict spending limit, and expecting her to ignore it as was usual. James made it clear to Sue that he had no intention of attending the race meeting and he would invent a last-minute excuse for himself.

The next day, the household assembled in the kitchen for breakfast, even Sue had bothered, which surprised Jazzy, as she had not seen her since the birth. Even more shocking was Pat: his long hair had gone. He now sported a very short crew cut, which accentuated his most obvious feature.

"Mickey did it," he announced, "just in case!" James peered quizzically at Pat. Michael piped up, "I wanted to do them as well," pointing to Pat's eyebrows, "he wouldn't let me though; he said he needed them to talk." Sue was looking blank, not being aware of the previous day's events, "I hear I'm taking you shopping today, I hear, "Pat was looking straight at Sue, "are you?" She replied, pointing to herself looking a little amazed.

"Yup! I'm really looking forwards to it," he replied sarcastically through a mouthful of half-chewed cornflakes. Sue disappeared instantly to prepare herself for the outing, deserting her plate of food of which she had eaten almost nothing. A thoughtful James belatedly asked Pat: "In case of what, may I ask?"

"In case they are looking for a long-haired, redheaded bog-trotter with a ponytail, driving a big black Mercedes, sir!" he answered in a military fashion, standing up quickly and looking straight in front.

"Sit down you fool, you're not in trouble. You weren't seen, were you?"

"No Sir, as I said just in case!"

"Just be vigilant, now relax and eat your brekkie like a good boy." James smiled at Pat, "a bit touchy this morning, aren't you?"

"Probably me hair not used to it yet sir!"

James turned his attentions to Michael, "How's your leg?"

"Not too bad, I can cope," he replied, proffering up the injured limb. Jasmine, who had been sitting quietly, listening to the breakfast banter butted in, telling all present that she thought

Pat's new hairstyle was, "very smart," and then turning to Michael, she insisted that his leg needed re-dressing straight after their meal. "I will give Pat a list of medical supplies to pick up while he's out, that first aid box is almost empty," Jasmine added. In fact she was really getting in extra, as she expected they might be needed in the very near future.

Sitting together they finished their breakfast in total silence; Jasmine blamed herself for the situation, regretting the deaths she believed she had partially caused; Michael was angry and sore, punishing himself for being clumsy and getting shot, annoyed that maybe he wasn't alert enough; Pat was missing his hair, feeling light-headed and strange, and James was planning, mentally visualising different scenarios, then plotting suitable counter measures. The spell was suddenly broken by an irate Sue, who shouted running down the stairs, shrieking at James, "That fucking crying baby is driving me fucking mad! I can't hear myself fucking think!" she screamed directly at Jasmine. "Do something about it, you lazy cow, do it fucking now!" she demanded, stamping her foot in temper. Jasmine looked shocked and slightly guilty for a second before scurrying off to tend to the noisy infants, leaving James Michael and Pat staring at one another, amazed by the unwarranted outburst of bad language.

The immediate needs of the boys were tended to, and both babies were sleeping contentedly, when there came a gentle tapping on the door. It was Michael, attending as instructed to have his leg re-dressed. Jasmine beckoned him in and told him to sit, offering him a chair and a stool to rest his injured leg on; he obeyed, taking the seat with a pained groan. She noticed that he looked more uncomfortable than he did at breakfast.

"Is it getting worse?" she asked him.

"It's certainly not getting any better," he said, nodding yes with a painful grimace. Carefully the bandage was unwound, for although Jazzy had put on a special Vaseline-covered non-stick gauze over the injury it still stuck and had to be dampened and peeled slowly off, pulling savagely at the torn flesh.

"Lucky you don't have hairy legs," she said, trying to take Michael's mind off his obvious agony.

"I haven't grown up properly yet," was his witty reply. Jasmine laughed a little, and then tutted, as she exposed the angry-looking wound.

"I've ordered some antibiotic cream, and you will need it, come and see me when they get back from their shopping trip. Don't forget!" She carried on, and bathed the area with a strong salt solution, calling it, "nature's healer." Then she swathed the leg with some freshly cleaned strips of linen.

Michael gingerly tried out his newly dressed limb, determined not to favour it, and almost succeeding, but still showing a slight sign of a limp.

"Don't tell the others that it's hurting me, will you?" he asked appealing to her.

"Not if you don't want them to know, I'll keep it between us, I won't say a thing." Michael hobbled to the door, and then, as soon as he thought that he might be seen, he pulled back his shoulders and strode out of the room as if he was on parade in front of the Queen.

After lunch Sue emerged from her bedroom. She had spent several hours excitedly preparing herself for the shopping trip. In obeisance to Muslim tradition, a large pale green silk scarf was carefully thrown over her head, making a stunning contrast to the full length kingfisher-blue silk gown that hung in luxurious looped folds down to the floor, wearing no more than a subtle hint of make-up to complement the outfit. Sue looked fabulous as she swept out of the building through the opened front door to the awaiting, recently acquired new car, a silver BMW. Sue paused for Pat to open a rear door for her to enter, he obeyed with a large mocking bow. An annoyed Sue glared at him as she took a seat in a very ladylike manner, swinging her legs in so as not to expose any part of her ankle: he closed the door with pretend reverence and then assumed his seat at the front. The ever-watchful Michael accompanied James to see Sue off on her outing, both waving a thankful goodbye as the car zoomed speedily off in a cloud of dust.

James laughingly remarked how he thought Pat's driving had not improved, and as he was in mid sentence he received a subtle prod in the ribs from Michael to attract his attention, at the same time, and whispering through the side of his mouth, "Don't look now." James instinctively did. "Don't look!" Michael reminded him, James duly cast his eyes downward whispering an apology, "Over my left shoulder," Michael said turning to face James as though they were in deep discussion, "about three o'clock, a bloke on a bike," "I see him," James replied.

Michael added "I've seen him before, a couple of times, once in Tabriz, when I was doing a recce, and yesterday here, I wasn't sure then, but I am now."

"Did he see you?"

"He might have done yesterday, but nobody saw me in Tabriz, not until the proverbial shit hit the fan."

"Do you think he's one of her relations, maybe a cousin?" questioned James.

"No, Jasmine's uncle was giving him money when I saw him there, lots of money, they acted like strangers," Michael added as they nonchalantly turned together appearing as if though there was nothing of importance to keep them outside, and then went back indoors.

Michael had found a place upstairs in the apartment where he could see out without being seen. The man outside was making an attempt to be inconspicuous, fiddling with his bike, and then pretending to examine a nearby car, walking around it then kicking the tyres, his amateurish attempts drawing attention to himself rather than deflecting it. James entered the room, asking if the man was still there.

"Yes," came the reply, "he's changed hats three times, he definitely isn't very good, he sticks out like a sore thumb, I'll go and do him if you want."

"No! Not yet, you are not in any condition to anyway, just keep your eye on him."

So Michael, glad to be sitting down resting his throbbing leg, kept watch, taking many notes of the comings and goings.

After two or so hours Jasmine brought him some refreshments, which he refused, not wanting to fill his bladder and causing him to have to leave his post. More hours passed, the unerring Michael had made several pages of notes, charting the watcher's movements and any possible contacts, even a crafty pee in an alley was written down. Importantly an ancient Ford had passed the man on three occasions, and each time the man seemed to secretly acknowledge it with almost unnoticeable A-

O.K gesture. As dusk fell the watcher changed shifts and was replaced by a tall, very dark Arab, dressed in black clothing, making him almost invisible in the gloomy street. He had been driven there and deposited by the Ford, and after a speedy conversation the men swapped places; the original spy was whisked away in the decrepit car which spluttered from the scene amidst a cloud of acrid smoke and dust. All the events had been written down meticulously by the tired, hungry and wounded Michael.

Night had fallen when Sue and Pat returned from the shopping trip. Laden to the gunnels with bags and boxes they both struggled through the door, she was bubbly and excited; he was just tired and bored. All Sue wanted to do was to unpack and admire her purchases, which she proceeded to do without delay.

"It's like Christmas, isn't it?" she squealed trembling, and tearing at the parcels. James simply ignored her immature behaviour, and carried on as though she was absent. Without any delay he told Pat about the watchers, asking him to have a subtle, but close look, commanding him not to start anything.

Obediently Pat went outside, immediately opening the car boot and fiddling about for a couple of minutes, finally returning carrying a bag of tools. James was eagerly waiting for Pat's conclusions, out of sight, at the side of the front door.

"Sitrep?" he inquired as soon as the door was shut. Pat had plenty to report, "Firstly there are at least two, one up the road and one over there," he indicated their positions by waving a flattened hand, "secondly, they are both armed, they each have pistols, and one of them definitely has a rifle, lastly they aren't professional, and last of all, I hate fucking shopping, it bored the tits off me." James was being distracted by Sue, who kept asking him insistently what he thought of this, and then "Do you think this suits me...?" and so on. He turned on his heels, glared menacingly in her direction, and yelled at her to "SHUT UP!" pointing out that he was too busy to be bothered by such trifles. Sue flounced out of the room in a huff, having gathered up all her new purchases and leaving a sea of wrappings strewn all over the floor. James looked mightily relieved, "That's better, what was the last thing you said?"

Pat repeated, "I hate fucking shopping, it bores the tits off me, sir."

"Oh yes, I remember. What do you think then?"

Pat replied sensibly, "All as I said sir, two visible, could be a third; they're just watchers with guns, no real danger."

"I wish I had your eyes Pat," James noted, smiling at him.

"They wouldn't suit you, anyway you'd hate the eyebrows."

James laughed, thinking how Pat could always see the funny side of even the direst of situations.

"Can I get some grub now? I'm knackered!"

"Go on, I've got to grovel at her ladyship's feet, anything to keep the peace."

Tearful and fuming Sue refused to accept James's apology, saying that he had spoiled her day, and he had embarrassed her in front of Pat. She was crying and stamping with temper, annoyed that he didn't bother to see what she had bought, telling him that she hated him. "All you care about is your fucking Arab whore!" she shrieked.

"Do you mean Jasmine?" he replied calmly, knowing his indifference would infuriate Sue even more.

"Yes I fucking do! You fucking wanker, I'm never going to talk to you ever again, now fuck off cunt!"

"Judging by your attitude I assume it means that you won't be interested in going to the races the day after tomorrow then. OK, I'll go and cancel your flight then." James knew exactly how to play Sue, and when he turned to leave, her attitude completely changed. He had realised years before that bribery was always a handy tool in his marriage to the fickle Sue.

"I didn't mean it," she pleaded coyly, "I was just a little upset, you know it makes me mad, when you shout at me, I'm sorry." Her wheedling apology fell on James's deaf ears; he'd heard it all before, but he had her back under control.

Upstairs Pat, refreshed after his arduous task, arrived to relieve Michael's watch. On having been briefed on all movements and handed the notes, he went to take the vacant seat; noticing a stain where the wound had wept through the dressings, he urged Michael to have his leg re-dressed.

"I think I will," he said, leaving the room and walking stiffly, partly due to sitting for a long while, but mainly due to his injury.

He hobbled straight to Jasmine's flat, knocked, waited and then waited some more... after a seeming age she answered looking a little flushed and dishevelled. Michael twigged instantly, offering to come back later.

"Don't be silly, come in. I'll get some hot water." He entered and sat on the same chair and putting his foot on the same stool that were ready and waiting for him. James was there looking sheepish. He shrugged at Michael, who looked an apology back to him, then he gently rolled up a baggy trouser leg, revealing the swaddled limb.

"Sore?" James asked as he was leaving.

"Not too bad!" Michael lied convincingly to reassure his boss of his fitness for duty.

Jasmine came back into the room with towels and Dettol-smelling hot water, she put down her burden on a table and started undoing the stained linen wrap, the ragged gash was still sticking to the gauze, but not quite as badly as before, and the wound was no worse, if not a little better than the last time she saw it.

"Nature's healer!" Jasmine said looking pleased with what she was seeing, and then very carefully she dabbed away the dried blood and matter. "It really needed stitches; it's too late now though!" she added, still cleaning the open slash, peering closely, and pulling out tiny pieces of debris with tweezers, "I can see now it's not bleeding anymore." Michael was quiet throughout the treatment, opting to concentrate on being brave and not show any outward signs of pain. Jasmine bathed the whole area once again with a strong salt solution, dried it and smeared the newly bought antibiotic cream all over it; she wrapped the wound with brand new sterilised bandages and secured it tightly with broad strips of Elastoplast.

"How's that?" she asked, looking for Michael's approval; he got up from the seat, walked around the room and declared, "Much much better, that's great!" His face told the story, it really did feel better, and he wasn't bluffing like he had been before.

"You're an angel!" was his comment.

"And you are named after one," she retorted with a small giggle.

"I'll go and tell James we've finished," he winked, gave her a toothy grin then left, walking almost, but not quite, normally.

The next day passed without incident. Sue was in a really good mood, busy fussing about planning her forthcoming trip, flitting about, doing her nails, hair and other girly things. As promised, James had arranged her flights and hotel, instructing her to behave as if she was to be his representative, reminding her to apologise on his behalf, saying that he was ill and sorry that he was unable to attend. Once again he reminded her that behaviour was to be of the highest standard, and she was not to let him down under any circumstances. She agreed to the terms willingly and then happily skipped about her business, packing luggage and preparing for her much looked forward to trip.

Michael felt much better; he and Pat took turns watching the watchers, assuming their purpose was nefarious they worked out defence schemes, often with their heads together poring over scribbled scraps of paper, like naughty schoolboys plotting mischief. James had lots of work on; he closeted himself in his office, only making occasional trips out of it to check the ongoing situation, reluctantly returning back to his humdrum work. Jasmine spent her time looking after the children and cooking for everybody, except Sue, who was on a new faddy diet she had read about in one of her glossy magazines.

Evening fell and all was as it had been. Nothing had changed outside; the watchers, having their every move observed and noted, Pat concluded that there were definitely at least three of them, two probably just hired thugs, the other, who seemed to be controlling them, either a relation, or the corrupt cleric employed by the family. Nobody knew how the men had got to know the whereabouts of Jasmine. They made the assumption that Michael had been followed, they had no reason for suspect otherwise, until James unexpectedly called a meeting.

He summoned Jasmine, Michael and Pat to his office, and addressed them much as a headmaster would a class: "It's my entire fault. Like an idiot I confided in my friend, I told him every last bloody detail, I thought I could trust him, Xavier is the Judas, I think he took a payoff." They all looked amazed, except Jasmine who said, "I'm sorry James." Inside it was no surprise to her as she was a very good judge of character. Pat muttered under his breath, but still audible, "French bastard!" Michael kept silent, his thoughts were obvious.

"He's used me, so it's my turn to use him. I've fed him a load of rubbish to report, I'm going get that two-faced so and so," James said trying, not to swear, which he rarely did. "I have let slip that Michael's leg is really bad and Pat is going to take him to the hospital, hopefully they'll take the bait and walk into my trap." They all thought it was a good idea.

"How did you find out sir?" questioned Pat.

"By mistake really, I tried to phone him when Michael got shot. His receptionist said he was away on business in Tabriz. I put two and two together it came to four, so I phoned my American contacts, and his name cropped up, Bobs your uncle!"

"He'll kill the receptionist," chimed in Michael.

"If I don't kill him first," grumbled Pat.

"No! Leave him, the Yanks want him, he's not popular in high places, I can't say why, it's hush-hush," James said, putting on an overly posh voice, obviously imitating one of his superiors.

The next morning Sue departed on her trip with the pomp and ceremony being observed. To put on a show for the watchers everyone lined up like her very own private entourage, all apparently saddened by her leaving. She teetered to the car, waving and smiling as she went, faithfully followed by the suitcase-laden, reluctant chauffeur that was a grouching Pat. Waiting while the baggage was stowed away, she then gestured for the even more unhappy manservant to open the car door for her. Begrudgingly Pat obeyed, and then flounced into the driver's seat, started the car and roared off like a bat out of hell, leaving the assembled company blinking and coughing in the resulting cloud of debris thrown up by the screeching tyres.

Unknown to Sue, the staged departure had its effect, drawing the watchers out of cover, allowing them to be assessed accurately. Michael's professional eyes didn't stop scanning and rating the opposition, looking for any visible weakness. When he turned to go back in, he exaggerated his incapacity, limping markedly and deliberately looked pained for all to see. The first part of the trap had been laid, now for stage two.

The atmosphere in the house was much better with Sue out of the mix, happier and more relaxed in a tense sort of way. On his return Pat was thunderous, his eyebrows down to his cheeks and muttering English and Irish verbal abuse, berating Sue openly, referring to her as "Lady Muck," calling her, "a selfish cow," among other unutterable Anglo-Gaelic obscenities.

"Is that my wife, you're talking about?" asked James.

"Yes sir, sorry sir!" Pat replied in a military fashion. James smiled reassuringly.

"Don't worry, I think she's been getting on everyone's nerves, myself included." The three men retired to their observation point, to discuss how they were going to lure the men in, and how they were going to strike They pored over sketched plans and went over their notes until, after twenty or so minutes, they all agreed, then repeating slowly their individual roles, they shook hands and went about their tasks.

Michael went to see Jasmine, to get a new dressing for his leg. She was pleased with him, he wasn't showing much sign of lameness and the etched lines of pain on his face had almost gone. Pat stayed on guard, still making notes, and James resumed working, shut out of sight in his office. After lunch the second part of the plan swung into action: Jasmine made a show of opening a downstairs window directly opposite to where one of the watchers was hiding: leaning out she shook imaginary dust out of a cushion, then deliberately forgetting to shut the window properly, she returned to the others, whispering, "Was that all right?"

"Perfect!" James and Michael answered simultaneously. Just as dusk was gathering, Pat took Michael out to the car; his limp now exaggerated so much he was almost being carried, his face screwing up with the pretended agony of walking to the car. Pat got in the driver's seat, started up and drove off sedately around the corner and then out of sight, straight into an alley a hundred yards behind the buildings. As quickly as possible both men alighted, then followed their pre-planned route to the back door of the lodgings. Michael, still hampered by his injury, was much slower than Pat, who galloped ahead like a loosed greyhound after a hare, arriving minutes before his struggling compatriot. Once in, they crept into the room next door to the one with the opened window. Upstairs in the apartment, the now heavily armed James remained on watch alongside Jasmine, who was there to act if needed as messenger. Sandwiches and bottled drink had been placed at both hiding places, just in case it was going to be a long night, which it was.

It was twenty-seven minutes past two precisely when the first signs of action started, the three men outside were joined by two more.

"Do you know them Jazzy?" James asked, motioning her to have a look in the street. Jasmine peered out, opening her eyes wide to let in as much light as possible, and after allowing time to acclimatise them to the gloom, she tugged at James's sleeve, uttering almost silently, "Yes, they're my cousins from Tabriz."

He whispered back, "Go and tell the boys!" and then as an afterthought, he reminded her, "Go quietly, keep to the planned route, and come back to me straight away." Obeying, Jasmine scuttled silently off on her mission to where Pat and Michael had been taking turns dozing in short shifts; when Jasmine arrived, panting, she gasped out the news to the now wide-awake pair and then, without a sound, disappeared back upstairs, there to be locked in with James and the children.

It was three o'clock when the action really started. The men crossed over the road running crouching, bent-backed and straight-legged, trying to remain unseen, one at a time, at even intervals. Pat was ready and waiting just inside the adjacent room; Michael took a position near the bottom of the stairs, his dark skin and black clothing making him invisible in the shadows of the night. The silent tension in the house was palpable, taut like a guitar string ready to snap. All of a sudden there was a small noise, sounding much louder than it actually was, alerting the patient defenders that the bait had been taken and that action was imminent... then the scraping of a boot on the window ledge, an uttered curse, the noises people make when they're trying to be quiet, then the click, click, of weapons being readied. Michael was counting the seconds from the first sound, *fifty-eight... fifty-nine...sixty...* allowing the attackers time to establish their foothold. At first a single shadowy shape emerged tentatively from the front room with the conveniently open window, then a second and a third, and finally a fourth. Moving in single-file, they moved gradually forward into the newly painted hall, foolishly making themselves easy targets against the pale wall.

Michael opened fire first: bang! Bang! Bang! Three flashes illuminated the startled intruders; the leading collapsed in a heap with a loud groan. The remaining three men returned shots, firing wildly in the direction of roughly where the flashes had come from. Looking to escape, and on seeing the open door, they bolted for it, straight into the arms of an eager Pat: Pop! Pop! His gun, a specialist low-velocity weapon, was much quieter than normal, but was only efficient at very close range, another Pop! Pop!

"Two down!" he shouted, and then one of the fallen men shot back at him – two bullets whizzed past him, he felt the hot wind as they passed close to his cheek. Ducking and running, he shot prone man at point-blank range, hitting him in the neck, then kicked his abandoned gun out of the dying man's reach to the other side of the room. The remaining man, fearing for his life, tried to run away when he saw his comrades so professionally dealt with. Michael's gun burst to life: bang! The last intruder was down, felled with a bullet in his groin; moaning pitifully, he tried to crawl away to hide, only to be despatched mercifully by Michael: bang!

In less than two minutes the conflict was over, three already dead and one dying. Pat had left the scene, hot on the tail of a fleeing and terrified fifth assailant. Everything seemed eerily silent after the tumult; Michael turned on a single lamp to inspect the full horror of the carnage, and at the same instant James shouted from upstairs, "Sitrep?"

"All OK boss. Safe!" he replied. On hearing Michael's assessment James raced down to survey the damage. "Christ! What a mess!" His observation was correct; there was blood and guts everywhere. "Where is Pat?" he asked fearing the worst.

"Gone after the other bloke," Michael replied unconcerned, "we've got a live one through there," he motioned with his head towards the crumpled heap that was a human being, "I thought you might want a chat with him." The man was lying face down in a pool of sticky congealing blood, groaning with each fitful breath, the unmistakable sickly smell of gore and his recently voided bowels clung to the dying man. Michael turned him face up with his foot. The injury to his chest was obvious, frothy pink bubbles formed, then burst where the bullet had hit him. As James bent to speak to the prostrate man, he breathed his last, moving him was the last straw, the final pain too much for his broken body to bear. He died without being questioned.

Pat was in his element, chasing an armed opponent, thriving on the danger it presented. It was a quiet night, and the streets were deserted, Pat was alert, and his body was tingling as he listened for any telltale sounds that might betray a hiding man, and then he heard an engine started not far away, about forty yards as the crow flies. His car was twenty-plus yards in the opposite direction, he stopped cocking his head on one side to listen again, this time to work out the direction it was travelling in, it was definitely heading out north. With his senses bristling, Pat ran at top speed towards the car he had left in the alley, rounding the corner expecting to see the silver B.M.W. he had left there earlier.

To his horror it had gone, and very recently, as he could still smell the petrol fumes lingering heavily in the night air. He kicked a nearby bag of rubbish, "FUCK!" he shouted, and then, "Fuck! Fuck! Fuck!" He sprinted to the end of the alley, ran right, and then left, jumping high in the air, trying to get a better chance of a glimpse of the errant vehicle. Seeing no sign of it, he decided to give up the futile chase and head back to the house in order to check on his comrades.

Pat arrived back panting thinking himself that he needed to get fitter. James opened the door. Breathless and wheezing Pat gasped out his words, "I didn't get him, some bastard has nicked the fucking car, it's nowhere to be fucking seen."

"Look behind you," James pointed behind Pat to the parked silver car. "We need it here to clean up with, you've made a bit of a mess in there, but we only need to make it a bit more presentable and I'll get the laundry men to do the rest," he said, gesturing to the front room. When they entered; Michael was rolling a corpse onto opened grey refuse bags. Jasmine was on her hands and knees mopping up blood and faeces, crying as she did so, not being used to such foul and gory scenes. She looked up at Michael, her eyes brimming with tears.

"Be careful with him. He's my cousin," she pleaded sobbing.

"The cousin who wanted you dead Jazzy," James reminded her.

"Still, my cousin." Carrying on with her grizzly task, Jasmine's tears splashing onto the wet tiled floor, leaving clean spots among the diluted blood. Meanwhile Pat assisted the struggling Michael, wrapping, then trussing the stiffening bodies with broad brown parcel tape, and then carrying them to the car, having to make extra haste, because of the fast approaching dawn. Quickly all four deceased were crammed into the roomy, BMW, two in the boot, the other two on the back seat which Jasmine had covered with some old curtains. Pat offered to drive, as Michael's leg had been hurting him, aggravated by his overnight crouching and exertions, so the pair left, hurtling through the awakening streets, off far into the desert, leaving James and Jasmine to finish clearing up after the carnage.

About mid-morning, a banging on the door awoke the exhausted pair. All was back to normal indoors except for the one room, where Pat had shot the second two intruders. A huge obstinate bloodstain had soaked into the carpet, yet fortunately a suitable rug removed from the front bedroom did the trick, and as luck would have it, it covered exactly the offending area. James rushed to the window and looked out, using the secret observation position they had used to watch their assailants the night before.

"Police," he told Jasmine. She looked frightened, "Don't worry!" he told her, "they know me." James smartened himself up, put on his jacket, then calmly went down and answered the front door. A crumpled smiling policeman stood there. "Hello Saeed," James greeted him in a familiar manner.

"Good morning Mr Cahill," he spoke reasonable English, marred by hissing noises caused by his missing front teeth, "it has been reported to me that shots have been heard near here."

"Shots? Oh yes, I heard some noises in the night, they woke me up, I thought it was a car backfiring though. Would you like to come in and have some coffee Saeed?"

"No thank you! I must get on with my work," he left cheerfully, blissfully unaware of the massacre that had taken place the night before, and unquestioningly he accepted James's sketchy explanation.

Jasmine was just finishing bathing the happily fed boys when James returned to tell her about the meeting with the policeman. She was still dreadfully upset by the events, barely being able to grasp the fact that it was actually real, not just a horrible dream. Both infants were tired, with their bellies freshly filled, cleaned and happy; all they wanted to do was sleep, so Jasmine put them to bed. Happy that the household had returned to something approaching normal, James took the opportunity to console Jasmine, telling her he would kill a thousand people rather than having a single hair on her head hurt.

"His name was Gholam," she cried again, "he was such a lovely boy."

"Did you see your other cousin?" James's voice was gentle and sympathetic.

"Only once, across the road, last night," she answered obviously needing to be comforted, so he started to comfort her.

At first he was just standing embracing her, patting her back in time to his heartbeat, and then she looked up into his eyes. He stared intently back into hers, reddened and brimming with tears, but still beautiful, appealing and innocent. He kissed a single tear away, then another; she responded, kissing him back lovingly, softly at first, but gradually the kisses were getting harder and hotter. His comforting hand had stopped comforting and started caressing and squeezing, she responded, aroused and willing, steering him effortlessly to the bedroom, shedding her clothes as she went, drawing him to the bed, laying down, naked and lovely, imploring for love, the vision indelibly burned into his brain there for the rest of his life. In a trance he removed his clothing, unable to take his eyes of the wonderful-looking woman who wanted him so badly. The lovemaking was meaningful, as she wanted to say thanks to him. James lowered himself gently next to her, kissing and licking the purring Jasmine, who responded to each touch, arching her back more and more, tightening the skin on her breasts, making them small and tight – and then, unable to resist his foreplay, she climbed on him lowering herself down, holding him against her, and then thrusting down heavily, accepting all at once, causing a great groan to issue from her lips, slowly rising and sitting rhythmically, increasing speed, judging the moment, timing herself, then sitting hard, causing them both to come together.

Greedy Jasmine wanted more, she looked at the exhausted James laying there flaccid and tired, his spent body unable to oblige, so she started on herself, first rubbing and stroking, building herself up to another crescendo before collapsing on James to repeatedly kiss him and gasp out her grateful words of love, which he was barely able to answer, the emotions of the last few days, leaving him drained in mind and body.

"I love you!" he uttered faintly.

"I love you too!" she responded and without making a sound, suddenly being overtaken with an all-consuming weariness, they just fell into a deep sleep, there on the bed, naked, embracing and hopelessly in love.

Half a day passed before Pat and Michael returned, with the car newly washed and polished, both inside and out, all scrupulously cleaned, any evidence destroyed far away in the desert, either burned or buried. Their initial responsibility was to report to James, telling him every detail of the journey, the disposal, the clean-up, and then the trip home – everything, no matter how small was carefully related back to James. One important item of interest not to be overlooked was that they had passed the abandoned old Ford on the road to Al Majma'ha fifty miles north of Riyhad.

"I think it was dumped, not broken down, it still ran, it had a quarter of a tank of petrol in it," explained Michael.

"Nothing wrong with it!" added Pat reinforcing what Michael said. James told them all that had happened, all about the clean-up at the house, and the visit from the police, everything except the details of the afternoon nap, which he thought might be too much information for them to cope with. Jasmine had rustled them up some food, which they demolished with gusto, the hungry men not having had anything substantial to eat for some time. Lunch finished, Jasmine insisted on dressing Michael's damaged leg, which desperately needed some urgent attention. Afterwards the tired and sore Michael took to his bed, needing to rest and regain his ebbed strength. Meanwhile the always faithful, ever watchful Pat returned to his duty, on guard protecting his only true friends.

The next several days were quiet. Michael's leg was healing well, Pat was still jumpy and watchful, and his eyes rarely strayed from the street. The more he thought about the situation the more he believed it wasn't all over; he was convinced there were still at least two more men, now his sworn enemies, waiting for the chance to pounce, to avenge the deaths of their comrades. He knew that his fears were founded, as did James who had learned that a corrupt Shia imam had been paid by Jasmine's rich uncle's family to spuriously pronounce a fatwa on Jasmine as part the personal vendetta held by his descendants.

Jasmine was blissfully happy; her uncle's family were back in Iran, licking their wounds and mourning their dead, the children were healthy and thriving, Sue was away, leaving James entirely without her distractive presence, peace and harmony had been restored, at least for the time being. Jasmine had always been curious about James and his ability to find out information with just a single phone call, and also she wondered what were the real reasons for Pat and Michael's presence as obviously they weren't merely drivers, they were more like hired guns. The first opportunity for Jasmine to ask James the burning questions arising as they were lying in bed the night before Sue was due back, all had been quiet and without incident, they were happily chatting about life in England when Jasmine took her chance.

"What do you really do?" she asked, and then she told him of her misgivings. James was taken aback, "I can't tell you much! But I will be as honest as I can, I do work for the trade mission, not all the time though, some of my time I just try and keep things calm, look after British interests over here, so to speak." James's considered reply annoyed Jasmine a little.

"What do you mean by that?" she said flashing an angry look at him.

"I mean that things are changing; revolution is in the air, certain people want the West thrown out of the whole of the Middle East, and they are stirring things up for us, using ancient laws and religion as the tools, corrupting the true teachings of Islam, turning people against us, calling us Crusaders, blaming us for poverty and all their woes." His voice was trembling with passion.

"In which there must be some truth! Do you hate Islam?" she asked, looking directly into his eyes, searching for any signs of untruth. "I love Islam! I love all that is good in it, but hate the bad, like anything; different people see things different ways."

He paused to think. "I've met lots of very good people over here, and I've met a few very bad ones, unfortunately the bad ones turn sweet to sour, like the proverbial bad apple." She knew he meant every word. "About Michael and Pat, they are what you see, professionals and drivers of a sort!"

"Heavily armed drivers!" Jasmine smiled and changed tack, "Xavier isn't French, nor is he a doctor you know!"

James was shocked; he looked at Jasmine amazed by her statement. "How do you know that?" he asked.

"He's Iranian, and a bad actor, only a fool would believe he's French!"

"I did." James replied. "How do you know he's Iranian?"

"My parents were from Tabriz, I lived there! And I've seen him before; when he speaks he gives himself away, by his mannerisms."

"I've only just found out myself, you should work for me, good pay you know," he said, impressed by her ability to work people out.

"I couldn't stand the strain, too much sex for my liking!" she said as she turned over to go to sleep.

The next day, at the crack of dawn, the two men James referred to as the laundry men arrived carrying a new carpet, which had to fitted before midday, as Sue was due back at two. On James's instructions she was not to be alerted to any of the preceding week's events under any circumstances, and everything had to appear to be completely normal. The men who came to fit the carpet were part of a specialist clean-up team, employed by the same organisation as James, who they respected and knew well. No questions were asked as they speedily went about their task, completing it quickly and efficiently, Pat and Michael paying the pair a visit, apparently having met before in similar circumstances, as they were all on first name terms, obviously pleased to see one another. For half an hour they sat and reminisced about past experiences they had shared. Chatting, laughing, drinking mugs of tea and eating biscuits, Michael proudly showing them his latest injury, while Pat explained most of how the carpet got so damaged, his busy eyebrows adding extra meaning to each word, the time came for them to leave, so after more handshaking, and back-slapping the men went, leaving the re-carpeted room looking as it did before, but smelling and feeling much different, all new and full of the aromatic bristle of static electricity.

Pat had to pick Sue up at half past one, so mumbling and cursing he left, walking grumpily to the car and sped off in the customary manner on his errand. Sue arrived back precisely on time, a clock indoors striking two as the BMW drew up outside. Pat begrudgingly opened a back door allowing the excited Sue to alight, who swept through the front door imperiously, leaving the unhappy man to cope with the baggage,

"Hello everyone, I'm home!" she called, announcing her arrival as though she was expecting a retinue of servants to be waiting obediently for her. Pat was floundering in her wake, carrying her stack of luggage, now larger than when she left. Dropping it all deliberately, he apologised instantly for his clumsiness, a wry smile giving his real intent away. James arrived to greet her.

"Good flight?" he enquired.

"Yes dear! How's your week been?" she asked kissing him on the cheek like an old maiden aunt would.

"Nothing special!" he replied smiling inwardly.

"Something's different!" she sniffed the air as a dog would when it scents a rabbit and then poked her head into the freshly fitted room, "New carpet?"

CHAPTER 3

1982

For the next few months everything stayed much as it was before, Sue pretending that her child didn't exist, never even bothering to talk about him let alone visiting the infant, who was never further than only just a handful of steps away. Sue carried on exactly as she had been used to, off and about, a function here, a race meeting there, rarely spending any time at home, preferring to be mixing with the good and the great, rather than indulging in the inconvenient drudgery of a family life.

James carried on working relentlessly, either sitting at home, ploughing through piles of paperwork or on the telephone speaking to different people from all over the world, arranging deals, or off on trips, visiting oilfields, refineries and pipelines. Most of his working time was spent with rich sheiks and other wealthy dignitaries, needing reassurance on their future dealings with Britain. The unpredictable political climate in the Middle East was scaring them, pacts and alignments had to be forged and then cemented together by friendships, huge financial deals greasing the wheels of commerce, and keeping all parties warily happy. However, James's other hat, the one shrouded in secrecy, was always conducted out of sight, on a special telephone, that was always kept shut away, secured in a drawer in his desk, behind the always closed and locked door of his office.

Jasmine spent her days caring for the two, ever-growing children, the elder, Ibrahim, was overlarge and sullen, always hungry, demanding and starting to discover enjoyment in bullying his smaller, younger cot mate Peter; never before bad two such different chicks shared the same nest. Peter, a small baby, bright and inquiring, ever interested in the world about him, his bright blue eyes twinkling, showing signs of his amiable nature, whereas the seldom awake Ibrahim showed no sign of any interest, other than eating or paying unwanted attention to poor unlucky little Peter. Never did Ibrahim appear to be happy, his surly nature noticeably growing day by day.

Michael spent his time working with James, driving him all over the place, sometimes undertaking a round trip of a thousand miles or more. James preferring to travel by land as internal air services were both unsafe, and unreliable. The BMW had been replaced with a dark-green Range Rover that was specially converted to cope with desert conditions. Michael loved it and treated it like his best friend, always polishing and dusting it, checking its oil and water every day, caring for its every need. Meanwhile Pat perpetually stayed near to Jasmine, never letting her out of earshot, always armed with two guns and a small dagger, his favourite and main weapon, a Beretta 17, a high powered accurate light weight pistol, the other, a Beretta 950 B, a four inch long close range mini gun. Yet the knife was a real killer's blade, small and light, honed razor sharp with an evil serrated back edge, designed to inflict as much damage and bleeding to a victim as possible.

Things were getting more and more dangerous in the Middle East, tensions were growing by the day, a greedy Saddam Hussein was avariciously eyeing up his neighbours, the wealthy oil rich Saudi Arabia and equally affluent Kuwait, threatening them as he had threatened and then attacked Iran. His expansionist ambitions seemed likely to plunge the whole region into all-out war, involving Israel then possibly the whole world. Terror reigned, frightened people sought solace from where ever they could, the mosques were full to capacity, the faithful seeking guidance from the eager clerics, most of whom were trying to give hope and comfort to the quivering masses. A few however preached words of hate, making use of the fragile situation, conjuring up a new common enemy, the Western world, its values, its religion, its worth, sowing the seeds of discord, then praying for the harvest.

James was, as usual, closeted in his office, planning measures to ensure the stability of his industry, the vital lifeblood of the whole of the Arabian Peninsula, which also happened to be the basic commodity needed for Britain to function as something like the world power it once was. James was busy thumbing his way through a great pile of neatly stacked paperwork, methodically scribbling down the points of interest, each being rated on a scale of importance and urgency, when Pat knocked and then entered the office. Standing erect as he waited to be acknowledged, while James finished his immediate task, marking his page in the papers by very deliberately and slowly folding the corner down of one of the sheets, and then placing his notes as a marker at the same place.

Without looking up from his work at the patiently waiting Pat, James asked what he could do to be of assistance. Pat answered formally.

"That fucking Frenchman is here to see you, sir!"

"Do you mean Xavier?" James asked, looking bemused and surprised at the same time.

"Yes Sir, as I said, that fucking Frenchman."

"He's not French!" The answer came back, calculated to confuse the Irishman,

"He's not?" Pat queried, his eyebrows knotted like fighting ginger caterpillars.

"No. You've got more French blood in your veins than he has in his. He doesn't know that I know though."

"Perhaps his grandfather flew over Paris once, sir!"

Pat added as he left to fetch the visitor, smiling at his own wit, but still amazed at the startling revelation.

Xavier was ushered in by the unhappy Pat, who really wanted to slap the lying imposter twice, once because of the lie, and a second time because he pretended to have been French.

"A frog to see you sir," muttered Pat not quite audibly.

"'Ow are you, my dear James, I am so pleased to see you!" Xavier announced himself, his traitorous smiling eyes hiding his true feelings, "and how is the lovely Susan and the baby?"

"All fine!" came the cold reply likely to expose James's true feelings, so collecting his thoughts, and ignoring his real attitude towards the man he once called friend, he became warmer and more amiable, "Sorry, I didn't mean to sound sharp, I've got

81

things on my mind," this wasn't an untruth, as James was really seething within, imagining the pleasure in strangling Xavier with his bare hands. Yet, needing to use him for his own purposes and swallowing his pride, he embraced him calling him old friend.

Using his best acting skills, James related the story of the gunfight, knowing full well that none of the details were strange to Xavier. However, as he recounted the tale, he watched the Judas carefully, noticing how his body language revealed his uneasiness, and showed James the truth of his complicity. The only unknown factor was the question of his intentions and aims, and who was he really working for. James was curious, as there wasn't any apparent reason for the visit; perhaps it was purely to see how the land lay with him and find out what he was thinking? Yet a clue to his motive casually slipped out when Xavier's attentions dwelt on what James knew about the political situation in Iran, repeatedly asking, "What do you think?" and, "How would the British deal with Israeli intervention in any forthcoming conflicts?" It was all very chatty, but his intentions were obvious to James: Xavier was working for the Iranians. All James's answers were non-committal, making broad statements, his replies to the probing question were all ambiguous, saying much and revealing nothing, keeping his interrogator's interest keen, carefully hiding his knowledge of Xavier's real intent, trying to lead him into a real sense of self-assurance. After over an hour, the strangely pointless meeting drew to an apparently harmonious close; upon saying their goodbyes, they embraced like the old friends that James thought they once were.

As soon as the door closed behind the quisling, James summoned Pat, who was conveniently waiting nearby still watching at a window, close at hand in anticipation his boss's next move. "Take the car, and find out what he's up to," James commanded, "And don't be seen."

Pat tutted, looking a little chagrined, "I'm never seen!" he retorted, charging off on his errand, still feeling slightly hurt by James's doubt. Meanwhile all had to be reported back to James's superiors, so he contacted them, using the secure telephone he kept in a locked drawer in his locked office. Having given his superiors a brief outline of his suspicions, giving and then receiving sensitive information, he finally nodded his agreement, as if they were there and confirmed to them that he understood what actions they wanted him to take, finishing the call saying, "It's already done sir!" With that James put the phone down and then called loudly for Michael, who was standing watching, at the same window recently vacated by the now absent Pat. James was still shouting at the top of his voice as he unlocked the office door, only to be greeted by a softly spoken Michael.

"Can I help you sir? I believe you rang," he asked, his face splitting into a toothy grin.

"Yes you can, I want you to do something for me, and it comes from the top!"

James explained the whole situation to his trusted subordinate, telling him everything, suggesting that the powers that be believed it was probable that ragtag Iranian cells of insurgents were operating in the area, cynically attempting to destabilise the fragile peace between Saudi Arabia and Iraq, plunging the Saudis into the ongoing war between Saddam Hussein and the Ayatollah Khomeini. More than happily Michael accepted the mission to locate the insurgents, having to be reminded twice not to become single-handedly involved in a fight with them. as he was to purely observe and report back his findings to James.

One of Michael's innate talents was his ability to blend in, to become unseen, so the next time James saw Michael, he was dressed as an Arab, a very convincing one. He had turned up to receive any last-minute instructions before leaving, having donned a disguise, and assuming erroneously that he would be instantly recognised by his boss, using his own key, he entered through the back door, wandering nonchalantly up the back hallway towards the office. Oblivious to the fact that his appearance might cause alarm, he turned into the hall and came face to face with Jasmine, who had just delivered some food and drink to James. She was in a world of her own thinking about her happy schooldays when she bumped into Michael, instinctively Jasmine looked up at the uninvited Arab, and then suddenly fearing for her safety she screamed for James.

Her piercing shriek shattered the peace, waking the sleeping children and alerting the startled James, who jumped out of his seat, upsetting the recently delivered tray of refreshments with a crash, the metal tray sounding like a gong as it spun slowly and noisily to a gradual standstill. James scrambled in a desk drawer looking for his trusty service revolver; grabbing it, he ran up the hall, and was about to shoot the robe-clad figure straight between his shoulder blades, when the shocked Jasmine shouted, "NO!" Holding out her open hands imploring James not to shoot, screaming, "NO! Don't shoot him, it's Michael," and then the mystery figure turned round to see what was happening behind him, introducing himself, amazed that nobody recognised him. "It's me Boss! It's Michael."

"Christ almighty Michael, I nearly shot you!"

Jasmine recovered her composure first. "You scared the life out of me," she said, visibly shaking, "never ever do that to me ever again!" Her voice tremulous and wavering, "You nearly got killed Michael." James was also recovering, his heart still racing from the shock of the scream, "Good God Michael that was close!"

Michael was apologetic, realising how upset Jasmine was. "I never thought boss! I just needed to see if there were any new orders, and to show you my disguise."

"You did that all right, very convincing. I trust you speak some Arabic to go with it?"

"Enough to get by boss. I hope!" James doubted Michael's apparent self-belief in his linguistic skills, but chose to ignore his misgivings.

There were no new orders; Michael had somehow acquired a suitably shabby truck, to go with his equally shabby outfit; he took James outside and proudly showed the beaten-up vehicle to him. James noted that, together, they looked like one of the fruit sellers who plied his wares on market days in Riyad. Michael accepted this approval with a thank you and then left, the old vehicle kangarooing and spluttering out of sight as he went on his clandestine mission.

James returned indoors, where Jasmine was cleaning up the mess left by the upturned tray. She was on her hands and knees when he entered and, with her shapely arse stuck in the air, his thoughts instantly turning to sex, only to be brought down to

85

earth when one of the children resumed its crying. "I must go, Ibrahim won't let up until I do." So having shed her load of broken crockery and wet rags in the kitchen, she hastened upstairs to tend to the boys.

Jasmine's feelings towards the two boys were completely different; she really loved the happy smiling Peter, who was a pleasing child, whereas the irritable Ibrahim started to really annoy the patient Jasmine, who pushed back the unnatural urge she harboured towards her own son and tried to compensate by giving him extra attention. James made many attempts at being fatherly to his boys, but his well meant efforts were less than adequate; he took a genuine interest in them but found it very difficult as he just wasn't naturally the paternal sort. Jasmine appreciated his support and encouraged his participation in their upbringing, but in reality she might as well have been a lone parent. In general as a family they were happy, considering the circumstances in which they had found themselves together.

James's relationship with Jasmine had been accepted by Sue, and she became resigned to the fact that they were no longer a functioning married couple. In reality Sue's amorous attentions were secretly aimed elsewhere, so James gladly accepted her tendency to disappear, often for days, even weeks at a time. Also he had noticed that her style of dress was changing subtly, even when she was at home she would keep her head covered, and wear much less revealing clothes than she used to. It seemed strange that Jasmine appeared less and less like a Muslim woman whereas, contrarily, Sue appeared to be heading in the opposite direction. The real significance of it was missed by James, who didn't really care what she did, as long it seemed to the outside world that everything in their relationship was normal. His main concern was that her trysts might be a security risk, so he always was careful never to let her know any details about his alternative work, keeping virtually all of what he did secret from her.

Nothing of any importance had occurred up until the arrival of Pat. A week had elapsed since his last meeting with James, so he was eager to relate his observations back to him. With all urgency, the dust-covered green Range Rover roared up to the front door in its usual fashion, skidding to a halt causing an oversize irate pedestrian to take evasive action and amid a tirade of shouted curses, the monstrous man dived tumbling out of the path of the hurtling missile. At first it didn't seem that the fuming dishevelled walker wanted to engage in a fight with Pat, only when he noticed that the driver was weedy and slightly built did he courageously stride forward menacingly, puffing himself up to look larger than he actually was. Pat who was oblivious to the imminent attack, turned to open the door, exposing his back to the likely assailant when out of the corner of his eye he caught a glimpse of the impending onslaught. Swivelling round at speed, Pat stared coldly at the man with his piercing blue eyes and softly inquired, in perfect Arabic, if the man was up to date in his prayers as he wouldn't like to send him to meet Allah, otherwise? The deflated man, having identified real intent in Pat's manner, turned swiftly on his heels and scurried away as fast as his weakened knees could convey his large frame, much to the amusement of a small crowd of spectators, who were drawn there by the noisy commotion.

Unmoved by the whole event Pat entered the building without a fuss and went straight to see James, who was really pleased to see his other trusted comrade.

"I'm glad you're back!" James greeted him with a firm handshake, and then proceeded to describe the events of the preceding week, omitting nothing. The patient Pat listened intently to James, absorbing each point, inwardly bursting to tell all about his spying expedition. Having finished his tale he asked, "How about you?"

The dam burst. "That bastard Xavier is in it up to his fucking neck. When he left here he went back to his place, I had a squint through a window, he made a load of phone calls, then after a while he was picked up by a couple of really dodgy looking blokes. I recognised one of them, he spent some time watching us the other week." Pat's eyebrows were dancing with each word, adding intensity to his story. "Then he buggered off miles into the desert ending up at a camp, thirty miles north of Qiba." Pat sucked in a great gulp of air; he had been holding his breath all the time during the telling of his tale, and then having recovered he carried on, "I saw Michael there, and he's dressed like a local!"

"Did he find you?" James asked earnestly.

"Did he bollocks! I found him, I saw him herding half a dozen scabby goats!"

"Goats?"

"Yes scabby, mangy, smelly old goats! I followed him, and caught up with him a safe distance away from the camp, he's bivvied down and well hidden." He paused and breathed deeply. "He was bloody surprised to see me there, he sold them some mangy goats to eat, yuk! Then buggered off when Xavier arrived, he reckons that they are mostly a load of peasants pretending to be soldiers. It wasn't them that attacked us, he thinks the lot who were after Jasmine were separate, they have just joined forces with this other bunch, I think helped by your ex-mate, that greasy lying frog bastard Xavier whatever his fucking name is."

Pat had finished his story and was breathing hard, waiting for a reaction, when James asked, "How did you recognise Michael?"

"I've known him years, his walk, probably, I don't really know, I've never known him to stink like that though!" They both laughed.

"He takes his undercover work seriously, doesn't he?" James mused.

"Sure does, he must if he's prepared to rub goat shit all over himself!"

"You just keep on watching Xavier, that's your job, stick to him like glue, and don't let him out of your sight! Where is he now?"

"He's back at home in his pond eating slugs or snails, or whatever frogs eat, I forget, but I checked before coming to see you," replied the earnest-looking Pat.

"Right get back to him as soon as poss., then stay on his tail If you see Michael, tell him to stay put as long as he can, we really need to know what he they're up to." Pat left moaning and muttering about Xavier, calling him a traitorous bastard and wanting to blow his lying head off. James shouted to the diminishing voice of the Irishman, reminding him, "don't forget, I want information, not his head on a plate!"

"O.K.! I know." The faint reply floated begrudgingly back, making James smile inwardly to himself, knowing that his orders would be carried out exactly to the letter.

Sue returned the next morning, arriving unexpectedly, she alighted from a battered old black London taxi driven by a suitably beaten-up old toothless Arab, who with all formality and grace opened the door like a prince's chauffeur, allowing Sue to glide effortlessly into the building. The old man limped in hot pursuit, carrying her bags and begging to be rewarded for his effort. Obliging, she placed a pile of coins into his filthy claw like hand. Satisfied, he departed walking backwards, bowing and thanking her as he went, imploring Allah to bless her, all the time his greedy eyes were fixed on the little mound of cash grasped in his talons. On hearing the Sue's noisy arrival, James poked his head out of the office; the sight that met him left him utterly speechless, the transformation was complete. Sue was dressed from head to toe in a dark blue flowing robe, not dissimilar to the one that Jasmine wore when she first arrived, her head completely covered, with only a suggestion of face visible.

James gasped in amazement, "Sue! I assume it's you in there?"

"It's me!" The curt response came coldly forth, issuing from deep within the voluminous garment, "I've converted to Islam." Sue's explanation caused James to laugh mockingly. "It's got nothing to do with the rich Arab you've been gallivanting around with, I suppose?" James's voice was tinged with a touch of jealousy.

"I love him!" came the spontaneous reply.

"More like his money!" James snapped back, his control almost deserting him.

"I want a divorce, I want to be free!"

"Free to roam about in that tent?" he declared, motioning to her drab attire. "Free to do exactly what you want? I don't think so!" He trembled with rage, annoyed that the possibility of a messy divorce could be an enormous embarrassment to him and likely to jeopardise his standing with the British stuffed shirts who were his peers.

"No! It's not possible, what about our arrangement? We agreed." James was sounding more reasonable.

"We agreed yes! But everything changed when I had your fucking brat, and you moved your fucking floozy in to my home." Sue's voice was venomous, her words spitting each consonant out fiercely. James bit back, "That's very convenient for you, any excuse to get your way! You knew the score when it all happened; once again you've changed things to suit yourself, you're never wrong!" James's reply had more than a ring of truth, and Sue knew he was right; spinning on her heels she stomped off, billowing in her gown like a small angry thundercloud, about to unleash its malevolence onto any unsuspecting innocent that happened to get in the way.

Exactly at the wrong moment poor Jasmine wandered innocently out of the kitchen, laden with a plate of sandwiches she had just made for James's lunch. Oblivious to Sue's arrival, she unintentionally walked straight into the departing irate female, who, on seeing her object of hate, spat a string of obscenities aimed directly at her bemused face, and then suddenly, in a flurry of kicking and punching, Sue attacked the amazed Jasmine, causing the meal to fly uncontrollably up into the air and land with a crash some six feet away. As quickly as it had started the confrontation ended: Sue bustled off, her footsteps clicking around the corner, into the sitting room and out of sight, leaving the almost still intact Jasmine staring incredulously at James.

"What's going on with Sue? Why is she dressed like that? What did I do to upset her?" Jasmine asked, whilst examining her bruised and battered shins.

James related the whole tale back to her in full detail. The shock of the attack had worn off, and Jasmine started to react, at first with tears of pain and then with tears of anger. Mostly she was angry about Sue's attitude to Peter, referring to her as callous and unfeeling, little did she care about what Sue said about her. James comforted her, offering his shoulder to the sobbing woman, who gratefully accepted it, hiccupping softly into his neck as she recovered from the bout of crying, leaving indelible black mascara stains on his shirt collar where Jasmine's tears had dried.

The situation remained tense in the household. James spent most of his time upstairs with Jasmine, only venturing down to work in his office when necessary; his relationship with Sue was completely finished, she refused point blank to even talk to him. Sue spent her time making calls to her unnamed admirer, giggling like a silly fourteen-year-old schoolgirl down the phone, coquettishly blowing imaginary kisses to him. Sue had decided to study Arabic with the aid of self-help compact disc and permanently walked round with a mini speaker stuck in her ear. At other times she buried herself in her newfound religion, learning passages from a wonderfully crafted copy of the Koran given to her by her rich mystery man, spending time finding out what was expected of her and the etiquette required for her to conduct herself with decorum as a Muslim woman. Sensibly, Jasmine kept completely out of Sue's way in order to avoid any more possibly violent confrontations with the belligerent woman, keeping herself busy upstairs being a good parent to the boys, fussing Ibrahim, trying to reinforce the fragile bond between them, attempting to make him happier, and less stubbornly sullen. Peter, on the other hand, was permanently a joy, always chuckling and gurgling and enjoying his infancy, wholeheartedly loving the person he believed to be his mother.

Far away in the desert Michael was hunkered down, staying invisible to the group of terrorists he had been ordered to watch. Sensibly he haphazardly deposited his transport half a mile away in a wadi, careful to immobilise the shabby truck so that it appeared to be abandoned, much like the numerous other vehicles discarded and left in the area. Michael's provisions needed to be regularly topped up by Pat, who visited him whenever the mission of following Xavier brought him into the vicinity, which it fortunately did every few days. The visits from Pat took the same pre-planned format; Pat would approach Michael's hideout from behind on its left-hand side until he was ten feet away, then enter humming a rare ancient Irish folk song known to both of them, and used by them before as a mutual recognition signal. Once there, they would exchange news, share some food and a flask, and then Pat would take over the watch in silence, while Michael grabbed a well needed proper sleep. Normally after having overseen about three or four hours of training the inept group of would-be insurgents, Xavier would prepare to leave, generally in the two-seater pickup truck that he arrived in. However on this one particular occasion he arrived in a large decrepit four-wheel drive Land Rover Safari. Pat had assumed that it was a forced change of transport, his usual one having probably broken down or something similar.

The hidden pair had followed their normal routine until it appeared it was time for Xavier to leave, and this time it was much later than normal. Pat awoke the well-rested Michael, shaking him violently out of his deep sleep, then putting his hand over the startled man's mouth, he whispered closely in his ear, "They're on the move, they've loaded the jeep with a whole heap of hardware, and it looks as though six of them are going to leave with Xavier driving them." Michael was rubbing his eyes trying to absorb the information. "They're very nervy, they've got sentries out and one's about twenty feet in that direction—" Pat made a gesture with his flattened hand, indicating where the sentry was "—we'll have to do him if we want to get away fast." Pat's eyebrows worked hard in his excitement.

"I'll do it now!" Michael volunteered, "I'll need to get out soon anyway, I'm dying for a crap!"

Stealthily Michael left the security of the hide and, as if from nowhere, he boldly approached the unsuspecting sentry. The man was dressed in a camouflaged ex-United States Army military uniform, only a black scarf tied around his head gave any sign of his real identity. The jumpy sentinel at first looked bewildered and then frightened by the grinning stranger's bold approach; he responded by pointing his wildly shaking AK-47 at the advancing man, all the time looking edgily over his shoulder hoping for some non-existent assistance to come to his aid.

Starting to panic, the nervous guard was just about to call for help when Michael threw his blade, which struck the shocked man directly in his jugular, severing his windpipe. Looking surprised and with a rasping groan he crumpled in a heap, spinning a bright arc of blood into the air as he died almost instantly, not having uttered a word. Michael picked up his knife, nonchalantly wiping the blood off on the dead man's sleeve, removed his black scarf and tucked it in his pocket; and then dragged the corpse out of sight to a natural hollow and hastily covering it with sand. On his return to the hiding place the waiting Pat announced, "They're ready to leave; I think there are only five going, including Xavier." Then after a pause he noted, "You were quick! Did you have your crap?"

"Yup! I crapped in the hole I buried the raghead in." Michael replied, pulling the scarf out of his pocket and handed it to Pat, "This was on his head," they studied the black scrap of cloth which had some white writing in Arabic script on it.

"Means nothing to me, I think it's a quote from the Koran," was Pat's only observation as he returned his gaze to the men as they moved off.

Dusk was gathering as the Land Rover readied to leave the encampment. Four heavily armed men, all with similar black headgear tied on, approached the already heavily laden wagon, depositing all their personal weapons in the back, then they waited for a couple of minutes for the identically clad Xavier to arrive, whose seniority was denoted simply by a pistol casually worn low on his hip, much like a gunfighter from the old western films. Joining hands, the men bowed their heads in prayer, then they got in the vehicle and disappeared off into the gloaming, its overloaded engine complaining bitterly as it struggled to get through the soft, yielding desert sand.

Michael assured Pat that he was happy to stay where he was, but Pat, who was the more experienced, insisted that it was more prudent to keep together and follow the group of recently departed insurgents into the desert. Pointing out to Michael that, when the remaining occupants of the camp missed their dead comrade, they would surely search for him and discover the hideout along with whoever was within. Although equal in rank, it had been always accepted that Pat was the senior, so having come to an agreement, they gathered up their gear, and hastened to the hidden Range Rover. Tracking a car at night, in the pitch black of the desert, was relatively easy, providing the followed vehicle kept its lights on, which was imperative, as even in the best of light the poorly made roads were hazardous to say the least, being littered with obstacles, including the deceased transportation of less careful drivers.

The journey took the pursued quintet slowly south-east at first, to a town caller Shaqra, thirty miles north-west of Riyad, where they liaised with an old, overlarge dark-coloured American car, driven by a lone occupant. After the exchange of what appeared to be a few heated words, one of the armed five from the Land Rover changed cars and joined the individual who had apparently been waiting a long time for him. Fighting clumsily in the dark to retrieve his weapon and pack from the back, cursing and struggling in the gloom, dropping his gun noisily more than once he ran furtively to the Chevrolet, which left quickly, heading back towards the city, its throaty roar fading into the black desert night. Simultaneously the slightly lightened Land Rover headed off in completely the opposite direction.

Now Pat and Michael were faced with a dilemma, whether to stick to James's instructions and stay with Xavier, who they thought had driven off in the Land Rover, or to follow the Chevrolet. Considering their options they decided to follow Xavier in his slow moving, straining, overloaded transport, due north into the now lightening desert. As the road was straight and continuous for about the next sixty or so miles the need to have visual contact was not completely necessary, so Michael and Pat stopped for a short while. Michael tended to his beloved car checking everything, the oil, the water, tyre pressure, topping up the petrol by carefully decanting some from a green jerry can; he even cleaned the windscreen, after first having to scrape off the many dead flies. Happy with his efforts, he stood back to admire his work, grabbing a quick bite to eat out of his bag, and offering to share it with Pat, who in return poured him a cup of tepid tea from his flask.

"I hope you washed your hands?" Pat asked as he took a curled and dry cheese sandwich from Michael's grubby mitt.

"Why do you ask?" Michael replied, turning his hands, first palm up then down, to be inspected by his complaining travel companion.

"After you shit on that bloke," Pat answered, grinning at Michael, who looked up from delving into his bag for the other sandwich, putting Pat's mind to rest by adding, "don't worry, I pissed on them afterwards!" The pair fell about like schoolboys, amused by their black sense of humour. Still laughing, they clambered back into the car; Pat offered to drive, as he hadn't driven to date, only to be refused, Michael not wanting to relinquish his most familiar role, so with all urgency they sped off after the ever slowing, overburdened, failing Land Rover.

Day had broken, and the rising sun felt warm on the cheeks of the pair of pals, as their powerful new car was cruising along at high speed along the straight dusty road, when suddenly the eagle-eyed Pat screwed up his face and squinted up the road, into the distance, knotting his ever-busy eyebrows, he exclaimed excitedly, "They've broken down, they look totally fucked!"

Shading his eyes from the glare of the reflected sun, Michael peered ahead to the horizon where he could just about make out the stricken Land Rover.

"You're right, they've bollocked up their motor," he said.

Pat was cheered at the prospect of action. "Stop here and I'll yomp up there and have a quick recce. I'll be about a hundred and fifty yards off the road, on your left, and if they get their motor going I'll be ready to join you quick smart."

So armed and ready, Pat left, adopting an energy saving half-running half-walking gait as used particularly by the special forces. When he got within a safe viewing range he could see their problem: the poor overworked truck had completely given up the ghost. It was on fire, and flames were busily spreading from under the greasy sub frame. The panicking occupants were out, trying douse the inferno by throwing mugs of water filled from a bottle on to it and having absolutely no effect. When the eager hot tongues started licking up the sandy coloured sides, the hapless fire-fighters realised that their efforts were doomed to failure and they all took to their heels, blindly sprinting in terror for the nearest scrap of cover. Crack! Crack! Crack! The ammunition was going off; the air was full of the angry wasp-like, buzzing sounds of un-aimed bullets haphazardly flying in all directions, causing Pat to stick his head down as low as possible, and getting a mouthful of sand to boot. Suddenly, after a massive orange flash of light, there was a colossal BOOM! The car all but disappeared, leaving nothing but a black oily mushroom cloud marked where the failed vehicle once stood; soon after the explosion its charred bent remains showered down like a hail of red-hot shrapnel, causing the cowering spectators to cover their heads, to shield themselves from the deadly rain.

The smoking debris had barely hit the ground by the time a high speed Michael arrived on the scene. Alerted by the initial sounds of the exploding ammunition, he had thought that Pat had got involved in a fire fight. Fearing for his friend's safety, he had driven to the site of the incident as fast as he possibly could. He slewed the massive car round as he arrived, cleverly using it as a barrier between himself and any would-be opposition. He jumped out almost before it had fully stopped and then, pointing his gun at nothing but the empty soot-stained road, he shouted out for Pat, whose calm appraisal came floating from somewhere behind the worried Michael.

"God's tits! That was some explosion, homemade HMTD by the smell of it!" The familiar voice heralded the appearance of a stunned and slightly sooty Pat, who came staggering out of a nearby depression to take a defensive position next to his comrade. "I think they've lost the lot, everything! They're fucking off into the desert."

"What happened?" asked the perplexed Michael. Pat filled in all the missing details back to his intently listening friend, chuckling all the time, completely dumbfounded by the utter hopelessness of their opposition. "We'll have to find them," Pat stated, after having finished his lengthy tale, then adding, "They can't get far, we can't just leave them, they'll have seen us!" They agreed it was necessary to eliminate the escapees, so after having first immobilised their own vehicle by removing the rotor arm, they collected a pair of assault rifles and raced off in full cry, on the heels of the terrified and deafened absconders.

Trailing in fresh desert sand is easy, especially when the quarry is clueless, as it was in this case, and in their panic to escape the group of men had kept bunched together, leaving an easily visible great furrow ploughed in the virgin sand by their hurrying feet. Pat and Michael were highly trained in all forms of warfare, and were able to quickly cover large distances, using the minimum amount of energy. It didn't take them long to get close enough behind the tiring men to see them clearly, especially with Pat's superb eyesight, who pointed out the escapees, puffing his words to Michael between deep breaths, "There's only three blokes and Xavier isn't one of them. I'll knock one down and see what they do." Without any hesitation the two men removed the rifles from their backs, lay down in the sand and took careful aim at the unsuspecting distant targets.

"I'll take the shot!" Pat insisted. "And you aim at the bloke on the right, in case I miss him OK?"

The silenced weapon made no more than a soft crack as the sand in front of the muzzle simultaneously puffed up in a tell-tale eddying swirl of dust, informing them that the bullet was on its way. The distant retreating man fell stone dead in a heap, shot through the base of his skull, leaving a telltale bullet hole as the only sign on the back of his head, but at the front his face was completely missing. The remaining two escapees, on seeing their comrade fall, apparently shot from nowhere, instantly put their hands high in the air, trying to surrender without a fight. Both men were wandering around in circles, looking at each other confused, not knowing what to do as they couldn't see anyone to yield to.

The first to appear on the scene was Michael, still dressed as a local, his appearance gave hope to the frightened pair, who desperately prayed that he was there to help them, and then from behind him came the advancing mean and threatening, stern-faced Pat. At the sight of him all expectation of clemency evaporated, they fell to their knees pleading loudly for their lives, without mercy, Pat shot the noisiest captive with his handgun, hitting him in the right thigh. The bullet passing through his upper leg into his calf, screaming in pain, the terrified prisoner stared at the two savage wounds, and started to try and staunch the copious amounts of blood pumping from them. Suddenly in a display of what seemed like concern, Michael rushed to tend the injury, putting a makeshift tourniquet around his leg, managing to stop most of the bleeding.

Pat trussed the other captives hands together so tightly with the prisoners own belt it caused his hands to take on a bluish tinge, then patted him condescendingly on the head saying, "We need to have a little chat, don't we? Speak English do we?"

The other nodded affirmatively.

"Some small bits," he replied.

"Right, where is that arsehole Xavier?" The scared man looked blank; Pat repeated the question this time in Arabic, but the man ignored what he was asked and stared vacantly into the distance. Pat looked at Michael who shrugged his shoulders and nodded. He then loosened off the tourniquet slightly from his prisoner's leg, just enough to allow the blood to resume oozing out of the wounds. Shrieking and pleading to be spared, the Arab gabbled the answer in passable English:

"He went off in a Yankee car!"

"Where to?"

"To Riyadh, he has some unfinished business." The captors looked at each other. "Fucking hell!" Pat exclaimed loudly, "we'd better get this over with." The terrified men understood English and knew their fate. "My turn to do the dirty work," Michael volunteered to finish the job; Pat jerked his head in the direction of the quaking men." Better make it quick, we need to get the fuck out of here!" Knowing what was about to happen, the tied-up prisoner started praying loudly while the other promptly fainted with fear and blood loss so that he lay in a pool of his own congealing gore. Michael shot him first, a bullet through the side of his head put him out of his misery; then, casually approaching the other, he raised his gun slowly to the centre of his forehead and pulled the trigger. Turning his back on the convulsively twitching corpse, he announced in a matter of fact way, "Job done, we fucked up following Xavier though, slippery little cunt!" Feeling worried about their amateurish error, they left the scene, jogging off together back to the Range Rover, then back to James and Jasmine.

Back in Riyadh, everything was normal. James got up to start work early, yet his thoughts were really with Pat and Michael, wondering how they were faring on their missions. Locked in his office, he just aimlessly shuffled papers, pretending to work and achieving absolutely nothing. Relief came when Jasmine brought him his breakfast, presented on a tray with a single flower lying across a piece of paper with kisses on; she was happily in love, and James loved her back. Their sex life was very active, they made passionate love, most nights, sometimes very noisily, much to the annoyance of Sue, who would lie in her bed fuming at their audacity and cursing their very existence.

Sue was becoming more and more bizarre. She had started to wear her Muslim veil all her waking hours and had destroyed all of her Western-style clothes, including many of the expensive shoes which she used to love. Her hatred of James and Peter had grown monstrously and she would spend hours dwelling on their imaginary guilt, building it up in her head, out of all proportion, allowing it to consume her mind, which she was quite clearly starting to lose.

Secretly both James and Jasmine feared for the safety of the boys, recognising that the unstable Sue was perfectly capable of doing something dreadful. However, this particular morning Sue was relatively happy, she had planned on going to Bahrain, to meet with some rich friends and holiday for a week on their yacht. Now that Sue was a Muslim and her clothes were few, she marvelled at the ease of her packing, not even filling a single suitcase which was closed with ease. Having allowed much more time to complete the task, she sat near the open window and listened to the sounds of the busy streets below. Gazing blankly into the distance, Sue's thoughts drifted back to the time when she was young and carefree. The happy memories calmed her tortured soul. Suddenly, a warm gust of wind, bearing the scent of cinnamon-spiced oranges, ruffled the curtains and broke the spell as it blew some papers on to the floor. Turning in her seat, she bent down to retrieve them; as she did so, she felt a hard thump in the centre of her back just below her shoulder blades, causing her to fall forwards, face down. Her breath failed her, she tried to scream but couldn't and then mercifully she passed out.

Outside her taxi driver had arrived to pick her up, and was waiting outside until it was exactly the appointed time arranged by Sue, when he knocked on the front door, it was opened by James who was passing by it at the time.

"Mrs Sue is ready?"

James looked around at the empty hall." Apparently not!" he replied his voice quizzical, as it was very unusual for Sue to be tardy, especially when she was off on one of her jaunts. "I'll get her for you, go and wait outside." For security reasons James never would leave anyone strange alone inside the premises, so he ushered the grubby little man out, shutting the door firmly behind him. Jasmine came down, curious to see who had just arrived, and when James informed her of the strange situation she went to seek the missing Sue. After knocking tentatively on Sue's door she gently pushed it open, poking her head into the room to see where Sue was. At first it appeared that she was asleep on the floor, her body was in the foetal position, lying curled in the hot sun that streamed through the open window. Concerned by the unusual behaviour Jasmine inspected Sue closely, noticing a small patch of fresh blood near her underneath arm. Shouting loudly for James to come and help her, Jasmine rushed to tend to the stricken woman. At first glance it appeared that Sue was dead, her body was lifeless and limp, but Jasmine found a faint pulse just detectable in her neck. Once again her medical skills were tested in aid of Sue, whose injury she adjudged was probably not serious enough to be life-threatening.

James entered the room just as Jasmine started to call for him a second time. He quickly inspected the fallen Sue, then ran to the window and snatched the curtains closed, nearly ripping them off the pole.

"She's been shot!" James declared, pointing to a nearby sofa where a long tear in the fabric from the ricocheted bullet gave testament to his theory. Knowing that the injury required professional attention, James went to his office to phone for medical help, leaving Jasmine to nurse Sue. She was reluctant to disturb her, but the position Sue was in made dressing the injury almost impossible, and not knowing how long it would be before assistance arrived she reluctantly decided to move her. Sue had started to regain consciousness, moaning and wailing piteously as she came round. James had returned, so the two of them proceeded to very gently roll the stricken Sue on the same appropriately sized rug that James had commandeered from a bedroom to cover up the bloodstains some months before. The moans turned to shrieks as they eased her onto the makeshift stretcher and then, mercifully, Sue fainted with the pain. Jasmine took this opportunity to attend to the wound: it wasn't deep, but it was severe, the bullet had hit Sue at an angle, just to the left of her spine, hitting and gouging out a neat piece of rib as it bounced off her backbone into the couch.

The first aid completed, all that there was to do was wait for the medics. James had been engrossed in the task at hand and he had forgotten all about the waiting taxi driver. Suddenly remembering him, he galloped off in the direction of the front door, peering out and optimistically hoping the man had gone, he saw the driver was still there, stubbornly waiting to pick up his fare. James beckoned to the scrawny cabbie, who was obviously half-asleep as the seat was reclined back as far as it would go, and his filthy sandaled feet were crossed on the dashboard. On seeing James he leapt up startled, then scurried expectantly over to the open door where he was handed a small wad of money and told, in no uncertain terms, to disappear. Following his orders happily, and clutching his gift, shouting a torrent of thanks running backwards and bowing the man jumped in the cab and hurtled off.

James returned to where Jasmine was tending Sue, who was now conscious, grumbling that her legs were cold and needed covering up to keep them warm. In fact they were already under a small throw that had previously graced the back of the damaged couch. James looked puzzled for a second or two, then Jasmine leaned over and whispered closely in his ear, "I think her spine is damaged, she can't feel a thing in her legs."

"Christ! That's bad, very bad, isn't it?" James asked, knowing the answer, and before Jasmine could reply the noise of an American military ambulance roared up with lights flashing and sirens sounding. Interrupting them as it screeched to a halt outside the building, and three burly servicemen hurled themselves out and running through the already opened door to where James beckoned them to follow him to where Sue lay.

Two of the men were trained paramedics, the third, a slightly older man, was a doctor. James had used his authority, and telephoned his friend at the local base for help, who dispatched the medics without delay, gladly accepting the opportunity to leave the base they raced to the scene, happy for once to have a real emergency to attend. Their findings were bad news for Sue, the doctor suspected that she had a fractured spine, so after a large dose of morphine, they moved her on to a spinal board, carrying her to the ambulance and whisked her off to a military hospital, once again not sparing the blaring sirens and flashing lights.

A full hour after the events that had in all probability crippled poor Sue, Michael and Pat arrived back, ignorant of what had befallen. Without ceremony they burst in through the front door and ran to find James, who was in his office with Jasmine. Pat announced sheepishly how he had lost Xavier, calling him a slippery little bastard and worse, telling them breathlessly that he was armed, and probably on his way to where they are, and after retribution.

"He shot Sue!" James announced coolly.

"Sue, why Sue?" Michael asked. "Is she dead?"

"No, she might as well be though," James said ruefully and explained everything that had happened during that morning.

"I'm to blame sir." Pat was beside himself, annoyed that he had let Xavier through his clutches. James however was understanding, realising that to follow both groups of insurgents was impossible. "You can't blame yourself, you couldn't have done more."

"I could have shot the greasy fucker when I had the fucking chance," he looked apologetically at Jasmine. "Sorry about the language miss."

She smiled her forgiveness back to him.

107

"You'll get your chance, that's for sure!" James reassured the fretting Irishman, who couldn't help but look pleased at the prospect of gaining his sweet revenge.

Michael and Pat reported the whole chapter of the events in the desert, and produced the black scarf. As if to corroborate the story James inspected it, and was about to make a comment when his desk phone rang. Listening intently,, James nodded as he agreed with the caller, whom he then thanked before he replaced the receiver.

"She's not critical," he informed the others. "Her back is broken and it's very unlikely that she'll ever walk again. They're going to fly her to Lakenheath from there she will go to Addenbrokes in Cambridge, to a specialist spinal unit."

"I feel dreadful!" Pat added still feeling guilty about the injury to Sue, "no time for that, we've got to get Jasmine out of here," James said butting into Pat's moment of self-pity.

"Why's that James?" Jasmine asked.

"Sue was shot by mistake, they were after you!" James for the first time in his life looked panicked. "That phone isn't secure, it's probably tapped. They might know Jasmine is still alive and well."

"And living here!" Pat finished on a whimsical note.

CHAPTER 4

1983

James was away in London, organising long-term care for Sue, who had taken to her new situation very badly, and had attempted to commit suicide several times. The most recent attempt had almost been successful: only a diligent nurse saving her when she noticed that Sue's actions were unnaturally slow and her speech was slurred, at first the nurse thought that Sue had suffered a stroke, but on immediate investigation she found, still clutched in Sue's hand, the remnants of an assortment of drugs that Sue had been storing rather than taking. Even though her stomach was pumped almost instantly, she still hovered between life and death for several hours.

During her hospitalisation, Sue had no visitors except for an old aunt and James. Her new boyfriend in Saudi heard about her plight and totally lost interest in the relationship, declining point blank to come to Cambridge to see her and refusing to even write to her. Sue spent most of her time crying and blaming James for everything that had happened, little knowing that the bullet that apparently changed her life so drastically was really meant for Jasmine. The aged aunt stopped making visits, fed up with Sue's venomous tongue, making ridiculous allegations, implying that, somehow the elderly relative was complicit in the shooting. Even highly trained the nurses and medical staff hated her. Nothing was right or good enough, not even the special food James arranged to be brought in was to her taste, she was lost in self-pity, her only solace was her ever-growing faith, and she was keeping occupied by burying herself in the teachings of Islam.

Back in Riyad Pat and Michael had been very busy. James had arranged a safe house for Jasmine and the children, Pat's feeling of guilt kept him always at her side, he promised to protect them and keep them safe out of harm's way. Michael had gone off in his disguise in search of Xavier, not to eradicate him, but to investigate his intentions, promising to keep him alive if possible, knowing that Pat desperately wanted him for himself.

The new house wasn't a house at all, it was more of a seedy little two-bedroomed flat, in a rundown old apartment block in Durma, a suburban town southwest of Riyad. The other occupants of the building were some of the dregs of society, convicted felons, thieves and fraudsters. Jasmine was there in complete secrecy, once again she and her family were isolated from the outside world, hiding away, frightened to be seen. Because if any of her dubious neighbours got the smallest sniff of her wanted status, they would sell her whereabouts as quickly as a blink of an eye. So, covertly sneaking in at the dead of night, she installed herself, Peter and Ibrahim into the flat. The front door and hallway were kept suitably shabby, only for the benefit of anyone who might glimpse in. Yet the rest was spotlessly clean and well furnished; all that they needed was there, including a well-stocked food store and freezer.

As always Pat was there, keeping guard over the precious trio. Never did he appear to sleep, he was like a cat, one eye open all the time. Jasmine missed James dreadfully, but understood that he had to be at Sue's side in her time of need. One day when Jasmine brought a lunch to Pat, she referred to him as Patrick, he looked straight into her face and smiled, his blue eyes twinkling beneath mobile eyebrows!

"That's not my name miss!" he informed her laughing out loudly.

"It's not! What is it then?" she asked, thinking that was having a joke with her.

"It's Philip, my mother named me after a bloody Greek duke!" Pat honestly appeared to hate his given name.

"You're lucky it wasn't Wellington!" Jasmine laughed surprising him with her witticism.

"I love cooking!" he added out of the blue, "French cuisine is my speciality," his gaze had that far away look.

"I thought you hated the French!" Her question brought him back from the distant place he had gone to. "No! I don't hate anyone in particular." his voice took on an indignant tone.

"Not even the Muslims?" she queried.

"No I don't hate the Muslims, I hate the men who want to make war over religion, and hate for hate's sake!" His voice wavered with passion. "Don't forget I was born in Ireland, both my father and brother were killed over nothing!"

"Over nothing?" she repeated it back to herself, thinking about her own family. "Why?" she asked.

"Because they were Protestants in a Catholic area." Pat looked visibly moved by his memories, so Jasmine, seeing his grief, piped in deliberately changing the direction of the conversation:

"What's the favourite thing you like to cook?" The question worked, plucking Pat instantly out of his melancholy and back from his sad musings; he went into a whole list of things he liked, some of the dishes Jasmine had never heard of.

"I'll cook for you tomorrow," he said. If you promise not to tell anybody my real name."

"I promise," she said, meaning it.

Jasmine's impression of Pat had changed completely, no longer did she think he was just a hard-nosed killing machine, she had glimpsed through the veil he hid behind, and she realised that within his granite exterior there lurked a sensitive soul, who had suffered grief, much like she had, they had more in common than was at first apparent. He did cook for her, a dish he called, "unknown variety of strange frozen foreign fish *a la* Philip, *avec les pommes sauté et petit pois*." It was delicious! And she never did tell anyone his real name.

The walls of the apartment were paper thin; every noise from the adjacent flats could be heard clearly, and sometimes it seemed that there was actually somebody in the same room as they were. This worried Pat as, in his words, there were spies everywhere, so each time they wanted to talk freely, the radio was automatically turned on, making eavesdropping impossible and giving Pat a lifelong loathing of Arab music. His long conversations with Jasmine started to reveal the reasons why she was so badly wanted by the Iranians. It wasn't as it first seemed, motivated purely by the outrage of a spurned spouse. Pat suspected that it was all to

112

do with her father's relationship as a trusted aide to the Shah, and he believed that unwittingly she possessed some very sensitive information that could possibly compromise some very senior minions of the Ayatollah. Jasmine's parents had been very heavily involved in the support of Shah Pahlavi; and they knew many who had withheld their allegiances until the outcome of the Iranian Revolution was settled. Most of them were corrupt, and had accepted financial incentives from the United States and backed Shah's government in order to buy their loyalty, belatedly changing their minds and coming out on the side of Ruhollah Khomeini.

Jasmine still had a small diary, kept as a memento of her father, one of her few treasured possessions retained when she escaped from her uncle in Tabriz. One evening she told Pat about the precious keepsake, when she was describing to him the events that led her to meet James.

"I'd like to see that!" he asked, pretending to only be half interested in it, and without any hesitation she went to fetch it from a secret hiding place, asking Pat to look away and shut his eyes as she did so. "I've always kept it hidden! It's got my poor dead father's writing in it, it's all I've got left of his." She explained her voice was filled with sadness and remorse. After shuffling about for a few moments she told Pat that could open his eyes, sweeping an escapee tear from her cheek as she produced a small embroidered bag of trinkets, from which she pulled out the little book. Momentarily caressing its tooled leather cover lovingly before handing it to Pat, who opened it with much care and reverence. After gently flicking through its gold-edged pages Pat

113

announced excitedly, his eyes almost on stalks, "I think quite a few people would be interested in this! Has James ever seen it?"

"I've only ever shown it to you, it's only numbers, isn't it?"

"More than that miss, it's an insurance policy," Pat replied, his eyebrows knotting as he pawed through the leaves of writing.

"If so he had six more of them!" Jasmine said sadly. "Where are the rest? Do you know?"

"I didn't have much room in my little bag, so I only took one when I escaped, that one was my favourite. I left the other six, I couldn't manage much when I left, and that one was the prettiest colour!" Pat knew that it was a key to many mysteries and it needed to be examined by experts,

Back in London James had been very busy. He had made suitable arrangements for Sue's care, all her needs had been catered for, both physical and emotional. He found for her a well appointed bungalow, situated in the better part of South Croydon, which had been specially adapted for wheelchair users, and had support staff housed nearby. He had also spoken to the leaders of a local mosque, who agreed to look to her spiritual needs, first having accepted a large donation, with the promise of more money to follow.

His visits to see Sue in her new home were becoming more and more unpleasant for James, her rantings and spitefulness alienating him and driving him further away than ever before. Thinking that she was as settled as she was ever going to be, the time came for him to tell her his decision to return to Saudi, and back to the ever-loving arms of the beautiful Jasmine. Completely satisfied he was doing the right thing, he embarked on his final visit to see his unhappy wife. James had enough of his efforts being snubbed, so, having braced himself for the expected torrent of abuse, he entered the room where Sue was sitting in a brand new electric wheelchair practising steering it. Manoeuvring the vehicle to face James square on she looked hatefully up into his face, "It's your entire fault, I pray Allah will forgive you!"

"I've come to say goodbye, I need to return to Saudi, to work." James informed Sue, pausing to wait for the sharp reply, which didn't come, "I know why you're here, you want a divorce! You can tell me, I know it, I've seen it coming!" He remonstrated with her that was not the reason for his visit, but she wouldn't listen, insisting that he wanted to cast her aside, and go back to his, she almost said whore, but she stopped herself and carefully said, "lady friend."

"I never want to see you again!" she said calmly, "no need to divorce me, because I've already started proceedings against you, Mr Hafez has helped me anyway, we were never properly married, not in the eyes of Allah" James was amazed, and delighted at the same time; amazed that Sue was happy to relinquish her hold on him, but delighted that he was free to get on with his life without her. Sue dismissed him from her presence with a regal wave of her hand, and as he turned to leave she called him back, telling that there was one more thing: a present for Peter. She gave a parcel to the open-mouthed stunned James, saying, "It's a copy of the Koran, make sure he gets it, he must be aware of the true faith."

"I will give it to him I promise." James said as he was just leaving when Sue suddenly returned to her old ways, telling him to, "Fuck off!" Shouting other abuse at the confused James, who left knowing that Sue was going barking mad.

James returned to Riyad on a searing hot day in August; as he left the plane, the heat hit him like a wall, the sun glared blindingly off the white concrete and the tarmac shimmered like a huge mirror, causing him to blink and squint as he cast his gaze around to locate Michael, who should have been ready and waiting with transport for his impatient boss. James was very eager for the latest news of Xavier, and even keener to see Jasmine. All the time he was away he yearned to feel her body next to his, his carnal needs were great and Michael was late.

Suddenly, through the distorting heat haze, James could just about make out a distant speeding Range Rover hurtling, without a care towards the airport, scattering a group of goats that were grazing on the perimeter's brown scrub that lay to either side of a beaten-up, downtrodden chain link fence. On seeing an appropriate gap the driver plunged the car across the divide, catching and dragging a length of mangled wire and rubbish behind the vehicle before it skidded to a halt alongside James, who felt rather pleased to see it was Michael abusing the government property. "Sorry boss, I'm a bit late, I got held up by your Yank colonel mate, he had some papers you wanted, and I had to wait ages for them!" Michael looked blacker than he used to, making his toothy grin look even whiter, he was smartly dressed in a new pale grey chauffeur's uniform and looked every bit the professional driver. Gathering the luggage, Michael put it in the back before opening the door for James, and then kicking the wire and debris free of the back bumper, he jumped in and drove off at high speed using the same gap that he arrived through. Scattering the same, now re-formed, herd of goats that he had terrified on the way in, leaving their minder hopping from one leg to the other, screaming oaths and curses in the direction of the racing missile, irked that he had lost valuable snoozing time in gathering them back together, causing his morning nap to be interrupted and peace disturbed.

The breakneck journey was interesting, James queried why Michael didn't use the proper gate, and why did he look so black, he answered simply, laughing as he did:

"One! The gate would have been too slow, they would want to see papers and things. Two! I've been racing around in the desert, chasing your mate, and I've got a suntan!" He pulled up his sleeve revealing a very black arm, "And three! You don't get that from a bottle!" Giggling at his own humour, Michael took the time to explain exactly where he had been and what he had been doing during James' absence.

His given task was complete; he had discovered that Xavier was employed by the new Islamic Republic of Iran, who were fundamentalists and opposed wholeheartedly to any forms of westernisation.

"Where is he now?" James asked, concerned that Xavier was still working for Jasmine's cousins. "He's pissed off for the time being, he thinks that job is done." James looked relieved, "my mind's been working overtime!" Michael nodded knowingly adding his take on the situation, "his greed will be the end of him! He still thinks you're his friend, he's not aware that we know who he is, we can use that!" The rest of the short journey from the airport was completed in silence, both James and Michael musing on the recent revelations.

The first stop was the home James had shared with Jasmine, it seemed empty without her, and still smelled faintly of her perfume, mixed with stale disinfectant, reminding him of the recent tragic events. Michael brought in his luggage, along with the files supplied by the Americans. On seeing them James said he wanted to take a look at them in his office, so obeying, Michael took the papers and placed them on James' desk ready for his scrutiny. At first he wanted to leave them for another day as he felt tired from his journey, but he was attracted by the title of one of the documents, called simply *Persons of Interest*. It was a dossier which included names, photographs and descriptions people that the CIA thought might be of use to James. He thumbed through the papers until he saw a face he recognised; it was that of Xavier, along with several of his aliases. At one time he claimed to be the son of the corrupt ex-prime minister of Iran Jafar Sharif-Emami, "Mr Ten Per Cent," as he was known. On reading further, it appeared that his most recent pseudonym was Doctor Xavier Dubois, a name he adopted shortly before he contrived his meeting James, assuming the role as a doctor because he briefly went to medical school. Apparently and seemingly unimportantly his real name was Hafeez Ali Abbass, originally he was in the pay of the American-backed Shah of Persia's government, but defected when it was overthrown by the new Islamic Republic of Iran. Fearing for his safety he threw his lot in with the revolutionaries, and became a major player in the eradication of his onetime co-workers, the Shah's supporters. His inside knowledge and testimony led to the executions of many of his ex-colleagues, ingratiating him with the new regime, and keeping him safe for the time being from the executioner. His latest brief was to find new recruits, to work for the Ayatollah's cause, and to destabilise either the Saudis or Kuwaitis whenever possible. James was intrigued by the information supplied, and assumed it explained much, including how Xavier, knowing that James was highly ranked in the oil industry, had deliberately manoeuvred into his life with a sole purpose to subtly glean information, useful to further his disruptive purposes.

Fortunately James had never spoken about his professional work, nor did he mention the more clandestine nature of his other employment. However he rued letting Xavier into the inner sanctum of his personal affairs, where he found the opportunity to feed off Jasmine's plight, and use her situation to advance his own. Feeling ashamed at his own naivety he proceeded to scrutinise the informative documents deep into the night, learning much, sharing the details with Michael, who had stayed all the time by his side.

It was two thirty in the morning when James remembered that Jasmine had been expecting him to arrive at midnight. He had become so absorbed in his work that he hadn't stopped reading the papers, nor had he bothered to eat or drink since he received the files supplied by his American friend. He nudged Michael, who was half asleep, mesmerised and bored by the unfamiliar paperwork.

"We've got to go!" James prodded the waking Michael harder, making him jump, and then gathering his senses and stretching he asked, "Where to?"

"I'm late! I promised Jasmine that I would be there by twelve, she'll be worried!" So without any hesitation they raced off the short distance to Durma.

Jasmine was waiting, pacing up and down like an expectant father, fretting over the absence of James, supported and reassured by the ever-faithful Pat. On their arrival Michael stayed in the car while James, not wanting to disturb the locals, crept furtively in and tapped quietly on the door. Opening it slightly, Pat peered through the crack to find an anxious-looking James waiting to be let in. Almost pushing past his friend, James burst into the hall to see a fearful Jasmine staring to see who it was. Forgetting her need for invisibility, she ran up to him and flung herself into his arms, relying on him to catch her without harm, which he managed with seeming ease. In reality he was exhausted, he needed to sleep after his long journey, but there was another more important duty to perform first.

Without being asked, Pat left to join Michael, leaving the two lovers together, reunited after having been parted for over a month. Hand in hand they entered the bedroom, Jasmine hushing James, whispering to him, making him aware of how much she'd missed him and reminding him of how thin the walls were. She led him to the bed. Hastily stripping off their clothes, James fought with his complete outfit, whereas Jasmine only had on the bare essentials to cover her modesty – which she quickly removed, exposing her complete nakedness to her lover, whose fatigue instantly disappeared with the vision. Throwing herself on the bed, she beckoned saucily to the partially naked James, who was hopping, trying to discard a stubborn final sock. In his efforts he tumbled forward onto the bed and almost squashing Jasmine in the process. Deftly she avoided his falling body, leaping out of the way and knocking over the bedside lamp with a crash; she put her fingers to her lips, as if to hush herself, and then laughing at her guilty look, he pounced on her naked body. They only made love the once: it was quick, both of them were over eager, and the foreplay was virtually non-existent, James came almost at once, his groans muffled by Jasmine's hand placed over his mouth. Looking in his eyes she saw he was completely tired out, and still staring passionately, she manually accomplished her own climax, so that he could rest, satisfied he put his tired head in between her breasts and drifted off into a deep, well earned dreamless sleep.

Before dawn had broken, Pat awoke the sleeping couple. Tapping gently on the door of the bedroom, he cleared his throat and reminded James that he had to be elsewhere. Refreshed after his two hours of satisfying sleep, and after a brief discussion with Pat concerning the discovery of her father's book, he kissed his darling Jasmine goodbye and, with her permission, he left, carrying the small diary, leaving Pat once again guarding his most treasured possession. Michael was ready and waiting, he knew that for secrecy's sake James had to depart before daybreak, prior to the waking community spotting him, and perhaps soliciting unwanted interest in his movements, thus alerting possible enemies to the whereabouts of Jasmine.

Michael drove James back to his office, where he had been co-ordinating the hunt for Xavier. Dawn was breaking, and the hustle and bustle of the waking day was starting, traders, merchants and early bird customers were milling about making the return journey back to the building much slower, and causing the large car to take evasive action several times. On arriving back Michael's first duty was to practice his catering skills, James went into his office, to continue where he left off the previous night, and as he was just beginning to get deeply involved with the dossier, the mouth-watering smells of breakfast disturbed him, and in no time Michael produced a simple repast of omelettes, toast and coffee. Sitting together, they both consumed the welcome meal and, as neither of them had eaten for hours, they agreed that hunger made the most basic of foods delicious. Their meal finished, and after a short digestion break, the time arrived to resume with the task at hand to find Xavier.

For the first time since he had it in his possession, James picked up Jasmine's father's diary; opening it, he was surprised to find it wasn't a diary at all. It was a handwritten list of transactions, times, dates and names, with descriptions of places where they had happened: it was political dynamite. The little book implicated many of the Ayatollah's top aides in corruption, and collusion that went deep into the heart of Iran's Revolutionary government.

This is it! This is want they want!" James's voice squeaked uncontrollably with excitement. Amazed at the outburst, Michael looked up from some other papers that he was studying. "What is it? What have you found?"

"I've found the key to this whole bloody mess!" James replied regaining his composure, and then explained carefully to Michael some of the intricate details of the ledger, how the information it contained would cause havoc among the leaders of Iran. "If they get hold of this, heads will literally roll!" James declared while leafing through the little booklet, when suddenly he snatched up the dossier supplied by the Americans, shuffled through it, and then put a page next to the open book, he pressed his finger hard down, pointing to a name for Michael to read, "Hafeez Ali Abbass," and then he pushed his other forefinger on to the page from the dossier, keeping his hand over the photograph on it.

"Hafeez Ali Abbass." Michael repeated slowly, and then James revealed the picture: it was Xavier. James berated himself, "I should have twigged last night, I should have remembered; it's all come back to me, I must tell my bosses, and see what they want me to do about it." James was thinking out loud and, gesturing for Michael to go, he opened the drawer that contained his secure telephone. Obeying his boss, Michael left the room so that James could make the call in private, retaking his position in the chair by the window where he had previously kept watch, and resumed guarding his friend and master.

It was almost two in the afternoon when the situation changed, James was still closeted in his locked office when a small car drew up outside the building. Michael's interest was immediately aroused when, much to his surprise, Xavier alighted and started approaching the front. Jumping out of his seat, Michael ran to the office and hammered on the closed door; opening it quickly, James poked his head out, to be confronted by the excited Michael, who mouthed silently, "Xavier's here!" his lips exaggerating each inaudible word. "He's here now, outside! Waiting to come in!"

"That's convenient! Let him in and just follow my lead, you're armed I trust?"

"Of course I am!" Michael answered, patting a bulge in his jacket, and proceeded quickly to the hall, to let the unsuspecting Xavier into James's web.

On opening the door, Michael greeted Xavier politely, "Good afternoon! Mr Cahill is in his office, come with me!" He insisted, with a gesture, that the guest should walk in front of him. The unsuspecting Xavier, dutifully obeying, strode into the office where a chair was already waiting for him. Satisfied that the prey was safely in the trap, Michael shut the door and stood with his arms crossed, barring the way out.

Blissfully unaware that he had been rumbled, Xavier sat and waited expectantly for his host to open the conversation; James looked sternly up from his papers, like a headmaster about to deliver a caning to a miscreant pupil. "I won't keep you a moment," he said. Very deliberately gathering the papers together into a neat pile, James tapped their ends on the table to straighten them out and put them to one side of his in tray, revealing the all-important little book for Xavier to see. His eyes almost popping out of his head as they locked onto the miniature ledger, instantly recognising it; he looked up at James, then nervously behind him to the guarded door, fidgeting agitatedly in his seat he cleared his throat and spoke, asking if Michael could make a cup of coffee for him.

"No! He's working at the moment!" James's replied coldly.

Starting to look panicky, Xavier scanned the room, hoping to spot an escape route.

There wasn't one.

"You know what it is, then?" James asked, already knowing the answer.

"What, what is?" Xavier was acting dumb and very strangely losing his false French accent which had disappeared altogether.

"The book that would condemn you to death! I've read it and it appears that you worked for SAVAK, in direct opposition against the Ayatollah Khomeini and apparently you were paid by the Americans, your answer, quickly!"

Not giving Xavier time to think, James brought his fist down on the desk, making the frightened man jump, and then, looking at Michael, he nodded. Understanding the signal, Michael punched the trembling man from behind, hitting him in his ear and making it bleed.

"Now!" James bellowed, moving his face to within inches of his victim's. "Tell me or I will let Pat loose on you, and he wants to hurt you lots, and I mean real pain," he shouted, spitting the words out, making Xavier blink, "Tie him up!"

Michael strode forwards purposefully and trussed Xavier's hands with two thick black plastic cable ties, roughly twisting them behind his back, throwing him out of his seat, pulling them so tight that Xavier cried out in pain. "Sit him there, and let him speak!" Michael dragged the terrified man by a handful of his curly black hair, across the room, to the chair indicated by James. "Go and relieve Pat, tell him to come here," James added turning to glower at the seated prisoner while Michael left as instructed, stealing the little car as a perk into the bargain.

James continued with the interrogation. "Come on Xavier, or is it Hafeez perhaps? What have you got to tell me, be quick! Pat won't be long, firstly why did you pick me as your target?" James was now speaking calmly. "You'll tell me sooner or later, it might as well be now!"

Xavier was stammering with fear. "I didn't target you! I saw you at Rafah, when you met your whore, I was there!"

Angered by the insult, James hit him twice in the mouth. "Call her whore just one more time, I dare you!"

"Jasmine, I meant to say Jasmine," he blurted out her name, spitting blood and teeth as he did.

"You were at Rafah! What were you doing there?" James paused waiting for the answer. He repeated the question, this time more forcibly. "Tell me and I won't hurt you, tell me now!"

What little bravery Xavier possessed deserted him all at once; he talked freely, hoping to avoid further pain. James had got it all wrong, Xavier or Hafeez had been friends with Jasmine's uncle, they both were heavily involved with the Shah's pro-Western regime, but defected when it looked probable that the Ayatollah would gain control of the nation. Jasmine's uncle had grown very wealthy from the proceeds of corruption, and he knew about his loyal brother's books, that contained evidence of his complicity. Partly because of their refusal to join the revolution but mainly to gain the incriminating booklets, Jasmine's parents were murdered by her uncle aided by Xavier, who, along with many other conspirators were recipients of the bribery and corruption logged down in them. Xavier had worked for the Shah's own Gestapo-like secret police, the SAVAK, torturing and then eliminating Khomeini's supporters, he had taken bribes to spare some of his victims, who he eliminated anyway. Jasmine's father, knowing their value, had sent the books to her while she was in London, and told her to keep them safe, telling her that they were important business ledgers, thus they weren't found when her parents were murdered. However she brought them back to Iran when she was summoned by her uncle, who was unaware that they still existed, until six of the seven were discovered after Jasmine had run away.

Xavier had been paid to find Jasmine, along with the missing book number five; pursuing her trail he eventually found her working at Rafah where she met James. Unable to act because of the high level security at Rafah, Xavier followed James to Riyad and befriended him there, hoping that he would be able to complete his mission when James met up with Jasmine. When he discovered how important James was to Great Britain, he tried to use him to gain information for his own cause, and he posed as a doctor to gain information and to gain free access to people's homes, as everyone trusts a doctor. The meeting with insurgents was to recruit temporary assistance, he promised to repay them however they wanted, if they helped him find the book and eradicate Jasmine. Everything seemed to be going to plan until he made the visit that resulted in him being where he was now.

Thinking he'd been summoned to dispense some summary justice on Xavier, Pat drove back as fast as he could, arriving just as the prisoner had finished telling James his traitorous tale. Looking murderously at the cowering Xavier, Pat leaned towards him menacingly as though he was about spit in his face. Instead he just spoke quietly to him.

"I killed your men, all of them!" he yelled before bending further forwards to peer closely into the quaking man's face and whisper, "And now I'm looking forward to killing you, very slowly, that'll be lots of fun! Won't it?" In a fleeting moment of bravery Xavier shouted back to Pat, "I shot his whore!" Calmly Pat bent his head so close that his nose was touching Xavier.

"Did you now! It was you that shot her, was it?" Then drawing back Pat savagely punched him in his already bleeding mouth, causing more blood to run freely, soaking the front of his shirt and trickling on to the floor, and then Xavier fainted.

An unhappy Pat desperately wanted to kill Xavier there and then, but James had promised to give him to the Americans, along with the book, his way of thanking them for their co-operation. The Americans' aim was to solicit Xavier's help and feed selected information to get back to the Ayatollah. Their methods of gaining co-operation from prisoners was much more sophisticated than the British, so all had been agreed and blessed by James's bosses, who needed to keep their allies on side to support their interests the region. Pat was in a rage: he was swearing and cursing, promising that one day he would get his revenge on the man who had escaped from his surveillance to try and murder someone who was under his protection. Kicking a waste paper bin so hard in his temper, that it flew in the air, across the room and hit the unconscious Xavier, who moaned feebly on being struck. James managed to console the fuming Pat, explaining how diplomacy worked, and that sometimes things had to be done to keep things working smoothly. Accepting the inevitability of the situation, Pat calmed down and apologised to James, who readily accepted it, knowing the guilt Pat had felt following the shooting of Sue, which had affected him so badly.

Grumpy Pat and acquiescent James sat together waiting for the Americans to arrive, drinking some tea, made unusually by James who did it by way of a small apology to his fuming subordinate. Xavier was awake and groaning, unaware that he wasn't about to be killed by Pat, thinking that drinking tea in front of him was a new type of subtle torture being inflicted on him, before the final act.

The next several hours passed slowly, the three men sat together in James's office, Pat unerringly watched Xavier, hoping that somehow he would make some kind of move that would give him cause to inflict more harm on the swooning, tightly trussed prisoner. James had taken his turn on guard, watching out for the Americans to arrive and collect the captive. Eventually after what seemed like an age, a large jet-black wagon arrived, its windows blacked out, so that any occupants were invisible to any persons outside the vehicle. It drew up very close to the front, leaving the minimum distance from the car to the house. On its appearance James rushed to undo the front door, in order to allow the visitors quick access into the hallway, three men alighted and speedily entered through the yawning portal. Two were large, young and burly, the third was an older and smaller smartly dressed man in a pale suit, all wore reflective sunglasses and had close-cropped, buzz cut hairstyles, the younger two both were wearing brightly coloured loose-fitting Hawaiian shirts, and called the older one, "sir!" On seeing the senior man James greeted him warmly, shaking his hand and called him Arnold, who replied in a real old-fashioned Southern accent, drawling his words lazily together with a nasal twang.

"Hi James, I've come to relieve you of that bastard Hafeez!" James escorted his friend and contact, Colonel Arnold Becket into his office, to meet with the captured Xavier, who had mysteriously fallen on his face during James's brief absence. Pat was looking innocent, but inside he was smiling as he roughly dragged the whimpering man back to his seat.

"He tried to get up without permission sir!" James smiled at the blatant lie, but the fall hadn't seriously hurt Xavier, who was now bleeding profusely from his nose.

"What have we got here then?" Arnold asked, scrutinising the battered prisoner. "Want do you want me to call you, Xavier? Hafeez? Or maybe Mr Sharif-Emami?"

The blood-stained man looked up at his questioner. "Hafeez is my name!"

"Your names have cropped up a lot recently; they're getting to annoy me! We need to sort this out, don't we?"

Xavier nodded affirmatively, turning his head away from the inquisitor, who roughly grabbed his curly matted locks and snatched his face back to face meet his. "It's rude to look away when someone's chatting nicely to you, isn't it?" Arnold turned to Pat and drawled, "He's so goddamn impolite to me, do you want him?"

Pat answered truthfully, "I'd love him, but he wouldn't survive my questions sir!"

"OK my boys can deal with him! Let's have look at this book, James?" James handed it to Arnold, having retrieved it from a locked drawer.

"It belongs to Jasmine, please look after it Arnold, it's all she's got left of her father's."

"Don't worry James; she'll get it back in one piece, cross my heart!" Sitting down next to James the two men studied the pages, all watched silently by Pat, the two burly American heavyweights and a frightened, trembling Xavier, who was still unsure of his fate and was muttering prayers.

Having seen enough for the time being, Arnold put the little booklet down on the desk, scratched his head, and then stared, wide-eyed, at James.

"Jeeze! That sure is some red-hot shit, wow! My bosses are going to love you!"

As ever, the modest James corrected Arnold, "It's Pat you've got to thank, he's the one who realised how important it was."

Pat was embarrassed by the attention, so he passed the plaudits straight over to Jasmine, telling the colonel it was her that suspected its value; he was lying, but it made him feel better. The Americans hung around until night had fallen, so they could smuggle their prisoner out under the cover of darkness, so thanking James and Pat they dragged the stumbling gagged captive to the huge vehicle, and drove off into the night. Satisfied with the result, the two comrades left to share their news with Michael and Jasmine.

James and Pat drove straight back to the safe house in Durma, where they told their tale, of how lucky they were when Xavier came walking unsuspectingly into the hastily laid trap set by them, and how when he was challenged he told everything, of the coincidences that resulted in the private war between him and Jasmine, the significance of her father's book, and how it was the key to several mysteries. Pat was still bemoaning the fact that Xavier remained alive, and was now totally beyond of his reach, in the hands Americans. James told Jasmine that Xavier believed he had shot her dead, and wasn't aware of anything to the contrary, and explained that he had lent the book to the colonel, who promised that as soon as possible it would be returned intact.

Together, the four friends discussed the events right through the night, never daring to speak much louder than a whisper, frightened they might be heard by the neighbours. Jasmine was used to keeping silent, but the others struggled not to speak normally when they were together, raising their voices in moments of excitement, regularly being hushed by Jasmine, who kept them awake and alert with numerous pots of coffee. The subject of Jasmine's future came up; it was mutually decided that she should remain hidden away until the heat had died down, and that could possibly be for a long time, as there was still a current fatwa out on her. She realised that it was necessary for her safety, but she still felt imprisoned along with her innocent children, having committed no crime, her mind dwelt on her future, suddenly to be brought back to the present, when Ibrahim noisily awoke, demanding immediate attention.

CHAPTER 5

1989

The months passed quickly. Jasmine was still incarcerated with the two children in the apartment she called her dungeon, the boys were both mobile and regularly got into mischief, the older Ibrahim had grown quickly, and was twice the size of his half-brother Peter who was the best part of seven months younger. Ibrahim was very demanding, and he had learned that if he threatened to make any undue noise his mother was prepared to bend to his will in order to quieten him quickly, thus he became utterly spoiled, always getting his own way, and getting worse by the day. Jasmine had found it very hard to love him, but she forced herself to try, and was starting to actually believe that she did. However a more sinister side of Ibrahim had come to light; he revelled in torturing his smaller sibling, regularly biting or scratching Peter who stoically accepted the bullying as part of his lot, causing Ibrahim to become inventive, and whenever his mother's back was turned he would steal Peter's toys and ruin them, pretending that Peter had done the crime himself. Sometimes he would take his food, and if he didn't eat it himself, he would throw it on the floor and blame his deprived brother for the act. Occasionally, when Peter had been subjected to a new form of abuse he would cry, and as was Jasmine's wont, she would pick him up, and soothe him out of his tears, making Ibrahim even more jealous than before.

When James first met and fell in love with Jasmine he bought her a very expensive, early hand-illustrated edition of *The Thousand and One Nights,* the beautiful copy was one of her most prized possessions and she treasured it, keeping it hidden with her other precious relics. On special occasions she would read passages from the book to the boys, first in Arabic, as it was written, and then translate it into English, pointing with her elegant fingers to the appropriate illustrations as she did so. Peter loved it; he used to listen intently, instinctively watching Jasmine's mouth as she formed the complicated words, eager to learn all the time. Ibrahim, on the other hand was disinterested, and usually struggled to escape from the boredom, to pursue something more interesting, like destroying one of Peter's toys.

Some nights James would creep in to visit Jasmine. Although he rarely stayed for more than just a few hours, his passion for her hadn't waned, but he avoided too much contact, frightened that he might alert unwanted interest, and inadvertently lead unwelcome elements as to Jasmine's whereabouts. They made love whenever possible, the ardour in their relationship hadn't lessened and their lovemaking was still red hot and steamy, but much quieter than it used to be. Jasmine's appetite for sex was still insatiable, she always needed a little more than James could provide, but she didn't mind as she loved him with all her heart, and worshipped the ground he walked on. Jasmine only saw Michael or Pat very rarely, sometimes either one or the other would bring provisions when James visited. She preferred it when Pat had shopped for her, as his taste in food was far superior to Michael's or James's; he would bring delicacies like smoked fish, olives or dried fruits, so when she saw Pat Jasmine would request some of her favourites, and he would never forget, always bringing them with him the next time he saw her.

Jasmine filled her long lonely days with reading, anything that she could get her hands on, and one day, when she had run out of suitable literature and she remembered the small copy of the Koran that was Peter's only gift from his real mother. It was still wrapped in the original paper that it arrived in; carefully undoing the parcel, she revealed the most wonderfully crafted book that she had ever seen, even more beautiful than her beloved *One Thousand and One Arabian Nights*. It had an intricately embossed and tooled maroon leather cover studded with silver and gold, and each corner was protected with precious metal, keeping them square and perfect. The pages were of the finest vellum, filled to capacity with fantastic handwritten script that must have taken years to write, and must have been worth a king's ransom. Unable to stop herself, Jasmine started reading, finding it very difficult as the writing was very small and it strained her eyes, never before had she read the Koran, and found the marvellous writings poetic and perfectly wonderful. She wasn't a practising Muslim but she still appreciated the superb work of a literary masterpiece.

Both boys had started talking, although there was a differential in their ages, their standard of literacy was at about the same level. With that in mind, Jasmine decided to educate them as if they were the same age, treating them exactly alike, but she soon realised that Ibrahim's slowness was holding Peter back, as he was ready to gallop ahead of his dullard brother, so when Ibrahim showed little or no interest, as he normally did, she would focus her attentions on the always willing Peter. Because of the need to be quiet she would often read, making virtually no sound, again Peter would watch her lips as she silently formed the words, repeating them quietly to himself, practising the sounds they should make.

When Jasmine thought the boys were old enough to understand basic religion, she brought out Peter's copy of the Koran. She read from it as she had done before, first in Arabic, and then in English, often repeating the most important passages so that the meanings could be properly understood. As she read, and tried to explain the deeper meanings, she grew to realise that Islam was a more peaceful religion than the one of violence she had experienced living with her uncle and cousins, when she became confused having seen such dreadful deeds committed, all in the name of Allah.

The next time Jasmine saw James, he was with Pat who had been shopping for supplies and as usual she made them a pot of coffee on their arrival. As they sat together to drink the beverage, she mentioned her misgivings and confusion about the teachings of the Koran, questioning how peaceful teachings could be misinterpreted and manifest itself as violence, Pat butted in telling her of some of the inconsistencies that he had witnessed in Ireland, of how outwardly peaceful Christian priests could preach death to their neighbours, because their interpretation of the same Bible differed slightly. He cited the Lollards of the fifteenth century, who believed that the bread and wine of the holy sacrament weren't actually the body and blood of Christ, but were in a spiritual sense, and only symbolic, telling Jasmine that, for their beliefs, they were burned at the stake by the thousands. James listened open-mouthed to the profound conversation, never before realising that the down-to-earth Pat was so sensitive.

"That was very informative Pat! I didn't imagine you were so well educated."

"Even you don't know everything about me; I've seen dreadful things done in the name of Christianity. I lost friends and family at home, in Ireland!" Pat became sullen for a moment, his eyebrows still and covering his eyes as he thought of the events of long ago. Suddenly he leapt out of his seat and announced that it was time for him to go, he didn't look at either James or Jasmine, and he just left, with a suspicion of tears in his eyes.

The pair of lovers just looked at each other amazed by Pat's profound speech, and surprised at the depth of feeling he harboured deep within his hard exterior. Taking hold of Jasmine's hand, James tugged her towards the bedroom, and to the ecstasy it promised. They made hot tempestuous love twice that night, for once James completely satisfied the greedy Jasmine, who lay on top of the bed wet and exhausted in the blissful afterglow of meaningful sex, while for once James slept soundly by her side, utterly spent from his physical exertions.

After the strangely contrasting events of the previous night the morning had broken, and James was gone. The boys needed washing and feeding, the long day's routine had started, and Jasmine, still moved by Pat's heartfelt attitude to religion decided, when the possibility arose, she would stand up for the rights of Muslim women all over the world, and resolved herself to never again wear the niqab or burka, the most concealing of the veils, and promised herself to bring up both Ibrahim and Peter with a balanced view of Islam.

The days turned to months, the months turned to a year, nothing much changed. Jasmine and the boys were still closeted in the same home, with the same routine. Jasmine was educating the children according to their individual abilities, Peter was always keen for more information, he learnt readily, and could memorise complicated facts, without any trouble. Poor Ibrahim was left toiling behind, struggling with simplest things, regularly going into great sulks, mainly because of the frustration he felt, as he watched Peter race past him, but partly due to his innate awareness of his mother's difficulty to love him. Ibrahim was large and fat, his petulant swarthy face was given a malevolent look by his pale greeny blue scheming eyes, set deeply in their sockets, a permanent frown betrayed his true surly nature. On the other hand Peter was small and slight, bright and happy, his blue eyes twinkled happily, and he always had a ready smile to charm those about him.

Peter's older brother still tortured him on a regular basis, becoming subtly more and more savage, until one day when Peter found Ibrahim defacing one of his favourite books, flying at his miscreant sibling, Peter hit him squarely in his face, continuing the attack, until the beaten lump of a boy ran screaming to his mother – who, terrified by the clamorous cries of the child snatched Ibrahim into her arms and soothed him to silence. Peter was sitting silently sobbing, trying to repair the damage to his book, his tears rolling down his cheeks onto the torn pages. Jasmine saw the reason for the uproar, and all of a sudden she realised her true feelings towards her real son: she despised him.

James arrived that night with good news, but before he could tell Jasmine she blurted out everything that had happened, all about Ibrahim's bad behaviour then sheepish with guilt, she confessed her feelings she harboured towards their irritating son.

"He drives me mad!" she told James, "he sulks, he never listens, and he tortures poor little Peter mercilessly all the time."

Concerned for Jasmine, James asked, "What do you want me to do?"

"I think he needs professional help, he needs to go outside and mix with other children."

James agreed with Jasmine that something had to be done and then, without giving it further thought, he told her his news:

"My divorce from Sue has come through, I'm free!" And then getting down on one knee in an old-fashioned way, James clasped Jasmine's hand and asked her to marry him. "It will solve all our problems, we can move to a house with a garden, and if you're my wife nobody would dare to harm you, you'll be protected!" Jasmine agreed that it would be a solution, but she didn't want James to marry her for the wrong reasons and then, out of the blue James said the magic words:

"I love you Jazzy! And I need you, please be my wife? Please say yes?"

Knowing that James really did want to take her as his wife, Jasmine pulled him to his feet, led him to the bedroom and gave him the answer as only a loving woman could do.

As was normal James had gone by the time Jasmine woke up, she was stirring still in a semi-stupor when she noticed a small mysterious parcel on the bedside table, it was simply addressed, "darling Jazzy," so she opened it, inside there were two things, one was a magnificent dark blue sapphire solitaire ring, the other was her father's book safe and intact. On seeing them Jasmine broke down into an uncontrollable fit of crying, happy about her forthcoming marriage, mixed with sadness remembering her mother and father. She clutched the precious little booklet to her breast and wished that her parents were alive and could share her joy, yet she rejoiced in her luck as she was going to marry for love, to a man of her choice who treated her as an equal and loved her in return.

All went according to plan; Jasmine and James got married and moved home to Ar'ar, a large town about thirty miles from the border with Iraq. Its situation on highway eighty-five, the trunk road that ran a thousand miles from Bahrain to Jordan and the fact that it had an airport made it an attractive place to live in. They rented a large house with a walled garden and an annexe. For the first time for over four years Jasmine and the boys were free to go outside, she felt liberated and safe once again. To Peter and Ibrahim it was a new experience, and for the first time they played happily outside together, especially now that Peter had gained the respect of his older brother, who decided to practice his torture skills on any available insect that was unlucky enough to wander across his path; Peter on the other hand spent his time trying to save the innocent creatures. Their cessation of hostilities was holding, at least for the time being. Often Peter would go missing, he had discovered an old wooden chicken coup that served him as a den, where he could read in peace. It was shady and cool; in it he had a crate that served him as a table and a tin of paint he used as a seat, it was his own private place, where he could hide away from his tormenting older brother.

Jasmine and James were happy, their full-time relationship worked very well. James, by his own admission wasn't the best of fathers, but he made the best of efforts and tried to interest himself in the boys' upbringing; Jasmine knew that he really wasn't cut out for fatherhood and admired his attempts to fool her into believing that he was. Their sex life was fantastic; James chose to work much more from home, and he wasn't permanently exhausted from travelling hundreds of miles, leaving him much more energy left to expend in the bedroom.

Pat had taken up full-time residence in the annexe adopted the role as personal chef to James and Jasmine, he was in his element in the kitchen, and revelled in cooking fantastic meals for them. As there was an airport nearby, the supply of fresh produce far exceeded what he had been used to, and he was able to obtain food that was generally unavailable. He spent lots of time with the boys, regularly giving them long lessons in the art of self-defence, which they both enjoyed, especially Peter who would practise until he was so tired he had to stop. Most of all, they liked it when Pat told them stories about mediaeval times, accentuating salient parts by wiggling his fascinating eyebrows. Ibrahim would listen to the tales with some interest, and appeared to enjoy them, whereas Peter was totally rapt by them, hanging on every word and conjuring pictures of knights in armour, damsels and dragons in his head. Peter started to call him Uncle Pat, which he liked, as he had no family and was glad being involved as a member of one. Michael visited Pat on a regular basis; he still drove James whenever he was required to and was always on standby. In the past year his marital status had changed and he lived happily as man and wife with a cuddly little West

Indian woman called Minnie, who worked in Ar'ar as a secretary at an oil company.

Everything remained quiet and normal; Peter and Ibrahim were falling out on a regular basis, their differences usually being patched up by Jasmine, but on the most recent occasion Ibrahim had discovered the den and a stash of Peter's books. Jealous of his hiding place he tore up some comics, then went to the kitchen, stole some matches, and set light to the shredded pages. The resulting fire far exceeded Ibrahim's expectations, instead of the little pyre that was desired the flames grew uncontrollably in the tinder-dry conditions, consuming the crate and started to set alight the wooden building. Overawed by the degree of his success, Ibrahim ran screaming from the small shed, closely followed by a large flash and boom where the paint in the tin had exploded and sprayed the fleeing child with spots of hot green gloss. Fortunately, the ever-ready Pat was on hand, alerted by the bang he rushed out to fight the fire and was soon joined by James, who sensibly brought with him an extinguisher from the house.

It didn't take long to put the fire out and, satisfied that there was no more that he could do, James left Pat dampening down the smouldering remains of Peter's den, whilst he went to seek the culprit. James found the lightly scalded Ibrahim in floods of tears hiding behind his crying mother, who was ignoring him and consoling the distraught, sobbing Peter instead. Upon refusing to admit his crime, Ibrahim was dismissed to his bedroom after receiving some soothing lotion for his burns and some dire warnings about his future conduct. Peter was feeling better; he had been promised some replacements for his lost belongings.

Happy at the prospect, he disappeared still clutching the book he had been reading before the conflagration had interrupted him.

Jasmine was still in tears and James had difficulty in calming her. "I can't cope with him!" Her voice was being punctuated with deep sighs. "He's horrible, when you're not here he's too much for me, especially now!"

James looked quizzically at Jasmine "especially now?"

Jasmine answered expecting James to be upset by her reply "I'm pregnant! At least I think I am!" Jasmine added, hoping it couldn't be possible.

"How long since your last period?" he asked, reassuringly patting her back to comfort her.

"I've just missed my second, but I feel different!" James consoled her reassuringly saying that it would all be all right and that he would get her to a proper doctor. "What about Ibrahim? I mean it when I say I can't cope with him," Jasmine blurted out, having recovered her composure as most of her tears were because she was worried about telling James of her suspicion, and, now that she had, she felt mightily relieved by his reaction.

It was July 18th 1989 when Ibrahim and Peter were summoned to James's office. Peter was only seven years old and Ibrahim was just a little older. James sat, while Jasmine stood next to him with her hand on his shoulder.

"You're both going away to school!" he announced sternly. "Ibrahim you're going to a school in Al Medina, where you are going to be taught to behave properly, you've got to learn now, before it's too late!"

Upon hearing this news, Ibrahim's face crumpled, first into tears of self-pity, then of rage, and when it appeared that he was going into hysterics James reached over and slapped him across his face, abruptly halting the episode and causing him to run out of the room to hide. James then looked at Peter and in a much softer tone he said, "You're going to a school that will prepare you to go to university one day, where you can read until your heart's content. You will live there, but it's not far away and we will visit regularly." Peter had mixed emotions about going to school, part of him didn't want to leave the security of Jasmine's side and he loved the lessons she gave him, but he was eager to learn, and realised that her ability to educate him further was limited as he knew that she was struggling to find new things to teach him. However he was resigned to the fact that school was best. Ibrahim was desperately unhappy at the prospect of going to school, he blamed everyone, and especially Peter who he said made him look bad, because he was so good. In his spiralling black mood, Ibrahim told Jasmine that he hated her and James for making him go, and, meaning it, he sulked from the time he was told until the time he left to go.

It was three weeks later when the fateful day arrived for Ibrahim, whose behaviour had been dreadful. He had begged repeatedly not to be sent off, but James insisted that he must go and in retribution he found and tore up Jasmine's copy of *One Thousand and One Nights*, knowing how much she cherished it.

Early one morning Michael arrived driving a new white Range Rover that James had purchased a few weeks before; it had been specially modified for desert conditions, complete with air conditioning, special tyres and a winch. Michael was more immaculately dressed than usual in his freshly pressed chauffeur's uniform; a peaked cap was magically stuck on the back of his head, giving a touch of humour to his appearance. Plump little Minnie was hanging on his arm, apparently frightened to let go of him in case he disappeared, and there to lend a hand if necessary, to control the irate youth while Michael was driving. Ibrahim had refused to say goodbye to James, Jasmine or Pat, who was the unlucky individual who had drawn the short straw and got the unenviable task of dragging the hysterical boy kicking and screaming out of the house. Minnie was still clinging avidly on to Michael's arm with one hand, while carrying Ibrahim's suitcase in the other. The pocket dynamo surprised everyone when she let go of Michael, grabbed the child and tucked the reticent boy, who was almost as big as she was, under her other arm and conveyed him and his luggage to the car, clamping him so firmly with the lusty arm his struggles and screams instantly stopped. Michael looked over to Pat, smiled broadly and then shrugged, drawing attention to the brute strength of Minnie. Without further ceremony, the deceptively tough little woman threw the subdued lad and his luggage on to the back seat and plonked herself next to him in case of further incidents. Looking somewhat amazed by Minnie's feat of strength, Michael got in the driver's side, started the car and then drove off out of the gate like a whirlwind. In a puff of dust Ibrahim was gone, leaving his audience both relieved and amazed by his departure; except for Jasmine that is, who was suffering from dreadful pangs of guilt.

The next week it was Peter's turn to depart from the household. All were there to say goodbye including Minnie, who had taken a shine to the friendly little boy. He was packed and waiting near the front door and James was giving him some last minute instructions about life away from home when Jasmine scooped him up into her arms and kissed him, pressing her wet cheeks against his. Manfully he asked her not to cry, as it was likely that he might do also: he wanted to be brave not like Ibrahim. Shocked by his eloquent fortitude, Jasmine put him down and dried her eyes to suit his wishes. She had two special presents for him, one was the precious copy of the Koran that once belonged to Sue, and the other was a new edition of *One Thousand and One Nights* bought by Jasmine to replace the one ruined by Ibrahim, and always intended to be given to Peter. Uncle Pat gave a small box of toy knights to Peter telling him to look after them as they were all he had left from his own childhood saying, "They're to remind you of our little stories!" Pat's eyes were moist, pretending that an invisible fly had flown into them; he turned away and removed the non-existent insect, having regained his composure he wished his young friend "good luck!" And then he stood back so other farewells could be said. All done, brave Peter left in the car with Michael. Without a tear in his eye he waved excitedly through the rear window to the swiftly diminishing band of family and friends, who were waving back through a billowing cloud of disturbed sand and debris.

Peter enjoyed the journey, his inquiring mind taking in all the sights, from a verdant small oasis to a band of nomadic Arabs with their camels and all their gear wandering, seemingly aimlessly, through the desert. All the time, he fired questions at Michael, who was concentrating on staying on the poorly marked dusty track and failed to answer most of them. They were heading to Al Uwayqilah a small town situated just south of the Iraqi border, about fifty miles east of Ar'ar where James and Jasmine lived. The school he was going to attend had been founded about thirty years before, to educate the influx of children whose parents were attracted to the area because of the oil boom but now it was only used by the sons of well-to-do British parents, who could afford the exorbitant fees. Its reputation was very good, and those who attended were expected to go very far in life.

After roughly an hour of travelling, Michael eventually drove up to the school entrance. To Peter's young eyes, the buildings looked odd as they were stuck in the middle of the desert, five miles north of the main town and were surrounded by a high white wall originally built to discourage any raids from being attempted by wandering tribesmen. There was only one entrance, which had an intercom situated on the massive pillar supporting the right-hand ornate black wrought-iron gate. Driving right up the gateway, Michael alighted from the vehicle, pressed its button, and was instantly answered by a very English highly educated female voice. Leaning close, he listened for a moment before he stated his name and business, which obviously satisfied those within as,, with a whirr and a creak, the great portal gradually opened, allowing just enough time for Michael to get back in the car and drive in, before it closed automatically behind them with a noisy clank.

Michael drove carefully up the stony driveway, thinking that it would be prudent, as there were signs pointing out that they were inside the school grounds and care should be taken, so taking heed he approached with great caution. On either side of the road there were amazingly lush-looking lawns, green and well groomed with stripes where they had been mowed. Ahead was the school itself, square and brilliant white, like a giant sugar cube, glaringly bright in the strong sunshine; above it, on a white flagpole with a gold finial, the Union flag flapped lazily. At the front the gravel drive opened out into a circle, so that any vehicles that arrived there could deposit their shipment directly adjacent to the pillared porch.

Outside the main door there was a reception committee comprising of two sombre-looking teachers, one tall, one short, both dressed in dark suits and full academic dress, with mortar boards tilted forwards on their heads, shading their eyes and hiding their features. Accompanying them was a short, dumpy, rosy-faced nurse wearing a perfectly laundered white uniform, whose immaculately pressed folds appeared to be sharp enough to cut her black-stockinged legs which looked as though they once belonged to a grand piano. The late arrival of another woman completed the welcome party; she was a middle-aged, tall and willowy woman, smartly dressed in a pale green suit, who stood with her knees slightly bent, making her appear to stoop. Some glasses perched on the end of her nose and a clipboard clasped under her arm gave the impression that she was the school secretary.

Getting out of the driver's seat, Michael went round to open the door for Peter, yet he was already out and introducing himself and Michael to the assembled company. Having finished with the formalities and shaken all their hands, Peter politely stood and waited for instructions. The four members of staff, who expected a frightened small boy, were standing amazed and speechless at the boldness of their diminutive new pupil. The nurse was the first to speak, announcing in a broad West Country accent that her services wouldn't be needed in this case; in fact she was only present in case, as often happened, the new recruits became over-awed by the new experience and needed help.

The tall teacher led the way, bidding Peter and Michael to follow, which they did, closely followed by the secretary with the short teacher who was barely able to walk, stumbling lamely behind the party. Peter opted to carry one of the smaller pieces of luggage himself, the rest he left to Michael. Obediently, he followed the staff through a polished hallway to an office where he was told to take a seat and wait. Michael, meanwhile, had been conducted upstairs to unburden himself of Peter's belongings, following the short hobbling teacher up a magnificent wooden staircase to dispose of them in the dormitory. Meanwhile Peter was still waiting patiently seated in the chair swinging his skinny little legs to keep himself amused. The office smelled strongly of lavender polish, as all the furniture being waxed and buffed to a deep immaculate shine and everything Peter saw was scrupulously clean and gleaming.

After a few minutes the tall teacher and the secretary entered the office and sat opposite to Peter. They introduced themselves. He was Mr Burrell the headmaster, a peaky tortoise-like man whose head was on a long scrawny neck and looked as if it would disappear in to his overlarge collar at any moment. The school secretary was his wife, who immediately asked Peter if he was ready to answer some questions. Agreeing, he said that he would be more than happy to, so the headmaster commenced.

"Can you read yet, if so how well?"

Peter was indignant. "Of course I can!" he answered, and was handed a sheet of paper with some large writing on it to corroborate his reply. He looked at the scrap of paper dismissively exclaiming, "I can read books, sir!"

The headmaster leaned forward in his seat and peered questioningly at the boy. "What books have you read then lad?" Peter reeled off a list of what he had read. The master was used to poorly home-educated children, and looked doubtful about Peter's claims. He went to a shelf, took a copy of *Pride and Prejudice* off it and, pointing to the opening passage, he handed it to him saying, "Read this!" So he did, reciting the line out loud, "It is a truth universally acknowledged, that a single man in possession of a good fortune, must be in want of a wife." He pronounced the complicated words accurately, once again amazing the teacher and his wife. A whole list of questions was asked to assess Peter's educational standard, which they agreed was very high. So having really impressed his inquisitors Peter left the office to say goodbye to Michael, who was ready to leave; he shook hands with Michael, who duly departed.

For the first time in his life Peter felt alone, stranded in a strange place surrounded by unfamiliar people, away from the reassuring presence of Jasmine. Inside he wanted to cry but he thought that it would appear weak, so he fought back the tears and followed Mrs Burrell on a guided tour of the facility. Firstly, an increasingly fidgety Peter was shown around the downstairs, and then by-passing the office, he was shown the first aid room where the nurse tended the sick or injured, the dining room where he was to eat, the kitchens and then, lastly, on the ground floor, the two classrooms where there were pupils were sitting quietly in lines, listening to their teachers. Having to stand in front of each class of roughly fifteen students apiece, Peter started hopping from one foot to the other as he stated his name and gave a brief history of his life so far. Reading the situation correctly, Mrs Burrell, used to young children, showed him the downstairs lavatories, he was grateful and accepted the chance to empty his bursting bladder. The next part of the tour took him to the dormitories; the rooms had six neatly made beds individually accompanied by a small wardrobe and a lockable bedside cabinet. The white sheets were turned down precisely the same distance over the brown blankets, at the end of the dormitory there was a door to its own bathroom, everything smelled of disinfectant and was scrubbed spotlessly clean.

Peter was left on his own to unpack his belongings and put his valuables in his little bedside locker. All done, he reported to the office for further instructions; it was early afternoon so there was enough time left in the day to have his first lesson, it was English which made him happy. Taking his seat, he listened to Mr Vincent his form teacher. The lesson was very basic and his fellow students were obviously finding the tuition too difficult to understand. Mr Vincent appeared to be frustrated by the pupil's inability to comprehend, and was showing signs of a bad temper. He was a stocky square-faced, gruff-looking redheaded man in his late thirties, his chalk-stained black gown billowed as he strutted up and down with annoyance, giving a touch of menace to his demeanour. Turning, fixed his gaze on the new boy, then raising his rich smooth voice he asked the previously unresolved questions, Peter stood politely and answered them all correctly.

"There you are!" he roared poetically as he turned his eyes heavenwards and exclaimed, loudly projecting his voice towards the heavens, "Oh wise and mighty Lord, thank you for this gracious bounty!" His mood changed completely around, he now appeared happy, pleased that he had found an apt student. As the lesson drew to a close Mr Vincent summoned Peter over to him, tapped him gently on the head and remarked affectionately, "There's a lot in that little noddle boy!" Then telling Peter to follow the others, he suddenly bellowed a famous line from Shakespeare and stomped off, his chalk stained black gown flapping in his wake. Peter became an instant hero to the other boys; he had defused the potential time bomb that was one of Mr Vincent's bad moods, saving them from verbal torture, the next lesson.

The schooldays were all very similar for the first few weeks, Peter was miles ahead of all his classmates, his knowledge was very wide-ranged, and he had the ability to shock all the staff being able to correctly answer most questions asked of him. One red-hot day in mid August a foul stench pervaded the whole school, the drains, as often happened there, were blocked once again, the usual plumber was unavailable, and in his stead a local replacement had been sent. Peter was in the front hall, having been summoned was waiting to see the headmaster, when suddenly the front door burst open, a stern-faced Mrs Burrell accompanied by a bemused Arab lugging with him huge bag of tools appeared through it. She strode to the office gesturing to the Arab to wait where he stood. Apparently not understanding, he continued to follow her. She gestured again, this time pointing to the floor where she wanted the man to stand; this time he obeyed and stood where he was told. Happy that she had at last got across her message, she went into the office and soon emerged dragging her husband, she pointed at the tradesman saying, "He doesn't speak a word of English, he just stands there grinning like a Cheshire cat!"

Mr Burrell spoke a small amount of Arabic but struggled with the plumbing terminology until, realising that his attempts to communicate were hopeless, he looked to the heavens and begged for divine intervention. It came when a small voice asked if it could help. The innocent question further annoyed the already fuming teacher, who spun round with a face like thunder to see that it was just a small boy who was offering to assist.

"Do you speak Arabic then, little boy?"

"Yes sir! I do," Peter replied looking nervy. Taken completely aback by the reply and speaking in a softer tone he asked if Peter could possibly translate for him.

"Yes sir, I can." So speaking perfect Arabic Peter translated the teacher's every word. The Arab now having a full understanding of the problem meekly followed Mrs Burrell to tackle the offending pipework.

Resuming his seat the lad was inwardly smiling until, at precisely the appointed time, Peter was summoned into the headmaster's office, he felt a little apprehensive, but he knew that he hadn't broken any rules and he wondered what the meeting could be about. Feeling a little nervous, Peter stood in front of the desk and, thinking that he might be in some kind of trouble, he started to fidget. Seeing his unease, Mr Burwell reassured him and told him to relax before he went on to explain the reason for his summons.

"I want to talk to you about your education; it appears that sitting with the others in class is holding you back." He went on to tell Peter that he was going to be put in a private room, and allowed to work unsupervised. He looked up and added earnestly, "I need to thank you for your help earlier on. Have you got any more surprises up your sleeve, I wonder?"

After the next day's breakfast, Peter resumed his tuition. Mr Vincent escorted him to a small gloomy storeroom, still half full of stacked ancient furniture, which smelled musty like stale celery and old boots. The windowless little room had a polished desk with a new chair pushed against it. A long old-fashioned table stood nearby, with all manner of books piled high upon it and a green angle poise lamp standing conveniently next to them. Mr Vincent handed Peter a list of tasks to perform, apologised for having to leave his favourite pupil to his own devices, and then on opening the door to depart and face the class of inept pupils, he deliberately misquoted a line from Henry V, "once more into the breach, dear boy, once more!" Swinging round he left shutting the door behind him; Peter could still hear the rest of the line, fading away, as the voice of the master disappeared, to attempt to teach the class of backward students.

Peter spent most of his time at the school closeted in his own private classroom, teaching himself, once again isolated and alone in a virtually silent world, rarely talking, only hearing small scraps of conversations as pupils or teachers passed by his door. No matter how hard Peter tried to mix with the others at playtimes, but he failed to bond with them as they looked on him as a sort of aloof outcast that was be too good to be in their company. His only friend appeared to be Mr Vincent, who regularly would poke his head round the storeroom door to check on Peter's progress and mark his work. Then quoting a suitable line from literature, he would depart. Inside the little prison, each day seemed to merge with the next, even at weekends the lonely Peter preferred to closet himself away to study, often spending hours, perfecting his Arabic by reading his copy of the Koran rather than to mix with his unfriendly classmates.

James and Jasmine were regular visitors; they would bring him sweets, books and new items of clothing, he was growing fast, and quickly catching up with the others of his age. Jasmine too had grown, and become much larger around the middle, he knew she was pregnant, but he waited for them to tell him. The visits were short, but Peter enjoyed them and they always had some news, either about Pat, or sometimes Michael. On one occasion their news was grave, James and Jasmine sat down with Peter to explain, how Saudi Arabia's neighbour Iraq was becoming threatening, the actions were likely to destabilise the whole peninsula, and conflict had become a real possibility. Jasmine took this opportunity to tell the boy about her pregnancy saying to him that James was sending her to England to have the baby, as a newborn would slow everyone down if a war started in the area, she didn't want to go, but good sense dictated that she must. James said sorry to Peter, as he would not be able to visit for some time, he had many things to organise and lots of places to inspect, and for extra security in the tense times, he had arranged for Pat to come to the school and work, masquerading as a gardener, so that he would be at hand in case there was an emergency.

The time arrived to say goodbye, Jasmine made an extra fuss of Peter, giving him instructions about nothing in particular, straightening his collar, and removing imaginary specks from his jacket. Not knowing what to say, James just shook hands with his son, coldly stood to attention and merely told him to take care, patting him on the head and calling him old chap.

For the next few weeks everything changed at the school, the teachers hurtled about like demented bats, their black gowns flapping and flying as they busied themselves preparing for a possible hasty withdrawal, and making as much as they could secure, hiding the bulky valuables by burying them under the veranda at rear. The pupils were subjected to daily air-raid drills and the whole situation was very nervy. However, Peter carried on as normal, reading and learning all that he could, staying for long periods in his room, and speaking as little as possible.

Pat arrived late in December. Most of the students and some of the staff had gone home to their families for the holidays, only Mr and Mrs Burrell along with Mr Vincent and two other pupils had remained at the school during the vacation. Peter was very excited to see Pat who told him all the gossip and updated him on all the events that had occurred while he was absent; talking a lot about Michael and Minnie, and how much Ibrahim hated the school he attended. He had been given the use of the Range Rover; James had acquired another for his own use, much to the delight of Michael who loved new cars. Pat was a very welcome addition to the company, keeping them all amused, teaching the boys kung fu, and telling them hair-raising tales, frightening the lads at bedtimes with horrific ghost stories, his busy expressive eyebrows and exaggerated Irish accent kept the youngsters fascinated and quiet for hours. Often Pat would flex his culinary muscles and, on 25 December, he cooked them all a fabulous four-course Christmas dinner, ably aided by his new close friend Mr Vincent, or Brian as he was called. They had much in common, as they both had served in the military at the same time, Pat been actively involved, whereas Brian was a non-combatant in administration, but their interests were similar, and they got on very well.

CHAPTER 6

The new term began in mid-January. Almost half of the pupils failed to turn up, the threats from Saddam Hussein deterred many of the parents from allowing their boys to attend the school, which was so close to the border – you could almost throw a stone into Iraq. The unsteady teacher had retired through what was rumoured to be alcohol related ill-health, and the dumpy Cornish nurse had disappeared off the face of the planet, never to be seen again, leaving enough staff to cope with just one class, as well as Peter's self-tuition. The whole place was much quieter, Mr Vincent's pearls of wisdom sounded much louder than they did before, and often could be heard echoing around the half-empty building.

After a couple of weeks panicking the school resumed to a semblance of normality, lessons carried on regardless, and Peter took to his room to study. In February Peter received the news that Jasmine had given birth to another son, and she and the baby were both well. James was away in Kuwait overseeing a new method of drilling horizontally for oil, and as soon as possible he promised he would fetch Peter and take him somewhere safer. All remained peaceful, Easter came and went, and the summer of 1990 arrived.

The sabre-rattling had become more and more frenetic; Saddam Hussein accused Kuwait of stealing Iraqi oil, and subsequently claimed the country as part of Iraq; he also blamed Saudi Arabia for being American puppets and was massing a colossal army of troops in the east threatening the valuable oilfields he so coveted. Over to the south-east of Iraq, the Kuwaitis seemed blissfully unaware of being threatened, and their idiotic generals had stood their army and air force down the month before.

July was drawing to an end, an oppressive stifling heat lay over the region, there was a sort of heavy static in the air, like prickly heat. Tempers were frayed and several minor squabbles had broken out in the school, everyone had been affected, even the ever calm Mrs Burrell got involved in a heated spat with her husband, loudly accusing him of losing her desk diary, which she found almost instantly in a pile of her papers. For safety reasons Peter had been told to join the main class, so that all the students were at one place in case of a sudden emergency. He missed his own room, but he mostly missed the silent solitude where he could concentrate on his studies, so he found himself a quiet position out of sight in the corner of the classroom as far away from the other pupils as possible. In amongst the other children, Peter found it very difficult to become completely absorbed in his work as his attention kept wandering off the subject at hand. Often, he would lose concentration and, instead of paying attention to his own work, he found himself listening to the mellifluous voice of Mr Vincent spouting his marvellous quotes. One day the class hadn't been paying close enough attention to the lesson, and when asked a pertinent question none of them could reply; so thrusting his hands forwards and rolling his eyes Mr Vincent shouted an apt line, to express his annoyance at the class.

"You blocks, you stones, you worse than senseless things!" Not really thinking about it, Peter finished the quotation to himself, but just loud enough for the teacher to hear, "Oh you hard hearts, you cruel men of Rome, knew you not Pompey?"

Mr Vincent heard, dumbfounded and asked Peter, "How knew you that, fair youth?"

"Murellus to the cobbler! Julius Caesar, sir! I've just finished it," Peter replied nonchalantly. The teacher sat amazed and satisfied, rocking back in his chair he exclaimed, "Out of the mouths of babes and sucklings!" A spell of complete silence fell over the class, the pupils were happy that the gathering tempest of one of Mr Vincent's famous moods had been averted and, feeling satisfied with his brightest pupil's knowledge, the smug teacher returned to his chair, rocking it backwards on two legs, happy that his teaching was not all in vain.

Not a sound could be heard in the room, where silence reigned and a pin could be heard dropping, when all of a sudden the peace was ripped apart. Four low-flying jets roared twenty feet above the glaringly bright building, causing the walls to shake, the windows to rattle and Mr Vincent, in his surprise, to topple unceremoniously backwards off his chair. At first he thought that Armageddon had been unleashed on the unsuspecting gathering; hastily rising to his feet and with his ears still ringing, he raced to the open window, hoping to get a glimpse of the guilty aircraft and loudly shout an appropriate quote in their approximate direction: "Cry havoc and let slip the dogs of war!" Then turning to the class, he bellowed instructions, "Air-raid drill! No running! Walk calmly!" At precisely that moment Pat came running into the room, to tell the terrified children, who thought that they were about to be bombed, not to worry as the planes had gone, and they were American anyway. Panic over, the lesson resumed amid a heightened feeling of tension and fear, nothing was learnt.

The next day it was hotter and even more oppressive, the headmaster summoned all the adults to his office for a meeting, he had received news. War was inevitable; Saddam Hussein had ratcheted up the rhetoric and had threatened to hurt American interests in the region. His army on his eastern border now numbered thirty thousand men and he had demanded ten billion dollars from Kuwait, for the reimbursement of lost revenues from the Rumailia oilfield. In response, Kuwait had only offered nine billion, leaving Iraq with no option but to save face by declaring war. Mr. Burrell decided this was the time to announce his escape plans: the school owned an old twelve-seater Safari Land Rover, once used to take the pupils on outings. Using it, he proposed to head to Jordan with as many students as he could, and, if possible, Pat would take everyone else in his. Mrs Burrell and Mr Vincent both volunteered to remain behind if necessary, and wait for help. Pat asked how long would it be before the proposed departure, saying that he needed to go back to Ar'ar for his gear, he needed the maximum of five hours; the planned exodus would be hopeless without him so they all agreed, knowing exactly the real reason he was really there for.

Pat emptied the Range Rover of all unnecessary equipment, and then departed on his mission at a breakneck speed; the main reason for his trip was to pick up Minnie. He liked her, and had promised Michael that he would look after her in his absence, knowing he would never be forgiven if he ever deserted her. On the empty roads, the seventy-odd miles took Pat only just over an hour; he screeched to a halt outside the house where Minnie and Michael lived, uttering a small Irish prayer of thanks when he saw that she was still there. Alerted by the noisy arrival of Pat, and fearing that Michael was in some form of trouble, she ran to the car for news. On seeing her concern, Pat leant out of the window of the still-running car and hurriedly filled her in on the details, he told her to grab a few things and be ready to go in half an hour, then without any more explanation, he roared off on the second part of his errand.

Pat returned easily within the allotted time, Minnie was ready and waiting for him, throwing a couple of carrier bags full of her belongings into the back of the car, she jumped in next to Pat, and then they raced back to the school. Minnie was more up to date than Pat of the situation in eastern Iraq. There had been reports of Iraqi commandos infiltrating across the Saudi and Kuwaiti border, and a warning that snatch squads had been sent out to grab the Western hostages Saddam needed to act as a human shield at the main military sites and the Iraqi army headquarters. The pair travelled back to the school at a good pace, but still not quite with the same urgency that Pat had driven with to find Minnie, taking more time and care to ensure they got back to the school in one piece; however, the whole round trip still only had taken three and a half hours.

Pat and Minnie arrived just as the staff were assembling the pupils in the hall ready for departure; the boys stood in tidy lines each with a bundle of belongings neatly placed at their feet, the headmaster and his wife both had bulging suitcases packed and ready. Mr Vincent, who had nothing he considered valuable enough to take up the precious space in the vehicles, stood with no luggage at all. Annoyed by the sight of so much bulky luggage, Pat strode up to Mr Burrell, snatched up his suitcase, emptied its contents on the floor then looked closely into his face and whispered to him, "Travel light, the more weight, the slower we go, these bags could get us all fucking killed!" Not used to being sworn at, the shocked teacher answered shirtily, "They're my valuables!" And before he could say anything else Pat spoke even more quietly and very slowly, "Then bury them in a safe place, we haven't got room for a load of FUCKING CLUTTER!" the last two words came out loudly, making the master jump backwards as he nodded in hasty agreement to a limit of two small items, that could be carried in one hand was all that would be permitted. The problem with the luggage settled, it was time to go.

Everybody was gathered, ready to leave, Mr and Mrs Burrell were to travel in the Land Rover with eleven of the smaller boys, one was to sit in the front with the adults, another four were to sit on the back seat and six were to sit on the side seats at the rear. Pat was going to drive the Range Rover with Minnie, Brian the three remaining largest boys and Peter. Pat was in the process of making the final checks before leaving the compound when his eyes came to rest on the Union flag, hanging limply on its pole over the school.

Pat gave Mr Burrell strict instructions to travel northwest along highway eighty-five, warning him to go easy and take care not to overwork the ageing car, reassuring him that he wouldn't be far behind, and the speedy, much newer Range Rover would easily be able to catch him up in no time anyway. Pat wanted to retrieve the flag, which he thought might come in useful, scuttling off, he climbed up the stairs, through the door to the roof, and then because of his military training he instinctively scanned the horizon. A small cloud of yellow dust marked where Mr Burrell with the first contingent of escapees had just left, and were heading north-east to get to the main highway.

Having gained possession of the flag, Pat's sharp eyes lit on two distant specks coming from the north and heading straight in the direction of the school. Although they were barely visible and kept disappearing behind dunes and the shimmering heat haze (which made the hot desert sand ripple like a sea of water), Pat's sharp eyes could just about make out that they were sandy coloured army trucks with canvas-covered backs. Travelling at speed, their spinning tyres created two large palls of dust and debris which confirmed that he was right and that they were making a beeline for the school. Pat surmised they were probably Iraqi troops attracted there by either the recently removed British ensign, or the glaring whiteness of the school buildings.

Fearing the worst, Pat hurried downstairs, back to the car full of anxious people, who were in their seats eagerly waiting to get away to join the others. In haste, He explained the situation, hopefully suggesting that the approaching vehicles were probably an over-excited Iraqi border patrol harmlessly straying south into Saudi Arabia but, just as he had finished his sentence, a burst of machine-gun fire told him that he was wrong. Unknown to Pat the leader of the approaching group of men had spotted him on the roof, and the gunfire was meant to intimidate rather than kill.

It was too late to escape, his first thoughts were of concern for the safety of Minnie and the boys, Minnie insisting she was able to care for herself, dived her hands into a carrier bag, she brought out a large calibre pistol and a box of ammunition, "Michael was worried about me and he gave me these!" Her West Indian accent rolled the words of her tongue, and she almost sounded happy at the prospect of using the weapon. "He taught me to use them as well!" she added, nodding positively.

"Will you look after the lads for me?" Pat asked, knowing what her response would be.

"Of course I will!" Minnie replied, oozing out the answer full of confidence. Another burst of fire rent the air, this time backed up by a small explosion causing a shower of rubble to patter down near to the boys. Minnie looked at Pat and then to Brian, smiled a brave smile and then, clutching her gun, she ushered the terrified children into the school to find a safe place to hide. Two of the younger ones had burst into tears and, along with their hurrying feet, their sobs could be heard disappearing into the depths of the school, all held together by the soothing tones of Minnie.

Knowing that the situation was serious, Pat shrugged at Brian, wiggled his eyebrows and duly announced his hastily constructed plan, "I think we've got to fight our way out!" Having said that, Pat leaned deeply into the back of the Range Rover, sticking out his backside as he did, and with his voice booming from somewhere inside the car, he asked Brian to help him with a large box of weapons that he had picked up from his lodgings, when he detoured from the journey to pick Minnie up from Ar'ar. "It is easier to put in than get out!" He winked at his new comrade in arms. "I mean that box of goodies, not what your dirty mind is thinking!" they both laughed, Brian had begun to wax lyrical – "We few, we happy few!" – when a sudden a small explosion burst close to the men, interrupting the apt quote from Shakespeare's Henry V. "A light mortar I think?" was Pat's only comment as he calmly went about his business, ignoring the danger.

Pat knew a great deal about weapons of all types and had collected many during his stay in Saudi, most of which were in the heavy box that the men carried between them as they ran for cover.

On finding a safe shelter, out of sight behind a low garden wall, Pat opened the crate with his knife. After rummaging among the contents for a few moments, he produced a Russian-made assault rifle and offered it to Brian, who accepted it, felt its weight, and then after a quick lesson on how to use it, Brian practised cocking and firing it. "Point it, squeeze the trigger and hope!" Pat had no confidence in his trainee, and he gave the instructions without much hope of success. The final part of the tutorial was succinct, and straight to the point. "They'll come directly at us, through the gates, if they had any heavier weapons they would have used them by now, so blowing a hole in the walls isn't an option to them, we'll set up a crossfire. I'll stay here, and you get behind that door, just follow my lead!" So obediently Brian loaded his gun took a box of ammunition and then ran bent-backed to position himself, out of sight, behind the front door.

The gate was about a hundred yards in front of the two waiting men. Pat, along with his mini armoury, stayed in position and had selected his favourite old sniper rifle to deliver the first volley. Lying on his front, he splayed his legs wide for stability and propped the muzzle of the gun on the top of the wall to keep it steady and waited, and then waited some more. Dusk was gathering, and the men who were waiting outside the perimeter erred on the cautious side; several times Pat had brief glimpses of their bronzed faces peering around the gate and then disappearing as quickly as they appeared. In truth it seemed that they were not at all sure of what action to take. The men outside seemed frightened to cross the open ground and expose themselves to harm, fearing they would be walking straight into a trap, and they didn't have the firepower to attack from a distance.

All at once several poorly aimed mortar rounds announced something was about to happen, bursting fairly close to the Range Rover, but hitting nothing of consequence, they were quickly followed by one of the trucks haring through the open gates and zigzagging wildly across the lawns as it came. The driver's efforts were good but Pat was better: first licking his forefinger, he leant forwards and wetted the front sight before he aimed his rifle, held his breath, allowed for the sideways movement of the wagon, and squeezed the trigger, hitting the driver in the base of his neck, causing blood to spurt all over the shattered windscreen, obscuring the passenger from view and preventing him from meeting a similar fate. The driverless lorry halted abruptly, slewing half round, exposing the cloth back. Pat accepted the opportunity with both hands and fired blindly six times into it. Taking it as a cue, Brian started blasting as well: the helpless remaining occupants, caught in the merciless crossfire tumbled out from under the canvas, making an attempt to try to reach the safety beyond the gate. Tripping and stumbling in blind panic, they ran for their lives, only to be scythed down by the relentless accuracy of Pat's rifle. With a total of fourteen shots, he had ruthlessly killed twelve men, wounding none, letting not one escape, and making a statement of intent to the rest of the enemies waiting outside the gate.

Knowing that the opposition were now aware of their defensive positions, Pat dragged his box the twenty-odd yards to the school and flopped down next to the inexperienced, visibly shaken Brian, and he panted out his new plan. The dark desert night was approaching fast, which would be to their advantage. Without starting the engine, Pat decided he needed to quietly winch the car closer to the school, in readiness to load up Minnie and the pupils for a speedy breakout. After that, and under the cover of inky darkness he was going to sneak out and place some timed explosives on the wall at the back of the compound. When Brian innocently asked where they were going to get the charges from, Pat pointed nonchalantly at the box, "You'd be surprised what I've got in there, why do you think it's so fucking heavy?" Brian nodded, accepting Pat's eloquent explanation. "They'll come for us as soon as they can see, so by first light we'll be loaded up, and be ready for when the charges blow, hope like hell they think we're going to scarper through the hole in the wall, and then fuck off through the gate, agreed!"

Brian responded with a simple nod, "Agreed!"

Everything had been put in place, it had taken Pat over three hours to complete, Minnie and the boys were waiting anxiously crouched low in the car. Pat had insisted that Brian was to drive, as he had set up a firing position in the rear luggage compartment ready to shoot at any possible pursuers. As Pat had planned, the gateway started to become silhouetted against the lightening sky that heralded the forthcoming dawn; he was looking at his watch and counting backwards, marking each number with a wave and then indicating the last five seconds with his splayed hand, folding down each finger in turn, five, four, three, two, one – and then promptly on cue, an orange flash followed quickly by a deafening explosion. Then allowing exactly five minutes to give the besiegers enough time to investigate what had occurred out of their sight, on the opposite side of the enclosure, the moment arrived for Pat and the others to make their escape bid..

Brian had waited apprehensively gripping the steering wheel for what seemed to be an eternity, and on Pat's command he tried to start the Range Rover. Not being used to its controls he let the clutch out too quickly, stalling the powerful engine. However on the second attempt and to everyone's relief it leapt to life and then, with a lurch it roared off, amid the metallic crunching sounds of the unfamiliar gearbox, swerving violently to avoid the deceased truck as it hurtled through the gateway on its bid for freedom. The plan almost worked perfectly; the remaining lorry was just visible disappearing around the wall to the far side of the grounds, on its way to discover the reason for the explosion when, unluckily, a sharp-eyed man aboard truck spotted the fleeing car, and told the driver, who instantly skidded round, causing a great plume of sand to fly from the tyres, as it then sped off in hot pursuit of the escapees.

On Pat's advice, Brian drove with no lights, deliberately heading westward, into the gloom, to join the main highway; the car handled the sandy conditions quite well and would easily be able to outstrip the lorry on the road, but on the soft sand it was no match for the eight driving wheels of the truck which gave it the advantage, and it was catching up very quickly. But the bright sky behind it made it an easy target for Pat, who, from his prepared position in the back, shot five rounds quickly through the pursuer's windscreen, hoping to kill one or both of the front-seat occupants, the effect was devastating. The vehicle flew out of control and careered off to the right, crashing nose first into a deep depression in the soft sand, instantly halting its forward momentum and flipping it over onto its roof, spilling the diesel, causing it to burst into flames, incinerating all the unlucky occupants in a fireball of burning fuel and exploding ammunition.

Shaken to the core, Brian drove to a suitably safe distance away from the conflagration before he stopped and changed places with Pat, who, as the more experienced man, was anxious to resume the role. Minnie was trying to console two of the boys, who were crying uncontrollably, overwrought by the recent events; the third lad was excited and garrulous, asking unwarranted questions that annoyed the still-trembling Brian, who poetically admonished him to silence. Peter stoically took all the happenings in his stride, showing a great deal of fortitude and bravery by trying to cheer up the distraught boys, but inwardly he worried about the safety of James and Michael. After the first few hectic minutes, the situation in the car calmed down somewhat; one of the lads had completely recovered his composure, although the other's muffled sobs could still be heard emanating from Minnie's tear-soaked, ample bosom.

Having covered several miles, Pat felt reassured enough to continue the journey in safety now that some semblance of normality had returned inside the Range Rover; he resumed driving with extreme caution, taking much care through the unknown part of the desert until, as was inevitable, he reached the normally empty highway eighty-five. Unusually, it was filled with an incredible assortment of slow-moving early morning traffic heading north-west along it, vehicles, camels, donkey carts and refugees of all shapes and sizes were traversing along the main road seeking safety as far away from Kuwait as possible. Pat joined in with the exodus of all sorts; some were civilian but most were the beaten military, who were escaping from the war zone, caused when the Iraqi army invaded oil-rich Kuwait under the leadership of the avaricious Saddam Hussein. It was the third of August 1990, and the war was only a day old, already the Kuwaiti military had capitulated, and the Royal Family had fled the country, leaving Iraq in charge.

The road to Jordan was cluttered with confused and bewildered people, frightened that the war would affect the whole area and was likely to put them in danger; escape was their only option along with as many of their possessions as they could possibly carry. All eyes in the car were scanning for the old Land Rover that was the conveyance of the Burrells containing them with the other fleeing schoolchildren; initially the progress along the road was very slow, but as the journey went on, the traffic thinned and the quicker it became, as most of the fellow road users had left the highway to find shelter in the many villages to the south, away from the border with Iraq.

Pat made a detour off the main road to the house in Ar'ar, primarily to cater for the immediate needs of the travellers, but also in case James or Michael had been to it, or were still there at the house. When Pat arrived there was no sign of his comrades, so in a vague hope he left them a note, detailing the recent events, and stating their intended destination. While they were at the house Minnie hastily prepared some welcome food and drink for everyone, and during the meal Pat took the opportunity to address the assembly and inform them of the plan: they were going to head for the Jordanian border town of Turayf, and then they would wait for five days for the others. Following that, either with or without their friends they would head for the safety of Tel Aviv in friendly Israel.

Before they resumed the journey Brian had the idea to display the Union Flag which Pat retrieved from the school roof, on the back of the Range Rover, to make them more visible and aid the others in finding them. So as quickly as they possibly could, using some scavenged nylon rope, they lashed a discarded ten-foot length of steel water pipe to the back of the vehicle and tied the large flag to it. Happy with the result and suitably refreshed, they continued their trek searching for the lost Land Rover and the others. The break had worked in their favour, as when they got to rejoin the main road it had almost cleared completely, enabling them to travel at a great speed, making the ensign flap and crack noisily above their heads, adding an even higher sense of urgency to their mission. For fifty miles they travelled uninterrupted until they came to a town called Al Jalamid, there they gained news of the Land Rover and its missing occupants.

Because of the tensions, the security was much heightened, and many more than usual Saudi border patrols were on duty. One such patrol was coming along the road in the opposite direction towards Pat's vehicle, and on seeing the Range Rover they threw their truck across the road into its path, making Pat brake violently, throwing the passengers forwards in a heap, hurting two of the boys and causing the makeshift flagpole to bend. A very smart Saudi major alighted from the truck and apologetically approached the driver and the shaken passengers. Pat leaned out of the already opened car window and was about to give the smiling Arab a mouthful of abuse, when, out of the blue the man addressed him in good English.

"Mr Vincent, we've looking out for you!" Pat's curses didn't have time to leave his lips; he stopped to think for a second and then informed the officer that he was not Mr Vincent, and that the man next to him indeed was, once again the man apologised to Pat, and then spoke to Brian.

"We've been looking everywhere for you, Mr and Mrs Burrell's car broke down, and I arranged for one of our mechanics to fix it for them, they're approximately three quarters of an hour ahead of you." Brian asked how they knew it was them; he explained that he had been given a detailed description, and how he was always happy to help the English, because he had spent many happy months there, during his officer training at Sandhurst. Pat then asked the Major if he was prepared to help further? He agreed, so Pat asked him to watch out for James and Michael describing them both, and the type of vehicle they would probably be driving. Quickly he wrote down some details, and handed the paper to the officer who read it and nodded his willingness to comply, telling Pat that it was a pleasure to be of assistance, and then inquiring if there was anything else either he or his men could do for them? Pat declined the offer, thanking the man sincerely and then departed with all urgency in pursuit of the missing friends.

Because of the newfound urgency, they roared along the almost empty highway eighty-five, the Range Rover's bent flagpole straining in their wake with the remnants of the ensign buzzing wildly above, shedding small pieces of cloth as they went. The closer they got to Jordan, the fewer the vehicles there were to hamper their progress, so the faster they went, and after about half an hour Pat spotted a distant speck on the road, which he recognised as a Land Rover, but was it the one they were searching for? Pat accelerated the Range Rover to get a closer, and better, look and, as he got a little closer, he started to just about make out a spluttering old vehicle of the right type, partially hidden amid a haze of smoke and oil fumes exuding from the exhaust pipe. It was looking hopeful, and after a minute or two his hopes were proven to be justified: it was definitely them, and he had arrived in the nick of time, judging by the condition of the old twelve-seater Safari Land Rover, which was kangarooing and shuddering, and was making virtually no headway at all.

Poor, confused Mr Burrell was driving and he didn't have a clue that assistance was so close at hand, his rear view in the mirrors were totally obscured by the smoke that the car produced as it attempted to make forward progress. All of a sudden and without any warning Pat overtook the failing vehicle and swerved in front of it, completely halting its progress. Mr Burrell's initial response was one of horror, thinking that the worst might have happened, and then when realisation of whom it was set in, he became overjoyed and almost tearful, thanking any gods that might have listened to his silent supplications. The relief was enormous, help had arrived, and the day was saved. All the occupants got out of their respective vehicles, and swapped their stories of the escape, chattering like magpies, the pressure built up during the journey was being released, the emotional dam had burst amid tears of relief followed by grateful laughter. Peter stayed silent throughout, still worrying about James and Michael, imagining all sorts of dreadful scenarios, fearing that they had either been taken or were dead. He had tried to shake off his gloom, but every time he had tried to think of something different, he found his mind had returned back to his terrors.

Pat only joined in with the rejoicing very briefly, as his main concerns were directed towards the deceased Land Rover, and after a cursory inspection he had come to the conclusion that to effect another makeshift repair would be completely out of the question. As usual Brian was there, close at his side offering pearls of wisdom and other ideas, but most importantly giving moral support when needed. The answer was simple: the bent makeshift flagpole had served its purpose, and the flag was just a mere shredded tattered rag of coloured cloth, but the lashings of nylon rope were fine, and would serve well as a tow rope, so the two friends set about rigging a means of transporting both vehicles, and the whole company the last twenty or so miles, to Turayf and relative safety.

There was enough usable rope to plait into a suitably thick enough piece of only nine feet in length. After tying knots the two cars would only be six feet apart, so the rest of the trip would have to be taken very carefully. Brian would drive the Range Rover, with as many of the children as could possibly be crammed in. Pat had volunteered to guide the Land Rover which, without the engine running, would be awkward without power steering or brakes. Mr Burrell openly admitted he lacked the confidence to with the cars being so dangerously close to each other. All unnecessary objects were jettisoned, to reduce weight, and the two vehicles set off slowly to complete their trek.

They arrived at their destination late in the day; Pat went straight to the airport hotel, where he negotiated with the manager for five rooms, after explaining what had happened, and the fact that they were mostly British nationals swayed the argument in Pat's favour. So with promise of payment by the British government, and leaving the keys to the expensive car as security, the tired travellers were summoned by Pat into the hotel. Pat and Brian were going to share one room, the Burrells another, the other three were for the boys and, after a quick wash, they had just enough time to get downstairs and eat before the evening meals were finished being served.

The next morning everyone felt better, rested, showered and fed. At breakfast the boys' talk was of phoning home, to let worried relations know that everything was well with them, and to arrange getting back to their loved ones. Peter was still fretting over his missing father and Michael. Minnie sat with him trying to allay his fears but inwardly she also worried about the whereabouts of Michael. Mr and Mrs Burrell were distraught, their whole life was in tatters, their home, their jobs and life's work had disappeared, engulfed by the aspirations of a tyrant. Brian had no particular direction to go in, no relatives or friends to turn to, he had spent most of his adult life working away from home and the closest person to him was Pat, whom he had only known for a very short while.

They had stayed at Turayf for three days before Pat received any information about James and Michael; the helpful Saudi

Major assumed where Pat and the others would be staying and he phoned the hotel with news. He had used his resources to locate the whereabouts of the missing men, and was keen to pass on what he had heard. They had escaped from Kuwait and were anxious to reunite with the others; he expected them to arrive within a day to join up with his son and the rest of the escapees. Pat went straight to Peter and Minnie to tell them everything he had been told, Peter had been sick with worry, the longer he waited the worse he was feeling. It was a great relief when he heard the good news and his spirit felt lifted for the first time for ages. Minnie cried tears of joy when Pat told her that her beloved Michael was alive and well; she had a dream that they were both dead, and being superstitious by nature she believed it to be true.

At breakfast the next morning the assembly were sitting at their tables, Pat was on his second piece of toast and marmalade when his missing comrades walked into the dining room. Minnie was the first to see them; she was absent-mindedly buttering a slab of bread when she glanced up momentarily and noticed Michael smiling at her, she looked down to carry on with her task when all of a sudden it dawned on her who she had just seen. An involuntary loud shriek left her lips, that caused Pat to spit the half-chewed food straight at Brian, who was sitting directly opposite him. The rest of the company took some time trying to recover from the shock of the scream before they realised the reason for the outburst. A tired-looking waiter came bounding into the room to investigate the reason for the uproar; when he saw the hugging and kissing of the reunited friends, he shrugged, muttered something about the effeminate English and returned to his duties. After all the greetings were over James and Michael sat with the others and joined them at breakfast to tell their tale.

Peter, James, Brian and Pat sat all together in a row opposite Mr and Mrs Burrell and Minnie, who was clutching Michael's hands tightly, and she wasn't going to let him go. The newly arrived men duly started to relate the story of their escape. Nobody in Kuwait expected the invasion, the army wasn't even on a full alert status when it started, James had been working at an oilfield near to the border with Iraq when it was stormed by commandos.

Punctuated with sips of coffee and mouthfuls of breakfast, James told the whole story. The Iraqis attacked the compound during the evening on the first of August; Michael had felt uneasy all that day, everything had seemed too quiet and he had been experiencing that strange feeling you get when you're being watched. He told James of his concerns, who also felt that strange prickly sensation when something bad was about to happen., Agreeing that all was not as it should be, they decided to stick together and stay wary.

The attack came on both sides of the vast compound at the same time. Luckily Michael and James were at the front near to the main gates, they were alerted to the incursion when a cluster of local employees bolted past them in a state of blind panic, shouting warnings, saying the Iraqis had invaded. A burst of gunfire gave credence to their fears, and so, without any prompting, James and Michael scurried off to locate their car. Upon finding it, they made a hurried exit from the facility, leaving all their belongings behind with the invaders. Their ungainly exit was followed a hail of bullets coming from the insurgents, and later on the group were shown half a dozen holes in the rear door of the vehicle as testament to the story. They escaped using the same road as Pat and the others had taken, making a detour to the school to see if anyone was still there in need of help. Sadly they had some very bad news for the Burrells; the buildings were burning when they got to them, and the whole school showed signs of being ransacked and looted. There were no Iraqis still present, but evidence of their involvement in the arson was everywhere and the whole place was utterly ruined.

On hearing what had happened at the school, Mr Burrell sank back into his seat; he looked startled for a fleeting moment and then, clutching his chest, he collapsed on to the floor with a clump. He had been feeling unwell and stressed for some time, ever since the possibility of war threatened his life's work and his livelihood, and the news was too much for his troubled body to manage. His wife tried, but was unable, to catch him as he fell, so she quickly knelt down by his side and cradled his limp head in her arms. Knowing instantly that he was dying, she rocked him gently; her tears were splashing on his unresponsive face, she crooned softly to him and called him, "My darling Tommy," the name he preferred to be kept secret, and was only ever used by her in private. A doctor had been summoned, but all the adults knew that his heart had given up; his face had taken on a bluish tinge and his breathing was rasping and shallow. Minnie ushered Peter and all the children outside, she tried to keep their minds off the events that were unfolding in the dining room, to allow Mr Burrell to pass away in peace, with as much dignity as possible.

Mr Burrell died there in the dining room of a strange hotel, his heart broken, without uttering a single word, surrounded by new-made friends and his grieving wife, the first British casualty of the war.

James arranged a flight back to England for everyone, the British government were anxious to repatriate as many of their citizens as possible, knowing that the whole of North Africa could soon be plunged into all-out war. Within hours, the sombre party boarded a sandy coloured RAF Hercules transport aircraft for the journey home, along with the plain wooden coffin, that contained the late headmaster.

CHAPTER 7

The flight home took slightly over six hours. The plane was noisy, for the whole journey it rattled and juddered, at first it frightened some of the boys, but after a while everyone accepted the lumps and bumps as normal and carried on regardless. The passengers sat in uncomfortable hard seats along the sides of the aircraft in two rows facing each other. Minnie sat down next to Mrs Burrell, who stoically refused to show any more emotion, embarrassed that she had showed weakness back at Turayf, when her poor Tommy died.

They landed at RAF Brize Norton, a large military airport sixty-five miles north-west of London. It was a miserable early August day; a cold mizzley rain was blowing straight into their faces as they disembarked down the steps onto the glistening wet tarmac. A cluster of friends and relations of the boys were waiting for them, all huddled together like a herd of sheep, trying to protect themselves from the elements. The boys rushed to find their respective loved ones, jumping into the arms of relieved parents or friends. Jasmine was there, her radiant beauty shining out against the bleak wet backdrop. On seeing her, Peter raced and flung himself into the embrace of his adoptive mother, excited to see his new baby brother William for the first time.

James joined the family reunion, kissing Jasmine and then briefly inspecting his new son, once again pretending that he had an interest in his children.

All of a sudden the noisy hellos stopped abruptly, the assembly shuffled round to face the aircraft, and then as one they all stood to attention and bowed their heads to pay respect to the coffin that was being unloaded. Solemnly a small group of men appeared on the ramp at the rear of the plane; Pat, Michael and Brian were there along with a uniformed stranger, they marched carefully down the slope carrying Mr Burrell in the coffin; his mortar board and folded gown were placed on the top, adding extra pathos to the occasion and making it even sadder. Behind them came Mrs Burrell, whose tendency to stoop was even more exaggerated in her grief; she tripped slightly at the bottom of the ramp but regained her balance without fuss, bravely and without a tear she followed the pallbearers to a waiting hearse, where her Tommy was gently placed reverently by the men.

James had made all the necessary arrangements for Mrs Burrell, who had no home, nor did she have any relations in England, so James undertook the role, much as a son would do. He had arranged lodgings and some of the necessities she would need to live in England, he had even gone to the extent of approaching some of his high-ranking Saudi associates, to organise some form of reimbursement for the loss of the school. James's seemingly impervious exterior was showing some cracks prised open up by his ever-loving wife in Jasmine.

The day of the funeral arrived. As per Mr Burrell's wishes he was to be buried near Wymondham, a small market town a few miles south of Norwich in Norfolk. The *cortège* consisted of only two cars and the hearse; the sombre little procession meandered sedately around the country lanes where Tommy had spent his childhood before making its solemn way to the small rural church where he had been christened. They stopped at a moss-covered lychgate and followed the coffin into the damp-smelling old building. The vicar had never met the deceased, as was obvious during the eulogy, when he referred several times to Mr Burrell as Timothy. An apparently three-fingered organist wearing boxing gloves blasted out an unrecognisable version of *Amazing Grace* during the service, and then an equally unrecognisable rendition of *Abide with me* as the coffin was carried outside to the leafy graveyard. It was unseasonably cold and miserable, but a valiant robin took pity on the sad scene and struck up a few chords as Tommy was laid to rest, witnessed only by his few friends and his stoic, tearless wife Isabel.

James's reputation as being a hard man had disappeared quickly, or as Jasmine would have it, he was mellowing with age. He hadn't mellowed towards his oldest son however, who was still safely ensconced at the school in Medina, the second most holy place in Islam, and the burial place of Muhammad, making it decidedly unlikely to be targeted in the war. Ibrahim still hated the strictness of the school and desperately wanted to be back with his mother, and the leniency it offered, however James wasn't prepared to give an inch, especially when there was the well-being of a defenceless new baby to consider. Jasmine and James had spent their time settling into a new home they had bought in Whitton in Middlesex, a town conveniently near enough to Heathrow airport for James to continue with his work in the oil industry, flying instead of driving to his destinations.

Peter had been enrolled at a very select boarding school near to Bournemouth on the south coast of England; he was due to start at the beginning of the new term in early September, and he couldn't wait to resume his education. Michael and Minnie were going to go on a sabbatical, and travel to the West Indies to look up Minnie's extended family. Pat shocked everyone by announcing that he and Brian were going to set up a guest house in Surbiton. They'd got on really well ever since they had met, so they combined their saved money and invested it in a run-down old Victorian hotel, one they intended to update and hopefully re-open before Christmas.

Peter left his new home on the fifth of September 1990 to journey to his new school. He was only eight years and five months old, yet ever since he could talk he enjoyed being taught, and was hungry to learn. His early years of being closeted out of sight, hidden away from external interests with no distractions and nothing to amuse him except stories and reading books had accelerated his standard of learning far beyond that what was expected at his age. His reading ability was equivalent to that of a well-educated fourteen-year-old, he could speak and read Arabic as well as he could English, he had a workable knowledge of maths, and, thanks to Pat's input, he was also interested in history.

James was going to personally drive Peter the sixty-odd miles to Bournemouth in his brand new Jaguar. Jasmine was going to stay at home with William, so the goodbyes were said outside the house in Whitton. The farewell party only consisted of Jasmine with the baby who had been joined by their next door neighbour, a curmudgeonly old man affectionately known by his friends as

Wobbly Bob. He had befriended Peter during the summer holidays, and enjoyed the boy's inquiring nature; amusingly the old man always pretended to be grumpily contrary when answering the lad's well-aimed questions. The trio waved their farewells as the car smoothly drove off, taking Peter, his luggage and most important of all, the two books that gave him comfort and had stayed by his side through the travails that had beset his early youth.

They arrived at the new school just after midday; it was set in massive grounds and surrounded by all sorts of sports fields, with dominating white rugby posts shining brightly amidst the green of the well-groomed grass. The red brick building had once probably been a stately home, and sported twenty or so mullioned windows on the front aspect alone. The only obvious entrance had a massive studded dark oak door which creaked noisily when James opened it to enter. A deep Welsh voice greeted them, apparently from nowhere, as it echoed around the empty panelled reception area, inquiring if it could be of any assistance? James looked at Peter and then they both scanned the room to see if they could find the body that belonged to the mysterious questioner. All of a sudden a round ruddy face popped into view from behind a low wooden counter and offered an explanation as to why the owner of the voice appeared to be in hiding.

"I'm sorry to scare you, I was looking for my pen, it's down here somewhere!" The bodiless head then asked, in a rich baritone, if they didn't mind waiting while he looked for it? Scanning the floor in order to assist with the search, Peter's young sharp eyes spotted a glint of gold wedged under the edge of the wooden front, near to where the man was looking.

"There it is!" Peter exclaimed, pointing at gleaming object.

"Ah! Thank you my boy," the man responded, seemingly overjoyed to be reunited with his lost pen. He retrieved it and then stood up, revealing his massy frame and barrel chest.

"Mr Peter Cahill, I presume?" the man boomed realising who the lad was straight away. "I've been expecting you!" The teacher scanned Peter up and down with a critical eye. "Play rugby do you laddie? You look like a scrum half to me." He looked at James, bade them both to take a seat, and informatively explained what Peter's first day at the school would entail.

After getting Peter unpacked and settled into his quarters, he and James were given a school lunch and then taken on a conducted tour of the school and the grounds, after which James was encouraged to leave; so having said goodbye and waved to his departing father, Peter once again was alone in a strange place with no friends and no one to turn to. The only crumb of comfort still came from the two little books he always kept by his side.

Peter's first duty at the school, along with the new intake of another six boys of a similar age, was to attend a general knowledge test, designed specifically to discover what class would be suitable for each pupil. The lads had to sit for exactly one hour in total silence, and write down the answers to questions that were printed on three sheets of foolscap paper. While the other boys sat scratching their heads, struggling to resolve some of the difficult posers, Peter was happy, his head bent over the papers, busily completing the test as quickly as he possibly could, and after only thirty-five minutes he had finished. Placing his pencil neatly alongside his work, he looked up and folded his arms in front of his chest. On seeing that the boy had obviously completed the paper, the large Welsh teacher walked silently over to Peter and gathered up the test, looked doubtfully at him, and took it back to his desk to mark it. When the hour was up, the boys were instructed to put their pencils down and stop writing. In turn, they filed up to the master's desk to present their work to him. Each lad had to stand quietly while they were obliged to witness him marking their scrawls; the teacher used the red pen more than the black during the appraisal of the students' work, making bold red crosses across great swathes of the work, frustratedly tutting during the process. Peter was the last one to be summoned to the front, he dutifully stood on the same spot where the others had, and watched the master as he re-examined the work, which was all marked correct with a large tick.

Because of Peter's highly successful completion of the induction test, he was summoned to see the headmaster later that afternoon, Mr Griffiths; the Welsh master escorted him to the study where the head spent most of his school hours. Peter looked tiny as he stood alongside the large teacher as they faced the gaunt grey-haired headmaster whose sallow skin was deeply etched with the wrinkles that were testament to the hard life he had suffered, having pushed away the pleasures of life to sacrifice himself to the education of boys, and to his steadfast belief in the Christian church.

The headmaster was a doctor of Divinity and in deference to his degree, he always liked to wear a starched dog collar and be called Reverend Mason in obeisance to his strict religious beliefs. Peering over his rimless half-moon glasses, he looked somewhat incredulously at the new pupil, who had shocked them by his knowledge. "You're a very bright boy master Cahill!" the head's voice was faint verging on the point of being feeble, "what are we going to do with you, I wonder?" The two teachers openly discussed their quandary in front of Peter, and it was decided that he would be placed in a class with eleven-year-olds, because it was probable that the boys of the same age were likely to hold back Peter's educational progress. With everything settled and the school day finished, it was time for the evening meal, and then bed.

Peter found it hard to make friends at school, his classmates were up to three years older than him and looked on him as too young to mix, and play with. To the boys of his own age he appeared strange, the experience of life in Saudi Arabia making him more mature and worldly wise than his peers. They were also generally jealous of the favouritism showed to their brightest star by the teachers, so among eighty boys and ten staff Peter was still lonely, and to escape it, he once again buried himself in learning. The only respite from his own company came at the weekends when he discovered the enjoyment of cricket, and in the winter rugby. He was still a little small for his age, but the inner toughness he had developed during his early years served him well in the sports field.

Over the next few months at the school Peter settled in very well, he proved himself to be educationally ahead of the class he had been placed in, and he was moved up a year, the physical gap between him and his classmates was now even wider, making mixing even more difficult. His new form teacher was Mr Griffiths, a man who insisted on fair play, and didn't allow bullying of any kind, saving Peter from the unwarranted physical abuse that was sure to be meted out on the smallest and weakest boy in the class, without his intervention. Although he was still streets ahead of the other pupils in his group, Peter had learnt that if he appeared to struggle with the work at times the others would be more favourable towards him. When the boys played Peter still found himself on his own, exiled and alone, forcing him to become more and more self-dependant.

Contrary to his predictions, the war in the Middle East had gone badly for Saddam Hussein; he had been ousted from Kuwait by an American-led coalition of nations, his retreating army adopted a scorched earth policy and set fire to the Kuwaiti oil wells in reprisal, leaving nothing of value untouched. Saddam cynically made an attempt to involve the whole world in the war, firing missiles at Israel and Saudi Arabia, but his efforts were in vain, and his prized army met its fate on the, "highway of death," at the hands of the coalition air force. The war officially ended on the twenty-eighth of February 1991, but in James's words it was only a cessation of hostilities as in his opinion there was no specific answer to the age-old problems in the area. Because of the clashing ideologies, new wars were inevitable and many thousands of lives would be lost solving the unsolvable riddle, where the minority Sunni Muslims hated the ruling Shi'as and vice versa, not forgetting the poor Kurds who were somewhere stuck in the middle. Eventually in later years, after the invasion of Iraq in 2003 Saddam went into hiding in Iraq, only to be captured tried and found guilty of crimes against humanity and was executed in Baghdad on the thirtieth of December 2006, creating a vacuum waiting to be filled by those who wanted the power most.

During the intervening years Peter had grown up into a young man, he had grown well and had attained a normal stature. He had passed all ten of his GCSEs with flying colours by the age of twelve, and went on to take six A levels when he was only fourteen, allowing enough time before going to university to study German and higher Maths, so once again he buried himself in his studies, on his own, in silence, with no outside distractions. He still took a little time off study to play cricket and his very favourite sport rugby, which he gave up after damaging both knees executing a brave tackle on a large prop forward, an injury that plagued him for the rest of his life, leaving him with no other real interests apart from learning. Yet he remained an avid reader never refusing a new book no matter what the content was. He saw James and Jasmine regularly, spending his holidays and some weekends with them and his younger brother William who was, like Peter, a happy child. James still darted off on missions all over the world, and was often absent when he visited. Jasmine retained her beauty in her middle age, only a touch of grey in her raven-black hair and a few subtle wrinkles betrayed her age. To her, Peter was still her special little boy, and whenever she saw him she fussed over him like a mother hen tending a chick.

Ibrahim had eventually settled down in Saudi Arabia and was studying the history of Islam. He never contacted his parents and ignored Jasmine's many letters to him, forbidding them to come to Saudi to see him, and flatly refusing James's repeated offers to pay the costs for him to come to England to visit. Pat was happy running his guest house with Brian, James had called on his professional driving and other services a few times. As always, the reliable Pat obliged, travelling to far-off climes, ironing out little problems that irked British government. Michael and Minnie had moved to Watford in Hertfordshire and created a brood of four boys, all of whom were exact replicas of their father, only in differing sizes. Michael still suffered from the injury to his leg, there was apparently damage to the internal ligaments and tendons and he was blessed with a permanent limp.

Michael kept in regular contact with his ex-colleagues, and met up with them occasionally to reminisce. On one such occasion Pat arranged for all the adults to stay at the guest house, where he was going to provide them all with a special meal. James and Jasmine arrived first, at five o'clock, closely followed by Michael and Minnie, so after the customary greetings they were all settled into their respective rooms. The meal was going to be served at seven in the evening so James, as always, took the intervening time to quickly make love to his beautiful wife, their lust for each other hadn't waned over the years, and the relationship was still as red hot as when it began. After the meal had been eaten they all sat together, drinking and discussing the past. During the conversation Pat mentioned how he wished he had got his way with Xavier and blown his lying head off his lying shoulders. James piped in, abruptly halting Pat's rantings,

"He's still alive you know!" They all looked at James astounded. "He works for the Yanks, they turned him, he's an agent in Iran." Pat's eyebrows knotted with annoyance. "How do you know that?" he asked.

"Do you remember that American colonel, Arnold Becket? Well, he's now General Becket and, my friend, he keeps me in the picture! Which is more than the useless bosses in Jermyn Street do, they still don't have a clue!"

Pat was mumbling obscenities under his breath with his arms folded grumpily. Brian, who had spent most of the meal just listening to the stories, prodded him. Pat stood up, cleared his throat and shuffled his feet. "You all know that I've never been for speeches," he began. Brian prodded him again. "I don't really know how to say this, but I just thought you'd better know, Brian and me are a sort of couple!" Having said what he needed to say Pat sat down reddened with embarrassment by his revelation. Jasmine looked at Pat and then Brian, "It's about time you said something, we all knew anyway. Ever since I saw you both together I knew you were made for each other, good luck to you both!" The assembly all stood and clapped. Brian had something to say; once everybody had resumed their seats he stood up to make his announcement, "Firstly some bad news, Mrs Burrell sadly passed away a couple of weeks ago. Secondly, thank you everyone for being so understanding, we were worried you'd hate us forever."

The conversation became less intense, and amid the chit-chat Michael asked James if he knew how Sue was getting on. Jasmine heard the question and reinforced it, "Yes James, how is she? You never say!"

James answered hesitantly. "The last time I heard anything was a couple of months ago, her back's no better, and she's a fully fledged Muslim now. She contacted me, because I sent her Ibrahim's allowance instead of hers and she wanted his address so that she could send it to him."

"Go on!" Jasmine butted in, prompting James, knowing he was hiding something, "she also asked for more money to pay for a trip to Mecca."

"I suppose she saw one of my letters to Ibrahim then?"

"Probably!" James admitted.

"Did you give her any money then?" Jasmine pushed the reluctant James.

"Just a little!" James admitted, loosening up a bit. "She's turned really radical, she wants sharia law over here. She's got it bad, she wears the niqab all the time."

Jasmine interrupted. "Isn't it strange? Here I am a Westernised Muslim, who hates the veil, and there she is, a Western woman who's become a Muslim, and loves to cover herself up with one, bizarre!"

They all sat chatting into the small hours of the morning. Outside the sky was getting lighter and a few early birds had started to sing when the party broke up and everyone took to their respective beds. The next morning a late breakfast was served at ten o'clock: a green-tinged Brian served the fried, "Full English," to the sore-headed company, cooked by the equally jaded Pat. Only Jasmine was unaffected by a hangover, in deference to her Muslim roots, she only sipped alcohol the night before. All six sat down together in silence, forcing down the greasy meal, encouraged by the giggling sober Jasmine who kept telling them that it would do them good and line their stomachs. Just after midday the friends left the guest house to go their separate ways, so amid thanks, hugs and goodbyes the reunion was over, leaving Pat and Brian to get on with their lives together.

When Peter had finished school, he attained all top grades in all his A levels and thus the doors to any university in the country were opened to him. He opted to go to Trinity College Cambridge, the same college his father attended in 1965, thirty-five years before. Peter applied for, and was eagerly accepted to study Maths on a degree course, because ever since he first was introduced to the subject he understood it as a type of universal language, and wanted to explore its complexities further.

Peter started his studies at Cambridge in September 2000. Trying to be a good father James paid for the course and bought him a small house near Newmarket as a congratulatory present for his success, also giving him a decent allowance for living expenses. James expected Peter would be able to rent out his spare rooms to other students and make some extra money, so all in all his student days were exceptionally well financed. However Peter made the decision not to rent out his rooms, preferring peaceful solitude, rather than sharing with potentially noisy, drunken students.

In early September Peter arrived at the college to attend his first lecture, which was no more than an induction course, telling him what was expected of him as a student and the direction his studies should take, finally giving him a long list of reading matter to study. Luckily he was in the position to buy the expensive books, so he ordered them straight away, and to his great joy he received them, and buried his head in the complicated pages within days.

Peter spent little time actually at the college; he attended the boring lectures only when necessary, but preferred to stay at home studying on his own, away from any external distractions, often becoming so absorbed in his work, he would stay awake for hours at a time, quite regularly all night and day, until the problem was resolved. Because of his peculiar tendency to hide away from the outside world Peter became known affectionately to his fellow course mates as the hermit. His absence from their company, and his refusal to go out on drinking binges, perplexed them. He offered them an explanation, saying he preferred to study alone so he could concentrate, and he didn't like to drink as it befuddled his mind; they listened to his reasons and accepted him as an antisocial crank. The upside of the hours Peter dedicated to his studies and the alcohol-free clarity of mind was he sailed through his University days without any problems at all, taking only four years to complete his bachelor's and master's degrees, graduating with top honours.

CHAPTER 8

2003

During the years at Cambridge, Peter had been very frugal, he had spent little of his cash, having no rent to pay and eating mostly pasta mixed with tinned tomatoes and toasted cheese. He never went out drinking, and the generous allowance from James left him with a healthy surplus of money. In the rare event of him becoming bored of his studies, he put his mathematic skills to good use; he loved using equations and graphs to make hypothetical financial predictions on the stock market, and when he realised that he was very good at it, he bit the bullet and made his first speculative financial investment. His initial play on the stock market was relatively small; he had been watching a small private mining company in South Africa that needed investment to expand. In due time it announced a floatation date, and after exploring mathematical probabilities, and possible projections he ventured some of his capital to buy some shares in it. As Peter expected it had been hopelessly undervalued, and he met with great success, almost doubling his money in no time at all. The bug had bitten him: he continued watching, and investing in stocks and shares as a sort of lucrative hobby. As time went on his investments became larger and more daring; the resulting rewards were closely linked to the size and the risk factor with each speculation, and very quickly he started to become accidently rich in his own right.

Peter was completely successful, and all his efforts resulted in large profits, he was totally happy watching his bank balance grow; he had no outside interests, and nothing to waste his money on and was in real danger of becoming a miser. James realised what was happening to him, so he encouraged him to tie up some money in property, thinking it might give him another interest. Taking his father's advice he sought to buy a suitable house in the Surrey countryside. James organised a meeting between one of his acquaintances, who was a London estate agent, and Peter to initialise proceedings. Together they decided that the best area to invest was somewhere in the Haslemere area, and accepting their expertise Peter gave them the go-ahead to start the search.

A week after the meeting Peter was sitting at his computer in his study in Newmarket, he was completely mesmerised in front of the screen, watching the performance of some of his latest shares when completely out of the blue the telephone rang, snapping him out of his trance: it was the estate agents and they had found a possible house for him to consider. It sounded perfect and inspection of the property was arranged for the Friday two days later, when Peter was to meet their representative, Charles Hill, at one-o'clock in the afternoon, in the bar of a small hotel in Godalming.

Peter set off on a misty November Thursday morning to attend the Friday meeting; he had booked a room at the hotel for the night as he wanted to be fresh and alert when he viewed the property, and didn't want the tiredness of the journey to possibly affect his judgement. He drove the hundred miles himself, taking a whole four and a half arduous hours on the clogged M25 to bypass London. Tired and frustrated he eventually arrived mid afternoon to sign in to the Greyhound Inn, a lovely small whitewashed thatched hotel James had recommended, situated in deepest rural Surrey. The weather had been mild, and the multi-coloured autumn leaves were still clinging on to the nearby trees, making the pretty little building look as though it belonged on a jigsaw puzzle or a chocolate box. The hotel itself was famed throughout the south for its comfort and hospitality, and with good reason; it boasted about the fine selection of food on its menu, and was seeking its first Michelin star.

After Peter had booked and settled in to his room, had a nap and washed and changed, it was time for his evening meal; he went down from his room into the heavily beamed reception area to order his long looked forward to meal. After spending a few minutes perusing the excellent menu he placed his request. The waiter asked him if he would like to wait in the bar while the food was being prepared? He duly obeyed and took a seat in the corner facing the room. Peter amused himself watching the other guests and visitors as they drank their beverages and chatted amongst themselves. Unusually, and to appease the sommelier, Peter had ordered a glass of wine, and sat sipping the tasty vintage when a young woman of roughly the same age as he was came into the bar, something he thought only happened in fairytales happened to him, without even speaking to the girl, he fell in love with her at first sight. She was utterly beautiful, the way she walked, the way she flicked her silky blonde hair when she ordered her food, her perfect features and figure, in fact everything about her was perfect and he couldn't take his eyes off her.

Peter didn't enjoy his much anticipated meal – the wild smoked salmon stuck in his throat a little, the seared local venison he had been looking forward to so much had lost its appeal, and he just poked and prodded his food around the plate; his appetite had dissipated with the appearance of the beautiful girl. Like him she sat alone, eating and drinking, and in between polite mouthfuls of food and delicate sips of drink she was peering at some important-looking papers. For most of her meal she was totally absorbed in her work, but as people tend to do, she looked up as she lifted the glass to her lips, when her eyes met those of the gawping Peter and, after a brief millisecond of eye contact, he snatched his glance away from hers, pretending to be paying attention to a piece of food. Not being used to the attentions of women Peter felt his face reddening, so he finished his drink and raised himself from his seat clumsily exiting the room, tripping carelessly over his own feet, which, strangely felt larger than they did an hour before. He managed to reach his bedroom without any more incidents; his hands were shaking so much he struggled to put the key in the lock to open the door. With relief his weakened legs carried him far enough to collapse on the bed.

Overnight poor Peter barely slept. Bang went his hopes of meeting the estate agent fully refreshed, instead he tossed and turned all night, the figure of the mystery girl etched into his brain. He tried to take his mind off her by reading his copy of the Koran, but still her image haunted his thoughts; there was nothing he could do, so he resigned himself to lying in bed imagining the unobtainable. Wearily he plodded down to breakfast, where a smartly dressed waitress ushered him to a chair in the breakfast room, and as he took his seat, he momentarily looked up. Instantly his eyes met the same eyes that had kept him from his sleep.

"Good morning!" she said, looking beautiful, the risen pink wintry sun shining through a window behind her, creating a nimbus of light in her hair.

"Good morning!" Peter stammered nervously back, squinting against the light, inwardly cursing the torture he was going to have endure during breakfast. He was hungry and he coped with the meal without appearing to be a complete idiot. Mercifully the waitress offered him a daily paper, which he pretended to be engrossed in, only daring to steal an occasional sneaky glance at the lovely fellow diner. When he had finished the last few gulps of coffee, he shakily retired back to his room, to prepare himself ready to meet with the estate agent. Peter sat in the room and whiled away the time watching inane daytime television shows, trying to erase the indelible image of the beautiful woman from his mind.

One o'clock arrived, so Peter left his room, descended the stairs and made his way into the bar; there were a host of drinkers and diners, sitting and standing in the room, creating a buzz of noisy chattering. Scanning the crowd Peter attempted to spot the likeliest candidate to be Charles Hill the estate agent. To Peter's horror she was there, once again their eyes met, this time the glance was held for a little longer. The girl was sitting in the same corner that he sat in the previous evening, smartly attired in a dark blue suit, much as a businesswoman would wear, her hair neatly piled on the top of her head with less make-up on than she wore the night before, she looked a little different but it was definitely her, sitting expectantly clutching a sheaf of papers, peering around the assembly apparently also looking for someone. Leaving her seat she approached Peter. The nearer she got the more awkward and uncomfortable he felt. When she walked straight up to him, he was sure that she must be able to hear his heart banging uncontrollably in his chest, and then she spoke:

"Mr Cahill?"

"Yes." he stammered back to her as she offered Peter a hand to shake.

"Charley Hill."

His forehead knotted, perplexed "I was looking for Mr Charles Hill," he said weakly, his voice wavering and thin.

"People often think I'm a man, not when they see me, I hope?" She smiled cheekily at him, seeing his discomfort. "We've got go and look at this house haven't we? I'll drive, I know a short cut!" Peter was in no fit state to argue with her, he just meekly obeyed, following her to a sporty little convertible M.G.

"Top up, I think it's going to rain later!" the beautiful Charley announced, stamping her foot on the accelerator and darting off like a bat out of hell.

Peter was amazed; she drove like a maniac, even worse than Pat or Michael. Keeping her foot hard to the boards, the car sped along the country lanes with virtually no regard for other road users, she wasn't choosy, either side of the road was perfectly acceptable to her, as Charley adopted the straight line approach to get to the destination. Twenty hair raising minutes later, after hurtling at breakneck speeds through villages and along poorly made country roads. They screeched through a large stone gateway, along a gravel driveway up to a massive buff brick house partially covered with a scarlet Virginia creeper. Many of the leaves had fallen off, creating a crimson and brown carpet at the front, amid the emerald green lawn it was breath taking. A few large drops of rain started pattering on the cloth roof of the vehicle, the forecast rain had arrived.

The pair alighted from the car. The rain hadn't set in properly as yet and was only light, the dull sky promised much more to come, so Charley and Peter took the opportunity to inspect the gardens first. Discussing the merits of the lovely gardens they wandered around the well manicured lawns and borders, all the time she was bringing points of interest to Peter's attention. She was completely absorbed in her sales rhetoric, and Peter was completely absorbed in her; without keeping an eye on the weather, they reached the furthest point away from the house, completely out in the open, when the heavens opened and a sudden deluge of huge raindrops came falling out from the sky. Seeing that the torrent was unlikely to abate for a while, they ran hell for leather together to gain the shelter of the porch; the rain was so hard that, not only was it soaking them from above, it also was saturating them from below, where the drops were bouncing up off the ground. Dripping and wringing wet they reached the sanctuary of the porch. Charley spoke breathless after the run, "I don't know about you, but I'm bloody soaked!" Peter agreed, feeling a little more relaxed in her presence, and was able to speak back to her without tripping on his words.

"So am I!" he replied, emptying water out of a removed shoe.

"I'll have to dry out or I'll wrinkle and I'm too young for that!" she said, opening the front door revealing a brightly lit massive entrance hall.

Charley didn't suffer from an undue sense of modesty. Once safely inside she proceeded to remove her clothes, letting them drop like wet rags on the red and black quarry-tiled floor. For decency's sake Peter offered to leave but she asked why, as she still had to show him around the property? Underneath her blue suit Charley wore a pale cream slip that had made its best effort to become transparent with the wet And as most women are able to do she magically removed her bra from the armhole without undoing the zip. Peter's eyes came out on stalks, he tried to be polite and avert his gaze, but his stare was magnetised to her barely clad body. He couldn't help himself, he had to take a look and she caught him red handed gawping at her breasts. Her cold and damp erect nipples were easily visible through the see-through soaked garment, but she took it all in her stride, laughing naughtily when he snatched his eyes of her chest. His imagination the night before had let him down; she was even lovelier than in his dreams. Charley conducted the guided tour of the house virtually naked, showing him the rooms and views, as though it was normal procedure for an estate agent to show a potential buyer a property in the nude. Peter heard and saw almost nothing during the tour; his mind was elsewhere, back in the hotel, stripping off what remained of her clothes and then making passionate love to Charley and doing things he had only read about in books.

They finished where they started in the hall, the ruined suit was still damp, but the heat of her body had dried the undergarment, and Charley wanted to get dressed. Skilfully she put her moist bra back on, but she couldn't fasten the damp elastic without help, so with a twinkle in her naughty eyes she asked Peter to help to do it up for her. Obligingly he obeyed, but his hands were shaking so much that he struggled ham-fistedly with the hooks. Charley realised that Peter was very nervous, and she tried to make him feel more relaxed by turning around and grabbing his trembling hands, clasping them saying, "What do you think then?" Peter wasn't sure what she meant, and his puzzled look betrayed it, Charley deliberately played on the ambiguity of the question, "You know what I mean!" Peter still seemed confused, she paused and waited for his reply, prompting him with little nods of her head, mercifully she put him out of his misery.

"The house, what do you think of the house?" Charley resumed the fight of re-dressing damp clothes, affording herself a little smile of pleasure at her well-played flirting-game. Trying to appear unflustered, and trying to use the situation to his advantage Peter answered carefully, "I like it, but I would like you to show me some more, before I make a decision?" by this time Charley was just about fully clothed, and was hopping, trying to force the last wet shoe on to her foot.

"Fine. We'll discuss it over dinner tonight," she replied, gasping, still grappling with the reticent shoe. Peter couldn't believe it; he was going to spend even more time with the lovely Charley.

The trip back to the hotel was scarier than the journey going to the house. Charley was damp and uncomfortable, she needed to shower and change as quickly as possible and the urgency reflected in her awful driving. Miraculously they got back to the hotel unscathed, entering together they went up to their rooms, Charley reached hers first, as she opened the door she looked at Peter to remind him. "See you at seven; give me a knock on the way past?" Peter returned to his room, confused, not sure whether it was a date at seven, or just a business meeting. Still puzzling over the conundrum, he removed his still sodden clothes and showered, thoroughly scrubbing himself all over. Warmed and happy that he no longer smelled like a damp dog, he dressed ready for a dinner date with the woman of his dreams.

As instructed, precisely at seven, Peter knocked on Charley's bedroom door on his way past. From somewhere within, her panting voice invited him in, apologising for not being ready at the appointed hour. Obeying the summons, he gingerly entered the room. Charley was right, she wasn't ready, in fact once again she wasn't even dressed, she rushed around in just a flimsy dressing gown with a towel piled on her head, "sorry! Sorry! Sorry! I got involved with some work, and lost track of time. "Peter didn't mind, he enjoyed watching Charley, especially when she was wearing very little. "You don't mind waiting while I get dressed, do you?" Peter felt braver, "no, not at all," "I've been looking on my lap top and found some more properties to look at; the details are on the table, hang on I'll show you." She scurried back from the bathroom still in her dressing gown, and bent forward to show him the papers, the robe gaped open as she leant forward, revealing her naked breasts to Peter. Charley was fully aware that he was staring down her front, but, unmoved and uncaring, she carried on showing him the leaflets, secretly hoping he would make a move, but the unworldly Peter was too shy.

Frustrated by his reluctance to act she took the lead, "Peter, I don't know why, but I like you, a lot, as it happens, and I know you like me, it's probably too soon, but we are both adults, alone in a hotel room, and life is too short to miss opportunities to have fun." Staring intently into his eyes she waited for his answer, when it came it surprised her.

"I'm sorry! I'll be honest with you, I haven't got any experience with girls, and in truth I don't know what to do!" Peter's face was scarlet with embarrassment. "All my life I've studied on my own and never really mixed with others," he went on and started telling the now seated Charley his life's story.

She sat listening to the saga for over two hours, enthralled and amazed, but also saddened by the lonely young life he had lived. At times she was moved to tears, horrified by the violence he had witnessed.

Instead of dining downstairs as planned, they had some sandwiches and a bottle of wine sent up to the room, eating their meal together they sat swapping stories until the small hours. Peter looked at his watch and on seeing the time he made as if he was going to leave, she stopped him, taking his hand.

"Come on, I've got you here, and you're not getting away that easily," she said leading him to the bed. Letting her dressing gown fall, exposing her complete nakedness to an incredulous Peter, his practical sex education begun. Everything came quite naturally to the initially over-eager Peter, who wanted to rush through his first sexual experience. Understanding and careful, Charley calmed him down, pointing out that it wasn't a race, teaching him the value of slow, steady foreplay and some of the subtleties of making love, the apt pupil quickly learned off his able teacher.

Peter really enjoyed the classes, twice in the night, and once in the morning. Charley also enjoyed giving the lessons so much that she and Peter booked in for the following night to resume the tuition. Sunday morning arrived and after the couple had finished their well earned breakfast, they departed, having arranged a similar tryst for the next weekend. As had been the case throughout Peter's education, he proved to be a very good learner, and the search for a house became a regular event that always ended up with a suitable lesson.

Peter and Charley started to spend all their available time together; at Christmas he took her to meet James, Jasmine and his fourteen-year-old younger brother William. All his family loved Charley, especially Jasmine, who had been worried that Peter was in danger of becoming a recluse, and was overjoyed that the normally very reserved young man had been prised out of his shell by a beautiful girl. On the New Year's Day, it was Peter's turn to visit Charley's family in Sheffield, Peter opted to drive, for two reasons, firstly he wanted to try out a new car he had bought just before the holidays, secondly he feared that the odds of survival travelling all that way with Charley driving was very slim. The couple planned to start their journey early mid-morning. They had spent most of the Christmas break at Peter's house in Newmarket, and after a muted celebration the night before, they set off on the trip to Sheffield slightly later than planned at just past eleven in the morning. Fortunately the roads were almost clear and the new car, a large gleaming brand new Audi, performed very well, and it took them just under three hours to reach their destination.

Charley's parents lived in their own house, a few miles outside the city; they had struggled financially for years to buy the property and were very proud of their achievement. Her father had only ever worked in the coal industry and was embittered by its downfall; her mother was very particular and fussy, everything in the house had its place and was cleaned and dusted to perfection. Peter nervously pulled up outside the house, having been warned about Charley's parents' peculiarities. The house itself was as immaculate on the outside as it was on the inside, even in winter the garden was neatly trimmed, and the outside paintwork gleamed and sparkled.

Anxiously they approached the front door and knocked gently. A small neat woman in her late fifties wearing a floral pink pinafore dress opened the door and beckoned them in; she looked Peter up and down inquisitively and looked slightly disappointed. Charley broke the ice, "This is my mum, Helen." Peter offered his hand to her, limply she took it, and with a slight curtsey she shook it feebly.

"Your father's through in the living room, he's in a bit of a mood!" She spoke very quietly, as if she was frightened to disturb the peace and awaken a sleeping monster. Charley led Peter into the room where, sitting near the fireplace, stretching his hands towards the blaze was her father, who chose to ignore the intrusion and carried on puffing at his pipe. Charley strode up to her father, stood between him and the fire leaned forwards, kissed him on the cheek and spoke to him loudly, "Don't be so grumpy Daddy! I've brought my boyfriend to meet you." She grabbed his armchair and started to tug it round to face Peter, who stood shuffling his feet, waiting to be acknowledged. Begrudgingly the surprisingly old man looked up at Peter and grunted an unmeant hello.

"There, that wasn't too hard, was it?" She knew exactly handle her aged father. The strained introductions over, they all sat at a table and had tea and cakes. No one relaxed, Peter felt like an exhibit when David, her father, found out that Peter worked for himself investing in the stock market: he openly called him a Tory capitalist and worst of all, a Londoner. Charley scolded her father, in defence of her bewildered boyfriend, pointing that he was born in Saudi Arabia and lived in Newmarket. To the old man everyone born outside Yorkshire was a Londoner, except for Lancastrians – that was an even more despicable breed. Charley's bigoted father complained and whinged about everything Peter had done or said. Helen, who was obviously terrified of the old bully, remained seated saying nothing; she just nodded agreement with David and served the food, until with a dismissive gesture he indicated that it was time to clear away the debris. Helen meekly obeying the demand without question.

After three hours of torture it was time to leave, so pretending that they had enjoyed themselves Peter and Charley departed, their goodbyes being totally ignored by David. With relief they embarked on the journey home. Charley's was most apologetic about her father's behaviour, correctly calling him ignorant and self-centred. Peter felt tired and stressed by the whole affair, and asked Charley if she wanted to stop at a hotel for the night as driving at in the dark, in a strange car, was proving difficult for him. She agreed that it would be sensible, so they started looking for somewhere to stay. They were fortunate, finding some suitable accommodation at a pub in Ilkeston just north of

Nottingham. It was almost six o'clock when they finished booking in and paying for the room. They were hungry and they sat in the bar and shared a bottle of wine while they waited for the food service to start. Peter was still upset about the meeting with Charley's parents, wishing that he had been more proactive when dealing with the rudeness of her father, feeling as though he had condoned the old man's attitude to women by not complaining about it.

At seven the couple sat down to eat their meal, and were on a second bottle of wine. Peter's tongue had been loosened by the surfeit of alcohol, suddenly and amid the discussion of the day's events. Out of the blue, Peter announced that he was in love with Charley, to which she responded that it was about time, as she loved him back and she wanted to marry him. Aided by the wine, Peter's head swirled with happiness tinged with disbelief, he had never been so close to anyone before, and had only dreamed of getting married to such a beautiful and loving girl. "Do you really mean it?" he asked not being able to believe his luck.

"Yes, I mean it! I fell in love with you when I saw struggling to swallow your smoked salmon, that first night at the Greyhound." Her reply took his mind back to that very same evening, when their eyes met in the bar, and he had felt so awkward.

"I didn't sleep that night, it was all your fault. I couldn't get you out of my head, I wanted to marry you there and then." Without finishing the meal, she took his quaking hand, led him out of the dining room, upstairs, into the room, to consummate the engagement several times.

They had a quiet February wedding, attended by only a few people, three colleagues from Charley's work, half a dozen of her school friends, Minnie and Jasmine and Peter's younger brother William were all of the congregation. Unfortunately James was away with Michael, working abroad, somewhere in Venezuela and couldn't be there. Although Peter had offered to pay for all the expenses, Charley's father had forbidden her mother from turning up, and as normal she obeyed her tyrannical husband, without question. Pat was there as Peter's best man and Brian, being the only other available male, was bestowed the honour of giving the bride away. The ceremony was conducted at a small Saxon church near to The Greyhound, the lovers' favourite spot, and where they first met.

After the ceremony the company all went back to the hotel for the reception and to a meal of wild smoked salmon followed by seared venison. From that day in, their married life was blissfully happy, with Charley's help and plenty of spare money, Peter bought a lovely house near Haslemere in Surrey, and the couple set out decorating and furnishing it to suit their personal taste. At last Peter was feeling as though he had become a part of the human race, and no longer sought secure places to hide away and study in; his lovely soul mate had breathed new life into him and saved him from spiralling into the life of a hermit.

One evening in June Charley returned home from work later than normal. Recently she had been acting slightly strangely, and although she had reassured him that nothing was wrong, Peter was worrying a little about her, innocently wondering why she seemed different. On hearing her return, as was usual, he got up from his chair, intending to put the kettle on so he could make her a welcome cup of tea. Without bothering to take her jacket off she ran into the room where Peter had been sitting and working on some financial projections; racing up to him, she flung herself into his arms and screamed excitedly: "I'm pregnant!"

Peter stood, incapable of speech, his senses all befuddled, not knowing what to say. His lips trembled uncontrollably and then he started to cry tears of happiness, looking into his water-filled eyes Charley cried with him; their tears of joy ran from their eyes down their cheeks and mingled together, mixing on the newly polished floor.

The baby was due just after Christmas, Peter phoned all his family and friends to tell them his news; they were all overjoyed for the couple, especially Jasmine, who also wept happy tears when he told her. On the other hand Charley's parents, on hearing the about the forthcoming event, were angry; her father irrationally blamed Peter for stealing their twenty-six-year-old daughter away from them into the dangerous other world outside Yorkshire. The pregnancy went exactly according to plan, and according to the doctors was advancing normally, as was Charley's burgeoning waistline, that seemed to get larger with each morning. Charley was due to finish work on the fifth of October, and she looked forwards to the day when she was to become a full-time mother and homemaker. In the meantime, however, she and Peter were ecstatically happy busily preparing for the new arrival.

It was late in September. Peter had been absorbed all day in his work and was belatedly changing the date on an antique calendar, spending a little extra time appreciating the craftsmanship of the small ivory slithers that were engraved with the dates, his fingers dwelling on October, the month when he expected to be able to spend more time with his lovely wife, Charley – who was out, showing a potential customer a new property. As usual Peter wasn't interested in the time, and had no idea that it was getting late, when there was a loud knocking on the door. Answering it, he suspected that it was Charley, and she had forgotten her key. To his surprise there were two large, blue-uniformed police officers standing at the open door. Sombrely the men asked if they could come in. Peter let them in, his heart pounding uncontrollably in his chest, his sixth-sense making him feel uneasy about their reason for the visit. The taller of the two suggesting he should sit, hesitantly Peter obeyed, shaking, starting to fear the worst, and then the thunderbolt hit him: without showing any emotion the other policemen spoke, "It is with great sadness I'm here to inform you that a woman, we believe to be Mrs Charlotte Cahill, of this address, has been involved in an accident, and was pronounced dead at the scene, we are very sorry for your loss." Peter's knees failed him and he collapsed in a heap on the floor. He couldn't believe it, it couldn't be true, there must have been some kind of mistake. He knew she was still alive, he could feel it inside. Was it all real? How could it have happened, how could his beloved Charley possibly be dead, along with their unborn child and along with all their hopes and dreams for the future? Alas for Peter it was true, and deep in his heart he knew it, and also he knew, from that day on his sorry life would never be the same again.

The next week was the worst of Peter's life. Dutifully and without tears, he informed everyone who needed to know.

Jasmine and James came to stay to support their inconsolable shattered son, who was so recently the blissfully happy Peter. The lowest point came on the Tuesday when he was obliged to identify poor Charley's broken body which still showed the obvious bump that was their nameless unborn baby son.

The funeral took place at the same church where Peter and Charley were married only seven months before, conducted by the same vicar and attended by the same small congregation that were at the wedding. Charley's distraught parents stubbornly refused to come, and ignored James's personal pleadings for them to do so, her mother privately asking for Peter's forgiveness saying that it would be too much for the old man. So as her only family member, heartbroken and mentally shredded, Peter watched as the love of his life with his baby still in her battered womb were buried in a lonely, shaded spot underneath the massive branches of an ancient yew tree in the corner of the isolated churchyard. Helpless in his grief, unable to cry the tears he needed to, Peter stayed at the graveside for half an hour, trying to believe it was all untrue, expecting Charley to pop up laughing, pretending, playing a grizzly joke. Feeling that he needed to leave something of a personal nature with his one true love, he gently dropped his favourite book *One Thousand and One Arabian Nights* onto the coffin. With nothing more to be said or done, Jasmine led her Peter away. With a comforting arm wrapped around his waist, she ushered him to a waiting car, to help him pick up the pieces of his shattered life.

CHAPTER 9

2007

After the funeral Peter simply disappeared, not letting anyone know where he had gone; he had left everything behind, his two houses, his car, bankbooks, passport, all that he owned except for the clothes he stood up in, his warmest coat, his favourite shoes and his only comfort, the magnificent cherished copy of the Koran he had known since he could first talk. Everyone searched for him in vain; Michael and Minnie asked everybody they met, Pat and Brian handed out photographs to all their guests, while Jasmine and James cruised around his old haunts. They even advertised in the national newspapers all with no response. There was not a sign of Peter anywhere, he had just vaporised into thin air. Months went past without any sign of the missing Peter; there had been no attempts to withdraw any money from any of his accounts, he had completely vanished.

The truth was, Peter had suffered a total breakdown. he'd lost the will to live, and just wandered about aimlessly, going nowhere in particular, living wherever he rested his weary limbs. He had reverted to his old ways, of hiding away from the wicked outside world, skulking out of sight in doorways and derelict buildings, eating whatever was edible and available. Peter lost so much weight that his clothes now hung off his shrunken body like rags, and had developed a weary stoop and a shuffling gait, his damaged mind unable to repair itself. Peter rarely slept, all he ever saw when he closed his eyes was Charley's pale broken body lying in the mortuary, and the sad sight of the coffin going into the ground taking their future with it. Sometimes, when overtaken by weariness, Peter would occasionally sleep, only to wake himself up with his own involuntary sobbing. It should have been so different; he should be watching his baby grow alongside his beautiful wife, in their lovely new home. In his grief he never thought of Jasmine, James or the others, and was totally unaware of how his absence had affected them.

Peter presented a pitiful sight when people saw him, they would shrink away from him, assuming he would be either drunk or dangerous or both. Often teenage boys and sometimes even girls would throw things at him calling him a wino and worse. With no sense-of-purpose he just meandered around the country, travelling mostly at night, away from the public gaze, his eyes downcast so that anybody who happened to glance at him would not see the misery in his soul. Peter's unplanned wanderings eventually took him to Croydon, a town nine miles south of London. He didn't deliberately intend to go there, his feet just led him there. Finding himself a suitable shelter, in a derelict old warehouse on the outskirts of the town which he shared with some other homeless people. It was conveniently close to the centre for the inhabitants to go out and forage at nights, under the cover of darkness, and far enough away to be safe from marauding youths.

All the other lost souls, with whom he shared the makeshift home, tended to bury their sorrows into the hazy nether world created by copious amounts of cheap drink. Not so with Peter, who because of his place of birth and early years, generally avoided alcohol, and only imbibed a little very occasionally. He hated the effects of drink, having seen apparently normal people turn into monsters when they were under the influence of the demon drink.

One day, when Peter was on a foraging mission in the city centre, he was traversing along a particularly seedy alleyway, which happened to be another regular haunt for many of the city's down and outs, when he witnessed an organised gang of about six teenage boys attacking a group of three vagrants, who were sharing some bottles of cheap cider. The men were helplessly drunk, and the lads set about kicking the harmless trio. As was Peter's wont, he was lurking out of sight in the gloaming, and when he saw the assault his common decency took hold. Generally he was adverse to violence, but to save the powerless men from further harm he attacked the lads. Pat's self-defence lessons came into their own, and he felled the most aggressive youth with a single blow, quickly followed by a kick to the groin of a second. Seeing two of their best fighters so easily laid low by the shabbily dressed saviour, the rest took to their heels and fled the scene, leaving their fallen comrades to their fate at the hands of the ravening group of homeless people, who had been attracted there by the commotion. Attempting to remain anonymous, Peter slid away from the scene, back into the shadows to resume his mission, to find some food.

In the bigger picture, the community of outcasts were unable to understand Peter, his reluctance to drink, and his desire to avoid their company confused them, they accepted him, but they also were frightened of him. After the events that occurred in the alleyway, the incidence of violence towards vagrants almost disappeared and he had found unwanted fame amongst the motley community, when he so gallantly saw off the attackers. Peter refused to accept their plaudits, often turning down the offers of sharing drink or some such thing with them, preferring to be on his own and burying himself in any written matter that he could get his hands on. The others knew that he loved reading, and sometimes to show their gratitude there would be books or magazines mysteriously left at his chosen place of rest.

Eventually summer arrived after a very rainy May and June; Peter had been either wet or soaked for over six months, his lack of food and warmth, coupled with his permanently damp state had played havoc with his health. He had developed a twitch in his left eye, and had been suffering from a rattling cough since January. All his limbs ached, especially his poorly knees which desperately needed to feel the heat of the sun on them once again, with this in mind he found a suitable position out of the way on a grassy bank adjacent to the river Wandle, where he sat in the full sunshine, massaging his aching knees whilst reading and trying to understand the beloved copy of the Koran, given to him by his mother, and kept by him ever since he was a child. Peter was absorbed in a particularly obscure paragraph when apparently from nowhere, the friendly face of a quite elderly kind looking Muslim gentleman appeared peering over his shoulder, evidently attracted to the book.

"I noticed your copy of the Koran, it's a very beautiful copy," the man noted in slightly broken English.

Peter, feeling refreshed to be speaking to someone other than a drunkard, handed the book to the man for his inspection.

The fellow handled it reverently. "This is very valuable; may I ask where you got it from?"

He was clearly taken aback when Peter replied in an educated English accent.

"My mother gave it to me; it was a present to her from a sheik."

Deciding to test Peter's truthfulness, the man asked yet another question, this time in Arabic: "You are English and yet you read Arabic, where did you learn?"

Realising that it was a test, Peter replied back, also in Arabic. "I learned at my mother's knee, in Saudi Arabia. I am reading it, trying to understand the teachings of Islam."

The surprised man returned to speaking in English. "I may be able to help you there; I am an imam at the local Mosque," and then the man took a seat next to Peter and asked him as to where he was confused.

After a lengthy conversation, explaining some more salient points, the man, whom Peter had come to know as Imam Naseem Allam, got up to leave, promising that he could often be found there come rain or shine, at his favourite spot, there near the river, where he had his most private conversations with his God.

Taking up the kind offer Peter regularly met up with Naseem, who brought with him welcome, wholesome food to share during their discussions. Naseem was a moderate, and he taught the peaceful interpretation of the Koran, encouraging religious tolerance, wanting understanding between the different faiths, berating the firebrands who tried to whip up hatred towards non-believers. That whole summer they met, Peter telling the cleric all about his past, and the grief he had suffered when Charley was killed; it was all met with a sympathetic listening ear, giving him the solace he so desperately needed. Naseem explaining to Peter that it was all part of a bigger picture, and fate had led him on the path he was taking, calling it Allah's way. The debates were always quiet and informative, even on the occasions when the pair would discuss the Bible. Never did Naseem make any attempt to try and convert his pupil, he just did as he was asked, and that was to explain the deeper meaning of Islam. Their friendship grew, and their talks brought Peter out of his darkest despair into a lighter place, but still somewhere where it wasn't healthy to be.

The meetings continued until November until one day, when they had arranged to meet, Naseem failed to turn up at the appointed time, and Peter was worried, never before had his only friend let him down. Peter waited patiently until darkness had fallen before left the grassy bank; in despair he wended his disappointed and worried way back to his sleeping place, and tried to rest. Instead of sleeping he just lay awake fretting over the missing man, so as morning broke Peter made his way to the mosque where Naseem taught, and found a comfortable position, out of sight, waiting for a glimpse of his missing friend. During the morning several concerned looking groups of men gathered, and chatted in Arabic. From a very young age, when Jasmine used to read to him in virtual silence, Peter developed the ability to lip-read, putting the skill to good use, easily understanding the whispered conversations.

Apparently there had been a change at the top in the Mosque and Naseem had been brutally murdered in his bed five nights before. Several of the congregation suspected the involvement of Naseem's replacement, Imam Ul Haq, who had already installed a new radical regime in place of the old moderate one to take charge of the spiritual well-being of the attendees. Their concerned chatter reminded Peter of a time some weeks before Naseem confided in him and told him that he feared that some of the more disruptive acolytes of Islam, upset by his moderate tendencies, were attempting to overthrow the present regime at the Mosque, and a move was in the offing, but he was not aware of the severe nature of the change, and how it would affect him.

Interested in identifying the murderer of Naseem, Peter took residence in a small disused coal yard adjacent to the Mosque, where, from his vantage point, he could easily eavesdrop on the conversations that took place outside when the faithful had finished their prayers. After a week had passed he had only established that more than a few of the devotees suspected that the new imam was involved in the murder of Naseem, so Peter devised a plan to get closer to the members of the congregation. That night, when darkness had fallen Peter returned to the alleyway where some months before he rescued the vagrants from an organised gang of marauding young thugs, to call in the favour they owed him.

The homeless that lived there were pleased to see their estranged saviour, and gratefully informed him that they were still being left in peace. Peter wanted them to do something for him, and he asked if they were prepared to help him. After a brief meeting with all the sober ones they agreed that if they could, they would help him, so then Peter made his strange request. He needed some Arab clothing and a prayer mat urgently, and the only snag was that they had to be obtained from as far away from Croydon as possible, so that they wouldn't be recognised by any of the local Muslims. In return he promised that if he was in a position to help them again, he would. Without question they unanimously assented, saying that anything suitable they could find would be placed in the old warehouse, where Peter usually slept. Gladly they went about their task, pleased to have some real purpose in their lives. Peter was blindly unaware that, for the first time since Charley's death, he had regained some purpose in his own as well.

Three days had elapsed since his meeting with his homeless helpers before Peter decided to investigate to see if there were any clothes left for him. Making his way back to the place where he had lived for almost a year, Peter walked into his old home expecting no progress, but miraculously there to greet him was a neat pile of freshly laundered Arab garb, placed in the middle of a brand new prayer mat, a simple note informed him that it all came from a safe distance away, and was signed with a simple "thanks from us all." Selecting two suitable outfits, Peter placed them in carrier bags, hid the remainder of the clothes, rolled up the rug, tucked it under his arm and left to go about the rest of his unfinished business: to buy, with what little money he had saved, a nailbrush, a bar of soap, a razor and a pair of scissors.

Before dawn the next day he made his way to one of the local public conveniences, which he entered looking like the grubby vagrant that he had become. Once inside, he vigorously scrubbed and scoured himself from head to foot, to remove the ground in grime, washed and trimmed his hair and beard, shaved off his moustache, as many Muslim gentlemen do, and dressed in the recently acquired new clothes. Peter emerging refreshed and almost, but not quite completely clean and looking exactly like a follower of Islam, only his trusty battered brogues, and his remaining favourite book were all that was left of the sordid life the among the homeless.

Feeling somewhat transformed Peter made his way to the Mosque near to Croydon. He arrived just as a mullah was calling on the faithful to come and pray, as it was time for *Zohar*, the early afternoon prayer; Peter entered, removed his battered old shoes, ritually washed and joined the prayers, staying out of the way at the back, inwardly cursing his unsympathetic knees that creaked and groaned mercilessly during the lengthy bout of kneeling and standing during the supplications. After the devotions were over Peter mingled with the congregation in an anteroom. Apparently there were several newcomers and, when people asked him where he was from, he introduced himself with a name from his past, as Malik Atiq originally from Jeddah, but more recently he'd been living in Devises in Wiltshire. Peter spoke with an accent and they accepted him without suspicion. As he circulated among the gathering, he listened carefully to some of the conversations and attempted to lip-read some others, trying not to stare for too long as it might alert them to his intentions. For a week he regularly attended the Mosque and he had become no longer an object of their curiosity, nothing new was unearthed about the death of Naseem, but Peter had discovered that the attendees of the Mosque were much polarised in their opinion of Naseem's replacement, Imam Ali Ul Haq, a halal butcher with a newly purchased shop in Croydon. Some of the elders supported him, but most thought that his teachings were far too extreme for their taste. As one of the new regulars at the Mosque, Peter had been invited to attend a lesson that was going to be conducted after Friday prayers, by what the gossip suggested was going to be preached by a guest jihadist fighter, a long-time friend of Ul Haq's, who had fought against the Americans and the West anywhere he could in the whole of the Arabian Peninsula.

Friday arrived and Peter attended the special early afternoon prayers called *Juma'h,* after they were finished Imam Ul Haq got up to deliver the *Khutbah,* or the sermon. It started with a lengthy reading from the Koran, followed by the Imam's personal interpretation of the reading. At first the tempo was reasonably sedate, but as it went on the Imam became more excited, and started using inflammatory words calling America and its allies Zionist puppets, bent on the rape and destruction of Islam, saying that all who don't follow the teachings of the Prophet had spat at Islam, and their lives were forfeit, and it was the duty of each devout Muslim to fight the crusaders, and give up their lives in the cause. The Imam was mad with passion and he spat out the words with bulging eyes and imploring hands, eventually working himself up into a breathless frenzied finish before he sat down and the time came for the guest speaker to deliver his address.

The guest orator spoke with an Iraqi accent. His name was Abu Bakr, his speech was less animated but much more passionate as that of Ul Haq's, he implored the congregation, saying how the West was controlling the Muslim world, causing war and poverty, creating fatherless children and grieving widows.

How Jews had been plotting with the Americans against true believers. He said the perpetrators that brought down the twin towers in New York were martyrs that would live in bliss for eternity. He called Christianity a plague used as a tool by the Jews against the teachings of Islam. He ended by openly asking for volunteers to join the Muslim brotherhood that are fighting against tyranny in other parts of the world, asking for heroes to spill their blood in the cause, pleading for Muslims of all persuasions to unite, forgetting their differences and join his new group he called ISIS, "The Islamic State of Iran and Syria", dedicated to improving relations between the Sunni and the Shi'as and the formation of a giant fundamentalist Muslim state encompassing the whole of the northern Arabian Peninsula, strong enough to challenge Israel and the West, to be governed by clerics under the strict auspices of sharia law.

Abu Bakr's impassioned speech disturbed Peter deeply, causing his main concerns to suddenly shift from the cause of Naseem's death, to fears that there was a real threat to national security coming from the Mosque.

Although not obliged to attend the prayers and sermons, some women were there, and joined the gathering in the anteroom afterwards. The content of the speeches fragmented the assembly, most just wanted to live normal peaceful lives and didn't want to be associated with the extreme views of the clerics; some however were sympathetic with the speakers, and supported their opinions. One such was a woman, sitting on an electric mobility scooter, and clad from head to foot in a black niqab was expounding the virtues of the speeches, calling for Christian blood to be spilled, but when she noticed Peter, she stopped mid sentence and drove directly over to question him, "Do I know you? You seem familiar." Peter shrugged and replied, "No! I don't think so." He couldn't see who she was anyway, so he thought no more about it; she went away puzzled and wondering where she might have seen the young man before.

Over the next few weeks Peter suffered as many sessions at the Mosque as possible, the repetitive praying was playing havoc with his damaged knees, and it was to no avail as nothing new came to light about Naseem's murder. Yet Peter knew that he had been removed because of his moderate views, and to him it was certain that Ul Haq was complicit in his death. Different guests were regularly invited to speak on Fridays; their sermons were getting more and more radical, many of the young men who listened were becoming polluted and influenced by the vile inflammatory rantings, and started to openly offer up their lives, being promised all their hearts' desires in Paradise.

During his visits, Peter had noticed that many of the old moderate regulars at the Mosque were becoming noticeable by their absence and new faces were joining the congregation in their place, mostly originating from warmer climes, their freshly roasted faces and hands betraying their place of origin. Several could only speak Arabic, and Peter recognised some of the regional Middle Eastern dialects including both Iraqi and Iranian.

After the most recent Friday's *Khutbah* as usual the assembly gathered in the anteroom. The mystery wheelchair-bound woman was there, shrieking encouragement to the young men, exhorting them to leave the comfort of homes and to take up arms, swearing that if she was able to she would offer her life in the cause. Generally they ignored her but, elsewhere in the room, one of the firebrand clerics was taking note and wondering if she could be of any use to him. Peter was walking past her, trying not to catch her eye, when she suddenly drove her vehicle directly across his path and stopped him in his tracks; she peered up at him and asked, "What is your name?" Without pause he replied with the name he now used in the Mosque, "Malik Atiq."

"Where are you from?"

He answered quickly, "Jeddah, in Saudi Arabia, why do you want to know?"

Instantly she asked him another quick-fire question. "Were you born there?"

Peter quickly realised that he was being grilled by the unknown vile woman and he answered firmly, "Yes!"

"When?"

Peter was thinking fast, guessing where the questioning was going bearing in mind that he looked very much like James.

"Nineteen seventy-eight!"

He lied, imagining that the years' privations probably made him look older than he actually was. She raised her voice and declared, "That's it, I've got it, you're one of James's bastards!"

"Who's James?" Peter asked innocently.

"My ex-husband that's who, you're a bastard's bastard, that's what you are!" Peter was looking through the slit in her veil into her glaring bloodshot maddened eyes when he realised that the dreadful woman was in fact his real mother, the woman who had hated his very existence ever since he was born.

As quickly as he could without attracting too much attention, Peter left the Mosque, his heart was pounding and his stomach

227

was in a knot, he felt sick, his thoughts turned to the love he always felt from Jasmine, James and the others. All of a sudden he started to wonder how they were, how they were handling his disappearance, punishing himself for being so selfish, and for his irrational behaviour. Realising how it must be affecting their lives, he needed to speak to them urgently, frantic to let them know that he was alive and well.

As fast as his aching knees could carry him Peter went in search of a telephone kiosk. Shamefully all of the ones that accepted cash had been vandalised, and the rest were card only, so Peter lurked by one hoping to beg the use of a card. Four times his appeals were rejected, being subjected to racial abuse twice, and he became very desperate, when aid came from an unexpected source: an elderly Jewish gentleman, noticing his anguish, approached Peter and offered him the use of his phone card, apologising repeatedly because there was very little credit left on it. The gift was more amazing considering that Peter was dressed as an Arab, the sworn enemies of the Jews.

Hurriedly and very carefully Peter dialled his father's home number, not wanting to make a mistake and waste some of the precious credit left on the card. Peter's sad heart leapt with joy when he heard the lovely Jasmine's voice answering; overcome with emotion, she cried with relief when she heard it was at last her darling boy. Hushing her to silence, Peter garbled his message, explaining the reason for his haste; he told Jasmine exactly where he was so that she could come and get him, adding that she may find his appearance peculiar when she did, and was about to give the reason when the card ran out. Within the hour a taxi turned up for Peter. Everything changed so quickly, in a dream he got in it and travelled, in total silence, the short distance to Whitton. The cabbie tried several times to make polite conversation with his passenger, giving up his futile efforts with a resigned shrug. Fed up with being ignored by Peter who was worrying about what to say to Jasmine, finding it difficult to put the reasons for his actions into words.

Peter arrived at six in the evening; it was over halfway through September and already getting dark, the anxiously excited Jasmine was waiting outside in the cold, hopping from one foot from the other, trying to keep warm when the taxi drew up. Jasmine threw herself at her errant stepson as soon as he alighted from the cab and kissed him repeatedly, crooning with joy and happiness at the sight of him. Without so much as a goodbye, the taxi driver left without any demand for money, prompting Peter to assume that he had already been paid by Jasmine who dragged the overwrought Peter into the house, sat him down and fed him a hot meal that she had hurriedly prepared in readiness for his arrival. All the time that he was eating, she fired questions at him. Peter responded by telling her the whole sorry tale, starting with his worry that he thought he had gone temporarily mad like his birth mother was. He then told her about his unplanned clash with Sue, and gave the reason for his mode of dress. Having heard enough for one night, Jasmine poured him a hot bath, handed him some lovely fluffy soft towels, and pushed him into the steamy bathroom. where he lay in the water and soaked to remove the deepest of the ingrained, most stubborn grime.

With great pleasure Peter went to sleep in his young brother's bed, vacated while William was away at boarding school. For the first time since just before Charley's funeral, he experienced the comfort of clean fresh sheets, and after a long restful night he woke refreshed, leaving all the madness of grief back in the old warehouse that was his home for so long. The always practical Jasmine had kept some of Peter's clothes handy, in anticipation and hope of his return. In the morning after his ablutions Peter put on an outfit she had laid out for him, and went down to breakfast, where Jasmine was waiting for him. When she saw him she descended into a fit of giggles, pointing out that the clothes that fitted him so well before now hung loosely draped over his skinny frame. Peter looked down at his baggy attire and for the first time since the tragedy he laughed, and laughed loudly.

James returned two days later, coming home from his mission early to be reunited with his son, as always accompanied by the ever-faithful Michael who was still in his service. James was horror-struck when he saw Peter, the stress and strain of all his travails had taken its toll on his features, which now were etched with the lines of the sorrow obtained during his self-imposed exile, along with the slight twitch, that stayed with him for the rest of his life. Peter spent time relating the entire tale to his father, missing nothing out, dwelling on his experiences at the Mosque, talking fondly about his meetings with Naseem, how he suspected that the regime change led to his murder, his fears for the young corruptible men becoming influenced by the inflammatory sermons. Finishing, Peter told of the unexpected meeting with Sue, which caused the shock that shook him out of his depression.

James was extremely interested in the events at the Mosque, telling Peter that there was a current general alert concerning the influx of known extremists being smuggled into the country, and there was intelligence of plans afoot to organise a major terrorist event somewhere in Great Britain. The main problem that the security services were suffering from was the lack of any clue as to what the intended target might be. Having listened to James's concerns, Peter thought it would be prudent to tell his father the gist of the sermons, adding his opinion that seemed like a recruitment drive, and the young and impressionable were flocking to sign up to the cause. James listened carefully to Peter's assumptions, and asked if he would mind meeting with his bosses to tell them about his experiences, warning him to be careful as they were grumpy, very old-fashioned men who were a law unto themselves. He also told Peter of his concern that he probably wasn't ready to see them but it was imperative for the country to get them to listen, they were likely to be tough on him, and he didn't want him upset, but it was necessary for national security that they knew about the events in the Mosque, so, not really thinking about it, Peter agreed to attend.

CHAPTER 10

Two days after the homecoming, James took Peter to small premises off Jermyn Street in central London, to meet with two of James's superiors. The front office was very plain and old-fashioned which pretended to deal in bloodstock, and the walls were covered with pictures of racehorses past and present, and racks of dusty stud books graced a colossal bookcase behind a desk at the front. Sitting at the cluttered desk and sipping a cup of tea was an attractive middle-aged, dark-haired woman James referred to as Lou. Barely looking up from her drink, she pointed at a large oak-panelled door and indicated for them to go in, telling James that they were waiting for him. James opened the door with a shrill un-oiled squeak, and they both entered an equally old-fashioned room and sat silently at a neatly arranged huge desk, opposite two grumpy-looking grey-headed men that were both considerably older than James. Peter felt a little nervous while he waited for the starchy pair to convene the interview, and started fidgeting in his chair.

Attracted by his discomfort one of the men peered over a pair of half-moon spectacles cleared his throat and spoke to him. "Hello, I'm John and this is Graham. James has told us your story, but we would like to hear it from you."

Obeying, Peter duly recited the whole lengthy tale back to the pair, omitting nothing. John listened, leaning forward watching him very closely taking everything in, unquestioning and absorbed until the story was completed. Meanwhile Graham casually took notes, seeming utterly disinterested in the saga, occasionally bothering to take the time to look up from his writing to study scrawny-looking Peter.

For the whole time, James remained seated quietly next to his son taking it all in, saying and offering nothing other than moral support for Peter. Graham sounded bored by it all and, yawning overtly, suggested that it was time for a coffee break before they continued – and as if by magic Lou brought in four mugs, a pot of lovely-smelling coffee and a plate of Rich Tea biscuits. During the break the atmosphere became much more relaxed and the bosses sat and excitedly chatted about their high profile involvement in the London mayoral elections on 1 May. When the refreshments were finished, the business resumed, this time both men fired questions at Peter, not allowing him time to think, trying to assess his reliability, occasionally trying to trip him up. Yet Peter answered everything they asked as accurately and honestly as he could, and after a full hour's grilling John declared that he was satisfied that Peter was telling the truth. Agreeing, Graham apologised to James, saying that they had to be sure.

After the interview was over, John asked James and Peter to leave the office for a short period while they had a brief chat about the situation, Graham opened another massive oak door leading into a side room and asked them to enter and wait until they were called back. A long time elapsed before they were summoned back into the room with John and Graham. Retaking their seats,

John spoke directly to Peter; "Are you willing to go back to the Mosque and be our eyes and ears? We don't have anyone on the inside and we need one."

Peter thought for ten seconds and answered, "Yes, sir! If I can help you I will."

Scratching his shaven chin, Graham spoke again to warn Peter of what he was undertaking. "Understand well, it might be dangerous. If these men are what you think they are, we need to stop them."

"I've seen quite a lot of danger, sir."

"So we understand, we've heard a lot about you. Some very good men have vouched for you, and you come highly recommended."

Once again, Lou magically entered the room without being summoned, this time complete with a large sheaf of papers for Peter to read. Leaning over the seated Peter, she allowed her breast to rest on his shoulder as she pointed to some relevant paragraphs, indicating where he needed to sign his name. Accidently pressing her breast a little harder into his back and using her most seductive voice, she merely said, "Welcome to the club, sweetie. I've given you a new name. I have called you Burmese, like the cat, remember, Burmese! You only need it when you're contacting us, but don't forget it, you might need it, dear."

The car ride back to Whitton was quite interesting; James was forthcoming and candid with Peter, John was the head of the department, Graham was his deputy, he considered them both old-fashioned and fairly useless, but they always had the final say. James was Peter's immediate boss, and Peter had to report directly to him with any information. Peter would receive a salary, along with expenses as officially he was now a civil servant with the rank of executive officer.

Taken somewhat aback, he looked at James with amazement. "I get paid?"

James replied roguishly, "Yes, you're in now, Burmese! You're one of us, a full-blown clandestine operative; you signed the Official Secrets Act, and for want of better terms, you're a spy!"

"Why Burmese? And what exactly do I do, father?" Peter was inquisitive. "In fact, how do I know what to do?"

"Like everything here, it's all so very old-fashioned, I know it's stupid but I'm called Abyssinia, its Lou's idea, she's much more important than you think and she loves cats, all our new call signs are all breeds of cat. I know it's ridiculous! The call signs used to be famous ships, John used to be Golden Hind, Graham was Dreadnought I was Argo, but Lou thought they needed changing, so as head of internal security she changed them to cats." Peter looked completely dumbfounded, thinking it was like something out of an Ian Fleming novel. James carried on with his explanation, "And just do what you've already been doing, blending in, listening, make MENTAL notes, nothing written, and when you can, you report straight back to me!"

Peter felt very pleased with himself, "I'm glad I get paid, at the moment I haven't got a bean!"

James replied to Peter's latest statement with incredulity, "Haven't got a bean? You've got thousands! The investments you made before Charley's..." Thinking that he was about to put his foot in it, James stopped in mid-sentence, thinking how to couch his words carefully so as not to remind Peter of Charley and unduly upset him. "The investments you made before the accident have all, except one, performed brilliantly. I've rented out both your houses for you, and you, my boy, are sitting on a fortune!"

Peter's thoughts drifted back to happier days. "I still miss her so much, I really loved her," he declared with the hint of tears in his eyes. "I would have been a dad by now!" Peter felt himself drifting into a fit of depression, so suddenly, and very deliberately, he snapped himself out of his melancholy.

"Which investment didn't perform well?" he asked, pulling himself together.

"The plastics firm Nylorile, the managing director is sunning himself on a beach somewhere in the Greek islands and two of the board members are inside serving a six-year stretch." The touch of humour making them both laugh, breaking the spell.

On returning home James and Peter closeted themselves in the office and went through all Peter's forsaken paperwork, calculating and adding up columns of figures, going through his unopened bank statements, and finally arriving at a figure that had a long row of digits.

"Wow! That's a lot of money," Peter exclaimed barely being able to believe his eyes. James was also amazed when the final total was reckoned up. "You've got more than me, and I'm rich!" They left the office together laughing, with their arms over each other's shoulders, father and son, closer now than they had ever been in their whole lives. When Jasmine saw them, she clasped her arms around them both, happy, and knowing that Peter was at last healed. After their evening meal was finished they sat and watched television for a while until, finding the programmes boring, they retired early to bed. Peter lay warm and snug, musing on what might have been, and what tomorrow would bring. In the next room Jasmine and James quietly made love, as usual.

When Friday came Peter turned up at the Mosque. There was no apparent change in him except he was better fed, cleaner and had new shoes, inside; however, he was very different. He was happy, the weight of despair and loneliness had been lifted off his scrawny shoulders, and the telltale lines in his face were slightly less obvious. It was a different Peter who attended the normal prayers, kneeling and then standing, and facing the *Qiblah*, the plaque in the wall that indicated the direction of Mecca. When they had finished their devotions Imam Ul Haq stood up to deliver his sermon. As usual he delivered his acerbic message with gusto, but the direction of his hate had temporarily changed direction. Instead of berating anything associated with Western civilisation, he turned his attack on the moderates who frequented the Mosque, referring to them as the traitors in our bosom, and slaves to America, imploring the faithful to root out and destroy the poisonous weeds that polluted the choice seedlings planted by Allah.

Over the next few Fridays the topic stayed much the same, pointedly making the old guard feel unwelcome and unwanted. The Mosque had been subtly, but surely usurped by the new regime, the old voice of reason and integration had disappeared and the voice of intolerance and segregation was now the norm. After the sermons Peter noticed that the faces of the members who voiced their moderate views had all but gone, replaced by new faces, those of younger men, who freely expressed their radical opinions, and were prepared to threaten any who objected to their ideas. Peter made a decision to appear to support the new regime, rather than to alienate himself from them, and therefore become less able to glean information that might be of use to his father. He pretended that the preaching had swayed him towards the radicals, and voiced his support for them. His quick brain and swiftness of thought aided him, and before long he had gained their trust, and they allowed him to listen to some of the more inflammatory sermons. Peter had become generally accepted by the nucleus of the Mosque, and it became obvious to him that they were secretly planning some form of subversion, but the meetings of the inner circle were always held behind locked doors away from prying ears and eyes, making it impossible to find out more.

Peter was becoming frustrated by his inability to find out their intentions, and left always feeling as though he was not able to do his job properly. On the next meeting with his father he voiced his doubts. James was very understanding and advised his fretting son, telling him to be patient, to stay watching and waiting, reminding him that the more people involved and the closer it got to the event the more likely it was that they would slip up, so feeling buoyed by the conversation Peter returned to go about his business.

It was night time so Peter decided to make a detour and catch up with his old associates who lived in the alley near to the deserted warehouse. It was cold so he took some blankets, whisky and several parcels of freshly bought fish and chips to the old meeting place in the alleyway. To his relief there were several familiar grubby faces glaring at him, not able to recognise Peter clad in the unfamiliar Arab garb, they stayed put, gazing from their hiding places. To gain their confidence he placed the whisky down on the pavement, reassuringly opening it and, taking a sip, he then unwrapped some of the food causing the unmistakable smell of vinegary fish and chips to waft around the street. No more convincing was necessary; a shadowy figure glided out of the darkness, and approached the anonymous "Good Samaritan." Peter recognised him straight away as one of one of the people that he asked for help; he didn't know his name, so he just thanked him for the clothes and the prayer mat. The man instantly realised who Peter actually was and, within seconds, he beckoned to the others that were lurking out of sight. In all, six individuals swooped out from nowhere and descended on the food like hungry hyenas. It was eaten in no time, and they sat with Peter while they washed down the food with warming whisky. Giving them the blankets, he got up to depart, thanking them once again for their past help.

As Peter was leaving he had an idea. They had helped him before without question, and he wondered to himself if they would be willing or able to help him again. They were still passing round the half empty bottle, and taking it in turns to swig the liquor from it, when Peter resumed his position and sat back down with them asking if they were prepared to help him again. At first the group just sat and looked at each other, when the man Peter spoke to earlier volunteered to act as spokesman. Their self-appointed leader introduced himself as Simon; it was hard to tell his age, as he was buried in layers of foul-smelling clothes, and had a woolly hat pulled low down over his brow. He spoke well but was difficult to understand because he had a thick Northumberland accent. Peter wanted to strike a deal with

Simon, first asking him to speak very slowly so that he could understand him, and after struggling through a brief conversation it was agreed, A bargain had been struck. The vagrants would secretly watch the homes of the ringleaders of the Mosque in return for regular Thursday visits from Peter, with food, drink and other gifts. Peter was very pleased with himself, he had managed to recruit an invisible team of trustworthy helpers that nobody notices or even cares about.

Everything was relatively quiet at the Mosque. Friday's sermons had taken on less aggressive tones, but the talk afterwards was still of retribution for the rape of Islam, a term regularly used by Imam Ul Haq. The new faces were still arriving in dribs and drabs, and his mother still was full of hatred, berating herself for being an old crippled woman, whose infirmity prevented her from being able to take up the gage and act in the name of Islam. Saying that she and others like her relied on the young men to protect them from the evil that was the Western world and its plans to overthrow the righteous followers of the Prophet Mohammed.

Sue had adopted the Islamic pseudonym Adeeva, ironically the Muslim female name meaning pleasant and gentle. Peter's latest unplanned meeting with her happened when she skidded her mobility scooter across his path, glared at him evilly and spoke, "Hello bastard of a bastard!" Peter tried to ignore her, and walk around her, but she just cleverly repositioned her scooter stopping him getting away from her, "You've got a brother you know! Another James bastard, and the son of a black-haired witch!" Peter looked at her doubtfully, not wanting to show his hand, "Have I indeed, what's his name, then?"

"It's Ibrahim, and the witch deserted him at birth, he was brought up by holy men in Medina."

"Your imagining things, my father died in Jeddah before I was born!" Peter wanted to know more so he flattered Sue by feigning personal interest.

"How do you know these things?"

"I have letters from the witch, sent to me by mistake."

Leaning close, Peter peered through the eye slit in her veil, "I don't believe you, you're lying, prove it if you can!" Having heard enough, Peter turned on his heels and walked away, leaving Sue wallowing in her morass of malice, fuelled by self-pity.

The next week Peter followed the same routine, late on the Thursday night he visited the alley where his friends and allies lived. This time he gave them some kebabs he had just bought from a local takeaway, along with some bananas and more whisky. They devoured their repast sitting at a table Simon had hastily cobbled together from an old pallet and some crates, the sight bringing back some distant memories of his old den to Peter who sat with them, allowing them first to finish their meal and drain the bottles, before he then asked if they had any news for him. Simon, who was still the agreed spokesman for the group, apologetically told Peter that nothing of note had occurred, except for Ul Haq, who had many all-night meetings at his house with dodgy-looking foreigners. Peter felt satisfied with their information and promised to return the next Thursday, asking what food and gifts they wanted him to bring, and then, having taken some rather odd orders, he left.

Peter made his way back to a pokey little bedsit in a seedy part of Croydon that James had acquired to use as temporary base during the investigations; he retired to the uncomfortable bed in its musty-smelling room musing on what could possibly happen next. Eventually Peter drifted into a fitful light sleep, beset with visions of his poor dead Charley, ranting clerics, but most of all, his hateful and venomous mother. Laying in bed between the bouts of rest, Peter started to wonder if madness ran in families; his recent nervous breakdown was foremost in his mind, worrying that he might be destined to lose his sanity, as he suspected that his mother had. Early Friday morning an annoying vociferous blackbird heralded the dawn, rousing Peter from his semi-slumber and breaking his melancholy, opening the curtains he gazed out on a beautiful February day. A hint of early spring was in the air, the birds were happy. Peter felt glad to be alive, so he decided to find the spot where he had so often met up to sit with Naseem and read the Koran together.

Early in the afternoon Peter enjoyed his walk to the Mosque. Everybody seemed uplifted by the lovely day, and there was a sort of bustle as they went about their business, it seemed as though the shackles of winter were at last broken, and there was a general lightness of spirit. Peter entered the Mosque still buoyed by the feelings that he had just experienced on his way there; however they were destined to be very short lived, as the atmosphere in the building was oppressive with expectancy. There were many more people than usual, and the normal buzz of voices before prayers was non-existent. After the ritual ablutions, the congregation squeezed into the prayer room, faced the *Qiblah,* and made their supplications to Allah, standing and kneeling in cycles, exhorting the greatness of God, and finally wishing for peace to be with all in the room. When the formal praying was finished, the time came for the sermons to start. At first Ul Haq stood up and read some passages from the Koran, and finished unusually without further comment.

Shortly after the sermon was completed, a one-eyed, handless cleric stood up to speak, his presence being greeted with general acclaim, and, waving his imaginary limbs to silence the congregation, he prepared to start. Satisfied that the gathering was silent and ready to listen, he started his speech. He opened his oration by quietly explaining how he had sacrificed his hands in the holy war against America. He told the assembly that they would be waiting to reunite with him in paradise where all the martyrs of Islam would be waiting to greet those lost in their gallant cause, how their places in paradise would be assured if they take up the fight. As he was speaking he raised his voice slightly with each sentence, expertly exciting the listeners and starting to whip up their fervour. Calling the Americans cowardly baby killers, saying how they bombed schools, pointing with a handless arm to a poster of maimed dead children to reinforce his statement. Waving his stumps about wildly he referred to Britain as supporters of Jews, who wanted to overthrow the Muslim world. In his ranting, he called for the British Royal Family and the government to be attacked and killed while they slept in their beds. Ratcheting up the rhetoric, his sermon started to reach the climax that he had been carefully building it up to. This came in the form of a parade of volunteers, all prepared to swear before Allah, and witnessed by the congregation, to offer up their lives in search for justice for Islam. In total, six men and two women were ushered to the front of the room and, to Peter's horror, his mother was one of them, at the front on her motorised scooter, dressed from head to foot in her black niqab, apparently ready to give up her sorry unhappy life for her adopted cause. In turn they each swore their oaths, first to the Imams, and then the onlookers, stating that they were willing to become human weapons to be used for the greater good of Islam. Individually they were greeted with riotous applause, and were loudly blessed in turn by each of the clerics. The whole frenzied crowd of devotees spontaneously started chanting, "Death to the crusaders!" Amid the boiling pot of hate and blood lust the meeting came to a clamorous close.

During the aftermath the anteroom Peter's mother approached him; once again she drove her little vehicle up to him, nearly parking it on his foot. She looked at him, and he could feel the air of smugness about her.

"You wanted proof, here's proof," she declared, scrabbling in a bag and producing an old crumpled envelope.

Peter recognised the writing instantly, it was Jasmine's; she handed him the note to read, it was addressed to Ibrahim. In the letter she was asking Ibrahim to come home and join the family, offering to pay his expenses, pleading with him to answer her phone calls, begging him to forgive her and James for sending him away. It ended with the words, "your loving Mother" and it was signed Jasmine, spelled the Arab way with a Y. "Proof enough? That's the James who is your father, you look exactly fucking like him, and Ibrahim is another of James's bastard sons, your brother, and he's coming here to meet me, we have a lot in common."

Satisfied that she'd upset Peter enough for one day, with a little laugh of victory, Sue spun her small vehicle around and darted off to create mayhem somewhere else. Sadly Peter made his way back to his bed sit feeling slightly depressed, the preceding events giving him much to think about. He worried that his estranged mother in her madness was going to do something heroically stupid in the name of a false cause. He also worried that his half-brother, the erstwhile cot mate, would arrive and recognise him as little Peter, the one-time object of his bullying, and focus of all his childhood hatred. The despair in Jasmine's letter upset him, he knew how hurt she must have felt when Ibrahim refused to contact her and rejected her efforts to reunite the family. Weary and overawed by the revelations he traipsed his way back to the temporary home and, once again, he struggled with his fertile imagination and slept poorly.

All that night the horrors visited Peter, making the smallest problem lose perspective to become all consuming and distorted. Eventually after tossing and turning for hours he managed to find sleep, until his noisy little friend decided to sound reveille with whistles and chirps, snapping Peter out of his hard-found rest, awakening him to face the day. On Saturday morning he went back to Whitton to join his family for the weekend and to report his findings directly to James. As he turned down the side street to where James lived with Jasmine, he met his old friend Bob, who appeared totally unfazed, if not somewhat curious and slightly bemused, by Peter's strange new appearance, but still he gave Peter a warm-hearted greeting, disguised behind a lengthy moan about the harshness of the winter, making him laugh, knowing that despite the old man's apparent grumpiness, inside he really was pleased to him once more.

Jasmine was out shopping when Peter arrived in the house and had plenty of time to fill James in on the events that occurred in the Mosque, telling James about the letter that Sue had mysteriously acquired, and her willingness to sacrifice herself. He also told James about the impending visit from Ibrahim at Sue's behest, offering the opinion that she had possibly encouraged him to join the Mosque and act as an insurgent. When Jasmine came home, she was clearly very pleased to see Peter and, wrapping her arms around him, she gave him a motherly big kiss, telling him that he looked exhausted and should rest. In fact he was absolutely worn out, and he accepted the offer and took to his brother's bed and went to sleep, enjoying the peace and security of somewhere he at last could call home. For once he dreamed pleasant dreams; Charley and Jasmine were in them cooing over a cherubic baby reading his cherished copy of *One Thousand and One Nights,* Mr Burrell was with his wife tending a lovely garden full of glaringly bright flowers. Peter slept deeply for over six hours and woke up refreshed, awakened by the smell of dinner, that was ready to be served.

They all sat around the dinner table enjoying their food. When James told Jasmine about the events that Peter had witnessed at the Mosque, including the expected arrival of Ibrahim, she nearly spat her food out. "What? Here in England?" she blurted out, almost choking on a piece of unchewed potato.

Peter and James were surprised by her reaction. However, it was James who answered for them both, admitting some guilt. "Yes, Sue stole your letter to him, when I sent her Ibrahim's allowance by mistake, apparently she's been writing to him."

Peter butted in. "She told me that they had a lot in common, and she invited him to join her." James carried on speaking directly to Jasmine:

"I think she wants to get back at you, and the scheming bitch is prepared to use Ibrahim to hurt you!" He turned to Peter. "I'm sorry, I know she's your mother, but she is evil!" Peter replied reinforcing what his father had just told him, "I've looked in her eyes, and I've seen the evil. I think she's quite mad, she lies to me all the time, and she calls Jasmine a witch, and you a bastard!" James concluded the conversation stating the obvious. "Be careful. She's a very dangerous woman; she can turn on you in a heartbeat."

Peter attended the Mosque every day the next week, telling people that he was on holiday from work and wanted the time to catch up with his devotions. Really he wanted to maintain a close eye on the proceedings, so he turned up at most of the five daily prayer sessions each day except for Thursday, which he needed to enable him to keep his tryst with his vagrant friends. He discovered nothing new during the time spent getting up and down, on and off his poor aching knees; in fact the attendance during the non-holy days was poor, and the imams toned down their sermons, storing up their venom for Fridays when the Mosque was more likely to be packed with eager, more receptive listeners.

Night time arrived and Peter made his way to the meeting place loaded with the old selection of supplies ordered by his homeless friends. To his surprise there was no reception committee to greet him and his gifts. He expectantly walked up and down the alleyway twice before a meek little voice called him over. Obeying the summons and entered into one of the more derelict buildings, too inadequately weatherproof to be inhabited by anyone. A sorry sight met his eyes: the ringleader Simon was laying on a stack of damp cardboard, being tended by his second in command Isaac. He Groaning miserably at each touch; a fresh facial wound, which was still bleeding, and several bruises appeared to be the reason for his discomfort. Peter knelt at his side to find out what had occurred. Mustering his strength, Simon told him everything that had happened. Half an hour before Peter arrived, the little group had gathered to meet with him; they were waiting as normal when a gang, probably the same one as before attacked them, calling them scum and saying people like them weren't welcome on their patch. Simon stood up to them as he saw Peter do and received a kicking for his troubles. Happy that they had inflicted enough pain on their victim, the gang left; not, however, without first setting fire to the makeshift table beforehand and burning what there was of their property, promising to return the next week to make sure that they had gone. Handing out the supplies, Peter swore to return on Saturday with some replacements for their lost gear. Struggling with his bruised mouth, Simon attempted to eat the prawn curry and rice that Peter had brought as part of the deal, when he remembered that he had some news about the people they were charged to watch. Hampered by his injuries, Simon spoke unusually slowly:

"There are lots of comings and goings. Four Arab-looking men in a dark transit van are going round at the dead of night," he explained whilst manipulating his aching jaw. "They're going to either Ul Haq's house or the woman's. They're unloading bags and boxes, and the lights are left on so I guess they are working through the night." Simon winced as he took a stinging draught of whisky to wash down his meal. "One more thing, she's got a foreign visitor staying with her." Peter was happy that Simon's injuries weren't life threatening, and he had emerged safely from his state of shock, so he departed taking the time to remind Simon and Isaac to be there with the others on Saturday.

The time soon came round to return to the Mosque for Friday lunchtime prayers. Peter's sleep was uninterrupted because the bleak Friday morning discouraged the birds from welcoming the day, and silence reigned, at least for the time being. A sleety rain was blowing directly into Peter's face as he approached the Mosque, penetrating his clothes and making him shiver. For once he was actually pleased to get through the doors and out of the inclement weather to attend the devotions, cursing the cycles of standing up and then kneeling as his knees were hurting, aggravated by the cold and damp. Prayers were finished, and the normal hell-raising sermon was preached. Peter was only half aware of what was being said, his aching limbs and the fact that he had heard it all before, contributing to disinterest. He was amusing himself watching the wild gesticulations, and the crazy eye rolling of Imam Ul Haq, when he noticed a familiar face across the other side of the room.

Gulping in a noisy lung-full of air in disbelief Peter knew it was his brother Ibrahim. How could he ever forget the mean looking petulant face, and those deep set evil seeming green eyes? The face that tormented him for most of his early childhood, Peter was looking at his brother, and worryingly his brother was looking straight back at him. Peter snatched his gaze away from

Ibrahim, not wanting to alert him that he recognised his sullen unsmiling face. After the sermon was finished, Peter wanted to return home quickly, for two reasons; firstly he was cold and needed to change and warm up, secondly he wanted to avoid any possible close contact with Ibrahim, fearing that after twenty years he might still recognise the object of his hate. He was about to leave when Sue blocked his path, accompanied by Ibrahim. Sue spoke, pointing to and introducing Ibrahim, "James's bastard son! Your brother." Ibrahim didn't show any signs of recognition; his apparent dullard nature hadn't changed over the years, nor did his sulkiness. At the mention of James he screwed up his face in the same fashion that he did when he was seven, and couldn't get his own way. "My name is Malik Atiq and I was born in Jeddah, and my father is dead. Why do you think I have a father called James, and this man is my brother?"

"Because you look exactly fucking like him!" Sue whispered out the words almost silently, but still managing to say them without losing any of their spite. Ibrahim stood next to her unmoved by her outburst. "He doesn't look like anyone I've ever seen before and I don't remember what my parents looked like, so I can't help you, he's not Peter."

Sue peered up at Peter through her veil and stared straight in his eyes. "You've been wasting my fucking time, and I've fucking hated you since I first saw you!" she screamed, turning to move away, but Peter couldn't help himself, he had to reply:

"And I hate you! You bitter venomous old-dried up crone, take your motorised broomstick and go and bother someone else."

Having said his piece, Peter left to go home to his room, feeling ashamed that he had spoken to his mother so badly and guilty that he harboured such feelings of hate, not only to her but also to his estranged brother, who amazingly didn't recognise him. His mind was in turmoil. The confrontation had deeply upset him and, for one of the few times in his life, he felt that he needed to cry unhappy tears. So he did; running away, he found a bench out of sight to the world and, sitting there in the pouring rain, sobbed bitter tears of emotional pain. Once the torrent had abated he felt a lot better, as if the physical act of crying had soothed his soul; it seemed to close the pages on a frightful chapter of his life, and he felt renewed.

Saturday evening arrived and, as arranged on the Thursday, Peter went to meet up with his friends; Simon's injuries had started to heal and even in the gloom Peter could still make out the multi-coloured bruises on his face. Simon stoically accepted them as one of the hazards associated with his chosen way of life, and made no more of it. The band were very grateful for the replacements for their lost belongings, and as usual Peter brought some food with him. During the welcome meal Simon and his frightened company expressed their fear at staying where they were, telling Peter they believed the threats made by the gang to be real, so they asked their benefactor for help, which he agreed to do.

On Sunday Peter travelled to Surbiton to see his old friend and mentor Pat. He turned up at the guesthouse unannounced and rang the doorbell; he was greeted by Pat's partner Brian, who was his former teacher Mr Vincent. After two or three attempts to work out the identity of the familiar-looking Muslim gentleman standing in the doorway. Eventually he realised who the caller was and loudly announced to all that were in earshot,

"Before mine eyes I see a welcome vision! Behold! The prodigal son returneth to the bosom of his family!" Pat was delighted to see Peter, who explained the reason for his mode of attire, and the series of events that led him to come and seek Pat. He needed help with the gang of thugs that were threatening his homeless band of watchers. Pat, as always, came up with a clever plan; he was going to pretend to be one of the homeless, and when they attacked he was going to jump up and beat seven shades of shit out of them, problem solved.

Thursday afternoon arrived and the time came for Peter to introduce Pat, who had made a sterling effort and dressed in his scruffiest clothes, to the group of frightened homeless people he was there to protect. Pat joined the vagrants in the forbidden alley and sent Peter away to get the food so that everything would appear normal. The group of men sat together and talked, all the homeless men had woeful tales to tell, sadly they explained the reasons for their present situation, in return Pat kept them amused by telling some harrowing stories of his own, making them laugh, and the wait seem shorter. Pat found it amazing that they were all intelligent and articulate; they all, at one time or another had decent well paid jobs, but each of them had suffered personal tragedy which plunged them to their present predicament. He found their different perspective on life refreshing and enjoyed their company,

The time for the promised attack came, and exactly on cue ten foul-mouthed teenagers appeared at the end of the alley. The head yob, a skinny boy in a grey hoodie was the first to speak, he walked boldly up to Simon and announced his intent, "I told you lot to fuck off and not come back!"

As planned the homeless men backed off away from the advancing thugs, drawing them further into the alley, and when they were a suitable distance in, Pat came out of the shadows cutting off their retreat and asking in his best possible Irish accent, "Can I help you, ladies?"

Upon hearing the well placed insult from behind them, the boys turned round to see nothing but a fifty-year-old, weedy-looking Irishman blocking their path.

"Is it a fight you're after? Or might I be mistaken?" Pat asked with a little wiggle of his expressive eyebrows.

Taken aback by such cheek, the lads looked at one another, put off balance by Pat's audacity. After a pause for thought the head yob spoke again, this time somewhat less eloquently than before, "Fuck off you old cunt, or I'll pull your fucking head off and shit down the fucking hole!"

Quietly advancing towards the boys, Pat answered, "Will you now? That I would like to see!"

That was it, the loudmouth ran straight at Pat yelling obscenities, and was instantly floored by a blow to his neck. His main henchman, a great big raw-boned youth, ran to his assistance and met a similar fate, pitching face down on the gravel. The others, disheartened by the reversal, started to look for an escape route, and seeing none they rushed en masse to try and overpower the quiet scrawny Irishman. Their efforts were in vain and Pat easily turned the front runner upside down, the rest acted like skittles tripping and stumbling over their fallen comrade, ending up in a disorganised tangled heap of arms, legs, bodies and heads. Scrabbling to get back up on their feet, they ran off in blind terror as fast as their legs could carry them, leaving their two fallen friends to their fate. Pat beckoned to Simon asking him, "Which one of these heroes hit you?" Simon pointed to the ringleader. "How many times?"

"Six or seven!"

"Right, it's your turn, now!" Pat said, grabbing the semi-conscious head thug by the ear, and dragged him to where Simon was standing.

"I can't do it!" Simon didn't have the heart to hit the defenceless bully, so Pat did; slapping him like a girl would, hard across his face.

"Six... Seven... and one for luck," he added, slapping the yob once more, a little harder than the previous seven blows. The boy was crying, pleading for mercy, all witnessed by his horrified second in command. Pulling the lad to his feet again by his ear, Pat pointed him towards the entrance of the alley, and gave him a thunderous kick squarely in his behind, sending him tumbling back to his gang, and passing Peter on his way in, with food and supplies.

CHAPTER 11

The experience with Sue and Ibrahim changed Peter. He felt better equipped to deal with his emotions; somehow, the recent bout of tears, which he had not been able to shed when Charley was so tragically killed, had made him a better man. Other than tears of joy, he couldn't remember when he last wept, thinking back he suspected that it was when Ibrahim set fire to his den nearly twenty years before. For the first time since the accident he wanted to go to the churchyard and say the goodbye to Charley that he found it too difficult to do when she died, when he was unable to believe it was all true, and was lost in the sea of self-pity that almost drowned him.

It was on a beautiful sunny Sunday in mid-April when he paid his visit to Charley's grave; the birds were in full song, the trees were coming into leaf, and a few tardy daffodils gleamed brightly amid great sombre grey gravestones. Peter looked at them as he wound his way through, reading the names, feeling some pain for each bereft family that had once called the dead by name. He hesitantly walked up to the little mound in the turf, simply marked with a small wooden cross that was the last resting place of his beloved Charley. Collapsed onto his knees, he wept the hot bitter tears he couldn't cry before, seeing her face behind his eyelids, happy and smiling. Peter didn't know how long he had stayed there, beneath the branches of the old yew tree, lost in his deep thoughts, chatting to Charley and remembering the past. But eventually he had to leave, so he rose stiffly to his feet, took a step back and bowed his head in reference to his love. Suddenly his eye caught a glimpse of the corner of a neatly folded envelope tucked out of sight, and under a flat stone to prevent it from blowing away. Picking it up, Peter could see some of the writing was still legible; it was from Charley's mother, apologising for not attending the funeral, and expressed her love calling Charley, "my darling daughter." Peter felt happy that she had at last swallowed her pride and visited the grave, there in deepest Surrey amid the trees and daffodils.

Everything had gone too quiet at the Mosque; the nature of the sermons had been toned down, and the openly expressed hatred for anything western had all but disappeared. Thankfully Peter's mother was noticeable by her absence, as was Ibrahim. Peter still attended regularly and was still bemoaning the nature of the prayers, getting up and down on the hard floor was playing havoc with his ailing knees; the suntanned new members from abroad had vanished, and all seemed rather too normal for his liking.

Since the showdown in the alley, Peter's homeless friends were able to enjoy their chosen way of life in safety, the thugs had changed the object of their attentions and were now victimising the elderly, a section of society who were less likely to be able to fight back. Simon and his associates heralded Peter as their saviour, and offered their services, and those of others, on a more permanent basis, promising to keep vigilant and remain on watch.

Peter gratefully accepted Simon's promise of help, and in return he furnished him with a mobile phone, so that he could either summon Peter or inform him of any developments without too much delay. But still, all remained too quiet, like the calm before the storm.

The first sign of the approaching storm was heralded one day in late April, 2008. All the key players at the Mosque were keeping a very low profile or completely out of sight. Peter was ably going about his everyday business, watching and listening, trying to blend in with those about him, his homeless friends were feeding him the odd piece of information, and anything of he considered to be important enough he reported back to James. Peter was spending an early morning at his bedsit in front of the television enjoying a bowl of cornflakes and watching a breakfast news programme, when there was an item of breaking news flashed up on the screen; the country's terrorism alertness status level had just been raised from green to amber. He was watching with interest when, a few minutes later, Peter's phone rang, it was James, who asked to come and see Peter as he needed to speak to him urgently.

Peter remained at home, waiting for his father. He kept his eye on the television, watching the yellow high-lighted newsflash as it monotonously kept going across the bottom of the screen without changing until, after a while, the presenter interrupted an article about a bank's financial woes, suddenly announcing that as a follow-up to the breaking news, he was going over to Penny Gray, in London, for an update. The face of a very pretty young woman's face appeared on the screen and she was interviewing a terrorism expert. After asking several idiotic questions, replied with equally idiotic answers, the interviewee mentioned almost in passing that he believed the Americans had lost track of a shipment of Saddam's non-existent weapons of mass destruction that were on their way to be destroyed in Saudi Arabia, and it was thought that they were for sale to the highest bidder. Peter watched with interest as a hastily gathered team of pundits all gave their opinions, which all differed except that they all thought that it possibly the most serious incident since the attacks on the twin towers and the subsequent declaration of war on terrorism.

James arrived late morning and was fresh from a briefing at the head office in London. He was puffing so Peter surmised that he had been hurrying, he drew up a chair and sat at a small table opposite Peter, a kettle gurgled and spat in the background giving promise to a welcome cup of tea. James glanced hopefully in its direction and then he spoke, "Well that's put the cat among the pigeons," again he looked expectantly over to the kettle, and resumed, "I can't believe it! The Yanks have lost a load of weapons."

Peter got out of his seat to make some tea. "Yes, I know!"

"You know! How on earth do you know?" James asked, looking perplexed.

Peter replied, while pouring boiling water into a cup. "It was on television this morning."

James was aghast. "I can't believe they know, we've only just found out ourselves."

"The people on television said that they were up for sale to the highest bidder," Peter added matter-of-factly whilst handing James a welcome cup of tea.

"That's not right, they're trying to allay people's fears, American intelligence suspects that an Al Qaeda-type cell has got one over here, and they're nuts enough to use it!" James explained whilst idly stirring his drink.

"When did they go missing?" Peter asked, taking a sip of his tea.

"Six months ago!" James replied, trying to control a mouthful of drink.

Peter spat into his cup with surprise, making the contents leap out. "Six months! And we've only just found out!"

James and Peter worked all the next day, trying to verify what, if any possible high profile targets would gain maximum effect coming to the only logical conclusion that any weapon might be used on an attack on the mayoral elections in London. James reported his suspicions to his bosses in London, but they wouldn't listen, saying their security was impenetrable and it would be impossible to attempt anything then. James openly expressed his lack of faith in his superiors; he knew they were complete idiots, but they still had the capacity to amaze him by their foolhardy attitude to national security. Exasperated, James told Peter to be aware, as he had stirred up a hornets' nest, the shit was sure to hit the fan, leaving him wondering what new obstacle was going to be around the next corner.

As a result of James expressing his obvious doubts about the competence of his bosses, Peter was summoned to Jermyn Street for a briefing. Peter was in the same seat, in the same old office where he attended his initial interview; John and Graham were there, along with half a dozen others that he didn't know. At the front Lou sat facing the assembly, legs crossed; pad at the ready waiting to take notes, although some twenty years senior to Peter he still found her attractive and without really knowing it, his eyes somehow wandered up her skirt. Lou noticed him staring and looking a secret smile to him she then adjusting her attire by pulling at the hem to cover her knees, causing him to snatch his gaze away from her shapely legs to pay attention to the address. Doing his best to keep his mind on the subject, Peter listened to a muddled briefing delivered by Graham, who seemed confused and ill-informed as he delivered a speech about what Peter had already been told by James. Closing the meeting, Graham merely told the gathering to be extra vigilant, as there was a real likelihood of an attempted attack on a high profile target.

As the meeting was breaking up John took Peter to one side and spoke directly to him telling him to stay behind as he needed to speak to him in private. With his voice lowered and secretive John explained that both he and Graham were very annoyed with James, telling Peter that his father's idea about an attack on the election was preposterous and he was to ignore it. Suddenly changing tack, John asked him nicely how he was enjoying his new employment and how everything was going at the Mosque? Peter told him, saying that he enjoyed the work, but was worried, as at the Mosque it all seemed to have gone too quiet. The hell-raising speeches that he had got used to had stopped, and the warlike rhetoric had been toned down. John seemed to see no significance in the observations and merely told him to keep up the good work, and stay on the ball.

On Peter's way back to his flat he detoured to visit James and Jasmine at home. Primarily he wanted to tell James about the strange meeting in London, but mostly to sample some of

Jasmine's cooking. When he arrived, James was looking worried, he had just received a recent update on the present situation, and it was definite: a terrorist plot was definitely in the offing, targeting Great Britain, but nobody knew exactly what the target would be. Apparently An American intelligence agency had extracted some information from an unlucky soul that had somehow ended up in their clutches, and had died by his own hand before giving up all the details, leaving the story half told; and by way of a sort of apology they promised to send one of their specialist Middle Eastern experts to help solve the riddle, as they felt somewhat responsible for the lack of information and were embarrassed by their carelessness.

It was Thursday 24th of April 2008. Peter had been running about all day like a headless chicken, there were theories, and counter theories, but nobody really knew what to do. The telephones were red hot and Peter had spent all that day with one stuck to his ear. The authorities still ignored James's theory, and had no idea whatsoever of what they were looking for. They had no identifiable plan, indecision and hopeless confusion reigned, and the whole internal security system was in a virtual state of confused meltdown.

Amid the chaos Peter carried on as normal, and the time came to visit his homeless associates. After the latest incident at the alley, the men were totally loyal to Peter, and their commitment to him was complete. Keeping his tryst Peter turned up at the alley at the appointed hour, as usual he was laden with food and other supplies. Simon was already there, hopping up and down, anxiously waiting and eager to see him; during the day he had tried to call Peter on the mobile that he was given, but he had run the batteries down in his attempts as Peter's phone was permanently engaged. Simon had important news; there had been a significant increase in movements, Ul Haq had been visited five times the previous night, all callers were Arab-looking men, arriving in trucks or vans; they entered with heavy-looking boxes, and left empty-handed. Exactly the same thing had happened at the woman in a wheelchair's house, only it was only three times instead of six. Excitedly Simon rushed his story out, hardly pausing for breath, causing him to gasp loudly when he finished. Peter barely understood the garbled message and asked Simon to repeat what he had said slowly as most of the content of his speech had been lost in translation, his hurried Northumberland accent seeming like an unknown foreign language to those who were strange to it. Simon repeated his message very slowly, making a show of overly pronouncing each word, exaggerating his lip movements as though he was talking to the profoundly deaf. When Peter fully understood the content, he hastily plonked down all his presents, and instead of spending time with Simon and the others as he usually did, he bade them a hurried farewell, promising to see them the next week, reminding Simon to recharge his mobile and keep him informed.

Peter needed to speak to James urgently to keep him up to date with the breaking news. Phoning James first to let him know he was coming and as it would be foolish to discuss sensitive material on a possibly unsecured line, they agreed a personal visit would be in order. Peter arrived within the hour, finding James waiting patiently for him; quickly Peter told his father of the new developments, and James thought that were really significant.

Hoping to change head office's opinion of James's theory they immediately reported the new findings to the bosses in London, but unfortunately John and Graham were deeply involved in following a different line of thought, and although mildly interested all they did was to advise James just to stay watching and keep them informed. James was furious, calling them blind and useless, commenting about their inability to see their noses in front of their faces. Because of the bosses' apparent disinterest and tunnel vision, Peter and James decided to act for themselves.

The more they considered it, the more sure they were of the intended target, but didn't have enough manpower to do much about it. Peter and James had locked themselves away for half the night to formulate a plan of action and decided that it would be impossible to implement without help, so they decided to ask their old friends Pat and Michael to assist them in their bid to prevent a possible major catastrophe, agreeing that urgency was the prime consideration, and to seek out their ex-comrades the very next morning was the next step, so they retired to bed to get some much-needed sleep.

James undressed and sneaked quietly in between the warm sheets trying not to wake Jasmine; as if he did she would expect his normal services and he wanted to sleep well and wake up refreshed. Thinking he'd succeeded in not waking her, he turned his back to her naked body and closed his eyes. Within seconds her wayward hand miraculously found its way onto his groin and started to gently massage, she pushed her breasts into his back and whispered closely in his ear, asking if he wanted to fuck her as she felt horny and needed loving. How could he ignore such subtle appeals? It was no good, he couldn't resist her supplications, so he obliged. James and Jasmine assumed Peter would be asleep, so they allowed themselves to be a little noisier than they normally were when guests were in the house, only half-bothering to stifle their groans of pleasure. After quite some time James managed to get the sleep he so desperately needed, but not before satisfying Jasmine's always demanding appetite for sex. It was past four o'clock when he eventually closed his eyes; exhausted he slept well, the worries of the previous day, were all forgotten, lost in the wonderful sleepy afterglow of making love.

It was Friday 25th April, Peter woke up at around half past seven in the morning; the sun streamed through his half-closed curtains, and outside two blackbirds were fighting noisily over whose territory was whose, an early flight from Heathrow roared overhead, making the windows rattle, and plucking an irritable Peter out of his semi-conscious state. Jasmine was up; he could hear the kitchen noises of breakfast being prepared, so he got out of bed, washed and then as it was a Friday he dressed in his best Muslim garb, and then he went to join Jasmine. She was already sitting at a small dining table drinking coffee, offering a cup to Peter; the television behind her was turned on, and she was more listening to it rather than watching it. James emerged looking refreshed, and stretching his arms wide he announced that he had slept well; grumpy and tired Peter mumbled a sarcastic answer into his coffee cup, more to himself rather than to anybody else. "Yes Father! I heard you sleeping well; you kept me awake for ages!" Jasmine heard what he said, and went scarlet. James was blissfully unaware of what had befallen, and was surprised when she left the room in a hurry, and was closely followed by Peter in hot pursuit, wanting to apologise for his careless remark.

Catching up with Jasmine he told her that he was sorry, and the remark wasn't supposed to be heard anyway. They made up with a huge hug and returned to the breakfast table as if nothing had happened; James was still sitting there oblivious to any discord, but the day had started badly for Peter.

After the early meal was finished, James telephoned his old friends, who both agreed to meet with their ex-boss before lunchtime at a pub in Kingston, on the banks of the River Thames. It was twelve o'clock when the coterie was due to gather. Peter and James selected an isolated table next to the water's edge, and sat outside in the spring warmth waiting for their comrades. Pat was the first to turn up. Looking much as he always did, lean and wiry, his bushy eyebrows had turned grey, but were even more prominent than they used to be and appeared to be taking over his face, his hair was still slightly ginger and he still had the bearing of a hardened man. Next Michael arrived, immaculately dressed as usual, but the years had been less kind; what remained of his hair had turned white, he walked with a limp, a direct result of the injury he suffered all those years before, and he had developed a slight stoop, but inside, it was clear, he was the same old smiling Michael. The old comrades greeted each other like long lost friends, even though they were still in regular touch, chatting and laughing about some silly details of their lives apart.

While the hellos were in full swing Peter went to fetch the drinks order, three pints of bitter and an orange juice for himself, many eyebrows were being raised when, for all intents and purposes, a Muslim man went to the bar in a public house and purchased alcohol. A group of loud young men who were sitting in the pub decided to voice their opinions, one of them telling him to, "Fuck off back to Egypt!" Peter just looked disdainfully in their direction, and ignoring them he went about the business of delivering the drinks. The four men sat huddled together over their drinks and James explained the situation, he told them about John and Graham's reluctance to support any action, explaining how they were off on a wild goose chase after shadows, and weren't prepared to listen to anything he had to say. Both Pat and Michael chimed in with their views of the unpopular duo at head office, Pat calling them fuddy-duddy old wankers and Michael just nodded in an expression of total agreement. All the time Peter was ruefully watching the men enjoying their drinks, he really fancied a beer, but he thought it would be somewhat impolitic to be seen drinking in public, and then turn up at the Mosque smelling of stale booze.

It was past one when Peter got up to leave. Unfortunately the party of lads, who were rude to him in the pub also decided to depart at the same time. They had obviously had drunk plenty and were noisily pushing their way carelessly through the other customers when their eyes lit upon Peter, and when they saw he was only accompanied by three ageing men they thought it would be fun to bait the quartet. Initially their attentions were aimed at Peter, and they started shouting anti-Islamic abuse at him calling him, "Saddam's little helper," and "Sheik My Dick." Attracted by the commotion, the other drinkers watched on in dismay as the bunch of loudmouths bravely turned their attentions to the weedy-looking Pat, asking him if he was trying to hide from them behind the bushes, and then, laughed loudly, they pointed at his unique eyebrows.

Noticing that one of the yobs seemed to be laughing a little louder than the others, Pat slowly raised himself up from his seat and stood square on to the offending lad, and politely asked in his very best Irish accent, why he found his eyebrows so offensive. The youth answered the question, addressing the onlookers like an actor about to start a play, asking if they wanted to watch an old Irish cunt have his eyebrows pulled out of his fucking head? As he finished the announcement he bowed mockingly and then rushed at the ever ready Pat, who smartly side stepped him, and soundly clipped the back of his head on the way past, sending him hurtling straight over a low wall and headlong into the river Thames. The audience simultaneously burst out into uproarious laughter, and Pat bowed reverently to them, imitating his attacker and receiving a round of applause. Meanwhile the boy in the river was floating gently downstream, being followed by his concerned friends who were hurling advice and shouting for help. Luckily for the lad two men in a small boat were alerted by the noise and went to his aid, pulling the half-drowned, mud-stained youth unceremoniously out of the water by his hair. Peter's day had got a little worse.

After leaving the meeting at the pub Peter went straight to the Mosque for Friday prayers. After the laborious process of standing and kneeling repeatedly, he gratefully rested his aching knees and sat to listen to the sermon. Imam Ul Haq delivered his normal style of inflammatory speech to an unusually full house, everybody Peter had seen there before had returned, including Sue and Ibrahim. He also noted that the men, who were freshly suntanned some time before, had all topped up their tans, indicating their fresh arrival back into the country. After the sermon was finished six young men were summoned to the front of the prayer room and reverently presented with black scarves adorned with white Arabic writing. Because of the volume of people in the room Peter was closer to the front than normal, and as each individual was given his token Peter was able to lip-read the almost silent blessing conferred on them by the Imam. Peter didn't know what to do, whether to leave straight away and report the alarming contents straight back to James or to stay on for a short while and see if he could find out any more details about their plans. Deciding on the latter option, he stayed, listening and watching, hoping to find out more.

In the anteroom at the Mosque there was an air of pregnant expectation. The six men that had been honoured had left, along with many of the recently suntanned devotees. An excited buzz of anticipation was present, and something was afoot. As usual Sue liked to bait Peter, she looked on it as a little game she liked to play, in her warped mind she was getting back at the person she correctly believed to be Peter's father, and today was going to be no different. Approaching him menacingly on her electric scooter, she screamed directly in his face, "I don't like you! I think you're a spy, I can see you watching people and taking note, listening to conversations!" Peter tried to walk away, but she followed him, "I can see your prying eyes!" And then she hurried up to him to get close enough to whisper, "You're just like your fucking father, always spying!" Peter turned to escape from her whiplash tongue, and as he did she grabbed his sleeve attempting to stop him from getting away, she clung on to Peter tugging at him, trying to turn him round to face her.

All of a sudden, the buttons burst and his jacket flew open. The little copy of the Koran, which she had once owned and which he always kept with him, fell on the floor, right in front of Sue. She looked at it and then at Peter, she paused for a moment while the realisation set in, and then she quietly hissed even more venomous hatred staring intently at him. "Now I know exactly who you are; you're that fucking little brat that nearly killed me. You're Peter; I can see it all now, you're in league with James and that fucking witch!" Sue stopped to consider what other poison she could spit at poor Peter, "I know where they live, I will have my revenge, Allah will help me!" Still holding on to Peter, Sue wanted to continue the verbal assault.

Unlike his usual self, he enjoyed having his say without regret; "And you're nothing but a venomous old hag that will die miserable and lonely!"

Without thinking, Sue replied quickly, almost instantly regretting her outburst, "And very soon, I will be embraced in the arms of…" She finished without completing her statement, thinking that she already given too much away. Glaring hatefully at her son, Sue whizzed away, muttering dreadful obscenities under her breath. The day had got even worse than it was before.

It was past four in the afternoon when Peter reported back his findings to James who was at home with Pat and Michael, still discussing their plan of action. Jasmine busied herself keeping out of the way cooking in the kitchen. Peter burst in, interrupting the trio urgently announcing that something was going to happen and happen very soon. Breathlessly he informed about the sermon at the Mosque, and the content of the blessing conferred on the six young men: it was a prayer for those about to die. James asked what exactly the words meant and Peter told him the interpretation of what the cleric said, repeating them out loud for all to hear, "Very soon as chosen ones you will be walking the desert patterns with Allah, surrounded by all you love, with everything you need. To get all this you must not forget to say you're final words *"la Illam Illa Allah!" Allah is great.* Peter looked at the three men, who were listening intently to what he said, and decided an explanation was in order: "They're going on a suicide mission!" And then, feeling ashamed of admitting his actions towards his mother, he told them about Sue, how she discovered Peter's true identity and his belief that she also was going to kill herself in the name of Islam. Telling James how full of malice she was, and that she still harboured the desire of vengeance towards Jasmine and James.

Peter concluded his report saying, "I can't go back to the Mosque now, she'll have told them everything. If you want, I'll join Simon, and watch them with him, without them knowing."

James considered the offer, and thinking that it was a good idea, he turned to Pat. "You're a scruffy old sod Pat, how do you fancy being a tramp for a few days?" Then, looking at Michael, James told him what he was to do. "You can wait at home by the phone, I'll probably need you later." James didn't really mean it, but he was concerned about Michael's leg, as it was obviously hurting him a lot. James continued giving out some final instructions before going into his office to report back to his bosses, hoping to receive their go ahead. He returned some twenty minutes later in a thunderous mood, "I don't swear often, but they are effing useless, some smart-arsed Yank expert has fed them a line, and they won't listen to common sense. I've got to meet him tomorrow morning, so he can put me in the picture."

Peter butted in, "What about us?"

"You carry on as planned; just find out what you can."

Happy everyone knew exactly what was expected of them, the group broke up; Peter and Pat went in search of suitable clothing to pose as vagrants, Michael went home to Minnie, and the still fuming James joined Jasmine to warn her about Sue and her vengeful promises.

Darkness arrived early. It had turned unseasonably cold and the sky was overcast, there was a promise of drizzle in the air. Peter and Pat sat together, chilled and miserable watching Ul Haq's house from the doorway of a deserted shop some thirty yards away that Simon called number twelve and suggested was the best possible vantage point. There were several comings and goings that interested the pair, but nothing happened of real importance until a car drew up and deposited a small round man who furtively scurried up the path to the partly open front door and then sidled in. Pat nudged Peter in the ribs. "Where should I know him from! I recognise his walk!"

Peter responded almost silently. "Where from?" "I can't remember," Pat responded, scratching his head, "but I never forget a walk." There they stayed keeping their vigil, cold and wet, huddled together shivering in a doorway. As dawn was starting to break there was another incident of little note: a man arrived, entered the house and then emerged to go to work dressed in London Underground livery. Cold, wet, tired and utterly miserable, Peter's day had been a complete disaster.

Saturday 26 April dawned. The rain that persisted through the night had blown through, and the sun rose turning the sky bright pink, making the streets and houses strangely orange in the morning light. Peter was woken up with a poke in his ribs from Pat, who never seemed to sleep, alerting him as there was some movement at the house and the same car that arrived the previous night had returned to pick up its passenger. Pat wanted a closer look at the man, but his line of sight had been obscured by the vehicle, and it would be impossible to break cover without being noticed, so he had to content himself with another brief glimpse of the man. On seeing him once more Pat reinforced his previous conclusion, "I definitely know him; my old brain's slowing down, I just can't remember where from, he seems so familiar!"

Confused and still scratching his head, Pat followed Peter out of the relative comfort of the doorway, still wondering where he had seen the mysterious stranger before.

Back at Whitton James was preparing himself for the meeting with the American agent who was due to arrive at eleven. James asked Jasmine if she wanted to go shopping in London so he could have the house to himself, he was always honest with her, and she obeyed him without question. James had politely ordered Michael to drive her, partly for security reasons, but also to keep him involved and safely removed from the stress of the mission, as he was still worrying about his failing health. Michael turned up precisely at ten dressed once again in his cleaned and pressed old chauffeur's uniform which still just about fitted him although the trouser buttons at the waist seemed to be a little more strained, the jacket was craftily left undone and the hat was on his head at a slightly less rakish angle than it used to be, however it was the same old Michael that presented a very smart appearance as he drove Jasmine on her shopping trip to London.

Somewhere a distant clock chimed eleven o'clock and James was patiently waiting for his visitor, who eventually arrived thirty minutes late, making the always punctual James annoyed even before meeting his guest. At last a very black-looking car arrived and halted outside the house, the dark-suited driver opening the back door for the passenger to alight and strut with more than a hint of swagger towards the front door to ring the doorbell. James' jaw dropping when opening the door himself, he came face to face with his suave old adversary Xavier.

"Hello James, you look surprised. I bet you didn't expect to see me, did you?" Xavier motioned to the driver to wait in the car and James just stood speechless and open-mouthed staring at his unwelcome visitor.

"Yes It's me, I'm called Zavier Fikri now, and Xavier is spelled with a zed, not with an ex. As you know I work for the Americans, and I am to liaise with you about our little problem."

Having gathered his senses, James answered, "I heard who you were supposed to work for once before, and I often wonder who it really is you answer to." Xavier was totally unflustered by James's honesty, "I am a very special agent, working for the CIA, a specialist in Middle Eastern affairs, and I am telling you the truth." Xavier had aged considerably: he had lost most of his hair, and what he had left was silver grey, he had grown fat, his face was deeply lined, but his shifty beady eyes were exactly the same, still telling of his lying untrustworthy scheming nature. At the mere sight of him, James wanted to kill him where he stood. Enjoying the effect his presence was having on his one-time

273

antagonist, and wanting to aggravate him further, Xavier asked the question which he knew would do the trick: "How is the dear lovely Jasmine? Still as beautiful as ever, I expect, and keeping well, I hope?"

"Jasmine is still spelled with a jay, and she is very well, no thanks to you." Having finished the introductions Xavier asked if he could come in the house, which James declined, not wanting him to be able to see inside and get an insight into his life with Jasmine. "We'll just have to stand here on the doorstep and talk then, won't we James?" They stood talking for ten minutes and were about to finish the highly strained discussion when two tramps rounded the corner and came into sight. James just caught a fleeting vision of them before the larger one dragged the other back round the bend, out of view.

The acrimonious meeting ended with Xavier bidding James an ingenuous goodbye, annoyingly asking James to give all his love to Jasmine and nearly wearing a punch in his mouth for his trouble. James only just managing to control himself, as the vile turncoat left, having deliberately infuriated James, and smugly knowing that he had won the first encounter, Xavier left, waving and smiling with falsely polite, smug arrogance as he was driven away. As soon as the car had left Pat and Peter came quickly back into view and crept into the house, trying not to be seen by the neighbours. They joined James who was shaking with rage, in all the years he had known him Pat had never seen him like that before.

"What's up boss? Are you OK? You look pissed off."

James gulped audibly, "Xavier's been here, he's the Yank operative I'm supposed to keep up to date with our intelligence!"

A distant look swept across Pat's face. "You're fucking having a laugh, was that him who just fucking left? We ducked out of sight because we saw that car last night, at Ul Haq's!"

Peter joined in, "And I think I've seen him at the Mosque!"

The always matter-of-fact Pat made a valid comment." This is getting very complicated. My fucking head is going round in fucking circles. Who can we trust?"

"Only ourselves!" James replied succinctly. Badly disturbed by the re-appearance of the enemy he wanted to kill all those years before, Pat was all for chasing Xavier and his driver to kill them. James managing to calm him down, pointed out that neither did they have a car, nor did they know where Xavier had disappeared to. The three of them spending the next few hours sitting fuming in a moody silence; musing on the events of the day and waiting for Jasmine and Michael come home, to be told the bad news.

CHAPTER 12

The evening at Whitton was very tense; James explained everything that had happened, including Xavier's veiled threatening behaviour. She couldn't believe it after all those years it had all come back to haunt her, bringing back hurtful memories of unhappy times when she was hunted by Xavier at the behest of her evil uncle's family, ending in the tragedy that afflicted Sue, and sent her mad. But as ever, bucking herself up Jasmine accepted the situation, knowing there was little she could do to influence the events, resigned herself to take things as they come and deal with them as they presented themselves. Peter and Pat left to resume their vigil, after first seeing Simon to catch up on any developments. Michael hobbled back home to the arms of his doting Minnie, and as all seemed quiet for the time being. Jasmine and James retired to bed and yet again forgot their worries between the sheets.

Sunday 27 April arrived; the changeable weather lived up to its name and outside it was raining hard and the wind was making the drops pelt noisily on the windows. At eight o'clock Peter and Pat returned with nothing to report, the night had been quiet and without incident, the wind and wet had been blowing directly into their doorway and they were both frozen and soaked to the skin. After they had bathed, changed and warmed up Jasmine provided a full breakfast for them all and they sat at the table and ate their well earned food. The four of them discussed what had happened the day before. James came up with a valid point, "Sue must have seen Xavier at the Mosque, and she's hardly likely to forget him." He turned to Peter. "Did you ever see them together?"

Peter answered hesitantly. "I'm not sure, I wonder if he would know it's her anyway; she's always covered from head to foot in her veil."

Pat butted in. "She would know it's him though; I bet they're in it together, I think were watching the wrong one. Ul Haq is getting all our attention, while I think we really should be watching Sue!"

"We should really be watching them all, and we should be watching them now!" James added, complicating things.

"We are!" was Peter's simple reply before gulping down the last morsel of food and going straight to bed to grab some rest. Jasmine had invited everyone to Sunday lunch and, capably aided by Pat, went about preparing it until he had to leave to fetch Brian. James, meanwhile, had disappeared to contact his inadequate superiors.

James's report contained all that had happened; he told them everything that he thought they needed to know but excluded his knowledge of Xavier's past, and the fact that he had enlisted Pat's help. The bosses had nothing new to add to what James already knew, and they told him to wait until the London mayoral elections were over before he contacted them again, as they were too busy helping to organise the security arrangements to be pestered by trivialities, and had more important things to worry about. James smiled to himself with relief, feeling that the anchor that for years had been impeding his progress had at last been cut away, and finally he could follow his instincts without being baulked by officious idiots in suits.

As arranged they all gathered for lunch at one o'clock, Michael and Minnie arrived early, Michael's leg had not improved with rest, and his limp was very noticeable, cursing the injury, he blamed the previous cold day for its present state, expressing pleasure that the day had warmed up considerably. Flexing it, he announced that it was starting to feel better already. Pat and Brian turned up slightly late; they had fallen foul of an overzealous policeman who stopped them accusing them of crossing a red traffic light, remonstrations were useless, and Pat was obliged to accept a ticket. Brian who always had a ready quote for any occasion, spouting loudly. "A tyrant will always find a pretext for his tyranny!" Peter entered the room just as Brian was finishing the saying, "Aesop's Fables, *The wolf and lamb!*" Brian perked up, "There you are James all that money you spent on your brightest star's education wasn't wasted after all!"

Peter gave James a sideways glance and repeated, "What's this 'after all' father?" The assembly laughed together like the trusted friends that they were.

Pat returned to the kitchen and helped Jasmine produce a stunning Sunday meal of roast fore rib of beef for them all and they sat and ate together, talking about the events that brought them all together, taking time to pause for a moment to remember those who were absent. The chit-chat moved towards the present day and the prospect of an Al Qaeda terrorist attack on the country. The media was full of two main discussion points: the London mayoral elections, and the terrorist threat. James mused to himself, amazed how the powers that be were unable to link the two together. James expressing his incredulity, was amazed at how the powers that be, with all the information at their fingertips, were still unable to link the two together. With lunch eaten, digested and the conversation having gone full-circle it became time for everyone to go their separate ways, Michael offered to stay and help with the investigations, but James insisted that he went home and rested his damaged limb as he was sure to need him soon, so with farewells and hugs the party ended.

Pat and Peter went about their business early that evening, they changed clothes into their Sunday worst and plodded off together to join their little army of volunteers. Their first port of call was to Simon, who had taken up daytime residence in the doorway near to Ul Haq's house. With a mind on Simon's permanently good appetite, Peter handed him some fresh beef and mustard sandwiches as he asked if he had anything to report. Taking an enormous bite Simon mumbled "not much!" through a mouthful of food and wincing at the heat of the mustard. Swallowing another chunk of the sandwich, he casually asked whether the Ul Haq had some form of connection with the London underground as two individuals dressed in their uniform had been seen entering and then leaving that morning. Not seeing any particular significance in the revelation, Peter and Pat resumed their rounds to meet one of the other vagrants in their service called Billy, who was on duty in the yard near to Sue's house. When they found him he was fast asleep and smelling strongly of booze, so Peter prodded him with his foot, causing a great snore to issue from the hopelessly drunk man who was completely lost in his own private oblivion. Pat looked at Peter, shrugged, sat down and assumed the watch, peering expectantly through a crack in a decrepit old gate, waiting for something to happen.

The first signs of movement happened at about seven in the evening. The two friends were crouching uncomfortably behind the gate, taking turns watching through their little spyhole, when a smart new Yankee four-by-four drove up to the house driven by a lone man, He alighted and boldly walked to the front door with an air of familiar arrogance about him.

Pat had been racking his aging brain for nearly two days wondering where he had seen Ul Haq's Saturday morning visitor before, when suddenly Pat had an epiphany, banging his head with his fist he declared, "That's it! I know who it is!" Pat declared, making his voice hoarse, wanting to shout but keeping it to a whisper,, "It's that fucking lying, two-faced French cunt Xavier, or whatever his fucking name is now."

Peter looked at his colleague askance, whispering back, "It can't be him; he works for the Yanks, he's on our side now, isn't he?"

In reply, Pat, still wanting to shout but controlling himself, mouthed almost silently, "Does he fuck! They might think he does, but I think he has always worked for the highest payer. I should have blown the slippery little fucker's head of his slippery fucking shoulders when I had the fucking chance!"

Peter smiled at his colourful use of language. "I hope you feel better after that, there were more *fucks* than words in there Pat." Pat had a ready answer on his tongue. "Of course I fucking do!"

Peter smiled, thought for a moment and carried on talking. "Do you think that it's him that's been misleading John and Graham, he must have spoken to them?"

Pat answered without pausing for thought. "There's not a doubt in my fucking mind, he's playing those gullible old farts like fish on a line, we'll have to do something, it's a bit risky, but we'll have to bite the bullet."

Peter's response amused Pat. "Not literally, I hope?"

Giggling, Pat simply said, "Maybe!"

And, with the aid of Peter, Pat formulated one of his amazing quick and simple plans: he intended to snatch Xavier when he was outside the house, steal the car and question him back at Peter's bedsit.

They felt it best not to let James know of their intentions, so that he could honestly deny any knowledge if it went wrong, "plausible deniability," as Pat called it just in case there was any fallout from their actions. As the most senior and more experienced, it was agreed that Pat should take command of the situation, Peter promising to do whatever necessary. From where they were hidden it was much too far to rush their intended victim, so Pat hatched a plot to break into the massive car and hide behind the seats along with Peter, and hope not to be discovered. Happy with their risky new plan, they shook hands in agreement, and Pat scurried off to the car. Doing as he had been told Peter stayed exactly where he was watching for a whole two interminable minutes for Pat's beckoning hand to summon him to the car. Obeying the call, as furtively as he could, Peter crossed to join Pat behind the front seats in the giant American gas-guzzling monster. Luckily neither of them were big or fat, so with relative ease they squeezed themselves out of sight. Once they were happily ensconced Pat's voice piped up, "No farting ladies and gentlemen please?" as always adding a touch of humour to a dire situation.

They didn't have a clue how long they waited cramped, silently in hiding before the situation changed. Darkness had completely fallen when the first sign of action happened: two sets of footsteps could be heard approaching the car. Both Pat and Peter wondered whether their hasty plan had started to fall to pieces already, and felt relieved when the unknown persons got in the front, only bothering to pay attention to the back seat when one of them threw a couple of carelessly aimed bags onto it. The men exchanged a few heated words before the driver started up the vehicle. Bursting into life with a throaty roar, the pair in the back could very soon feel that they were moving. The driver and passenger were obviously continuing a discussion that they had previously started, and were gabbling in Arabic, speaking far too quickly for Pat's untrained ear, but Peter understood every word, gaining an insight into the real intentions of the insurgents. The conversation was about their fundamental differences in doctrine and lasted five or so minutes before Xavier's angry voice told the other man in English to, "shut the fuck up!" something Pat even understood.

In the front there was a moody silence, and Pat took it as a cue to announce his presence. "Hello Xavier. It's me your little old friend Pat! Remember me, do you? Don't even think of trying anything as I've got a fucking great gun pointing straight at your lying fucking head, so carry on driving, and keep your eyes on the fucking road, and tell your little minder what a bastard I am, and if he moves I'll shoot him too?"

Taken aback by the sudden intervention Xavier thought for a second, and then spoke. "He speaks English, and I warn you, he's younger and a lot better than you!" Bang! Without warning Pat shot the passenger, through the back of the seat, the bullet passing into the man's chest, piercing his heart and left lung, killing him instantly, his escaping last breath making a low whistling noise as it escaped through the entry wound.

"He's not now is he? I think he just died on the job! Now do as your told and FUCKING DRIVE! And keep your fucking hands where I can see them, on the fucking steering wheel."

Peter was still crouched next to Pat, shocked, shaking violently and completely stunned by the suddenness and severity of Pat's attack. His ears were ringing, and the man's blood was making his shoes wet. Also in a state of shock, Xavier drove on, still completely unaware of Peter's presence in the car, and was surprised when to escape the discomfort of being folded up, Peter raised himself from his position to straighten his legs and ease his aching knees. The sight of the apparent newcomer in the rear-view mirror offering Xavier a vain hope that he might be the voice of reason and spoke imploring him to listen.

"Tell him that I work for the Americans, you can't hurt me, I'm a very special agent! Tell him!" And then Xavier recognised who the stranger was. "Your Peter, aren't you? I know your mother and father, and I know Jasmine, and they know me." His pleading was falling on Peter's deaf ears.

"Yes, I am Peter, but I find it strange that you know who I am, funny that isn't it? And don't forget, you tried to kill them. I've heard all about you; you're not very good are you?"

Pat joined in the reminiscing, "Yes! I owe you, I haven't forgotten, you've been in my thoughts for years! Now shut up and drive exactly where I tell you." Peter gave Pat directions, who relayed them to the terrified driver, and he, fearing for his life, followed them to the letter. Obeying the instructions, Xavier drove the car up an unlit squalid-looking side street, some three hundred yards from the bedsit and halted, parking it in the darkest spot available.

It was ten in the evening; Pat got out of the car first and opened the driver's door, getting a good hold on Xavier's jacket to drag the reluctant traitor out. Seeing it as possibly his last chance to escape, Xavier struggled to free himself from Pat's grasp and make a bid for freedom, but his effort was in vain as no matter how hard he struggled he was unable to get the dogged Irishman to loosen his vice-like grip. His failed attempt being rewarded with a tooth-rattling clout in the side of his bald head, the hefty thump all but aiding Xavier's escape bid by almost spinning him free of his captor. Not wanting any more similar occurrences Pat decided to knock him out before going any further, so with a single blow to the back of his head he rendered the reluctant captive senseless. Peter found it difficult to alight from car, his recently cramped, over-prayed knees refusing to obey their commands and with great relief he managed the simple task, stretching his grateful limbs before joining Pat along with the unconscious prisoner.

Their problem of publicly conveying a resistant captor through busy Sunday-night streets, without attracting too much undue attention, was easily solved. Who would notice two drunken tramps assisting a comatose compatriot on their way home to their hovels? So Peter and Pat positioned themselves either side of Xavier, slung Pat's grubby coat on his back to hide his smartish clothes and manhandled him towards Peter's lodging. Most of the people still on the streets were fresh from the pubs and avoided the unsavoury trio; however, as luck would have it the same gang of yobs Pat last saw in the alley were about and fairly drunk. When they saw the apparently incapable vagrants, they forgot all about their last brush with the homeless and decided to bait them, the resulting rumpus causing a stir among the homeward-bound revellers, and attracting a crowd of onlookers. Pat couldn't help himself, he had to do something. Dropping Xavier on the ground and walked drunkenly, weaving up to the youth he knew to be the ringleader, lifted his head up and stared directly into his eyes.

"Remember me, do you, sonny boy? You've got a very short memory, haven't you, kiddo!"

Upon seeing who it was, the terrified boy bolted like a scalded cat, his hasty exit being closely followed by his fellow tormentors, their panicky plight prompting a spontaneous round of applause from the tipsy audience as they pointed and laughed at the fleeing youths. Happy with the result, Pat casually resumed his task of transporting the now semi-conscious groaning Xavier the remaining hundred yards to the privacy of Peter's temporary home.

It took them over a quarter of an hour to make the short journey from the car to the house; both Peter and Pat were exhausted, having dragged the unhelpful, portly Xavier through the streets and then up the stairs to the room. Inside the lodgings, there was a bed, an old-fashioned wooden table, an armchair and three dining chairs, all very tatty and from different sets. Taking pride of place in the apartment, an old television sat proudly on a rickety shelf in the corner of the room, on a rickety shelf. Brutally hurling Xavier on to one of the chairs, Pat tied his crossed hands tightly in front of him and pushed the seat close to the table. As he was still only partly awake, Pat suggested that Peter should fetch a jug or bucket of the coldest water that he could find. Obeying, Peter brought a saucepan full of tepid water.

"Now if you know where any tools are, I need some pliers, or whatever you've got?"

"Why?"

"Don't ask me Peter, you won't like the answer, just get them!"

Again doing as he was told, Peter rattled about in the cupboard under the foul-smelling sink for a while and returned with a mouldy old canvas bag with an assortment of ancient rusty carpenter's tools that looked as though they might have belonged to Noah when he built the Ark.

Xavier was now wide awake, soaked to the skin and tightly gagged with a strip of cloth; his frightened eyes were following Peter's moves, silently pleading for help. Xavier nearly fainted when saw the bag of tools as Peter plonked them on the table with a clunk. Using his best mock-French accent, Pat quoted a line he was told by James years before:

"For the birth, I think!"

Picking up a pencil off the table and pretended to puff at an imaginary cigarette, blowing non-existent smoke in the air. "This is going to hurt you a lot more than it does me!" Xavier was crying with fear, his muffled sobs only just audible through his tight gag and then Pat went to work on his terrified victim.

With a mind to break any resolve left in Xavier, Pat plonked the would be torture instruments just out of Xavier's reach on the table so that he could see what was in store for him. Turning to Peter knowing he didn't have the stomach for such barbarity, he told him to leave. In loyalty Peter decided to stay, but inside he dreaded what he was about to witness. Pat slowly and carefully inspected each tool in turn, feeling them and miming practices with each one: Xavier watched every move, his petrified eyes bulging and suffused with blood followed Pat with horror.

"Are you ready to tell me what you know?" Pat's voice was calm and cold. "Tell me when you're ready to speak to me." Pat was actually looking for some pliers to break one or two of Xavier's fingers, but his eyes lit on a bundle old large rusty screwdrivers. Carelessly picking one up, Pat twirled it in his fingers.

"Come on, we haven't got much time." Pat noted, turning to Peter. "What is the time?"

Xavier instinctively glanced at his wrist, and like a cat Pat pounced – stabbing the hand with the screwdriver, piercing it right through Xavier's palm into the table. Holding it in place with his free hand, Pat picked up a hammer from the bag and hit the tool driving it an inch into wood. At the sight Peter was instantly sick, holding his mouth to stop the vomit from spraying everywhere, he ran as fast as he could and locked himself in the bathroom. Knowing the gag would never be sufficiently tight enough to completely muffle the screams from the captive's lips, Pat wandered over to the ancient television and turned it on to drown out his sounds.

"Are you ready to speak to me yet?" Pat asked as he picked up another screwdriver and felt its point with his thumb as he looked at the blubbering Xavier. "It's a Phillips and not very sharp!" On the television in the background Benny Hill was putting his angels through their paces, and the familiar theme tune was playing as he speedily chased the scantily clad women around a garden. Staring coldly into Xavier's eyes, Pat picked up the hammer and placed the new screwdriver on the already spiked hand. He was just readying himself to strike again when Xavier started nodding feverishly and mumbling 'yes' through his gag. Pat loosened the strip of cloth just as a green-looking Peter re-entered the room, it was then Xavier started talking. He retold his tale of treachery, lies and deceit starting at the very beginning, from the time he worked for the Shah's regime, how he met James and used him hoping to further his career, the pursuit of Jasmine and her father's ledger, the accidental shooting of Sue, how he convinced the Americans to trust him, eventually becoming an agent for them. He freely admitted still working for the extreme Islamist powers that controlled Iran, and was proud of his work for them as a double agent, saying how easy it was to mislead the Americans and British, as they were prepared to listen to anything he told them. He got them to believe that the Al Qaeda plot was aimed at a rock concert at the 02 in Greenwich. At times Xavier started to show some reluctance during his confession, but Pat merely picked up the tools to get him to resume.

Peter was amazed how easily he had hardened to the spectacle of watching someone suffer dreadfully at the hands of another, berating himself for being so quick to accept it. Inside he felt sorry for Xavier, who was pleading for some water so Peter, probably for the first time ever, ignored Pat when he said Xavier couldn't have any, and fetched a beaker full for him to drink. Refreshed he carried on with his story. Punctuated with sobs and moans he told of why he took the assignment in England; how, when he heard the name, "James Cahill", it convinced him to leave the comfort of his office and assume the role of field operative once more, hoping to be able to settle old scores.

He was aware that the old moderate imam had been murdered to make way for the extremists, and knew that the Mosque was being used as a central coordination point for insurrection against Great Britain. Peter and Pat had been listening, absorbed by everything Xavier said, but Pat needed to know exactly what actual plans were in place at the present time, and he needed to know quickly.

"Enough of your fucking life story, but you're missing the point; I need you to tell me what you and you're fucking raghead mates are planning?" Xavier was silent. Pat's voice had changed tone, from softly inquiring and matter of fact, to forceful and demanding, "I see I'm going to have to hurt you again!" The room fell into silence as Pat rummaged in the tools for a suitable instrument to further terrify the quaking prisoner. In the background *The Benny Hill show* had just finished, and another old series was about to start, the announcer apologising that it was the last show of their great, eighties classics evening.

Xavier was watching Pat's every move, and when he picked out some fearsome-looking pipe grips and held them up for the captive's inspection, Xavier resumed talking, begging Pat not to hurt him anymore and told all. The plan was to blow up certain strategic parts on the underground, where the major Fibre-optic cables were vulnerable; the main aim was to disrupt communications as well as kill as many commuters as possible at the same time. Waving his new instrument of torture under his victim's nose, Pat asked how they were going to get enough explosive in position without being noticed.

"It's already there, they've been smuggling it in for weeks in their lunchboxes! There are millions of hiding places down there, you'll never find it!" Xavier's voice was getting weaker by the second, and he was on the verge of fainting, so Pat picked up the remains of the half-drunk beaker of water and threw it into his face, bringing him round.

"Which stations and when is it all planned for?"

Xavier smiled a weak smile, "I don't know exactly where, anyway you're too late, it's going to happen tomorrow in the rush hour, it's all in place ready to go!" The opening bars of *The Good Life* struck up in the background, mockingly striking a sharp contrast to the events happening in the room.

Pat knew that the tortured man had more to tell, but the urgency of the present situation dictated the next moves, which were to try and coordinate a rescue of the communications network in London along with the possibility of saving hundreds of innocent lives, Christian, Muslim and others.

CHAPTER 13

A distant church clock had just struck midnight, Monday 28th April had arrived; Peter's thoughts went back to his schooldays and one of Mr Vincent's Shakespearian quotes from *Henry IV,* when the boys were found staying up late "We have heard the chimes at midnight!"

His mind was cruelly snatched back to reality as Pat hurried by him, anxious to return to the American car hidden in a backstreet some three hundred yards away. The two men, still dressed as vagrants fought their way along the road supporting the stunned Xavier, appearing as they did before, like three itinerant drunks wending their sorry way back to whatever they called home. Arriving back to the huge car, they bundled the unconscious Xavier in next to his dead friend, behind the front seats, where so recently Peter had spent time crouched so uncomfortably in hiding. Xavier was in no condition to reveal any more of the treacherous plan, and Pat had no further use for him, and the only sensible thing to do was to kill him and get rid of the bodies to prevent the Americans from finding out about the treatment of their very special agent.

Pat drove three or so miles before he found a suitable place to get rid of the evidence of his inquisition. Screeching up an apparently little-used side road, Pat found an open space in the secluded wooded area he thought would be appropriate to get rid of evidence. Years before Pat had promised himself to have his revenge on Xavier and felt little pity for his hated, semi-conscious traitorous prisoner, who had in the past caused so much grief. Peter was mortified as Pat coldly dragged Xavier out of the car by his blood-stained jacket, suggesting he should pray, as he didn't want to send him unshriven to hell. Standing behind the prisoner he kicked the man to his knees and disregarding the stammered terrified pleas for mercy and snatches of prayer, he mercilessly slit Xavier's throat, being very careful not to get covered with the resulting shower of blood. At the sight Peter was sick again, retching, trying to void his already empty stomach, and only being able to produce strings of bile coloured mucus. As quickly as he could Pat bundled the still twitching body into the vehicle and started a fire on the back seat, feeding the blaze with anything flammable to hand, and when he was happy that it was big enough to do its job, he left with Peter to find a car to steal.

The pair sprinted at top speed for about two hundred yards before Peter's legs were unable to race further, forcing him to break into a hurried walk. They had been travelling for ten minutes when from behind there was an enormous flash, followed by a deafening boom. Peter looked questioningly at Pat who came up with a reason for the large explosion. "That lying little fucker was transporting explosives for them! We've been driving a fucking great bomb!" Peter had recovered enough from his sickness, and his exertions, to wheeze at Pat, "Well at least that will have got rid of all the evidence!" "And it will attract the police and fire services from all over London; we had better get the fuck out of here, pronto!" Pat exclaimed, knowing that he had to find to find a car before everyone in whole area was wide awake, staring out of the windows gawping at the emergency vehicles, haring to the conflagration with lights flashing and sirens blaring.

Pat estimated that they had a period of roughly five more minutes to steal a suitable vehicle before all hell was let loose. He was seeking the ideal car not to attract attention, nothing too flashy, neither too new nor too old, when his eyes rested on a Mitsubishi Pajero, a famously easy car to steal. It took him less than thirty seconds to break in and start it without causing any damage to someone's pride and joy. Pat was right, within no time at all, the air was filled with the clamour of dashing fire engines and police cars. Pat drove steadily and calmly past the rushing emergency vehicles in the opposite direction on his way to way to see James, and urgently report to him what he had discovered. The short distance to Whitton was covered in record time, away from the incident the roads were clear and the speed limit was ignored, causing more than one camera to flash, photographing the rushing stolen car.

When they arrived they were surprised to see the lights were still on in the house. Jasmine had retired to bed alone leaving James on his own in his office working, trying to solve the riddle of the mystery terrorist target, puzzling over the possibilities, and help was at hand. Pat tapped gently on the door, rousing James from his work; he seemed surprised when he saw Pat and his decidedly ill-looking son standing at his door they entered and quickly related the order of events that led to the fiery climax and their escape from the scene. One thing perplexed James; he wondered why, if all the explosives were already in place, were

Xavier and his friend transporting dangerous materials unnecessarily? There was no logical answer, other than there was another undisclosed target, which James was becoming more and more convinced that it would probably be the London mayoral elections on 1 May.

At the present moment James had more pressing concerns. Somehow he had to alert the security services that an attack on London's communication network was imminent without interference from either John or Graham at head office. He was fully aware that they would quash any of his attempts to foil the plot, believing, with the able assistance of the late Xavier, the main attack was to be aimed elsewhere. James could come up with only one answer to his conundrum; he was going to go over their heads, and speak directly to the Home Secretary. In the past he occasionally had need to contact some of the senior members of the government, so he knew the protocol and had no trouble contacting the Home Office. Using the word Abyssinian, his own private codename allotted by Lou, James's call was quickly accepted by the duty under secretary, who spoke to a senior under secretary, who in turn contacted the Home Secretary's aide, who eventually spoke to the sleepy Home Secretary himself, who in turn spoke to James. On hearing what James had to tell him, and after having it slowly repeated twice, so that he fully understood the context of the information, knowing and trusting James from before, he instructed the ever growing more frustrated messenger to take whatever actions necessary to try and prevent the attack, reassuring him that John and Graham would be forced to understand.

The whole procedure of contacting the powers that be, took over two hours, and dawn was starting to break when assisted by Pat and Peter, James addressed a hastily arranged meeting in his front room. In total a group of four agents, two communication experts and three senior transport police officers were ordered to attend, and be briefed on the situation. Jasmine did her part by providing some very welcome strong pots of coffee to the weary gathering, who so very recently were slumbering in their warm beds, only to be rudely awakened and dragged unceremoniously to Whitton, and the most important meeting of their lives. The first consideration was to identify the most likely locations on the Underground where the attacks might take place. Initially the older, more senior of the communication experts stood up and bumbled on about communications in general, speaking as though he was talking to a bunch of backward ten-year-olds. Butting in James reminded him that the situation demanded urgency, clearing his throat in annoyance; he laboriously listed thirty-two of the probable stations where an explosion might cause the most damage, giving brief explanations as to why, and then sat back down in a bit of a huff, with his arms crossed defensively in front of his chest.

Taking turns the policemen then stood up and reasoned why some of the sites might be ignored, some because of limited accessibility, others had a clean bill of health, having just passed one of the regular rigorous security checks, so the field had been whittled down to twelve possibilities. Six were in central London, and the other six others were out in the suburbs. The whole process was taking up far too much precious time, and James said as much, raising his voice and thumping the table to make his point to the assembly.

On seeing how anxious James was becoming the younger communication expert stood up, also frustrated by the direction the debate was heading. Without being asked, he loudly expressed his own opinion, "You're barking up the wrong tree!" Angry by the outburst, his older colleague glared menacingly at him, and told him to sit down and shut up. Wanting to hear what he had to say James interceded on the younger man's behalf; first looking somewhat sympathetically at the freshly admonished speaker, and then with a hint of a glare at his senior he called the meeting to order.. "No arguments please, let's listen to what he's got to say." With that the young man, who was in the process of retaking his seat, stood back up and introduced himself.

"Good morning, gentlemen. My name is David, and I am the operations manager for the communications company Reach Out. Unknown to most people there are six Underground stations, all on the outskirts of London, which contain specially designed as communication hubs called Sector Switching Centres, or as we call them SSCs. All the major fibre-optic cables that control London communications run through the tunnels that act as the already made conduits, and the SSCs are the distribution points, and if one goes down we can cope. If two go down, we're in trouble, if three or more fail, we my dear chaps, are totally buggered and London will be in deep doodoos! Nothing will work, no phones, no computers no communications!"

Peter rose from his seat and politely spoke. "Why are they on the outskirts, and not in central London?"

"In case a situation like this one presents itself, and also to equally distribute the fibre-optic network throughout Greater London. It's all very technical, but without them, everything grinds to an almighty halt! Before I finish there's one more thing of interest you should know, three or four weeks ago there was a security breach at one of the SSCs, and two over-interested underground employees were fired.

James pricked up his ears; he was very interested in what the man had to say. "What type of employees, and what did they do?"

"They were cleaners at Finsbury Park, and during a routine security check they were found to have postage stamp-sized scraps of paper that could easily be construed as parts of sketches of the area where the hub is located," he turned and stared pointedly at his boss. "Didn't they Mr Morgan?" His boss shuffled uncomfortably in his seat. James then asked, "Why wasn't it reported to us, or someone like us?"

"I was told that it wasn't important, because, apparently, the sketches weren't maps like I thought they were. I was told they were probably Arab doodles, they were very small and crude, it was hard to say. I personally thought that they fitted together like pieces of a jigsaw puzzle, but I was overruled!" Once again David looked at the agitated Mr Morgan. Pat and James spoke with one voice, "Arab?" James continued alone. "Where are these SSCs or hubs, or whatever they're called?"

"The main two are at Ealing Broadway, and The Elephant and Castle, other four are at Finsbury Park, Harrow on the Hill, Earls Court and Canary Wharf Park, there are a few more non-essential areas, but, if I wanted to do most damage to the communication network, these are where I would strike.

Incidentally the culprits were never sacked from Finsbury Park, they just disappeared off the face of the earth!'"

James wanted to extract a little more information from David. "Who knows about these SSCs?"

"Loads of people, they're one of those poorly kept secrets everybody knows about!"

James thanked David for his candour and took total control of the meeting, delegating jobs to the agents and even to the senior police officers, who didn't appreciate it too much. He arranged for specialist anti-terrorist operatives to be despatched from their base at top speed to the locations of the major SSCs. James made sure everything that could be done was in place before he left to see for himself. The neighbours were all awake and amazed at the unfolding events at the house, they stretched out of their windows to get a better look as the attendees of the meeting dispersed, leaving with police outriders, sirens and lights. Never before had such a clamour disturbed the backstreets of the relatively quiet suburb of London that had momentarily become the security centre of Great Britain.

James, Peter and Pat headed off in one car, followed by the most senior police officer and the younger communications expert in another, where they were going to liase with the security team supposedly already in position at the Elephant and Castle station. The rest of the informed group were despatched around London to the expected targets, to link up with the specialists and try and prevent the attacks. James, Pat and Peter were driven at high speed, in a souped up large white BMW chauffeured by a very capable speed-loving police officer, accompanied by three equally capable motorbike outriders. All four vehicles were flying to their destination with blues and twos turned on, the noise was deafening, but exciting as they roared to the famous landmark.

On the back seat of the luxury car, James and Peter sat either side of a noticeably quiet Pat, trying to discuss the problem above the din. Seeing that Pat's eyebrows betrayed that he was in a bit of a mood, James looked at him, concerned by his silence.

"What's up Pat, you look down in the dumps?"

"Don't worry, it's just me, I often feel down when I've been cruel," he explained, his sad voice full of remorse. "I'm not really like that, but it had to be done. I'm like Jekyll and Hyde, sometimes I hate myself, I joke about killing people!" Peter was still in shock over the violent deaths he had just witnessed, but, unwittingly, Pat had given a valid reason for them and it made Peter feel a little better, and he spoke trying to bring Pat out of his gloom, "What about Mr bloody useless Morgan?"

Pat instantly perked up. "I'd enjoy shooting him, fucking useless isn't the word for it, he's so bad at his job, he's a fucking danger! I don't give him much hope of still being in work tomorrow morning."

James added his two penneth worth, "He reminds me of my ex-bosses, they can work out the square root of a pickled egg, but can't get the lid off the flipping jar!"

"Ex-bosses?" Peter inquired.

"Yes, before we left, I made a quick phone call, I promised to keep the Home Secretary updated I don't think he was too chuffed with them, and amazingly they both have been feeling unwell and have taken time off sick, and for the time being I'm in charge of the whole shebang. So here I am, the first day on the job, facing being responsible for perhaps the largest catastrophe to happen to this country since the Second World War. Yours truly, signed crapping himself, your boss!"

In what seemed to be no time at all, the car drew up in front of the one of the two station buildings at The Elephant and Castle. Hundreds of frustrated would be commuters had gathered outside the closed and barred station, a carelessly chalked scrawl on a blackboard apologised for any "inconvenience caused," and promised a further update at seven o'clock. James looked at his watch, it was twenty-five minutes past six, and the rush hour was going into full swing.

"I don't think we have enough time. Let's go!" James shouted as both he and Pat jumped out of the still-moving car and started running, plunging into the throng of commuters, parting the crowd like Moses and the Red Sea. Close on their heels, the four policemen that accompanied them there were thundering up behind, leaving Peter, struggling with aching knees, and lagging hopelessly behind. As Peter hobbled into the station, he noticed a familiar face staring at him from the crowd, and before he could do anything about it, the man had disappeared in a blink of an eye, merging into the throng; it was the face of Ul Haq, probably there to gloat over the carnage he was expecting. As Peter entered the station he was overtaken by another group of heavily armed police, who galloped past him and hurdled the barriers, bravely racing to their possible doom.

Some way ahead of Peter, James had halted the small army of police, giving Peter time to catch up and join the body of men who were listening to him instigating a hastily thought up plan. He needed a situation report, so he was asking for four volunteers, one for each platform, to enter the station to reconnoitre ahead, before giving permission for the main body to follow. All the men agreed to go, so James selected four at random and gave them a sketchy briefing; he wasn't actually sure what they were looking for, as the communication expert and the senior officer hadn't arrived yet, but he simply told them to watch out for anything suspicious, and to take any action they thought appropriate. Allotting them each a platform, they scampered off down the tunnel, into the bowels of the station to do their duty.

They had only just disappeared down the lengthy flight of stairs when the red-faced tardy chief inspector Alexander Robson turned up along with an anxious-looking David. James gave them an outline of his plan, and was in the process of telling the chief superintendent about the instructions he had given to his men when from the depths, echoing up the stairwell, came a short burst of gunfire, followed by a blast of scorching heat and a rumbling boom, the resulting shockwave fortunately blowing everyone off their feet, and saving them from the stream of red-hot shrapnel fired up the tunnel like grapeshot from a cannon. Deafened, bewildered and burnt they scrambled to their feet, David was unconscious, and bleeding from a head wound sustained when he was blown backwards into a wall. Pat had been peering down the stairs, trying to be closer to any possible action when the explosion occurred; the storm of searing heat had not only scorched his face, and reduced his eyebrows to white patches amid the toasted reddened skin, but also lifted him off his feet luckily for him, his fall was broken when he landed on a cushion which happened to be the chief superintendent. James had been lucky; most of the force of the blast was absorbed by a large police motorcyclist who was standing directly in between him and the stairs, shielding him and falling on him, his padded leathers protecting him from being hurt. Peter was at the back and was totally unscathed except for the ringing in both ears and a twisted ankle sustained in his fall, adding to his lower limb woes.

Pat was the first to speak, looking around surveying the mayhem, blinking like a moulting owl with singed hair and white shadows amongst the red of his face, denoting where his eyebrows once were. Prophetically he announced shouting, because of his temporary deafness. "Fucking hell! That's fucking torn it!" The dishevelled police officer scowled at him, disapproving of his language, and was about to complain when James simply told him to shut up and bite his tongue, as there were much more important things to worry about.

Pat was on the verge of giving his admonisher a mouthful of abuse when, alert as ever, he suddenly darted off down the stairs without saying a word; and when James looked to see where he had gone, he could just about make out two figures appearing out of the dust-filled air. It was Pat assisting one of the volunteers back from the epicentre of the explosion, acting as his crutch, he managed to get the ragged, bleeding man back to James and laid him gently on the floor, placing his jacket under his head to act as a pillow. The man's sooty face looked up to James and his boss who were both bending over him and feebly mumbled, "They're all dead, it's carnage. They blew it up as a train was pulling in, there's hundreds down there!"

Within moments, floods of stunned, scorched and battered commuters started to appear, their shadowy forms emerging from the dust and grime like ghostly apparitions rising from the pits of hell. Peter stared at them, horrorstruck, thinking that at least six other sites were about to meet the same fate, if they hadn't already. He turned to his father, who was looking equally horrified, "We must stop the trains, it's the only way!" James instantly pulled his mobile out of his pocket yet, when he tried to use it, no signal flashed up on the screen. He asked Peter for his, and the same thing happened.

"The network's down!"

The quick-thinking Peter turned to the police constable that drove them there and asked, "Is your radio working?"

The man fiddled with it for a second and answered in the affirmative, and handed to him who handed it to James; he wasn't used to using one so he handed it back to the policeman who relayed a message destined for the Home Secretary.

"Tell him Abyssinian says shut down the whole Underground network, turn the power completely off!"

The chief superintendent remonstrated with James. "You don't know what you're doing! You can't do that! All those people trapped in the dark with no ventilation. There will be mass panic, and people will get killed!" James stared straight back at him, "I do know what I'm doing! It's my call and from what I've heard it's probably the only way to stop them from getting killed."

Pointedly ignoring the senior policeman's wishes, James seconded the helpful driver at his private radio operator to his service, to relay messages to all the other target stations, sending orders, and trying to prevent another catastrophe like the one he had just witnessed. In no time at all the emergency services had started to arrive in droves, and looking around him James decided that there was nothing more he could at the ravaged Elephant and Castle, so he had a decision to make, whether to go to Canary

Wharf or Earls Court, where the two nearest Sector Switching Centres were located.

His new private radio operator was familiar with the area and he offered some welcome advice, "Earls Court is closer, but Canary Wharf is quicker, the roads will be less crowded."

Thankful for some local knowledge to help him, James made his choice and shouted to Pat, commanding him to follow. Reading the situation, Peter had already started hobbling towards the exit in anticipation of his father's next move. As Pat overtook Peter, he realised the difficulty he was having, so grabbing his sleeve, he towed him stumbling all the way to the car they arrived in, through the burgeoning crowds of police, firemen, medics and injured.

James's new driver proved that his motoring skills would be better placed at Brands Hatch; being fully aware of the utmost need for urgency he sped apparently heedlessly through the crowded streets, even managing to impress Pat, who marvelled at his prowess behind the wheel. After a surprisingly short while the speeding car bumped up the kerb onto a spacious concourse in front of a large glass-domed portal, which was the entrance to the very space age-looking Canary Wharf Underground Station. A huge frustrated crowd were being herded and jostled some fifty yards from the doorways, being held back by a line of straining police officers, who soon scattered swiftly when the warning siren of the flying car alerted them. The expert driver skidding the vehicle to a halt just a few feet from the door and as one they all alighted together and entered the building.

Inside the foyer three groups of four specialist armed police had gathered, but without specific instructions they just stood aimlessly, not knowing what to expect or what actions to take. Each unit had a sergeant in charge, summoning them to him, James briefed them on the situation and made his decision; he was going to take one of the groups to Earls Court, and Pat was to take the other to Finsbury Park, leaving Peter in charge of the remainder. Wishing Pat and his father good luck, Peter gave a little wave to his friends and promptly led the quartet down the massive stationary escalators and deep into the ground. As previously arranged by James the power was off, and deliberately none of the emergency lights were switched on.

Near to the heavily glazed entrance there was plenty of light to see by, but the further in they got the darker it became. Peter wasn't someone who often carried a weapon, but he was fully versed in the use of them, thanks mainly due to his early years with Pat, and on this occasion he opted for a small semi-automatic machine, mostly because of its lightness, but also as it had a bright light positioned above the barrel. The men fumbled and groped their way down into the shadowy depths, passing confused commuters, as they emerged from the dark, with nothing but the light of their mobile phones to illuminate their escape from the pitch-black tunnel.

With trepidation, they entered the body of the station, which was strangely lit with an eerie pale greenish blue light, where the other commuters had followed the lead and also used their otherwise useless phones as lanterns. Confusion reigned everywhere zombie-like people meandered about in the gloaming not knowing what to do, or where to go. Peter had a fantastic advantage over the rest of the people down in the gloomy depths; during his homeless days, when he had spent all the daylight hours in hiding in the shadows and only venturing out in the dark, Peter had developed an ability to see reasonably well at night. Putting his enhanced senses to good use, Peter scanned the thronging faces, trying to spot anyone that stood out from the others, looking for any possible signs of malicious intent. Desperately, he rushed up and down, forcing his reluctant ailing legs to obey his commands, ignoring the agony he subjected them to by making them run. Followed closely by his armed retinue he raced up to strangers, peered into their faces, dismissing them as harmless he then rushed up to someone else. Peter was nearing the very end of the second platform when he glimpsed a man who was trying, but failing to remain unseen by lurking around a corner in the mouth of the tunnel, and hiding out of sight in the shadows. Attracted by the man's furtive demeanour, Peter positioned himself to get a closer look.

As soon as their eyes met, Peter recognised him as one of the volunteers from the Mosque and he, in turn, recognised Peter. Looking startled for a moment, and then a little frightened when he realised who the armed person was, the man shouted the first lines of an Islamic prayer and pulled what looked like a remote-control device out of his pocket. Instinctively Peter shot him, aiming his gun and firing, giving it no thought, hitting the man twice in the right side of his chest and instantly felling him. Responding, two of the burly officers jumped on the prostrate man to prevent any opportunity of him being able to complete his task, while the other two plunged around the corner to shine their torches on any others that could be about to seize the chance to gain glory. The sight that met them stopped them in their tracks, two crates of explosives had been strategically placed in an alcove opposite a doorway, and were primed ready to go. The shot man was fading fast, and Peter bent down and tried to question him, but the man was too ill to answer. He was only eighteen or nineteen years old, and still had downy cheeks, a black scarf was tied around his young head, and Peter quietly prayed in Arabic with him as the last light of life faded from his eyes.

Satisfied that the bomb was safe, one of the police officers was despatched by the sergeant with a message to switch the emergency lights on, and with a ragged cheer the utter gloom was promoted to something close to twilight. Allowing the would-be early morning commuters to leave the station and return to their homes.

In the half-light, Peter surveyed the location as it was being taped off with striped blue tape which announced that it was a crime scene and nobody was to cross it. He was in a state of shock, he had seen people killed before and felt sorry for them no matter what they had done, but never in his worst nightmares did he ever consider that he would be responsible for snuffing out such a young man, who had been lured into believing that his life was a fair trade for an act of war designed to hurt as many innocents as possible. Peter knew inside that his actions saved hundreds of people from being either maimed or killed, but he was still unable to erase the picture of the dying young eyes out of his head.

Dazed and stunned with his ears still ringing from the gunfire, Peter was escorted away from the site to a police mobile incident unit which had been parked on the concourse immediately adjacent to the glass dome. As soon as possible after the event Peter and the four police officers who were present at the shooting were obliged to be interviewed by senior officers. As the shooter Peter was interviewed first, and the police were completely happy with his account, hailing him as the hero who saved the day, but still he didn't feel better about the shooting. Peter limped past the four new friends who were waiting to relate their individual accounts of the events at the tunnel to the investigators. As he wearily passed them, they each in turn stood and shook his hand gratefully, pleased not to have been blown to smithereens.

Traipsing outside Peter plonked his behind on the nearest seat he could find, grateful to rest his weary painful legs while he waited for any news. For quite a while he stayed there worrying about his father and Pat, and musing on the shocking occurrences of the day, when he was approached by a very senior police officer in a heavily braided uniform, who questioningly asked him if he was Peter Cahill. Peter answered his tired voice managing just about to say, "Yes, that's me." The man smiled, pleased to have found him.

"I've some news from your father and his assistant," he said. "They're both fine. Unfortunately they were unable to prevent two of the other attacks, but they're on their way here to pick you up and tell you themselves, and I wish to offer you my personal thanks for your prompt action."

Peter started to get to his feet in politeness to the friendly man, who, on noticing how pained he looked, immediately gestured for him not to rise, telling him to stay seated as he had earned the rest. A welcome cup of tea and a plate of biscuits were brought to him from within the caravan; he assumed that the officer recognised his need for refreshment, and obliged him by having it sent out. Peter sat on the bench, keeping himself amused as he sipped his tea, by watching as the emergency services run hither and thither, at first apparently aimlessly, and before his eyes the disorderly comings and goings started taking on more purpose and, before long, out of the original chaos there came order.

Peter had stayed in his seat for some short while before the bomb disposal squad arrived; quietly and without fuss, they went about their business. Their first task was to have the police cordon extended away from the glass dome; they adjudged the original fifty yards too close and dangerous to any spectators in case of an explosion., Much to the annoyance of the police, they demanded it moved out another fifty to a hundred, forcing the position of the mobile station to also be changed, along with the now comfortable Peter, who was forced to forsake his ease and give up his seat. Still in a trance, he wandered back away from the entrance along with the multitude of nosing bystanders, when he suddenly caught sight of Pat's scorched eyebrowless face, scanning the sea of people. On seeing Peter alive and well, he waved wildly and, barging his way through the crowd, ran towards him. When Pat was close enough to Peter he clutched his arm and pulled him out of the throng, to be soon reunited with his anxious father, who was still accompanied by his commandeered driver. All of the men were delighted to see one another, amazed that had defied the odds by remaining alive.

All phone lines were dead, and communication was almost impossible, but, although overly busy, the police radios were still in operation, and Ian, the large-framed commandeered police driver was more than happy to act as James's own personal telephonist, allowing him use his. All day James had been in regular contact with the Home Secretary and a special priority channel for their private use had been set up. James needed to update him on the present situation, and with the aid of Ian entered into a lengthy conversation with him.

It had been agreed that there was little more to be done that day and it was decided that going home to rest was the best option, so much more sedately than before the trio made their way back to Whitton. The car was driven away from the turmoil without too much urgency, and James took the opportunity to tell Peter exactly what had occurred. The attack at Ealing had met with complete success, the switching station had been completely destroyed, along with eighty-odd commuters and many more casualties. The bomb at Finsbury Park had been partially successful, badly damaging the SSC, but there were many less casualties. The other two attacks had failed and both would-be perpetrators had been arrested in one piece and sent for interrogation. Pat chimed in saying that they should be handed over to him if they wanted them to talk. Peter thought to himself that they most certainly would, knowing his methods, and remembering the grizzly fate of Xavier.

During his lengthy conversation with the Home Secretary, James requested the use of a dozen police radios and their own secure channel to tide him and his men over until normal communications were restored. Receiving an instant sanction for his request, James deliberately sought out the grumpy chief inspector to oblige him, and after having to convince him with a radio call to one of the aides to the Home Secretary, the aggravated policeman begrudgingly ordered a sergeant to fulfil the requisition. After ten minutes, the man returned, complete with the desired items, and, grinning smugly, he handed them over to James in front of the senior policeman. Issuing a device to each one of his men, James retained some for the others who weren't available at that precise moment. Ian proved to be as good a teacher as he was a driver, and after a brief lesson James and Peter were able to use them with ease. In fact they looked more complicated than they actually were, but still a bridge too far for Pat who was totally inept when it came to any form of technology.

With the partial success of the attacks on the London tube stations, most of all the senior officials became more relaxed, believing that the threat to national security was over. James and his team had been congratulated from the top, as all the higher authorities realised that, without their prompt actions, the result would have been much worse. The Prime Minister had been advised that it was probable the explosions were supposed to be detonated all at the same time, to create as much mayhem as possible, and it was almost certain that the explosion at the Elephant and Castle was all but unpreventable. Yet the turning off of the power confused the bombers and saved three of the other locations from being utterly destroyed. James accepted the plaudits on behalf of his team, but was still aware that there was probably much worse to come.

CHAPTER 14

It was past three in the afternoon when they eventually departed on the journey back to Whitton. Peter noticed that outside of the car everything seemed different, the whole of the city was in chaos, all the major shops were closed and burglar alarms were going off everywhere, their ear-splitting rings and wails filling the air. Most of the traffic lights were out of operation, causing confused queues of traffic at junctions, where the puzzled drivers meandered about mixing with the bewildered pedestrians who frustratedly tried and re-tried their useless mobile phones. The businesses were shut and their employees simply gathered outside their places of work, perplexed with nothing to do and nowhere to go, even the busses weren't running to take them home, recalled in case of more attacks on the public transport system.

All three of the men had been up for hours, and they all needed to rest their weary bodies, especially Peter whose injured legs were grieving him sorely. It was with great relief when they drew up in front of the welcome sight of James's house, anticipating first some food and then bed. The house appeared strange, the front door was wide open and there was no smiling Jasmine to welcome them. James felt worried as he alighted from the car and a wave of dread swept over him, a feeling of horror consumed him; instinctively he knew that something was dreadfully wrong and his stomach knotted as he entered the gaping door into the strangely silent hall, Jasmine had gone! The house inside had been ransacked and there had very clearly been a struggle. All three of the others followed in his wake of the terrified James as he raced through the house, turning things upside down, frantically searching for his missing love. The men looked at each other amazed, trying to work out what had transpired, when Pat stopping dead in his tracks, cocked his head to one side, listening. Shushing the group to silence he held up a hand to quiet them, and then without warning he plunged into the back garden, full of hope the others followed.

A horrific sight greeted them. Lying in a pool of jellified blood was poor old Bob, the friendly next-door neighbour, beaten, bleeding and unable to get up off the ground, he was still conscious and he looked up gratefully at the welcome arrivals, worried that without rescue he would have perished there on the ground. On seeing the state of the fallen man, Ian, who as well as the driver of a police armed response vehicle, was also a qualified police first aider, called straight away for an ambulance on his radio, and carried out a cursory assessment of his condition. Adjudging that he was fit enough to be moved, Ian carefully assisted the unsteady old fellow into the house and on to the settee to administer to his considerable injuries. Although sore and still slightly dazed, he was lucid enough to retell a full story of what had happened. Quaking with delayed shock, Bob asked to have a smoke to calm his nerves while he retold his tale. Nobody in the company smoked so Pat raced round to the old boy's house to where he kept his cigarettes and soon returned with a packet of Super Kings. Lighting one he handed it to the eager Bob, who held out trembling hand to accept the smouldering cigarette, and after a giant drag on the glowing fag, he felt able to start his account.

Pausing to think, and surrounded by a cloud of grey blue smoke, Bob recounted what had befallen to the assembly. "I was pottering about in my garden doing some weeding when I heard a kerfuffle followed by a scream," he paused again to have another long drag at the shrinking cigarette. "I tried to call the police, but the phones weren't working, so I went round to investigate." Bob looked at the ceiling hoping for inspiration, tutting with exasperation James tapped his foot impatiently, wanting to get on with proceedings. "I took my hoe with me in case I needed a weapon. The front door was already open so I went in, two foreign-looking men were dragging Jazzy out of the living room into the hall. I tried to help her, and I hit one of the blokes on his head, and broke my hoe in half." He stopped for a moment and took another colossal draw on the cigarette stub, causing him to cough loudly with a rattle of loosened phlegm. "The man I hit let go of Jasmine and punched me in the head," Bob pointed to a shining purple lump on his forehead. "He knocked me down on the floor, and then kicked me in the stomach," he coughed again, cleared his throat and resumed. "I got up, but he chased me with the hoe. I tried to escape but I only got as far as the garden, I tripped over and he beat me up with the metal end of the hoe." Bob showed the several cuts and bruises on his head and shoulders, to give more credence to his account.

Consumed by impatience James listened to the tale, desperate to go and search for Jasmine he hurried Bob along, confusing the old-boy. Although equally as anxious to find Jasmine, Peter was in a much more rational frame of mind than his father and among the questions to old Bob, he asked if he had noticed anything unusual. He thought for a moment and replied that there was a dark blue Transit van parked in the road, with a woman in the front.

"A woman?" Peter's ears pricked up. "Was she a blonde, brunette, maybe a redhead?" Bob thought for another few moments much to the annoyance of a frustrated James.

"I don't know! Her head was covered with a black shawl." James looked at Peter who looked back at James, Peter said what they all were thinking.

"Sue!" Pat joined in. "Fucking hell! She always hated Jasmine; ever since they met she was jealous of her!"

James looked horror struck. "She always promised to get her revenge, Xavier must have told her that we would be bloody well tied up with the bombings, and she took her chance, the vengeful bitch!" Ian had been listening carefully to them, and not understanding completely what happened before, his voice of reason spoke.

"I don't really know what's gone on, but I do know that you need a plan, and on behalf of the chief constable I offer my services. After all, I have been seconded to you." Outside an ambulance noisily announced its arrival, waiting to take Bob to hospital, and the proper medical care he so badly needed.

The time was four thirty in the afternoon when the three men and their new conscript gathered around James's kitchen table. James had recovered slightly from the initial shock of discovering that his beloved Jasmine was missing, believed kidnapped by a long time enemy, his insane ex-wife the vengeful Sue. Making his best attempt to put his emotional connection with the problem to one side, and trying to remain professionally detached, he addressed the problem speaking to the men as one, "we know why, we know when, what we need to know is what Sue's intentions are, and where they've got her?" He looked hopefully at Peter. "Can you ask your homeless friends to keep their eyes open for us, and find out if they've seen anything." He then looked at Ian. "You're a policeman, can you go house to house and find out if anyone saw anything we don't know about?" James voice faltered for a second, "Pat can go with Peter he might need a helping hand! I've got people to see."

Having donned the old clothes they had not long before removed, Pat and Peter went to seek out and blend in with the homeless that had proved so useful; happy they looked scruffy enough, the pair went off on their mission with even more urgency than usual. Ian undertook the laborious task of going door to door, asking stupid questions to reluctant people, a job he joyously left behind four years before and promised himself never to do again. Yet in this case he was happy to make an exception to help his newest bunch of comrades in arms. James went about his errands, firstly to see Michael, to send him to act as bodyguard to James's eighteen-year-old student son William and then to seek his oldest son Ibrahim, to see if he could throw any light on the matter.

Peter was keen to seek out Simon as he considered him to be the most reliable and the ringleader of the local vagrant community and unknown to the high-ranking policeman. Peter had stolen one of the radios for him to use. Following his gut-instinct, Pat disappeared on his own secret mission, finding the watching place in the old disused yard, folding his slight frame into a neat shady spot behind the gate and observing all through the crack.

It took Peter over an hour to find Simon. Normally he would be asleep in one of two places during the daylight hours, but on this occasion he was nowhere to be found, so having given up his search Peter took a detour past Ul Haq's Halal grocers shop, he was wandering past, on the opposite side of the street trying not to be noticed, when a noise from a large heap of discarded cardboard boxes and rubbish in an alley between two uninhabited shops attracted his attention:

"Pssssst!" And then again, "Psssssssst! It's me! I'm here."

Peter soon understood that the familiar voice emanating from the heap of refuse was that of his missing comrade, Simon. Bending down Peter pretended to be interested in the pile of debris, mumbled quietly out of the side of his mouth, "What on earth are you doing here?"

The bodiless voice answered, "What you asked me to do, keep my eye on your mate in there. It took me ages last night to gather up all this crap!" Peter moved a torn cardboard box pretending to look interested in it, revealing a pair of eyes, staring back at him. "Put that back they'll see me! There's been a lot going on, Ul Haq's been running about like a scared rabbit. I tried to phone you but they're not working, what's happened?" Peter told him briefly about the events, and why the phones weren't working, and then told Simon he had better be on his way, because he thought that he had started to attract unwanted attention, promising to return later, after dark. Peter kicked the heap with apparent frustration, being careful not to make contact with Simon, and went on his way to find Pat.

Peter found Pat still keeping his vigil in the yard. He only just saw him crouching out of the way, making himself as small as possible. As nothing of note had occurred during his stay, out of boredom, Pat had been whittling at the spyhole, making it larger and giving him a wider field of view. "I can see better now," he added peering through his enhanced hole. "I've been bored shitless, it's been as quiet as the grave out there, nothing happened, so I've been thinking." Pat added as he started on some food and drink brought by Peter. Pat was in one of his philosophical moods. "It seems funny to me why they bothered to take Jasmine away with them, if they wanted her dead they would have done it there and then? It doesn't add up to me?" Peter gained some hope from Pat's observations; he hadn't considered that they wanted her alive as either bait, security or as a bartering tool.

Peter sat with Pat, watching and hoping until darkness arrived at around nine. Still nothing was happening so he bade Pat a disappointed goodbye, and hurried back to the shop as fast as his ailing legs would carry him, fretting with every painful step, cursing his aching knees, to where he expected to find Simon, and all he found was a closed, shuttered and locked shop, and where the pile of rubbish lay there was a simple note, scrawled in chalk on the pavement *back to d'way twelve!* Peter knew exactly what it meant even though it was in a crude sort of code. Simon liked to make things secretive, and he often spoke in strange riddles to test the recipients of his ideas.

Once again Peter made his way back, another half-mile, lugging his worsening legs all the way to the doorway at number twelve, near to Ul Haq's house; and at last he found Simon, crouching under an old coat this time, smiling up like a naughty boy. "I'm glad you found me, you got my message then? Your mate has been going back and forth all afternoon, a foreign geezer's using his van and he's been walking everywhere, and I've followed him, I'm knackered." Peter took the time to consider his own knees, and Simon carried on. "The wheelchair woman came to the shop with a delivery."

Peter perked up. "What sort of delivery?"

Simon thought for a second. "A carcase I think? Two blokes were with her, and carried it in wrapped in a sheet!"

"What did they bring it in?"

Again Simon paused to recall the scene. "His butcher's van, the blue Transit! Come to think of it was rather big to be a sheep or goat, and it wasn't stiff like they normally are! I think they're having some sort of meeting there, loads of them have been arriving."

"Why didn't you stay there then?" Simon sounded a little chagrined at the question. "Because I thought it best to follow your man, and I can't be in two places at once, now can I?" Peter apologised to the irate Simon, he knew that he needed Pat with him, and remembering his new radio he decided to use it:

"Peter to Pat! Peter to Pat over!" From the other end all that there were several clicks, and then suddenly the radio loudly burst into life.

"Fucking hell! Ah, yes, that's it!" was the only reply; this was Pat's booming voice, echoing noisily down the street, as he wrestled with the unfamiliar piece of technology. Quickly Peter located the volume knob and turned it anticlockwise, making the incoming message too faint. Readjusting it Peter made it just about audible enough for them both to hear. "Pat to Peter, can you hear me, over! Fucking hell! Click!" There was a few seconds silence, "Click! Fuck that's it!" Pat had just about mastered the device enough to have a very strange staccato conversation with Peter, punctuated with lots of unexplained expletives and unnecessary clicks, eventually Pat understood that Peter needed him to join him as soon as possible outside Ul Haq's shop, where he surmised Jasmine to be. Peter handed a radio to Simon, gave him a quick lesson in its use, and told him he needed a feline-sounding call sign. He thought for a moment, looked up to the heavens for help and with his honed sense of irony he declared he wanted to be called, "Alley cat!" Peter smiled at his offbeat sense of humour, asking him to carry on doing exactly what he was, and then he hobbled painfully back to the shop.

Strangely it didn't take too long for Peter to make the journey back to the shop, somehow his legs carried a little quicker than they did before, maybe it was the renewed sense of hope, or perhaps he had gone through the pain barrier and was becoming used to the aches? Nevertheless, with slightly more comfort than he had experienced recently he arrived at the location, and met with Pat, who was already there ready and waiting. Peter filled Pat in the details of what he thought might have occurred, and the intelligence supplied by Simon. Pat listened carefully, paused to think for a while, and made an executive decision.

"We've got to go in, no matter what!"

Peter looked straight back into Pat's blistered hairless face. "I think you're right, but how do we get in and how do we know what's in there?"

"We don't, we've just got to hope. It's about time that something got me anyway, I've lived a bit of a charmed life." Pat's less than positive prediction surprised Peter, and he asked, "What are the odds, do you think we've got a chance?"

Pat was honest. Not much, but I'd rather die trying!" So the teacher and student prepared for the worst, but still hoped to rescue the woman that was so dear to them both.

Staying out of sight in the dark, the pair of comrades crouched in total silence, each wondering if they were making the right decision, when very soon an opportunity presented itself to enter the shuttered shop. Ul Haq had arrived back. With a swift gait, he approached his shop furtively, trying not to be noticed, looking guilty as though he had no right to be there. Creeping up to the small locked door in the centre of the shutters, designed for pedestrians' use, Ul Haq glanced over each shoulder in turn, to make sure that the coast was clear and put the key in the lock. Like a flash Pat was on him, knocking him to the ground, and then without a sound he drew his gun stuffing its muzzle between the terrified man's bulging eyes, he threatened Ul Haq to silence, reinforcing his demand with a hushing finger held to his lips, he beckoned for Peter to join him. Using the shocked Ul Haq as a shield by bundling him in front of them, Pat followed by Peter burst through the little door into the butcher's shop. To Pat's horror the door shut automatically behind them with a click, cutting off any chance of escape, and in front of them, looking surprised by the interruption were ten young men with pistols, talking to Ibrahim and Sue. Realising that they were trapped and hopelessly outnumbered Peter looked at Pat, who shrugged with resignation back at him, and handed over their guns and radios to Ul Haq without a fight.

Another shock for Peter was the sight of the wheelchair-bound Sue standing unaided in front of the young men, all of whom appeared to be in a slight state of shock after the unexpected intrusion, looking over to the two captives; Sue could barely believe her eyes when she saw who they actually were. Gathering her thoughts she spoke to the men.

"Well, well well! What have we here then? If it's not the wonderful Pat! And my lovely little boy Peter. How Xavier's going to love it when he sees you."

By way of an apology at being caught Pat gave Peter a sideways glance, Ul Haq saw it and hit Pat in the ear with a confiscated gun, making it bleed. He went to hit again, when Sue interceded, "Leave him in one piece, Xavier doesn't want damaged goods. This one's got a debt to repay, and he owes quite a lot," She turned her attentions on Peter. "You're a naughty boy aren't you, you've been lying to me haven't you? You've been lying to a lot of people, and you're going to be punished for it!"

Peter looked back at her. "And you've been telling the truth I suppose? Or have we just missed a miracle?"

She turned to the young men. "Put them in with the witch." And without any more conversation they were pushed towards a large shabby-looking cool room, and were brutally shoved through the door. Peter almost retching when he was hit by the stench of over-ripe fruit vegetables and most of all the strong smell of stale fatty meat. The brief light from the opened door illuminating the inside, revealing boxes, bags and crates of groceries stacked between the hanging carcasses of goats and sheep. Gazing around in dismay at the cluttered interior Peter noticed the familiar face of his adored step mother Jasmine; alive and well, give or take some bruises and battering.

The door was shut behind them with a loud metallic clunk, plunging it into complete and utter pitch blackness. From out of the shadows Jasmine's worried voice appeared, sounding upset and hesitant. "I can't believe you found me, Sue's saving me for Xavier, he wants to finish the job he started all those years ago!"

Pat's voice emanated from somewhere in the gloom. "They'll have a very long wait; he's where he belongs, in hell! He's dead!"

"How's that?" Jasmine asked with a deep faltering sigh.

"I had to question him and he suddenly died!" Pat lied, neglecting to tell Jasmine the manner of his death to avoid the details.

Peter joined in. "We'd better keep that to ourselves, it might buy us a little more time."

"I can't believe Ibrahim hates me that much, he's in there with her, he just watched as they hit me with their shoes." Jasmine paused to sob. "You know Sue can walk!" She fell into a reflective silence, sobbed two or three more times and asked, "How are we going to ever get out of here, they're going to kill us, aren't they?"

Pat came up with a sort of answer. "Not without a fight. Two things they haven't reckoned on, first they're amateurs and they didn't search me properly, I've still got my little Beretta 950 in my sock. And second they didn't know that Peter's mate Simon saw us going in, and he'll be waiting to see us come out, and when we don't he'll tell James. So let's stay warm, keep our chins up and wait for help."

The little prison was too small and uncomfortable for three people, so Pat and Peter attempted to make a little more room by moving and then carefully re-stacking some of the crates, and as Peter groped about in the darkness his hand felt a light switch at the side of the door, which had been hidden behind a pile of boxes. It was a joy to all when suddenly the darkness was broken, and a wire-covered glass lamp sprang to life, illuminating the sorry group. Jasmine looked frozen, her face was bruised and her nose had been bleeding, the dried blood forming a dark bib down her front. Pat's left ear was badly swollen and had started to turn a shiny purple colour, the shoulder of his grubby old coat sported a redder, fresher blood-stain. Along with his scarlet, peeling eyebrow-less face, he presented a very pretty picture, and Peter just looked like your everyday tramp.

After pottering about for a little while to arrange their cell to gain maximum comfort; Peter gave Jasmine his coat telling her that after spending a year on the streets, freezing half to death, he found it plenty warm enough in the chilly store room. Gratefully accepting it Jasmine wrapped it around herself so that only her eyes were visible, making her look much as she did when James first met her. Arranging some sturdy crates, Peter made a sort of bench so he could sit in a position to ease the aches in his knees. When he was satisfied with his work, he sat and enjoyed a few pain-free moments with his legs stretched out as far as possible, supported in their middle by a crate.

While this was going on Pat scrabbled among the boxes searching for useful objects or any ready to eat food. He was tearing open and inspecting the contents of a likely-looking parcel, when his eyes lit on some very familiar looking thick dark brown waxed paper, sticking out of the poorly re-sealed lid of one of a pile of boxes stacked and hidden out of the way at the back. Even in the poor light he could see it was similar to the paper that new weapons come wrapped in, so Pat clambered over the piled crates to investigate. Opening the inefficiently closed carton, Pat pulled out something that looked a little like a small paint tin; then prising the lid off he sniffed the contents. Giving a low whistle he announced his findings, "fucking hell they're full of homemade explosives, TATP to be precise, triacetone triperoxide, it's about as stable as Sue, one fart and we're history!" Peter had never heard of it, so Pat explained, "It's easy to make and easy to set off, if you drop it it explodes, if you breathe on it explodes. In fact it will go off for no reason at all, it's as dangerous as it comes! That's why they're keeping it cool, to try and keep it safe."

"Is that what they used in the tunnel?" Peter asked thinking of the severity of the blast.

"No! That was mostly C4. It's got an unmistakable smell, you've got to use detonators to set that off, it's very stable you can set fire to it, it just burns!" Stopping to think for a moment, Pat came up with a plan. "Listen! If they've been making this stuff they know exactly how volatile it is and they probably think we won't find it in the dark, in amongst all this clutter, so we'll pocket some. They're hardly likely to search us on the way out are they?" Pat nodded to Peter. "We'll turn the lights off and wait for them to come and get us, hey presto! We've got some grenades."

Happy that they had some sort of plan, Pat and Peter went about putting everything roughly back as it was before, making sure that the boxes that contained the explosives were well covered, turned the light off, and then sat silently freezing in the dark, not even knowing what the time was.

Totally exhausted from the day's exertions, and completely unable to have any effect on the situation, Peter and Pat took the opportunity to grab a few moments of sleep. Very tired from the long arduous day, they found it relatively easy to drift off, leaving Jasmine frightened and being kept wide awake by Pat's sonorous snoring, wondering what next was going to happen and fretting about Ibrahim's indifference towards her. She had no idea how long she had been in the room, and she wasn't even sure if she had slept or not, when the door was suddenly opened with a blast warm wind, instantly rousing the easy to wake Pat out of his slumber and disturbing Peter. The sudden influx of light caused a temporary blindness to the prisoners, and they sat gulping in the fresh air and blinking trying to focus their eyes to identify the gaoler. It was Ibrahim, and another young man who was unknown to any of them, bringing some food and drink for the captives. Watched carefully by his accomplice Ibrahim doled out the victuals, first to Pat, then to Peter and last of all Jasmine, and when he handed her the plate, saying nothing and unseen by his colleague, he deliberately touched her hand and looked her in the eyes, smiled a secret half-smile and left closing the door behind him with a bang.

Pat was upbeat about the visit. "If they're feeding us, they're not going to kill us yet!" he said munching on a slightly stale unidentifiable meat sandwich and pulling a long piece of gristle out of his mouth to inspect it. Jasmine was quiet, taken somewhat aback by the fleeting incident with Ibrahim, and not sure what to make of it, but no matter what, she was pleased to have had the physical contact with her son. Oblivious to everything else, Peter was absorbed in pulling the revolting stringy meat of unknown origin out of the bread, so he could eat it without the filling. Roughly an hour later Ibrahim and his friend arrived back to retrieve the remains of the meal, and the same thing occurred, this time the subtle touch of the hand was coupled with a little wink, to suggested that Ibrahim knew something that he wanted to tell Jasmine but couldn't. Perhaps it was the remains of the affection he once had for his mother, or maybe he was merely expressing his joy in punishing her. Yet the touch from her estranged son gave Jasmine hope and a slightly more heart than she had a little while before.

Several hours passed. Peter wasn't sure of how many had elapsed before the door was opened again, a sudden shaft of light and a gust of refreshing air heralded the time for the captors to inspect their captives once again. This time two different men were standing at the opening. Jasmine had been expressing some bladder discomfort for some time and was anxious to be escorted to the bathroom to relieve herself, her wish was granted and taking it in turns the three prisoners were ushered by the guards to perform their ablutions. Being the most desperate Jasmine went first, taking mental notes of everything as she went through the shop, then up the stairs, along a corridor, past a room with two or three guards playing cards in, and onto a landing to the toilet. The whole premises seemed strangely quiet. On her trip through the building where she expected to see Ibrahim once more and to face the gloats of Sue and the curses of Ul Haq, but to her surprise the journey was conducted in peace. The bathroom had a very small barred window glazed with obscured glass, the exterior of the pane appeared to be very dirty, but, despite that, Jasmine was still able to see that outside full darkness had fallen, and she assumed that it must have been Wednesday the thirtieth of April, the day before the London mayoral elections.

Peter made the trip next, hobbling off slowly between the two escorts, who tugged and swore at him encouraging him to hurry, wanting to return to the game, giving time for Jasmine to brief Pat on what she had noticed. Telling him of the apparent lack of personnel at the shop, and gave him a sketchy idea of the layout of the upstairs. Taking it all in, Pat sat in the pitch black of the storeroom, wiggling his non-existent eyebrows, as if they were trying to aid him with his thoughts as he put the final touches to his desperate plan. As Pat plotted the escape bid he relayed the details to a closely listening Jasmine. "If it's dark it's more likely that James is out there, waiting for chance to make his move. He doesn't want to come charging in like a bull in a china shop, as we'd be the first casualties, wouldn't we? When I go to the bog, I'll kill the blokes with me, hurl a bomb in the room with the other ragheads in, cross my fingers and rescue you and Peter. Sounds simple doesn't it. But that's my plan, and I'm going to stick to it."

Ten minutes later Peter returned, two guards forcibly hurling him back into the store, moaning about how slow he was, kicking him as he tumbled forwards onto the crates he had used as his seat. Then grabbing Pat by his collar, the men dragged him to his feet and out of the room, slamming the door behind them, and once again plunged the store into utter darkness. Jasmine told Peter of Pat's plan, who thought it was a good idea to make an effort to escape, as he was sure that Ul Haq and Sue were sure soon to realise that Xavier wasn't coming to oversee Jasmine's punishment, and were likely carry it out without him. Sitting together in the total hushed silence of the claustrophobic confined space, Peter and Jasmine pricked their ears, listening and wondering what was happening outside the room with Pat and the others. The wait seemed like an eternity, suddenly there was a distant muffled boom – and after what felt like another age the door was flung open. Standing silhouetted against the light were the unmistakable figures of James Michael and Pat, who without any greeting or ceremony plucked both Jasmine and Peter out of the hole which had served as their prison and raced away, hauling them to the outside and freedom. Pat's plan had worked a treat, except for the fact that his makeshift hand grenade was more powerful than he thought, and instead of causing the small bang that he suspected it would, it created an enormous boom accompanied by lots of flame which had set fire to the tinder-dry bare floorboards, and the whole building was threatened to be engulfed by the resulting inferno. With the fire came the probability that the remaining crates of the notoriously unstable, homemade explosive, triacetone triperoxide, would explode and cause unthinkable consequences to all those who lived nearby.

Because of the impending danger to the surrounding residents, Michael had bravely entered their living quarters in the buildings and was rousing the dwellers to alert them to the imminent peril they were in, methodically clearing the occupants and advising them to get away from the area as soon as possible. Satisfied with his efforts he decided to make a hasty exit, and was running away from the conflagration as fast as his injured leg would allow him when the bomb exploded, engulfing him in flames and debris. Peter and Pat watched in horror as their lifetime friend disappeared amid the white-hot flames, certain to be killed along with the other less speedy members of the escaping tide of humanity.

CHAPTER 14

The explosion Ul Haq's butcher's shop had razed the whole building to the ground, flattening everything within fifty yards radius of the epicentre, including those bystanders who ignoring the warnings from James and Pat, had remained too close. Twenty-odd people were killed, including the badly burned heroic Michael, who died in Jasmine's arms. Michael bravely suffered a whole ten minutes of indescribable agony before succumbing to his extensive injuries and closing his eyes, muttering his last words, "Tell Minnie and the boys that I lo..." He wasn't able to finish what he was saying as his rigid body relaxed with a gasp, and a relieved smile crossed his face. Yet Jasmine knew that as his life left him he could see a picture in his mind of his beloved Minnie and his boys. Straightening Michael's partly cremated body into a more seemly position, Jasmine covered his happy-looking face with her jacket, all the time wetting her poor dead protector with her cascading tears.

James was more upset than anyone had ever seen him. He had been worrying about Michael's leg and didn't want him to get involved with the search for Jasmine. He simply wanted Michael to go and find his youngest son for him, but he refused, saying that William was perfectly safe where he was, and he insisted on coming to Croydon with James and joining in with his old comrades to find and rescue the only other important woman in his life. Michael had lied about his painful leg, convincing James that he was reasonably sound, and saying how hurt he would feel if he was left out of such an important mission, so acquiescing to the pressure James reluctantly agreed to let Michael be part of the undertaking, which ended up with his dreadful death.

Due to the lack of communications it took the emergency services an overly long time to appear at the scene. Yet when they did they dealt with the situation quickly and with consummate professionalism, attending to the fire, the casualties and then the dead. Having no time for lengthy explanations and also not wishing to be associated with the incident, James decided it would be sensible to disappear under cover of the confusion; so along with the others they made their way back to Whitton. A shocked Pat took the wheel of the Jaguar so recently proudly driven by his good friend and associate Michael, and in a trance he drove the few miles on a sort of autopilot, having no recollection whatsoever of the journey afterwards.

The time was a quarter past four in the morning on the thirtieth of April when the group of friends arrived back at James's and Jasmine's house. The journey was completed in stunned silence, none of them able to believe that the immortal Michael was at last gone. The bereft company entered the building and sat in the kitchen where Ian had been waiting for them to return, with no news to offer and feeling only horror on hearing about Michael. With none of them really knowing what to do or say, Jasmine offered to make some refreshments. However seeing the state of her Pat jumped up and volunteered to take over the chore from the slightly battered Jasmine, refusing his kind offer she told him she needed something to take her mind off the situation. Some welcome coffee was soon produced steaming and smelling lovely, and they all accepted a cup. Waiting until each person was seated with their drink, James then stood up, raised his cup and simply said, "Absent friends." The others stood with him and repeated the phrase with their cups held in the air and, simultaneously, took a drink.

Despite feeling dreadfully bereft, and as if he was personally responsible for Michael's sad death, James couldn't help but worry about the present situation, Ul Haq was missing with Sue and Ibrahim, leading him to believe that the Al Qaeda plot to disrupt the mayoral elections was still in place and would most probably be implemented by his eldest son and his suicidal ex-wife. There was a real possibility that the insurgents had much more firepower than just C4 and home-made explosive devices. He had managed to lose one of his best operatives, communication was difficult, and all considered he was losing the battle; the insurgents seemed to always be one step ahead. He had to act, but how? Resolutely Pat had shaken himself out of the gloom that descended on him when he saw Michael killed; he told himself that after the operation was over he would have plenty of time to grieve for his comrade. Deciding that the best way to honour his dead friend would be to strive even harder and successfully complete the mission, Pat applied his mind to the problems at hand and sat deep in thought, searching for an answer. Peter was in a similar state of mind, knowing the gravity of the situation, and applying his quick, alert mind to attempt to solve the conundrum that presented itself; together they sat, lost in individual thought, but with one purpose of mind, to outwit a suicidal company of brainwashed extremists, who had no concerns about any innocents who might become collateral damage in the pursuit of their goal. All that remained of the night was spent in thoughtful silence. Jasmine had retired to bed feeling overwrought and tired. She needed some time to come to terms with what actually happened at the butcher's shop, and she lay in bed trying to make some rhyme and reason out of the events that happened.

The morning of the last day of April was lovely, it was warm and the sun was shining from a clear blue sky. The leaves on the trees were all out of their buds and the birds were singing happily in their branches, all in all there was little amiss with the world, except the threat of the partial destruction of inner London. There was some good and bad news: the telephone services had partially been restored, but the national terrorism alert status had been downgraded from red to green and against all common sense the elections were going ahead, as planned.

James Peter and Pat were still in the same places as they were when they got home the previous night, still musing on the options that were open to them. Jasmine as usual provided some breakfast for the tired men, and they were gratefully eating the welcome food when, suddenly, out of the blue there was an urgent knocking at the front door, and with everybody else busy, it was James who rushed to see who it was.

Opening the door expecting to see a policeman or anyone similar, James was flabbergasted to see his youngest son William standing there, red-eyed and terrified, with obviously plenty to say. On seeing his father he rushed and hugged him, and shouting in his excitement, "Is mother alright? How's Peter? I've been to where the butcher's was, there's nothing there, I've looked everywhere! I want to help." Jasmine, Peter and Pat heard the commotion at the front door and rushed through expecting to see another unwelcome sight, and almost fainted when she saw William embracing James, who could hardly believe his eyes when he saw his mother, bruised, but still alive and well.

"Mother you're alive! I heard that you'd been captured by a terrorist cell and they were going to kill you and Peter!"

James was looking aghast at William. "How on earth do you know about everything that's happened? Who told you?"

William stared directly at James. "I mustn't tell you, I cannot tell you, I've sworn that I would keep their secret, they only told me because they thought that you were all in great danger! But they gave me a message for you, in case I saw you"

The reunited family's, joy to see one another was muted by the urgency of the situation, and they quickly went through to where they had been having breakfast so that William could tell his story.

When seen together it was obvious to all that William and Peter were brothers, but William was much bigger and burlier than his sibling. He was quite the school rugby star, and now he played for a half decent side in West Sussex, he looked rather like Ibrahim, only instead of fat, he was muscular and strong. He was darker than both his brothers but his overall appearance was very similar to his father's, whose stamp was plain to see on all his sons.

William sat down with the others to tell his tale, being careful not to mention any names. "This is the message for James," William began, before pausing for thought.

James drummed his fingers impatiently on the table, "Hurry up Wills, we haven't much time!"

"This is all I've been told. The attacks on the underground were a feint, to hopefully fool the authorities into believing that was their primary aim, and any success was a bonus. The main plot is to blow up the Axial centre tomorrow; an Iranian agent has supplied them with a 'suitcase nuke'. The bomber has been working in the offices at the centre for over six months." James wanted to know who the bomber was, but all William could tell him that it was a woman. The whole gathering knew exactly who it was, much to the sadness of Peter, who looked downcast at the thought. William continued with his informative saga:

"Al Qaeda have financed the attack in league with the Iranians, apparently the man called Ul Haq is the co-ordinator, and the bombers have all been brainwashed into thinking they're doing it for Islam, but there's no religious reasons for the attack, it's purely revenge to settle an old score against the United Kingdom and Bahrain, whose National Exhibition Company have just bought the Axial exhibition centre and officially they're going to take it over tomorrow, and tomorrow as you know it's going to be used as one of the three counting centres for the election."

William turned to Peter. "I've also got a message for you. A grubby little tramp came up to me when I was looking for you, at first he thought I was you, but when he realised that I wasn't, he asked if I was your brother. When I said yes, he told me that he had something to tell you, and he'll be at number twelve, whatever that means." William finished his lengthy messages and waited expectantly for the questions. Yet the assembly just looked at one another dumbfounded, finding it hard to believe that all the information they were struggling to discover was now in their grasp.

Peter had one more thing to ask James. "What exactly is a suitcase nuke?"

James had the answer. "It's an anti-personnel suitcase-sized nuclear bomb, which explodes with roughly the same force of five hundred tons of TNT. They were developed by the old Soviet Union, and hundreds went missing when the Communist Bloc broke up. Many were sold to tin-pot dictators like Saddam Hussein.

To James everything was becoming much clearer. At last he could understand the reasoning behind it all: it all went back to the early 1980s when the Shia-led Iranian Islamic revolutionaries wanted to radicalise the whole Middle East, and called for the overthrow of the Sunni-run westernised monarchies like Saudi Arabia, Abu Dhabi, Bahrain and many of the other Gulf states. Their bellicose demands were strongly opposed by the West, and the Ayatollah and his subsequent heirs never forgave the people who stood against them.

James was fully aware that in a new twist in the complicated modern-day politics, Al Qaeda had started using old unsettled scores, agitating the aggrieved, and then paying them to take actions suitable to advance their own beliefs and taking the credit for the resulting mayhem for themselves, and this was probably such an occasion. The only problem now was to find the bombers and to stop them before they could implement their plot.

The father, his two sons, Ian and Pat agreed a basic plan of action and as they reckoned they had no more than a day and a half before the expected attack, there were a few loose ends to tie up. Peter was going off to catch up with Simon, to find out what he wanted to say, and to ask him to undertake some more clandestine work for him. Pat was going to try and locate the missing insurgents, while Ian was going to stay to act as driver in the fast police BMW for James, whose immediate task was to try and speak to the Home Secretary, to inform him of the latest developments, and then to make a detour to Watford and see Minnie and personally inform her of Michael's death. Meanwhile, Jasmine remained at home protected by the young and eager William. Except for Pat they all agreed to meet back at Whitton at one o clock allowing enough time to complete their errands, unless something more urgent was to crop up.

The morning was lovely; the bright sun shone in the heavens, a warm breeze heated the air giving promise for a lovely day. The rush hour traffic had abated, leaving the air smelling cleaner than it normally did. The search for Simon didn't take very long, Peter knew that he would be one of three places at that time of day, but he suspected the favourite would be number twelve, the doorway near to Ul Haq's house where he liked to sit and watch from, and he was correct. When he arrived he glanced briefly into the gloom of the spying place, seeing nothing, until a bundle of old clothes thrown in the corner raised to its feet and spoke to him:

"Hello boss, I've been waiting ages for you, I see you got out of the butcher's OK! That was some bloody explosion; I scarpered when it went off, all those police and all." Peter was anxious to find out what Simon had to tell, but first he needed to thank him. Grabbing his grubby hand Peter shook it meaningfully, and staring into Simons surprisingly clear eyes he spoke. "On behalf of my mother and all of us—"

Simon didn't let him finish. "You've saved my skin before, it was my pleasure! Your dad seems to be a nice fellow though, he was so pleased when I told him where you were. I'm sorry about your black mate, I saw he was a gonner just as I was leaving. I lost a mate like that, not in an explosion; some blokes doused him in petrol and set fire to him, for a bit of fun, not a pretty sight!"

"You've got some news for me I hear?" Peter asked, trying to hurry things up.

"Your brother found you then? Christ, don't you both look like your dad, I thought he was you at first."

"The news?"

"Oh yes! The news, yes the news. Ul Haq and the woman in the wheelchair, who can walk, by the way, along with two likely lads, have loaded up the van and disappeared for the best part of a day now. Isaac's watching her place as we speak. One thing more, they were all wearing black scarves on their heads, except her who had hers tied around her neck."

With as much haste as possible Peter made his way back to Whitton, ignoring the beautiful day, not having the time to take it in. His one purpose was to report back as soon as was possible to his father to tell him that the birds had flown the nest. When he arrived back at the house, James and Ian were already there and the first thing Peter asked about concerned the welfare of Minnie. James related back the harrowing saga of how she initially took the news with disbelief, and when the realisation set in she broke down, into inconsolable floods of tears, bringing back to Peter the trauma he suffered when he received the news of Charley's accident and death. Peter always had been rather sensitive, but never prone to crying. Perhaps the recent chain of events had softened his resolve and he felt the need to weep. Partly feeling sorry for himself, but most of all he felt sorry for Minnie and the grief she and her boys were going to suffer. The worry about his real mother and brother, and his fear for Jasmine's welfare, and the dreadful scenes he had witnessed was all building up inside him, and manifested itself in a brief bout of tears. He cried for about two minutes, yet as though nothing had happened he wiped his eyes, straightened himself up and carried on as normal, telling James about the latest information from Simon. James listened carefully to what Peter told him and, upon the completion of the story, he ordered Peter to remain at home with him as he would need him as his secretary for the afternoon.

Lunchtime came and went; Jasmine and William had been asked to stay out of the way during the afternoon while several agents and senior policemen arrived. Peter was more than happy to act as James's personal assistant for the while, spending most of the time sitting comfortably allowed his knees to recover a little. Acting as doorman in chief, Ian welcomed people to the front door or ushering them individually into the office, where they stayed for a while closeted in with James before being despatched from the house with much urgency. Peter counted twenty-two callers in all, and the last to visit were two American Secret Servicemen who stayed considerably longer than the others before departing. Afterwards, James emerged from the meetings looking tired frustrated and irritable.

"The Yanks are very upset, they've lost one of their senior agents, and lucky for us they think Ul Haq's got him, but they are still convinced that we're wrong, and they insist the target is the O2 arena in Greenwich. However I've convinced them that it would serve both our purposes to find Ul Haq and arrest him, and heavens forefend they've agreed. Hallelujah!"

For the whole evening Peter, James and their new recruit stayed working together in the office, going round and round in circles, covering points, only to realise that the same points had been discussed a short time before; they were getting nowhere. On Jasmine's insistence they took a half-hour's break, when she cooked and served an evening meal, telling them that "cars don't run without fuel," and she was right. So they stopped what they were doing and all five of them sat the dining table, and not mentioning work or the present situation they ate the food, giving their brains time to stop racing so they could resume their work refreshed, and possibly with a new approach.

Feeling better after their break Peter and James returned to the work with new vigour. The pause in their thinking process had done its trick, and instead of the merry-go-round that they were on before they now found themselves approaching the problem from a different angle. Instead of perpetually wondering how the bombers were going to implement their plan, they decided to concentrate their thoughts on what Ul Haq's intentions were, and Peter came up with an idea.

"At the moment I think we're concentrating on the actual event, rather than the instigator of it. I think Ul Haq knows that we've marked him as the leader, and as I believe he's a complete coward, so I wonder what's he going to do next?"

Scratching his head to think, James paused to consider what Peter said, eventually coming up with his best guess; "I reckon he's going to get the hell out of it!"

Nodding his agreement with James, Peter replied, "Yes, and where can he possibly go? He's hardly going to stay around here, is he?"

James answered hesitantly hoping Peter was going to help him with his reply. "Perhaps he'll go back to Iran," James added and then gaining more confidence in his response, "yes, where else would he be safe?"

Peter listened trying to piece together more of his theory, "when and how's he going to get there?"

James was now convinced that at last they were on the right track, "He's going to fly home tomorrow morning, he can't go before, he's got to give them their last blessing, they're hardly likely to go ahead without it!"

Peter corrected his father. "Tomorrow after *Asr*, the mid-afternoon prayer. It's normally at about four thirty, they'll never go back to the Mosque though, so all that we have to do is find out where he'll give their last rites, and what time his flight is?" Yet there proved to be no way to find out the times of any flights as both the phone service, and the computer network, were inoperable, and as there was nothing they could do until morning they agreed that the best policy was to get some rest.

Happy with their conclusions both Peter and James retired to bed hopeful of a couple of hours' proper sleep before the trials and tribulations of the next day. William had generously forfeited his bed, slumbering on the couch so that his older brother Peter, who was still suffering dreadfully from his sore knees, could stretch out in the comfort of it. Ian took to an armchair to snooze, and James slid quietly in next to Jasmine, dreading that she might make her normal sexual demands on him. However, when he had made himself comfortable there were no wandering hands, no breasts subtly pressed into his back, she merely sighed, hiccoughed as though she had been crying and simply said, "I'll miss poor Michael, he been with us for so long, I hope he's an angel like his namesake. Poor Minnie, she's all alone now, I'll get William to take me over to see her tomorrow, she needs someone's shoulder to cry on."

James was about to tell her it was a good idea, but she turned her back to James to let him sleep.

At about four thirty the next morning, Thursday the first of May announced its appearance with a brief tempestuous storm, with thunder, lightning and huge pelting raindrops that hammered on the glass. The sudden squally wind vibrated the whole house, making the windows shake and the tiles on the roof rattle. After ten minutes of violence, and as though the storm had been switched off, calm was restored and everything returned to normal. James had already been seated at his desk for some time, pondering on what steps to take to prevent the bombers from getting through to their target. The day was expected to be one of the busiest of recent times, with millions of people to-ing and fro-ing, involved in the whole logistical nightmare of a city-wide Mayoral election, to say nothing of the thousands of people going about their normal business, all adding to the mayhem likely to hamper the attempts to thwart the insurgents. The whole household was astir, awakened by the brief but violent tempest. Peter had joined his father in the office to assist wherever he could, and while he was waiting for instructions he stood peering out of the rain-spattered window; dawn was breaking and the clearing sky had turned bright pink, the black cloud, that had so recently released its malevolence over their heads, was retreating to the east, and the sun promised to soon make its appearance over its fiery trailing edge. Watching it as it went, Peter prophetically noted that he hoped it was going to be a good omen for the day ahead.

Within minutes of Peter's attendance at James's side the phone rang, its strident noise making them both jump as it was still very early, and after the attacks on the Monday due to the chaotic networks, there had been no incoming calls until then. James picked up the receiver, handling it as though it was the poisoned chalice, fearing that it was news of the worst kind, feeling much relieved when he heard Pat's unmistakable voice on the other end. So that Peter could be party to the conversation James pressed the loudspeaker button and the irate Irishman's voice could clearly be heard by them both.

"I've been trying to contact you for ages, the fucking radio is useless and the phones aren't working very well!"

James interrupted wanting Pat to hurry up, as the echoing and buzzing line was very obviously unreliable. "Hurry up Pat I could lose you at any minute."

"OK boss, meet me at Ul Haq's house Peter knows where—"

Click! The half-finished call ended abruptly, leaving them both wondering when they were expected, deciding it would be best to go there straight away. Before leaving James and Peter took the time to say hurried goodbyes to Jasmine and William, who were readying themselves for the trip to visit Minnie, and departed on the precarious mission.

Ian volunteered to act as driver as this was where he felt he would be in the job he knew best. The early morning traffic was still fairly light, and the journey to Croydon took a relatively short while. It would have been even quicker had not the early stages been hampered by a slow-moving dustcart blocking the road, heedless of anyone trying to go on their way. Ian became annoyed at their reluctance to even attempt to allow them past until, much to the amusement of the men, he honked his horn at them and signalled that he was in a hurry to get on. Eventually, after ten or so minutes the noisy refuse workers pulled the giant vehicle over just enough for Ian to squeeze his car past, suffering a tirade of verbal abuse because of his demonstration of impatience.

The time was seven when James, Peter and Ian arrived at a street near to Ul Haq's house. The last hundred yards they covered on foot so as not to alert anyone of their presence. Pat was already there with Simon, hiding in the same doorway where Peter had spent so many cramped and uncomfortable hours. He was excited and eager to speak to them. "He's inside boss, he's been there since first light, the others have left, but I think one of them might still be in there."

James knew exactly what the next course of action was going to be. "Pat, we've got to find out what Ul Haq knows, so do whatever you have to, I rely on you to find out." Peter's heart sank, having witnessed firsthand Pat's merciless way of extracting information from unwilling captives. With a mind on Ian's employment with the police James offered him the option to either go and wait for them to return, or stay and probably be party to breaking the law. Opting to make himself scarce, and not jeopardise his future with the police, so with a quick cheerio and a good luck he returned to wait in the car before seeing something that would compromise his loyalties.

Pat was eager to fulfil Jame's wishes so, without any more encouragement, he scuttled off to break into his target's house, refusing Peter's and James's offer of help, telling them that he would be better off on his own, asking them to give him ten minutes, and then follow. All the while, wide-eyed Simon looked on, open-mouthed in dumb amazement, not realising until now the type of operatives he had got himself involved with, and he was curious to see more. Pat was prepared, earlier he had reconnoitred the house and had already planned his route into the building; Ul Haq made some amateurish attempts to beef up his security, but the locked and barred new back door had been hung in an old and rotten wooden frame that, although newly painted, showed signs of many repairs that dated back several years.

Pat's wiry strength had not deserted him over the years, and with two smart karate-type kicks the door flew out of its frame, hinges and all, the unexpected speed of his success causing him to tumble inward, almost tripping over the flying timber, and straight into the room where Ul Haq was sitting at a kitchen table with a frightened-looking young man. Pat was honed and ready for action, and before the two startled men could grasp what had just happened he was on them with his gun poked into the face of the terrified cleric. "Keep your fucking mouth shut and listen, tell him if he makes a fucking move I'll blow your fucking brains all over that fucking wall." Ul Haq speedily relayed a message to the younger man in Arabic, unaware that Pat knew exactly what he was saying, and he was telling him to wait for the opportunity, and as soon as he could he was to throw himself on Pat's gun, telling him that Allah was waiting to welcome him in Paradise. Without bothering to say another thing Pat aimed his weapon at his would-be-assailant: Pop! Pop! He shot the young man in the mouth, and then in the forehead, spattering dripping blood and matter all over the wall behind him. Then, in perfect Arabic, he told Ul Haq that if he dids anything else so stupid that he would be the next person standing next to Allah and his new friend in Paradise.

Alerted by the unusual noise made by Pat's weapon, that was more like the sound of champagne corks rather than a gun, Peter and then James went to discover exactly what had occurred. Rushing through the destroyed door they found Pat in total charge. Their arrival followed thirty seconds later by a nosey Simon, who didn't want to miss the action, and rushed into the room, instantly regretting it. Turning green, he ran straight back out and was instantly sick at the sight of the dead man and the gore, disappearing back to the streets where he hid from the horror in safety.

Ul Haq was already strapped in an upright chair, secured there by a leather belt that very recently used to hold up his trousers. The slumped corpse was bent forward, his sprawling arms spread wide on the blood-soaked table surrounded by the contents of a knocked-over box, which had contained twenty or so small spherical balls, made of tied and knotted condoms, along with one part full and six empty jars of honey, an unopened pack of Durex, some scissors and at a safe distance away, a package that contained some hand-held electric control boxes, similar to the ones used for electric garage doors. James was curious when he saw the little rubber-covered parcels, and handed one to Pat, who dug a fingernail through the latex covering, and sniffed the contents. "Semtex! They're full of Semtex!"

Peter butted in. "They're swallowing it covered in honey, that's the way heroin or cocaine is sometimes smuggled by drug mules. I've heard that one woman in the States was caught carrying one and a half kilograms of coke in her stomach, she got through customs pretending that she was pregnant."

Pat gave a long slow whistle on hearing what Peter had to say. "That would make a very big bang, but Semtex needs a detonator, and they'd have to swallow that as well." Again Peter had the answer. You've got to keep up to speed Pat, with micro technology they can make them as small as you want, you don't need a huge battery and plunger anymore."

Looking for clues, James started to methodically ransack the house and Peter started to cut open the remainder of the little packets of high explosive, looking for a micro detonator. Meanwhile, Pat set about the interrogation of Ul Haq. He started using his tried and tested method, by quietly asking some relatively simple questions, which were answered easily by the quaking trussed man who continually protested against his captivity, remonstrating with Pat that he was an important Shia cleric who had the ear of Allah, warning him of dire consequences if he was hurt. Ignoring his protestations Pat thumped him impatiently on both sides of his head, causing him to spit out his set of false teeth, which clattered on the floor as they span out of sight. In the background, and dreading what was going to happen next, Peter was flattening out the little plastic balls, eventually finding what he was looking for: within the middle of one of the balls of explosives, there was a small copper-coloured cube of approximately two centimetres across.

The questioning of Ul Haq had taken on a more aggressive nature and Pat, frustrated by his non co-operation, had resorted to downright torture, smashing one of his reluctant prisoner's fingers with the butt of his gun, causing a high-pitched squeal to issue from his lips, and even before the noise diminished Pat hit one on his other hand, splitting it all the way along, making his fresh blood mingle with the darkening red jelly that had poured from his dead co-conspirator's head wound and causing another loud scream. Ul Haq turned out to be an ideal subject for Pat's questioning technique, and was soon blubbering for mercy, promising to tell all in return for clemency, when Peter handed the small cube to Pat.

"What's this, and how does it work?" He showed the miniature device to the crying coward, who Pat had just punched in the mouth and then threatened to apply his bone-crushing skill to a third finger and, in a bid to avoid further pain, Ul Haq agreed to reply honestly to all questions. The cube was a small Chinese-made detonator originally designed for use with smart bombs, but had been altered by scientists in Tehran who had added a microscopic electric solenoid switch, triggered by the small control boxes.

Pat needed to find out everything he could. With a pricked conscience, his prisoner thinking he had already said too much, had stopped talking. So Pat grabbed a handful of the small parcels of explosives and started ramming them down Ul Haq's throat, one by one he made him swallow them, not bothering to lubricate them, allowing his bleeding mouth to ease them down, and holding his nose to complete the process. Last of all Pat took hold of the miniature detonator, carefully wrapped it in a small amount of the malleable explosive, stuffed it into the end of one of the discarded condoms, knotted it in, and very coolly snipped the end off: all done very slowly and deliberately in front his mesmerised captive's eyes. Ul Haq was still reluctant to speak, so without any more words, Pat savagely snatched hold of his nose, wrenched his head back to open his throat, dipped the little ball in some spilled honey and thrust it down Ul Haq's gullet using the barrel of his gun as a ramrod, causing a bout of retching with strings of blood, honey and mucus hanging out of the victim's gagging mouth. Pat was unsympathetic, speaking to the prisoner in his very best Irish accent. "If you're fucking sick, have no fear, I'll make you fucking eat it. Now, tell me everything I need to fucking know!" The last act of torture utterly broke Ul Haq's resolve and in a state of panic he told Pat all, omitting nothing.

During the savagery inflicted on the captive both Peter and James made themselves scarce, hunting through the house for any clues that might assist them in their quest. One thing they discovered was that Ul Haq was packed and ready to leave on the twenty fifteen flight from Heathrow to Beirut airport. On hearing the cessation of the noises of afflicted pain they returned to the room where Ul Haq was croaking out the answers to Pat's questions. There were five other human bombs. There were supposed to be six, and three were going to Alexandra Palace, and the other three were going to Olympia. Pat was satisfied with his reply, but there had been no mention of the bomb at the Axial conference centre so he asked him:

"What about the big one, then?"

Ul Haq looked surprised, he wasn't aware that Pat knew about the other bomb, and he remained silent considering his answer. The information was needed urgently so, once again, the inquisitor resorted to sudden violence, pistol whipping the battered man across the back of his head just hard enough to split his scalp, without rendering him unconscious. The desired result was obtained, and with his final act of betrayal the crushed man told Pat the rest of the stratagem and the reasons behind it.

The whole plot wasn't formulated on religious grounds; it was purely a vendetta, and the frustrated radical elements of the old Ayatollah Khomeini's theocratic republic were still harbouring a deep hatred for the West and their allies in the Middle East including Bahrain, who announced that they had purchased the Axial Centre as a status symbol in London. After a chance meeting with an unrelated group of militants, who were whole-heartedly opposed to the, "slaves of the West," and the, "puppets of America," an unlikely alliance was forged. The goals were the same, but the reasoning was different and funding their individual schemes was proving to be difficult, both parties agreed to join forces and create a plan for a high profile strike to rival the attacks on the twin towers large enough to make their point. The proposed use of the Axial complex as a counting centre for the election presented a perfect target, offering, "two birds with one stone."

Recruiting non-extremists to commit certain suicide was virtually impossible, so it was decided to manipulate the impressionable, disillusioned young Muslims and recent converts to do their bidding, using bogus imams to whip up blind religious fervour, naming the pro- Zionist West as sworn enemies to Islam bent on the destruction of the Muslim way of life, promising eternal life in Paradise to martyrs of the cause, and soldiers of Allah.

Peter had only a single question for Ul Haq: he wanted to know who killed his friend and saviour Naseem. To his surprise and without any remorse Ul proudly admitted committing the murder himself, calling it the execution of a despicable enemy of justice, who was a blight on Islam.

James needed to know where Sue and the other bombers were, and the answer wasn't the one he wanted to hear. Ul Haq triumphantly informed James that, having made peace with Allah, they had only a few hours left to make peace with the world. They had gone off before their missions, along with the enforcers that were there to make sure that they went through with the final act, and stopping them would be impossible. Pat dispensed a summary thump to reward him for his smugness, and then dragged him to the basement of the house and hurled him down the steps into the gloomy cellar, taking time to lever the main incoming water pipe off the wall and splitting it, causing torrents of water to cascade down the steps and begin to fill the underground chamber.

Ul Haq was pleading to be taken to hospital to have the explosives removed from his stomach, squealing at Pat, exhorting him to do his bidding, reminding him that he had told everything he knew and had no more to give. Ignoring his begging, Pat slammed and locked the cellar door, shutting off the rasped appeals and plunging the dank dungeon into utter darkness. Pat returned five minutes later, giving a ray of hope to the desperate incarcerated cleric, thinking that he might have taken pity on his prisoner and changed his mind, only to be thwarted when the body of his deceased colleague was tossed on top of him; and when the door at the base of the stairs was closed this time it was closed and barred for good, sealing in Ul Haq to consider forthcoming watery doom.

CHAPTER 15

Four precious hours had passed since the interrogation of Ul Haq, and midday was approaching fast. People were flying about everywhere excited about the election, happily going about their business, thinking that the terrorist threat had passed, blindly unaware that even greater incursions into their lives were carefully planned and without a miracle they would happen that evening. With hundreds of agents and law enforcement personnel on high alert, it was amazing that the planned attack remained hidden from all but the select few. The powers that be worried, that if the enormity of the planned event were to become general knowledge, the ensuing panic would seriously hamper and possibly prevent the authorities from combating the intentions of the suicidal insurgents. The dire situation made worse by the successful diversionary raids on the London Underground. These made communications almost impossible, causing all the anti-terrorist units to work separately instead of as a cohesive large force. However, James, Peter and Pat worked happily alone, away from the officiousness of over-careful stuffed shirts that had ruined more than one previous investigation.

Their new information was absorbed discussed and an agreed path of action had to be planned. The aim was to try and nullify the threat before all the bombers reached their destinations, but how to find their whereabouts was virtually impossible. To wait at the targets for the unknown likely suspects to appear was another option, but with the entire sites thronging with excited people, it would there again make identification of the insurgents unfeasible. They still had their less than efficient radios, and some of the telephone services were working again, but the reliability of communications was hit and miss. The whole situation considered, they were blindly tripping around in the dark, hoping for inspiration and clutching at straws.

The unsure trio driven by their willing conscript Ian hurtled round for hours inspecting all Sue's of old haunts where they suspected she might want to visit before giving up her life to Islam. They went to her home and then to the Mosque without success, they even went as far as St John's Wood, where the London Islamic centre was situated, all with no result. James was becoming desperate, not knowing where to turn, when Peter had an epiphany: after racking his brains for ages searching for a spark of inspiration, the obvious suddenly dawned on him, and he excitedly reminded them of a fact they all had overlooked. Sue still had her vendetta against Jasmine, and to complete her worldly mission she probably needed it to come to a satisfactory conclusion, and surely it would be better for at least one of them to wait back at the empty house in Whitton? The visual relief on James's face was obvious for all to see, now that he had a reasonable path to follow, and with much relief they made their way back to James's empty house, arriving at a quarter to six in the evening.

All was reasonably quiet in Whitton, the evening was lovely, and very warm for the time of year. Somewhere nearby an old-fashioned push-pull lawnmower could be heard whirring and clicking as it cut the grass, and the smell of somebody's barbeque burning perfectly good meat drifted on the breeze, an aircraft droned high in the sky and everything appeared to be well with the world. James was aware that the rest of the day was likely to be very long, and the group of men would need some food.

As ever Pat was more than happy to rustle up a quick meal for them all. By seven fifteen they had finished eating the repast, and were preparing to venture to the threatened Axial centre in East London near to the famous Canary Wharf, when Ian's radio suddenly crackled to life.

"Alley Cat to Burmese! Alley Cat to Burmese! Over!" Ian looked stunned, firstly because his radio was working, but most of all because of the strange message, not having been informed about the unusual call signs allotted to the operatives that worked out of Jermyn Street. Peter explained that his vagrant associate had demonstrated a passion for the obscure, and he had permitted him to adopt a cat-sounding name of his own selection, mostly tongue in cheek, but it worked as he knew exactly who it was. The radio crackled to life once again, this time the voice had more urgency about it.

"Alley Cat to Burmese! Over!" Ian looked skyward and handed the radio to Peter.

"Burmese to Alley Cat! Receiving you over!"

"Alley Cat here, the blue vans have been spotted in the derelict warehouse behind Jubilee Hall in south Croydon, over."

"Burmese here, you said vans, if so how many, and who saw them. Over!"

"Alley Cat to Burmese, three vans, all identical. Billy saw them, that's where he sleeps, over!"

Pat waggled his non-eyebrows at James. "If that's the Billy I met at the yard he's probably suffering from triple vision, and there's only one of them after all." Peter smiled, ignoring the gravity of the situation, knowing exactly what Pat meant. Frustrated that the return to Whitton was somewhat a bit of a wild goose chase, they got back into the white BMW and set off back to Croydon.

Without pausing to consider their own safety, Ian drove them faster than he had ever before, sirens blaring and lights flashing, skidding round corners, flying across whatever red lights promised to hamper their progress, scattering any unwary pedestrians who were too stubborn to be bothered by the wailing klaxon, amazingly arriving within a few hundred yards of their destination without causing any deaths either inside or outside the car. The last part of the trip was taken more carefully, as both the warning sirens and the lights had been turned off so as not to alert any possible terrorists of their approach. They halted the car a short way away from the Jubilee Hall, and walked the remaining distance to the deserted warehouse, approaching it very carefully to reconnoitre the lie of the land. Billy was correct, there were indeed three low-roofed, dark-blue Transit vans, almost identical except for the consecutive number plates; apparently the habitual drunk was sober for a change.

The four men crept to within a fifty feet of where the three vans were parked in a row, out of general view, just behind a seized and rusted roller door that was stuck open at a height of about six and a half feet above the ground, allowing enough headroom for them to enter. Several voices could be heard, echoing inside the roomy empty store, all praying in Arabic, bringing back memories of Peter's lengthy devotions and a sympathetic pain to Peter's slightly improved knees. It was eight thirty in the evening, and time of *Maghrib,* the sunset and second to last prayer of the Muslim religious day. After listening for a short while, the words *assalamualaikum warakhmatullah* could be heard repeated twice, signifying the end to the six-minute-long supplication, and very soon afterwards one of the vans started up and roared off, to urgently go about its murderous business. It was too late to pursue so James surmised that it would be best to deal with the ones that remained as quickly as possible, but how?

A conundrum presented itself: the prey was in their sights, and its route of escape could easily be blocked, but what could four lightly armed men do to prevent maybe a dozen heavily armed extremist and suicidal brainwashed young men from completing their fell task, to kill as many of what they believed to be anti- Muslins Zionists as possible? The tiger's tail was well and truly grasped, and to let go would be a fatal mistake as would holding on, they needed a plan. James was whispering possibilities and asking questions to the others, trying to come up with a suitable idea to stop the terrorists from reaching their targets, when Pat produced one of the remote controls he had pocketed from off of the table in Ul Haq's house. He fingered its casing in thought for a moment and then turned to James.

"I wonder if this might work at this range?"

Peter and James looked doubtful, so Pat removed a tab of plastic that was designed to isolate the battery from the workings of the device, pointed it at the nearest vehicle, a red LED flashed indicating that a signal was being sent... initially nothing happened, so Pat waved it about hopefully. The answer to Pat's question was answered; it did work at that range.

The closest van seemed to swell like a balloon for a millisecond, and with a blinding flash and a deafening boom it burst, disappearing upwards, revealing the second vehicle that instantly followed suit. Seemingly in what seemed like slow-motion he bent and twisted remnants of the chassis and bodywork of both vans started raining down, rebounding of what still existed of the roof, that now boasted a great hole above where the explosions happened, along with the shattered remains of the occupants, sickeningly spattering the hidden men with globs of gore and matter that, moments before, belonged to human beings. Peter felt sick, wondering whether the sundry pieces of flesh that hit him were those of his mother or brother; his heart sank, thinking that they might have met with such a grizzly end. Once again in his life, a deep sadness could have easily engulfed him, However Peter was still well aware that the work was not finished, and he could not permit himself the luxury of grief; without hesitation he shook himself of his fleeting bout of melancholy and followed the others, who were about to leave the scene in pursuit of the remaining party of insurgents.

Suddenly and most unexpectedly from somewhere behind the departing group of the slightly , blood-spotted crew, a large mellifluous voice issued from the yawning burnt building, causing each of the four to look behind them back at the scene – to witness the man known to Peter and Pat as Billy staggering out of the building, startled, smoke-stained and three parts naked, rubbing his watery bloodshot eyes, having been plucked so unceremoniously from his drunken stupor by the enormous bang. "Fucking Nora, I was having a lovely dream!" was his only audible comment, spoken in the most educated of English accents floated across the short expanse of waste ground to the ears of the departing quartet, creating a touch of humour to a dreadful situation.

In haste Ian, who was fitter than the rest of the others, sprinted to the BMW and had started it up. It was ready to go by the time James and Pat arrived, Peter, as now was his wont, brought up the rear, hampered by his ailing lower limbs. Once they were all in the car Ian pressed the accelerator pedal down hard, glueing the speechless passengers to the back of their seats and keeping them there with the G force. Driving like a maniac Ian, followed James's instructions and headed directly to their destination at the Axial Centre in Docklands, almost as far east in London as you could get. Once again Ian was worth his weight in gold, his ability behind the wheel reaching new heights on the journey as he sped through the metropolis, breaking all the speed limits as he went, his local knowledge being a godsend, haring down side streets and back alleys to avoid the known bottlenecks and other probable hiatuses in the traffic flow.

They reached the massive multi-storey car parks quickly, and immediately set about the enormous task of searching the buildings for the remaining Transit van, which they suspected contained the suitcase-sized nuclear bomb – small enough to be carried, but large enough to flatten and pollute huge swathes of

Docklands and render most of East London a no-go area because of radioactive pollution. With all the latest information at his finger-tips James suspected that it was his mentally disturbed converted ex-wife Sue, along with his embittered Muslim son Ibrahim, were the insurgents who had been given the dubious honour of detonating the device to make a statement to rival, and possibly outdo, the bombings of the twin towers in New York 2001, seven years before, and with great sorrow he urgently sought them out with the aim of eradicating them, and their equally radical enforcers, before they could go ahead with the murderous act.

James only had Peter, Pat and the newly conscripted Ian to help him with the colossal task of searching for the proverbial needle in a haystack, as all of the others that worked for the many security services were all busy occupied with different aspects of monitoring the gigantic logistical task of overseeing the vote collection and counting for the London mayoral elections that were about to reach their climax within the next hour. People were thronging everywhere excited by the party-like atmosphere generated by the high-profile event that had captured the imagination of London as a whole, ignorant of the fact their lives were in deadly peril.

The four men split into two groups in order to expedite the search. Peter teamed up with the new associate and novice Ian, while James joined his long time friend and partner in crime Pat. Fearing they might never meet up again they all shook hands and said some heartfelt goodbyes, hoping upon hope they were wasting their breath and would soon meet up to laugh about the sincerity of the moment. James and Pat alighted from the car at the entrance to the orange car park, while Ian drove Peter to the purple to start their search there.

Pat raced off in one direction, at James's bidding, not wanting to hamper the amount of ground coverable by his fitter colleague, while he went off in the opposite direction, running on tiptoes to make himself as tall as possible to improve the chances of spotting the sought vehicle. After half an hour of frantic searching there still was no sign. The task was hopeless, the tide of ever-changing traffic gave them no chance of locating it, with cars and vans of all sorts coming and going, with drivers going round in circles, seeking the rare vacated parking places, quickly filling them gratefully relieved to have found one. The fruitless search complete, the pair met up at the same point as where they started, and made the decision to enter the main part of the huge centre and resume the quest in the spacious central area where famous bands, competitions and many large scale events had previously entertained thousands of spectators.

The sight which greeted them was awesome; the gargantuan arena was filled to the brim with milling people darting in all directions, because of the recent purchase of the facility by Bahrain National Exhibitions Company there were many Middle Eastern men and women amongst the throng, adding an extra complication to the already difficult, if not impossible search. James espied a vantage point from which the area could be scanned from above, so wasting as little time as possible, and ably aided by Pat, he slid through a previously locked door marked "STAFF ONLY, PRIVATE", climbed a long flight of stairs and burst noisily through another door at the top, onto a light gantry over the main body of the hall.

Two overly large Arab gentlemen, proudly sporting shiny new security badges with their photographs on dangling from their lapels, were on watch, standing leaning over the low parapet surveying all below them. Attracted by the loud interruption they turned to see the uninvited interlopers and immediately challenged them. James offered them an inspection of his own identification card to allay their fears, and made his best efforts to explain why they were there without giving too much away, even attempting to speak in Arabic to try and give them a sense of confidence, but it was no good, the men weren't for listening.

The larger of the two decided he was going to forcibly eject Pat from the area, and made the terrible mistake of grabbing the weedy Irishman's jacket with the idea of impelling his slight frame back through the door and down the steep stairs they had just come up. Pat looked over to James, who was still remonstrating with the other Arab, and asked a simple question as he was being urged away. "Go on boss! What do you want me to do now?" The answer wasn't the one Pat really wanted to hear, as he didn't want to hurt the innocent man who was only doing his duty.

"Whatever you have to, Pat!"

Immediately the words left James's lips, and like a cougar – which incidentally was Pat's call sign – he turned the large individual's strength against the man and sent him flying past his captive, stumbling over the low safety rail, and unfortunately plummeting onto the crowd some sixty or seventy feet below, squashing seven of the unfortunates he landed on. Seeing his fellow's demise, the other guard charged at Pat with a mind for revenge, and raced to subject the little man to a similar fate. Yet he didn't allow for Pat's swiftness of foot; he tumbled past his side-stepping target and, with a loud bellow, he also flew over the edge landing some twenty feet from his dead co-worker, and killing even more unwary members of the audience.

The effect down in the hall was devastating. Terrified people were shrieking and screaming, causing a general alarm, only a very few actually knew what really happened, and after the recent events at the tube stations, the widespread panic spread as individuals started to flee from the two heaps of dead and dying humanity, causing a large-scale stampede to ensue. The desperate tide, fearful of becoming embroiled in a life-threatening situation, ran blindly to escape the carnage, clearing the whole area within minutes except for those who were not so concerned with saving themselves: those who were about to make the ultimate sacrifice and forfeit their lives in a false cause.

James and Pat had chosen their vantage point well. Peering over the parapet they could see everything, as the strange tableau unfolded beneath them. All they could do was watch as the two small circles of clear space, where their victims had landed, started to grow, gradually getting larger and merging as the frightened people hastily retreated from the danger-zone. Within moments the whole area cleared revealing just a stubborn few that stayed behind. Standing on their own were a group of five men and a mobility scooter-bound woman, all dressed in Muslim apparel, each wearing black scarves wrapped tightly around their brows, except for the female who had hers draped around her shoulders. The small assembly appeared confused, aware that they were now in full view for all to see. Strangely a very burly member of the group seemed to be standing against his fellows, holding up his hands as if imploring the others to cease what they were doing. From behind them on their left-hand side, Peter and Ian were approaching, furtively creeping up on the insurgents, only visible to the man standing alone. James and Pat looked on, still powerless to help, mesmerised and silent, impotently watching as the fate of thousands of innocent people was decided before their eyes.

Unable to find the van in the purple park, Peter and Ian, followed a similar course of action to the others, and had just joined the main hall when the tumult started. Not realising that James and Pat were the cause of the stampede, they headed against the tide toward the epicentre of the escaping multitude, assuming that was where the extremists had announced their attentions to incinerate the whole building along with those still in it, when Ian's trained eyes noticed the little party that looked to him to be suspicious – and as the room cleared it became obvious that they had found Sue, Ibrahim and four others that were the object of the search.

Approaching carefully, so as not to cause them to panic, they got to within fifteen feet when it became clear that there was dissent was in their ranks. One of the would-be bombers was standing between his five comrades and the heavy case that he, being the strongest, was charged to carry. There was no time to think, two of the terrorists, the lone man was standing against had drawn their guns and appeared as if they were about to shoot their dissenting colleague, so without a second thought Ian opened fire, hitting them both, fatally injuring one and felling the other, the noise of the shots still echoing around the massive hall well after the two had fallen. Drawing his own gun in support of

Ian, Peter's gaze instantly looked on to the familiar face of his estranged brother Ibrahim, who unbelievably was the one preventing the others from reaching the suitcase he suspected that contained the bomb. Sue started screaming at Ibrahim, "Fucking do it you cowardly cunt! Do it fucking now, before it's too late!" Taking everyone by surprise, she leapt up from her scooter and still shrieking obscenities ran towards the bomb to detonate it. Without thinking Peter shot her, hitting her in the right-hand side of her chest. At first her mad eyes looked at Peter startled, and then casting her gaze at the blood pumping from her injury, she slowly collapsed on the floor and losing her precious scarf in the process. Horror struck by his actions, Peter ran to his stricken mother, to try and administer to her: she merely looked evilly up into his terrified face and wheezed, venomously:

"I always fucking hated you! You bastard, from the day you were born I knew that you'd fucking kill me, and it seems I was fucking right!"

Peter was in shock. He had saved many lives, but was watching his own mother die, shot by his own hand, and a feeling of remorse swept over him. "I didn't mean to, it was an accident, I'm sorry!" He knelt down by her side, took his constant companion, the precious copy of the Koran, out of his pocket, and started to read an apt passage to ease her passing. With her last words Sue still had no forgiveness in her soul. "Save you're fucking lies, I curse you, and everything you fucking do, bastard of a bastard!" With these malicious words issuing from her foul mouth she died, still trying to reach the dropped sacred scarf and knowing, in her heart, she had failed to complete what she considered was her final allotted earthly task.

As if in a surreal nightmare Peter raised himself up from his dead mother's side to survey the carnage she had wrought. Ibrahim was assisting Ian in restraining the two remaining bombers, and a helpful member of staff was sitting on the third and injured man. James and Pat had arrived on the scene to assist where possible, and Pat took over the role undertaken by Ibrahim, giving him a chance to speak with his father and brother to explain what he was actually doing getting involved with the whole episode. Ibrahim was about to start his story when James hushed him to silence, embraced them both, at long last being able to show his affection for his sons by wrapping his loving fatherly arms around the pair of estranged siblings, pleased that they were all still alive when he thought that there could only be one possible result, and not the one he was hoping for.

The sight in the hall was like a scene from a horror film.. Blood and guts everywhere, in all eleven deaths had occurred when the two who fell from the gantry crushed several of the people below, killing seven and injuring three. Ian shot two of the Islamist extremists, one fatally, and Peter had shot and killed his mother Sue. Before long everything in the area descended into chaos. The British security services and the police had arrived at the scene of the carnage in droves. A cordon of terrified-looking constables surrounded the suitcase waiting for the specialist team to come and deal with the device, while other equally scared individuals were taping off the whole area with blue and white tape. The more senior policemen were running about like headless chickens, as several high-ranking government officials were due to come and inspect the scene, including The Home Secretary who had been informed about the near miss, and was more than satisfied with the result, allotting no blame to James and his team over the deaths although, later on, there was bound to be an inquiry into the whole affair. James felt a great sense of relief that it was all over, with as few casualties as was.

After about six more hours at the centre Ibrahim, James and his team were allowed to leave, not without having to use his high rank in the secret service and his familiarity with the top members of the government as a lever to prevent Pat from being arrested over the unfortunate demise of the two security guards. The journey back to Whitton was a sombre one; Peter was inconsolable, fretting over Sue's death, piling the guilt on himself, her final dreadful words having their desired effect, stabbing at his heart, stealing from him the vain hope that she might have retained a modicum of love for her only child. Pat was as bad, wishing upon wish that the innocent lives he caused to be lost could be undone, and miraculously they would spring back to life to save him from the terrible pangs of remorse he was suffering from. Although Ian had been fully trained as a fast response firearms officer, and had passed all the police courses on the use of guns, he had never actually shot and killed a real person before and was in a state of shock over the death of the man who threatened Ibrahim – who was dying to tell his story but didn't feel the time was right. James was attempting to convince himself that, although bloody, the result could have been a lot worse, which was quite correct, but with the pressure of the actual situation, combined with the lack of sleep his assessment was somewhat distorted, and the whole event would seem clearer after a well earned sleep, back home in his own bed next to his beloved Jasmine.

First light was breaking when the little group in the car wearily turned down the side street to where James lived with Jasmine, but instead of his house standing proudly, with its neat hedge, small lawn and flower beds, there was nothing but a smoking ruin, being guarded by two tired-looking police officers. Struck by horror at the unexpected sight, James and Peter jumped out of the moving vehicle, overcome by the spectacle that met them and fearing for Jasmine and William, they raced up to the nearest policeman and was about to ask about their whereabouts, when the badly bruised old Bob, who had been on guard at his bungalow window, patiently waiting all evening for James's return, limped painfully up to them, holding his hands up in a gesture, telling them everything was all right.

Jasmine and William were alive and well, albeit slightly singed. Cynically in a last act of defiance, feeling frustrated by her personal failure to gain revenge on the main focus of her hatred. Sue had paid one of the non-suicidal militants to fire bomb the house at a time when Sue thought Jasmine would probably be asleep inside. The halfwit bomber found stealth impossible, and alerted the household with his clumsy efforts, and at the present he was languishing at the local police station after having been rugby tackled and knocked senseless by William, when he saw the perpetrator fleeing the scene, after having set the incendiary's fuse. William had made a valiant effort trying to prevent the conflagration, but found the flammable agent too potent to control, so frightened that Jasmine might become trapped indoors he bravely fought his way back into the inferno and rescued his mother, guiding her through the flames to safety. At the present they were both at the local hospital having their injuries tended to. Bob appeared much relieved after he told his tale. Without accepting any thanks or answering any questions he turned round and, with a quick grumble about his painful injuries, he plodded off, shuffling lamely in his slippers back to the cosy bed that had beckoned to him for the past several hours.

The house along with all its contents were cremated, nothing of value remained intact. James was thankful that no more injuries had occurred, but his main concern was to find Jasmine and William, primarily to make sure that they were both hale and well, but also to inform her of his and Peter's wellbeing, as well as Ibrahim's surprise arrival. It was with great relief when a taxi drew up bringing Jasmine and William back to the rubble that not so long ago was their abode. At first Jasmine didn't notice James and Peter smiling their welcoming smiles as she alighted from the cab, as her complete attention was focused on the miserable ruins of her home. Having to rub her sooty eyes in disbelief when she noticed her entire family standing in front of her, complete with the person she never expected to see again, her missing oldest son Ibrahim.

All the misery of losing all she owned and the pain of her burns was forgotten. She yelped with joy and squealed with pleasure when she saw them all, running into their arms, hugging and kissing all that was dear to her. Pat and Ian felt a little uncomfortable as they witnessed the emotional family reunion, So Pat announced he was going to find an all-night café and get some breakfast. Ian's local knowledge once again came in handy, as he knew of a nearby one that was famed for its fantastic fare. None of them had eaten for hours, and it wasn't possible to get any food locally, so they all piled into the spacious white BMW and, with blues and twos waking the early morning layabeds, they hurtled the half mile to Jackie's Café.

All seven sat together, the policeman, the Muslim, a singed and bandaged young man and his mother and three tired, slightly blood-spattered and smoke-stained others. Together they painted an unusual picture. Ibrahim felt it was time for him to offer his explanation of how and why he came so far to get involved in such nefarious dealings.

While Ibrahim was away at the very strict religious school in Al Medina, he was deliberately isolated from all outside contact, and the letters from his family weren't given to him so as not to subject to any influences other than the teachings of the mullahs. Because of his poor and petulant attitude he was locked away in solitude, where he had plenty of time to consider his behaviour towards his family and realised the folly of his ways, regretting his selfish actions and changing his views for life. The teachers were all very old school, and they beat the pupils regularly until they could recite certain passages of the Koran off by heart. It wasn't until the regime at the school changed to a more moderate one that he received the missing letters including the most recent, a communication from Sue. Until then he was unaware that his family had any interest in him at all, still believing they deserted him he was reluctant to try and re-establish the relationship. Subsequently regular contact with Sue was established, fuelling his fears, she told him that his parents hated him so much they sent him to the savage school to get him out of their way, and wished him dead. So feeling betrayed and confused, he spilled his heartfelt thoughts to her, expressing hatred towards his family. It became apparent that she also harboured similar feelings towards Jasmine and James.

The longer the relationship continued the more disaffected and extreme Sue's letters appeared to be getting, and when the talk started to mention martyrdom, and parts in the Koran which in her opinion supported radical actions like the destruction of the twin towers in New York as a symbol against the Zionist West, the more he heard the more Ibrahim became concerned and worried Sue might be involved in a similar action. He took the letters to the new more sympathetic mullah, who advised him that in his opinion his family still loved him, and to become associated with radicals was anti-Islam, how some of the international atrocities carried in the name of Allah was polluting the doctrine, turning much of the world against them, eventually possibly leading to a religious war. The mullah's advice to Ibrahim was to do as much as he could to prevent any event that might worsen the relations with the West, and Ibrahim took him literally and with the mullah's blessing joined the militants in England with a mind to disrupt their plans.

He went along with them and voiced his support for their cause and, with Sue's support, they eventually accepted him and let him into the main part of the plot. That was to set off a small nuclear device, supplied by Xavier, in the most recent of Bahrain's purchases and their flagship status symbol in London, the Axial Centre on its opening day – which happened to coincide very conveniently with London mayoral elections count there. On discovery of the enormity of the plot, he had no other option than to stay playing the role of suicide bomber until the very last moment, when he showed his hand and prevented the detonation.

Ibrahim had found William on Facebook and had been in regular touch with him, making William swear to keep their communication a secret from the family, not wanting to open up old wounds and possibly upset the relationship between James and Jasmine. It was Ibrahim that alerted William as to Jasmine and Peter's predicament at Ul Haq's butchery, hoping that he could find James and alert him to the danger.

Jasmine listened to the story intently, feeling both guilty and sad about the torment and anguish Ibrahim suffered at the school, pleased that the temperament he showed as a child was only due to the strange conditions he found himself in, and elated that he was back in the bosom of the family, welcomed by all.

The next day was Friday, the Muslim holy day. Peter and Ibrahim, to seal their new found brotherly bond, decided to go to the Mosque and pray together, and they knelt side by side, devout Muslim and unsure Christian appealing to Allah to bring peace to the world, imploring him to look kindly on their supplications, hoping he would lend an ear to their heartfelt prayers. There they stayed, still together after all the dreadful happenings, defying the odds, thwarting the obstacles that the fickle hand of fate had put in their path, surviving to live another day, now re-united hoping for better days ahead.

Epilogue

In thanks, understanding and respect of the multitude of vagrant people who wandered aimlessly about, shunned by the society they were once part of, Peter set up a drop-in centre for the homeless in Croydon, ably run by his new manager and friend Simon, who he put in total charge of the facility and gave a suitably large budget to finance it without the need for outside financial assistance.

James retired from the service and moved to Cornwall where he spent the rest of his days with his beloved Jasmine, still making love as often as his ageing body would allow him. All three of their sons visited regularly. They had become a very close-knit family, cemented together by the common danger that very nearly caused the deaths of them all.

Minnie remarried and settled down happily with a new man, never forgetting the lost real love of her life and father to her children, Michael.

Pat stayed with Brian, successfully running their guest house in Surbiton. However, Pat never strayed far from the phone, secretly hoping upon hope that it was going to ring and summon on his very special services, once again.

After all the excitement of the events surrounding the mayoral elections Ian gave up the boring police force and joined one of the secret services, specialising in anti-terrorism.

Over the next year Peter's life changed very little, "Burmese," stayed working from Jermyne Street under the auspices of his new boss, the cat-loving Lou. His life stayed relatively calm, dealing with comparatively small and insignificant incidents, until the unexpected and surprising arrival of the second horseman, whose name was conflict, and was bred from unresolved issues and hatred that been fermenting in unforgiving tortured minds for many years, manifesting in a major incident which changed the political dynamics of Great Britain for ever.